# MY IDEAL BOYFRIEND IS A CROISSANT

# MY IDEAL BOYFRIEND IS A CROISSANT

## LAURA DOCKRILL

Delacorte Press

All rights reserved. Published in the United States by Delacorte Press, an imprint of Random House Children's Books, a division of Penguin Random House LLC, New York. Originally published in paperback in the United Kingdom as *Big Bones* by Hot Key Books, an imprint of Bonnie Zaffre Ltd, a division of Bonnier Publishing, London, in 2018.

Delacorte Press is a registered trademark and the colophon is a trademark of Penguin Random House LLC.

Visit us on the Web! GetUnderlined.com

Educators and librarians, for a variety of teaching tools, visit us at RHTeachersLibrarians.com

Library of Congress Cataloging-in-Publication Data is available upon request.
ISBN 978-1-9848-4928-1 (trade) — ISBN 978-1-9848-4930-4 (ebook)

The text of this book is set in 11.5-point Adobe Garamond Pro.
Interior design by Casey Moses

Printed in the United States of America
10 9 8 7 6 5 4 3 2 1
First American Edition

For my same, my ride or die,
you are beautiful in every way,
thanks for saving my vegetarian bacon

# CONTENTS

# MY IDEAL BOYFRIEND IS A CROISSANT

# CRUMPETS

The first thing I ate after my asthma attack was a crumpet. OK. Not *a* crumpet. It was more a set. A set of crumpets.

"Can you push them down again, please? They still look raw."

"As if *that's* what you're thinking about now, BB, after you've just nearly died," Dove snaps as she pushes the crumpets back down into the toaster. "Besides, you don't get a *raw* crumpet, you idiot."

I am not one of those people that just *can't* eat. I can always eat. Even when I'm sick. Even when I'm sad. I can even eat when I watch people being sick on TV.

"Don't call me an idiot. You're lucky I'm alive. Push them down again."

I like my crumpets really toasted and slathered in thick butter. I like it when all the butter trickles into the holes of the crumpet and leaks through the bottom and puddles onto the plate, then you get to soak up the salty yellow pond with a warm sponge of crumpet innards.

"You know Mum's gonna make you go to the doctor's now, though, don't you?"

"Yep." I pull a clump of mascara out of my eyelashes and roll it into a little black ball like a squished fly. "And Dr. Humphrey is going to tell me I'm fat."

"*Overweight.* They don't say *fat* at the doctor's."

"Fine, *overweight,* then. Whatever."

"It's stupid anyway. Everyone is basically overweight on that stupid chart thing."

"You're not."

"On that chart thing I probably am." NO WAY IN HELL. Dove could make an HB pencil look fat. She leans her arms onto the counter, taking her weight. She hovers there, kicking her legs like she's tiptoeing on thin air.

"Although I do think those nonsense BMI chart things were, like, created in, like, the fifties when everybody was tiny. . . . Have you seen Grandma's wedding dress? It's like a dress for a doll. I wouldn't even be able to get one leg in that. The things are tiny; they aren't realistic anymore. These days even our feet are huge." I see smoke rise out of the toaster in foggy streams and I panic. "OK, they're done, pop them out now."

"I reckon you could've probably done this yourself, BB," she says, jumping down and dumping the clumpy warm discs in front of me.

"Dove, I nearly just *died,* the least you can do is make me some crumpets. Pass the butter."

# FINGERNAILS

We are waiting to be told I'm fat. Both Mum and I. And we chew our nails in the waiting room at the doctor's. We both know that we aren't chewing our nails because we are nervous, because we aren't nervous. We are chewing our nails because we both love to chew.

Mum just has more willpower than me.

I ADORE food. I was the sort of child that, if she ever got pocket money, instead of buying a toy or sweets, would go ahead and buy themselves a fully loaded jacket potato with cheese and beans.

"Don't touch the magazines," Mum says out of the corner of her mouth. "They're covered in diseases." I think about all the things I've already touched in the doctor's: the door, the bell thing, the banister. All the germs that are now in my mouth, dissolving on the eensy white dots on my tongue into some deadly sickness. I don't want to touch the magazines anyway. I HATE these types of magazines. The way they hoop those red rings around women's bodies on the beach, individually isolating their body parts like a lineup of cream cakes being judged on a baking show. Too fat. Too thin . . . Too cellulite-y. Too wobbly.

Too *real*.

You know, I bet you any money that all the women who earn a living out of drawing those red circles around celebrities' body parts are sitting on their own fat bums in some clammy office eating a packaged sandwich, hating themselves. What an existence. I'd much rather be the one with red hoops round my body parts than be the one drawing them.

*"Did you have a good day at work, darling?"*

*"Ooh yes, the usual, I got to draw loads of red rings on pictures of half-naked women and then put the pictures on the front of magazines."*

*"Ah, great, another productive day, then."*

Dr. Humphrey isn't there, so we have to see a nurse instead. I prefer a nurse anyway; I always feel they are less smug. More human being–y. One of *us*. This one is quite fat herself, so I'm hoping she doesn't have the audacity to go round mentally drawing red rings and pointing fingers.

"Most girls hate getting on the scales," she comments as I jump on.

"Not BB," Mum jokes. "I thought the other nurse might have warned you."

I roll my eyes. No. I don't mind getting on the scales because I've got nothing to hide, nothing to be embarrassed of and nothing to take me by surprise. I have a pair of eyes; I know my body.

"You need to lose weight," the nurse says. Oh, does she have to be so matter-of-fact? It's like her accent immediately gets more Nigerian. Well, I've heard it all before. Yawn. "It will help your asthma." She is wearing a really nice gold watch. It's thin and antique-looking; it looks beautiful against her dark skin, like it's in a velvet box. "And your blood pressure too. You are only sixteen, but you are at serious risk here, Bluebelle, of diabetes, of high cholesterol, cancer. And more asthma attacks."

All right, chill out. Aren't we all at risk of cancer? A girl from school won't eat packaged salad because of the risk of cancer. I mean, obviously she's absolutely batcrap crazy, but still. Cancer seems to be in everything.

"Hmm. I don't think I can lose weight."

Mum rolls her eyes. Again.

The nurse chuckles, kisses her teeth. "Of course you can, just move *more* and eat *less.*"

Wait a minute . . . sorry, I think I just heard the words *EAT LESS*? She makes it sound so easy. In fact, I'm gonna tell her that, but with sarcasm.

"You make it sound easy."

"It *is* easy. It's three meals a day, there's not *that* much room to go wrong. Eggs for breakfast, chicken salad for lunch, fish and vegetable and rice for dinner. See? Easy. Peasy."

No pudding. *Or* pie.

Dry.

She writes some stuff down on a little blue card. It's probably my weight, because it goes on for AGES. The end of her biro is chewed. See, she loves chewing too. A woman after my own heart. She raises a brow while she's writing, like she's writing out a cheque for someone who doesn't really deserve it. Then, staring me right in the face, she begins to speak, the end of the chewy biro pointing at me.

"I know *you girls.* You think because you have such a pretty face you can get away with being *very* fat?"

All right: *very.*

Firstly, I didn't think doctors and nurses were allowed to have

5

actual subjective opinions of patients' looks. It's distracting. They should see *all* the body parts as blank facts. *Arm. Head. Nostril. Liver.* You can't go around telling a patient that she's *pretty.*

"No," I laugh. "I think I have a very pretty *everything,* actually."

You weren't expecting *that* curveball to swing your way, now, were you? Ha!

She overreacts as if she's swallowed a fly and laughs, all smug.

"Excuse me. Well, you can look pretty in the grave, then."

Oh. *Ouch.*

Mum starts to cry.

What the *actual* hell? No. What's she crying for? I thought we had this under control.

"Mum, don't cry, Mum. Don't. You never cry."

"I'm not crying."

"Well, you are, look. Mum. That's tears. Look, all down your face."

"I just feel, I'm sorry, I . . . When you were little I used to tell you what a good girl you were for eating everything on your plate. . . ."

"Errr . . . yeah . . . 'K . . . *and* . . ."

"And now when you're stressed . . . maybe it makes you eat?" DO NOT SAY IT'S FOR ATTENTION. "For comfort," she adds. "And maybe I did this to you? It's my fault."

"You? You did *what* to me? I know I can be a greedy little pig, Mum. I eat the roast potatoes, the cheese, the ice cream, the white bread, the *everything,* Mum. You don't force-feed me. *I* make me fat, not you. And also . . . there's nothing to be sorry for. I like food and I like how I look; that's actually pretty rare for a girl my age. Most girls I know despise their bodies." I shake my head; why is she crying? "Jeez, Mum, if anything, you should be proud, really. Mum?"

6

"See," says the nurse, "you are selfish for being so fat. You are making your own mother cry." *Oh, shut the hell up, you.* I find myself getting caught in a silent debate with her. I am sticking up for my own fat.

"But I'm healthy. I eat so well. I don't get what the— Mum, don't cry."

"You cannot be eating well if you are this obese."

# WINGS

OBESE? Says the actually QUITE FAT HERSELF nurse. What does she EVEN know? She's not even a doctor. I HATE the nurse.

"Mum, I eat well, don't I? We're so *organic*. Tell this woman, please?"

"We do eat well at home." Mum defends us between sniffs. "But her dad and I, we split up. . . . We . . . well, we are separated, for the moment; it's not the first time. . . . We just . . . It's complicated . . ." She wipes her tears and looks at me. I'm looking at the slits in the blinds, the weird beads joining the material together, the filing cabinet holding the records of all the patients that have been told good and bad news on this red plastic chair. And then she throws me *right* under a bus. "You do comfort-eat from time to time, Bluebelle."

"No, Mum, I don't."

"That might be it," the nurse interjects. "Parents breaking up can be very stressful and upsetting for a *teen*." She says the word like it's a disease. *Teen.* She has her hands on her hips. "You need protein. Chicken soup and more exercise."

I think of my little sister, Dove, running freely over roofs and buildings. She's so light it's almost as though she has a pair of invisible wings stitched to her back. I think of my own wings, weighing me down like an overstuffed turkey.

Mum, glassy eyes peering out at the world, mumbles, "It's me and Dad."

Errr. No. "This has ZERO to do with you and Dad breaking up, *again*," I growl. "ZERO." Absolutely nothing. "It's not about you two all the time. You're both such attention-seekers. I was fat way before you two had problems. Can we just go home now?"

"I think the nurse has a point, Bluebelle. I think it's time we get this sorted."

"Mum! This is what we do, remember? This is our hobby. We come here, we get told I'm fat and then we go home. . . . I don't know why you're making such a drama this time."

"Yes, BB, but most times we come here you haven't nearly just died from an asthma attack."

I knew this would happen, that my parents would blame my enjoyment of food on their unenjoyment of each other. I can't help but feel the need to cut my eyes at Mum for stabbing me in the back fat.

The nurse begins to rummage around in her cupboards.

"Take this." She hands me an exercise book. "I want you to write down what you eat every day."

"What? I'm not a robot."

"Ha! Well, you eat like a feeding machine."

This nurse does. Not. Care. One. Bit.

I don't. Actually, IF I were a feeding machine, I would trade me in for a new one because I would want it to be eating ALL the time, which I DON'T DO.

"If you say you're healthy, I need to see it." She passes me the book; I pass it back to her; she presses it back into my hands like it's a game. "And if you eat as healthily as you say you do, you shouldn't have anything to worry about."

"Mum, tell her I don't need to write down what I eat. I don't need to be monitored."

"Just try it for six weeks," the nurse suggests. "Then come back to me and we can take a look."

"SIX weeks?"

"Six, yes."

"But it's the six-week summer holidays. Mum, no, tell her— I want to be wild and free to eat what I want."

"Not *this* summer, I'm afraid." The nurse dips her face down and raises her drawn-on brows. "You've had your fun."

NO. WAY. I'm not EVEN started.

"I'm not a child."

"In the eyes of the law, technically you are, Bluebelle," Mum butts in. "If anything serious happens to you, it's me who gets in trouble. It's just a food diary. It's a good idea. Just see it as you would a diary."

# THE FOOD DIARY

A diary. I could keep a diary. And I realise it might be my only chance. Right here, when Mum is feeling vulnerable and weak and this horrid nurse is here. I'm going to use this to my advantage and make Mum crumble right beneath her.

So I just go for it. It's now or never. . . .

"I don't want to go to college." Mum does a scowl at me almost exactly like the scowl of the young teen on the "Don't Do Drugs" poster on the wall behind her head. Clearly it's an effective advert. "I want to end school. Goodbye. Done. NO. MORE. SCHOOL."

"No way," Mum snaps.

The nurse *ooooooo*s like a bunch of kids would in a playground when someone trips up some stairs. She gets comfortable like she's watching a chat show.

"We're not doing this again."

"I've got it planned out. Even Julian from Careers says it's possible."

"Bluebelle, no, I don't care what *Julian* from *Careers* says. You aren't allowed to leave school; we've been through this. Do we have to do this at the doctor's?"

"Mum, it is possible, it's totally legit. I have to get an apprentice-ship . . . I can just do extra hours at Planet Coffee AND if I can get Alicia to fill out this application for a barista apprenticeship scheme thing I could potentially get paid for working *and* learning at the same time. . . ."

"So what is it you're telling me? That your ambition is to be a *barista?*"

"Well . . . no, I don't know, not yet, and even if it is, so what? I just know that there is absolutely nothing for me at that stupid school and it can at least buy me some time until I figure out what it is I want to do."

"You're just worrying about your exam results, Bluebelle. They're done now. I'm sure you did fine. You need to stop worrying about them."

"This is not about GCSE results." Secretly I am worried about my results. I fell asleep in my English exam because the poem was so dry; I don't know why they don't show us any good poems. And I *thought* I did OK in geography until I sat next to Diane at lunch and all of her answers were VERY different from mine and she knows everything. The nurse really cosies down in her squeaky chair now.

Mum adds, "And if the worst comes to the worst we know you will have done well in your art exam." I should have done, yeah, but art was actually the *ultimate* worst, though. Basically I had so much time left after drawing my fruit-bowl still-life composition that I filled the whole background in with black charcoal. I don't know what came over me. My creative mind betrayed me. My piece looked like it was hijacked by a goth. The image will haunt me for the rest of my waking life.

And THAT was when I had the stupid asthma attack. In art. The one exam I actually thought I'd be OK in. And everybody stood over me on the splattered grey lino floor, watching me struggle like a slug with salt poured on my back, whispering in their stupid girly whispers, not knowing what to do. MORE reasons for the stupid school to continue the rumours that I've been fatally impacted by my parents' split. "SHE WAS SCRIBBLING OVER EVERY-THNG IN BLACK CHARCOAL, MISS, AND NOW SHE'S HAVING A PANIC ATTACK AND DYING! SHE'S HAVING A MELTDOWN!"

I can't go back to that place. I just can't.

# SARDINES

"**M**um. Just hear me out." The nurse doesn't care—this is far more entertaining for her than dishing out hay fever tablets and sticking her finger up old people's bums to check for piles.

"Not now. We will talk about this later," she says to the nurse, not even looking at me.

"You said you would hear me out if I sat down with Julian from Careers."

"That was just to pacify you. Come on, let's not do this now."

"Pacify me? You're quite happy to sit here and talk about my body—that's not private, no? Or you and Dad breaking up, *again,* but you don't want to talk about my *life.* It's *my* future. Not yours. And I'm happy to talk about it in front of this nurse. I don't want to go to college. I don't want to go to university. I want to work at Planet Coffee. I'll do my normal hours plus the apprenticeship and take my time and think about what *I* want to do next."

"It's called a gap year," Mum says as if she's trying to show the nurse that she's all read up on this.

"No, Mum, because a gap is a gap between two of the same thing.

School and then more school. I don't want a gap. I want a severe cut. Finished. Over. Done."

"Bluebelle, school thinks you're going back in September; you can't just—"

"Why not?"

"Can you not just listen to the nurse and keep the food diary?"

"I didn't say I wouldn't keep the diary."

"Thank you, take the diary; now can we go, please?" Mum gathers up her handbag; I halt her like a traffic warden.

"I'll keep the diary, so long as you're OK about me leaving school."

"I'm not talking about this now." She tries to push past me like we've reversed roles.

"*You* didn't go to college, Mum."

The nurse glances at Mum. I didn't want to have to use that poisonous dart to be honest but she's driven me to it. Trump. Card.

"It was different then." Mum looks apologetically to the nurse for solidarity. Almost hoping the nurse might've also *not done* school.

"It's always going to be different, Mum. I wish you would remember that when it comes to this stupid BMI scale too. It was different then, that's why I'm being treated like a heifer when I'm actually not; it's just that times have changed and EVERYONE'S bigger. Course they are. Half the girls at school eat a box of fried chicken on their walk home. You should see the size of their boobs. But look at me, here I am just a hundred percent embracing it—that things are different. Everything's different. That's what makes life so exciting. Once upon a time, Mum, we were monkeys. As in actual real-life monkeys. We change. Now, do we have a deal?"

The nurse tries not to laugh and holds her hands up and shrugs. "Don't ask me."

"Have you spoken to your dad about this?" Mum asks.

*"Really?"* We both know Dad's opinion does not count.

"OK. Rules are . . . you keep the diary for six weeks and you need to talk to Alicia from Planet Coffee, you go to work without missing any shifts *and—*"

"There's *more?*"

"You sign up for the gym."

"MUM! NO!" *Don't laugh at me, idiot nurse.*

"You heard the nurse: move *more*. Exercise is good for you."

"But, Mum! I have asthma! You know this. I'm not allowed to do exercise; it makes me die. Even school doesn't make me exercise!"

"No, actually, exercise is good for everybody. If you have your Ventolin and you listen to your body, you should be fine," the nurse offers.

"See?" Mum raises an eyebrow at me. "And the only reason school doesn't make you do it is because you deliberately throw the ball into the boys' field behind so the girls can't fetch it back. You think I'm an idiot. You're doing it." She points at me. "Gym. Membership." She says it like it's a poem, like they are two words that rhyme, but they clearly don't. She wants to threaten me. It doesn't work. It's a crap poem.

"MUM!" I feel so betrayed. "Well, you're paying for it."

"Bluebelle, I don't have that kind of money. You work, don't you? You're the one that wants independence; if you want to act like a grown woman, then you can pay for yourself too. And that includes taking care of your body." She puts her hands in the back pockets of her jeans that fit her *too* well. Mum always looks good in jeans, like a Gap model. An older one, obviously, but a hot one still. "Some mums make their kids pay *rent*!" She makes the word *rent* sound all hard and sharp like a swear word. Then she looks at the nurse for approval, like she wants a gold star put on her jumper. She's showing off in front of her new friend. "We'd all love a gym membership!"

"I think I'm too young to join a gym."

"No you're not, you can be a member from sixteen, and some gyms even do a discount for under-eighteens." Mum's BFF, the nosy nurse, intervenes *again,* almost as if she's giving good news. I hate these two bad cops.

"Do we have a deal?" Mum pouts.

CAN I really see myself doing this? Big Bones keeping a food diary like some sad celebrity in rehab AND going to the gym? Except without the cool paid bit where some magazine prints it.

"This isn't a diet, you know. I'm not dieting." The only people I know who have ever dieted are ones I don't really like. And my dog. And he doesn't count because he's got four legs. Mum looks at the nurse.

"Deal," I grunt.

"Take the diary."

"Thank you."

"This diary is going to be a good read! See you in six weeks." The nurse celebrates with a smile so hard I see her fillings. They are the colour of sardines.

And I absolutely HATE sardines.

# BONES

Hi, nurse. Or doctor. Or whatever you are. Weirdo with too much time on their hands . . . Welcome to this scraggy notebook all about what I eat.

What you are reading is a promise. Between my mum and me. It's my food diary. So before you go around prodding the big judgemental finger, remember *you're* the one reading this. I know you're probs used to people sucking up to you, pretending they don't smoke half the cigarettes they actually do, but to be honest I'm kind of livid that I even have to write this stupid thing. I know this is your job to go probing round into people's private lives but I guess I just sort of, SILLY ME, thought that doctors and nurses were far too busy *saving people's lives* and stuff to have the time to read something like this. Unless you actually ARE the complete weirdo that gets off on this kind of stuff.

Yes, before you ask, I am fat.

Yes. I just called myself fat and that's allowed.

And . . .

I'm not greedy.

*I just love food.*
AND I'm not unhappy.
*I just love food.*
NO BIG DEAL.

# BIG

I like being big.

Because there's something *of* me. I feel *wholesome, there, alive,* 3D. I bolster myself; I look after *me*.

I'm not just fat either. I'm big all over. Tall. Chunky. Big. Strong. Like a Range Rover. It's how I was designed.

I don't even know what the obsession is with being small anyway, do you? It's all the girls at my school go on about: how to get thinner as quickly and as ferociously as possible. Honestly, they'll stoop to the wormiest, shallowest, ugliest pits of lowdom to get there and will stop at nothing. And once they've done all the starving one can do, overdosed on paracetamol and cranky coffee and nail biting— and their breath stinks like an old fish tank—they'll binge on 1,000 donuts, cry themselves into a frenzy and do it all over again. It's so tiresome and dull. Not one of the girls at my school sits down and says, *Right, great news, girls, I've found this amazing reel of wool, let's go and knit ourselves some sick cardigans* or *Hey, girls, this lunchtime let's climb a* tree or *Hey, girls, I think my next-door neighbour is an undercover spy . . . Let's stalk him and find out.* Not the ones I've met, anyway.

Is it a girl thing? Boys seem to want to be big. Full of bravado and banter and big and loud. It seems the world wants us girls to be tiny and petite and taken care of. What's all *that* about? You know, in some parts of the animal kingdom the female is the bigger beast. Women spiders eat the boy spiders after they've mated—*that's* how REAL it is in the animal kingdom. They know how to do it. Don't you just think that's cool?

So before we become friends or whatever you need to know that I embrace my body. It's mine. And I live inside it. And I take care of it. Don't read this because you want to perv on my size, indulge in my indulgence and think *how fat are we talking here?* I'm being honest with you, so please just accept that.

What I see in the mirror is a BEAUTIFUL, HEALTHY young woman with a positive attitude towards food. Sorry about me knowing how to speak like an actual expert but it's true. And that, to me, is no real reason why I should be writing some food diary . . . Get the people with eating disorders to do it, not me.

My real name is Bluebelle. But most people call me BB. I wasn't enormously thrilled with the nickname initially because it makes me sound like one of those posh blond girls that expects a flat white after school instead of a Coke like the rest of us. And wears a pashmina. Nobody puts BB in the corner.

Once somebody asked me what BB stood for. And before I could answer them back, they answered for me.

"Is it cos you've got big bones?" they suggested. "I mean, I'm not being rude but does the *BB* stand for Big Bones?"

And before you ask, yes, they *were* being rude. Because "big-boned" is the kind of term they give people like me. To try to reassure people like me that they don't *believe* it's our fault that we're fat. Like being fat's a bad thing. Truth is, "people like me"—meaning, oh yeah, hi, *me*—don't actually need your reassurance.

But the name sort of stuck. Because I like to own my fat. So that's who I am.

There are two *B*s in Bluebelle and two *B*s in Big Bones, which seems to make sense as I am double in everything.

So call me BB.

BB for Bluebelle.

BB for Big Bones.

# CROISSANTS

I meet Dad at the Pelican Cafe near him, although I reckon he'd rather go to the pub because he's obsessed with Guinness, which is basically freezing-cold beef stock. It tastes like blood. I'd prefer to go to Planet Coffee actually because the cakes are better there but the staff always forget I'm not working and make me do work stuff, so I'd rather not.

Apparently you could live off Guinness, fish and chips and oranges for the rest of your life and get all the vitamins you needed. Cos Guinness has so much iron in it.

I'm not really sure why Dad is so weedy, then.

There's a quite big thing I need to tell him.

That I'm not doing school anymore.

But I'm not stupid. I know I need to tug on those daddy heart-strings first, which I should tell you are very easily tugged. My dad is a failed actor/drama teacher, so he's very sensitive and always has lots of time for sob stories. And his constantly watering eyes are always ready for a good cry. Although that could be because he's quite old for a person-my-age dad. He had me "later in life," you see, and old people's eyes tend to water quite a lot.

"That's a nice . . . errr . . . What is it . . . a shirt . . . type thing, shows off your curves." OH PLEASE. CURVES. You mean thick chub rolls. Thank you very much. Then again, Dad's most over-used phrase when he used to take me clothes shopping was "It does nothing for you." Which he probably thought was a nice, quiet, polite way of saying, *My God, kid, you are seriously fat.*

I sniff my top lip—it's a habit I'm going through, don't worry, I don't like it either—and say, "I had an asthma attack."

"What?" he shrieks. "Oh God, BB, when, where?"

"At school."

"Nobody called. Does school have my number? Did Mum come and get you?"

"No, she was at work." Mum is a community programmer at a theatre. She has to involve the "locals" with "outreach" work and make all these plays up about knife crime and politics.

"For f— *Course* she bloody was." He's trying to SOMEHOW pass the blame on to her. If she was at home he would have said "Course she bloody was, why wasn't she at work?" My parents take turns to be positive and negative magnets to try and attract one another, but they never seem to be the right + or − at the right time. Always repelling, taking turns to point the finger. "Why didn't you call *me*?"

"Errr. Maybe because I was in the middle of having an asthma attack?" God, thanks for asking if I'm all right.

"Your mum never said."

"I'm fine. Don't worry about it."

I don't know why he even suggested calling him. His phone is from the 1970s and has a battery life of nineteen years and could survive an apocalypse but he never has it on him. He doesn't even know how to use it.

"What do you fancy?" Dad asks. I look through the glass counter; it's like looking through a pet-shop window stuffed full of miserable-looking road-kill rabbits. I just reach for a packet of waffles by the till, knowing they can't be contaminated by this cafe's crappy efforts. "I think I'll get myself a croissant," says Dad.

The croissants here are pretty dry. In fact, appalling, to be honest. OK, they aren't as terrible as the ones that come in little cellophane bags on aeroplanes that may as well be sweetened cheap bread rolls but they are pretty bad. No flakiness, no butteriness, no layers. The almond ones aren't even dusted and there're about two untoasted almond flakes on each. It's actually quite rude to even call them croissants. I think food only really works if people show they care with the detail. It would've taken somebody thirty seconds to toast those nuts. Almond croissants are meant to have all those white crusty guts pouring out of them like an overstuffed bean bag made of pastry, but *oh no*. The chocolate ones look like flattened sloths. I adore croissants; they get me out of many a hunger crisis. I mean, complete nightmare to eat in public because they stick to your lipstick and fall all down your clothes and the flakes love to cling to fabric. Truth be told, my ideal boyfriend would be a proper buttery, warm, well-put-together croissant: you could almost imagine the folds of the croissant opening up and closing around you, tucking you in for a great big puffy hug.

We sit back at *his* table, which he's already managed to make look like his poor little poet's desk. His glasses case and weird little scrawly notes in his scratchy little notebook all left out, some tarnished coins piled up into towers.

"I think my ideal boyfriend would be a croissant," I say to Dad.

"Oh no . . ." Dad shakes his head, taking my comment deadly seriously. "They'd cancel on you last minute, too flaky." He winks and takes a bite. "That's what I think of your boyfriends!" He laughs.

"You'd eat them?"

He clears his throat. "So . . . errr . . . w . . . what about you and . . . you don't have to tell me . . . but any . . . do you have any . . . I mean, it's not my business really but I just want *you* to know you can tell me if you . . . I suppose what I'm trying to say is . . . do you have a, have you got a boyfriend?"

"No." I feel sorry for him. He's so embarrassed; it's like Dad is trying to ask me out on a date.

"Oh, that's good. Not good, obviously, but not bad. Neutral, neutral." He backs his coffee. "Or girlfriend? I didn't ask that, do you have a girlfriend?" His eyes light up. Dad would *love* that. It would give him something to show off about at his drama classes, an extra political angle to tear someone down about during a debate at one of his wine and cheese nights with his friends, *Well, MY daughter's gay, so I'm the only one here fit to speak on this particular subject. . . .*

"No, Dad."

"You're dating *yourself,* then, are you?"

"Something like that."

"Me too at the moment. Until that mum of yours sorts her head out."

Hmm. Or YOU could try sorting yours out too?

"I think she's just jealous. You know?"

He wants me to agree but I don't because I know FOR A FACT that Mum is more jealous of the dogs than she is of Dad. I say nothing. He can dig himself out of his own grave. "Because I'm still treading the boards in a way, you know? I mean, I know I'm *teaching* theatre but I'm still very much hands-on with the actors and the space. I don't direct as much as I'd like to; always the way, isn't it? The higher up the ranks you get the less you get to actually get stuck in." He mimics digging into soil or something visual, then he chuckles to himself; I can see why Mum hates him. "She misses that, your mum. Her team isn't using her to her full potential, all that helping others and not herself. Of course the work they make there is of a pretty high standard. She was a great actor, stunning. I'd love to see her on stage again. It's confidence, isn't it? Age knocks it right out of us. Shrinks us to fragile . . . mice." He considers the mice comparison. "By the time you finally get your confidence, you die. Sad old world," he mutters. This is D-E-P-R-E-S-S-I-N-G, boy. "I'll never forget the day I saw her headshots, those eyes . . . I said to my friend, *I'm gonna marry that girl.* As the great man said, the course of true love never—"

"You've told me this." I chew the inside of my cheek. "Here, have a waffle."

# WAFFLES

These amazing caramel waffle things are divine. You just can't go wrong with them. You pop them over your mug of tea and they heat up. When you split the waffle it tears apart, the toffee arms grab at each other, like you are some evil cold-hearted giant separating mad lovers. Dunk in any hot beverage and the chewiness dissolves.

"Why didn't Dove come today?" Dad takes EVERYTHING so personally. So insecure, although he's too insecure to say it out loud so just makes everything about himself instead.

"She's roof running."

"It's called parkour, isn't it, that thing? One of the blokes in dance, his son does it. When I said Dove was doing it they thought I was joking. They were quite shocked that she was a girl." More shocked than the bloke doing *dance*? It's all so sexist and tedious.

"Ha! Everyone says that."

"Do they?" Dad frowns. "Is it dangerous, then?"

"I think it's cool."

"I think it's cool too." Dad fiddles with the sugar packets. *I hate sugar packets in cafes, so cheap-looking.* "But is it safe for a girl to go running around jumping on buildings and all that? I mean, she could hurt herself."

"Boys can hurt themselves too, Dad."

"I didn't mean that." He panics, as he always does when he talks about Dove and me being girls, and becomes a ginormous horned bull in a china shop smashing all the china up. "I mean boys too—is it safe for *anyone* to go jumping around on buildings?"

"Probably not."

"I mean, when I was younger we were performing protest theatre outside the Houses of Parliament, on the roofs of buildings, very powerful stuff. Of course the police hated us—we were a movement! A notorious army of guerrilla thespians raging at the system, but that was then. . . ."

"Yeah, yeah, you've told me before."

"She sent me this video but I can't get it to load properly on my phone." Like I'm surprised. "But I saw a bit; she doesn't even tie her hair up, you know?"

"She's like Tarzan."

"Yes, I suppose she is. Are you sure she's not rejecting me?"

"Why would she be doing that?"

"I thought she might be punishing me for moving out. It's only temporary." Whatever. I don't even take their breakups seriously anymore. "How's Not 2B?"

"Fine."

"I miss that dog."

Our dogs are 2B and Not 2B (good old Shakespeare again). Dad actually thinks that Not 2B might have a complex about the fact that he is *not* 2B, so he always tells me to love that dog extra hard and now the balance has shifted as if to say that *not to be* 2B is actually better than being 2B. *That* is the answer to the question.

Also 2B was once actually in a car insurance advert that paid more than Dad's entire salary for the whole year, so he is quite a major celebrity big deal in Dalmatian land. And paid for our central heating, so . . .

I smile.

"I'm sure he misses you too." That's probably true. But Not 2B's a dog, so it doesn't count. A dog would miss its owner even if he was a murderer. I wish Dad could be the person Not 2B thinks he is. . . . He probably sees Dad like some action-movie-star actor hero . . . not a broke, grey-haired wiry stick of a man with round tortoiseshell spectacles (he calls them that, not me. He also calls bikes *bicycles,* and Snickers bars *Marathons* . . . so you can just imagine the type of man I'm dealing with).

We watch the people. Polite smiles, *hello, thank you,* the cricking of a neck, pushing hair behind ears, sneezing into a tissue. A baby softly whimpers, a toddler stretches its legs out in cramped frustration in its pram and loses a shoe, a young-ish guy with a beard picks the shoe up but the mum doesn't see so he sort of gently props the shoe on the toddler's lap and orders an Americano to take away. I love humans.

"So guess what?" I say in a happy, don't-respond-badly voice.

"What?"

"I'm *not* gonna do school anymore!" I say excitedly, as if he should leap up in delight. He doesn't. He frowns. And his greying bobbly drama black clothes make him look like he's shopped for my funeral in a beat.

"You're what?"

"I'm leaving school."

"What about sixth form? I thought you got a place."

"I'm not doing it."

"What about university in the future?"

"I don't want to go. It's a pile of debt for something I don't want to study. I would literally be picking a course for the sake of it. I want to take my time."

"So take a gap year."

"No. Dad. You can't just take a gap year. I have to be in some form of training or education until my eighteenth birthday."

"Can't you just get on with your art and sewing and baking and stuff at school until you're eighteen and then let the world be your oyster? You don't have to rush."

"I don't like school, Dad. It's not for me. It's not my kind of place."

"You're not being bullied, are you?"

I think about the way some of the girls stare at me when I eat at lunchtime. Or in the changing room before PE. The red lines from my bra straps carving into my skin like scars.

"No, of course I'm not. I just don't want to go back. I've outgrown it."

"Outgrown school, eh? That's a first." He considers it. "I suppose it is possible to outgrow anything. A sunflower can outgrow its garden. . . . Of course, better to outgrow a garden than not see any sunshine at all. Left to wither and die because you're being overshadowed by the other plants."

"Or get strangled by ivy."

"That too . . ." He nods, visualising it, I imagine. "*Poison* ivy. What does your mum say?"

"I like the way poison ivy made you think about Mum."

"No it didn't," lies Dad. "I just know she'd have something to say about this. And of course, she has to grant you permission." Mum's not the queen gatekeeper. So annoying. "Well . . . what did she say?"

"She's not happy about it."

I feel like I actually see my dad's head go as clear as glass. The little mechanical wheels begin to turn and clank, he's seen a window here, to get close to me while trumping Mum. He plays with a little ball of foil he's found in his pocket. He relaxes methodically; it's all that acting, I guess, reading between the lines—all actors have to pretend they care about tiny things like rolling balls of tin foil. He starts to chew the waffle, using it like a prop; actors ADORE eating and acting at the same time. They think it's the ultimate proof of being a human being. If they could do a poo on stage they would.

"I don't know what she's talking about; she didn't go to college, neither did I, and look at us!"

Yeah. *Look* at you.

"I wonder if they'll be up for slurping a drop of whisky into this," he jokes with a deadly serious face and a leaning eye. I say nothing. He continues, "The whole thing's making a wedding cake out of a cupcake if you ask me." He always thinks I'll appreciate cake jokes. No fat person appreciates cake jokes unless they are on OUR terms. "I think you're old enough now to decide what you want to do with yourself." Even though it pains him to say this. "So what are you going to do? You're not going to become an *actor*, are you?" He pronounces the word *actor* like *goblin*, terrified at the prospect but also secretly quite proud of his profession.

"Hell no!"

"Nothing wrong with treading the boards, following in the footsteps of your *very* old man." Defensive, immediately. "English rose like you." SNORE. "So . . . what *is* the plan?"

"Be an 'alien' at Planet Coffee a bit longer . . . I dunno, bake?"

"No travelling or . . ."

"Maybe."

"You should learn the guitar. I always wanted to learn the guitar, like Bob Dylan. You know that my one regret in life was not learning the guitar."

*Your* regret in life, Dad, not mine.

"Maybe," I say, meaning probably most definitely actually not. "I'd rather perfect the art of the chocolate fondue."

"Of course," he says, but he's disappointed.

"It's not too late for you to learn the guitar, though, Dad."

"Nah."

He uses his bitten-down fingertips to collect some fallen grains of brown sugar. He can only use brown—it has to be wholesome. Farmhousey. I think about all the habits and bits and pieces of him that I don't get to see now I don't live with him anymore. Now that I don't know him like I used to. His choices are usually a safe bet. As long as the boiled eggs are organic, the juice is fresh, the coffee is proper and the booze is on tap, he's happy.

"So." He defrosts. "Then I'll have two girls running wild on the streets of London! What you got there?"

"It's a food diary."

"You're not going to write down any of the things I said about your mum, are you, like a reporter?"

"No, Dad. It's part of my deal to Mum to stop going to school, I have to fill this in every day, to show the nurse, because of my asthma."

"Deal to Mum? Bribing you, is she now? Unbelievable. That's that woman all over."

"The nurse made me do it." Dad folds his lips into a little ugly purse.

"So what is it? A string of love letters to food?"

"Yeah, basically. Mostly unrequited."

Dad pats me on the shoulder sympathetically. "You can always write down how I feel about your mum in there, if she'll read it—will she read it, do you think? Reckon you could tell her I still love her?"

"She knows you love her, Dad."

"And maybe you could tell her I looked really handsome today?"

"No, Dad, it's a diary, you have to tell the truth, that's the whole point."

# BAKEWELL TART

"You must think I'm stupid," Dove barks at me. "This is just exactly like the time you and Dad snaked me and went and got your ears pierced behind my back."

"I don't know what you're on about," I say. Which is another lie. Half of the joy of getting my ears pierced was because I knew Dove would be jealous. It's what got me through the burning ringing sensation.

"I don't get why you just get to *quit school*."

"I *am* older than you."

"Only by three years, and you're still meant to be learning."

"I *am* still learning." And then I say in a wind-up condescending tone: "You never stop learning, *Dove*." Always more patronising when you add their name at the end. I decide to leave out the bit that technically I'm desperate to become an unglamourous apprentice at Planet Coffee, because it's too good watching her squirm with envy.

"Oh PLEASE. It's not fair."

"Well, it's what's happening. School just isn't for me."

"School, actually, just isn't for most people, but you just get on with it. Why do you think you're such an exception to ALL the rules, ALL the time?"

"We could ALL be an EX-ception to ALL the rules, *Dove,* it's just about having the guts to not ACC-ept them."

"You're full of crap." She folds her arms. Her hip bones poke out like shark fins, making a little gap between her jeans and her body. You could balance a taco in there, balance it nicely while you stuffed it. Her belly button winks at me like an eye. "It's always about you," she shouts. "I'm sick of it!" And then she struts away, blond ponytail swinging after her like some hideous discontinued My Little Pony.

"That's not true!" I shout back. It's always about Mum and Dad; we ALL know that.

I love making Bakewell tart because it calms me down so much. Its creation, so gentle, is like building a sand castle or dozing off to sleep.

Make pastry. Chill it. Roll it out, measure it against your tin to make sure it will fit, line the tin with your pastry. . . . Then chill it again so it sticks to its shape in the fridge. Then blind-bake the pastry with those baking bead things (or you can use coins apparently, but I think that's kind of weird and might make it taste money-ish). Or rice, but I mean, what a waste.

Then you've got to make the filling, which is basically ground almonds, almond essence, sugar and eggs . . . and you heat it in a pan. This is the frangipane. I could eat this stuff for dinner every single night. IT IS AMAZING. It's sweet and tart and more-ish.

When the pastry has been baked, blindly, you'll be so proud of yourself, you might want to think about adding that new skill to your CV. Because it's actually, well, hard to make your own pastry and so tempting to not make it and buy ready-made. So in other words you're pretty much completely over the moon with your own self before you've even begun.

Smear a fat layer of good-quality raspberry jam on the bottom, then topple the frangipane mix over it. Scatter with flaked almonds and bake again. It smells like butter and amaretto. Like the house is a cuddle.

Serve the cuddle on its own or with custard or ice cream.

"DOVE!"

No answer.

"DOVE? ANSWER ME, YOU ABSOLUTE WITCH!"

"What do you want, you IDIOT?"

"I've made you a Bakewell tart."

"Made *me* a Bakewell tart or just made *a* Bakewell tart mostly for your greedy-ass self?"

Errrrrmmmm . . .

"There better be custard."

# AVOCADO

**I**T IS LONG writing a food diary. It's becoming the first thing I think about each and every morning and it is BRASSING my life out. I don't think it's healthy to look this *inwardly* at your own life.

"They don't even taste of anything," Dove says as she watches me scoop out the green flesh.

"Yes they do." Please don't ask me of what because I can't give you an answer. It's a bit like how tea just tastes of tea, which is kind of a nothing flavour but you need it. I reckon I'm only even questioning the way an avocado tastes because of this stupid logging-of-every-thing-I-eat life I'm currently leading. "It tastes of superfood smush."

"Do you think if you eat loads of a superfood you will be a super-human?" Dove folds into a backbend, the dogs sniff about her face.

"It's so annoying trying to hold a conversation with you when you're always moving like some hyperactive acrobat."

"It's called a crab. Look, watch this." She lifts a leg up, her toes pointing to the ceiling. I know what it's called. "Eugh, the ceiling is well dirty."

"It's called a superfood because it's extra good for you; it's a good fat. Like nuts. You know some people won't eat an avocado because they say it's fatty but they won't think twice about eating a cereal bar, which is full of sugar and crap. Avocado is nature's answer to cream and butter and mayonnaise; it's perfect. Much better for energy than all that junk food you eat all day, Dove. In fact, start carrying an avocado around in your pocket and watch your happiness go up."

Dove looks at me, stunned. "No thanks. If I wanted to walk about with an alligator egg in my schoolbag I would."

I think about the amount of crinkled-up chocolate wrappers and crisp packets Mum clears out from Dove's pockets before a wash.

For something to do while the water boils, I unwrap a roll of cherry drops that's been sitting on the table for an age. The white paper is all stiff and stuck to the little red sugary planet. I unpeel the paper and look to Dove; she opens her mouth like a lazy fish; I pop the sweet in.

"Ta," she says, and I hear the chink of the cherry drop clatter against the back of her teeth.

Then I do one for myself. Once the initial hardened crackly sticky bit has dissolved, it's as good as fresh.

We poach eggs. The trick is to use a frying pan with water rather than a big pot; it's the only way for perfect poached eggs every time. That way you don't have to crack the egg into a glass first. You just drop it in with confidence. You let the little angel bob around for a while, skimming the scum off the surface with one of those spoons with the holes in it, before placing the egg on a piece of bread to soak up all the unwanted excess water—you don't want that going on your toast. We have it on toast with chilli and I have avocado but Dove has Marmite and we both crumble rubbles of feta cheese on top too because (a) it's delicious and posh and (b) why not?

"What you doing today, then?" I ask her.

"Parkour. Want to come watch?"

"No, for the millionth time. I do not want to watch you Tarzan-ning it around London like some circus-act burglar. I've got stuff to do."

"Like what, being rude?"

"No. Actually." I cut my toast; a salt crystal cracks under my tooth and for a second I think it's eggshell but it's not, thank goodness, because eggshell loves to get stuck in your teeth and turn to sand, which turns to chalk and ruins your day by making you think too much about what it actually is and where it actually came from, like, errr, how about a chicken's body? Absolutely gross. "I'm going to work." And then I add, "Like a real-life actual person."

"Like an annoying person, more like."

"You're annoying. Do you think people like you springing round town? You're not the main character in a Batman film."

"That would be . . . Batman?"

"Fine, yeah, well . . ."

"Well, at least I'm not writing myself as the main character in some sad trashy novel that's only going to be read by a NURSE, about some fat girl who moans about her weight all the time and . . . doesn't . . . know what to do with her life."

She rushes the words out in a squeal, unable to even finish her sentence because she's snorting and laughing so hard. I pinch her under her arm and make a cow-bite bruise. We scrap about the kitchen giggling and tussling, smiling so hard.

"Ahhh, you dribbled on my head," I gargle. Dove is so vicious. "You don't need to actually grab my hair like that."

I struggle and claw at her face, dragging her eyes down into her cheeks. "WAAAAHHH! MUM!"

"Don't shout *Mum*; what are you calling out *Mum* for?" Dove wraps her arms behind my back and digs her strong knee into my back. For someone so tiny she sure can cause injury. The dogs begin to rally round us, barking, just to assess the situation and make sure this isn't something more serious.

"GIRLS! SHUT UP!" Mum yells.

We can't stop laughing. Exhausted from giggling, we continue with breakfast, elbowing each other in the ribs and winding each other up. We breathe to try to compose ourselves.

I take another avocado and slash its alligator skin open, carving the pebble heart out of it. I roll it into my hand like an oversized walnut marble, all varnished.

Oh my goodness grief, I very nearly forgot to tell you, somebody told me that apparently the stone of the avocado is the very best bit. You have to, like, roast it down or dehydrate it and then pound it to a dust and it's meant to be amazing. I don't know what you'd do with it after . . . sprinkle it on your cereal?

I need to stop taking up all my brain space with ideas like this. Really, I have to get thinking about my general life. Like what my existence is on the planet. Like, I don't mean to scare myself but leaving school is like leaving the womb for the second time, and now . . . things are about to get really actually real.

I wish superfoods did make you a superhuman. Then I might know what the hell I want to do with my life.

# CHOCOLATE SPREAD

One bad habit I have is to do with spread and jars. My room is quite often filled with jars of Nutella and chocolate spread and peanut butter all over the place with a knife or teaspoon rammed in. Now, as a nurse, you're probably gonna have a problem with this but don't worry, I'm not like a beast or anything, I don't just sit there and polish off the whole jar like a tub of ice cream—although I probably could do if I wasn't going to feel sick afterwards. I just like the idea of sort of reading a book or getting dressed in the morning and reaching over for a jar, unscrewing the lid and letting a blob of sweetness press onto the back of my teeth like clay and melt onto my tongue. It can actually take me weeks to get through a jar. A couple of times I've forgotten I have a jar on the go and begun a new one and the room becomes decorated with jars of Nutella like flower pots.

Don't you think Nutella is such a cute name for a baby? Like, if it wasn't the name of a most famous hazelnut spread?

# TRIFLE

Everything in my room orbits my bed. I believe a bedroom should be a sanctuary. A private place for peace and relaxation and comfort. And that is everything a bed is. My bed is actually a four-poster—don't worry, I'm not posh, but it came with the house and Dad was gonna throw it out because it had all that woodworm stuff and was rickety but I begged them to keep it. We treated it and replaced the screws, even though Dad says the rivets are just "rot" and "sawdust" and will one day collapse under me. But it's lasted me this long. The same as the house, really, which is just as old and rickety, stuffed with all the secondhand old things that nobody else wants. The crack down the side of it is getting bigger and bigger, as though the whole thing could split in two.

My bed is a heap of cushions and blankets and I nicknamed it "the trifle" because it's layer upon layer of excellent lux squidge that just keeps giving and giving. There's so many blankets that I rarely get to the sheet of the bed itself, I usually just find a soft spot and burrow myself into the comfort. Kind of like a cat would do, I guess. It really is the best. And yes, it still is rickety, but I find the creaks are now reassuring and soothing. Lullabying me to sleep each night. I like to lie in the trifle and look over and above, where I have made a canopy of blankets and fabric. Stitched waves of flowers and stars, palm trees, cartoons and curtain rags, flops of sari material from the market and off-cuts of tablecloth. I often forget to turn off the fairy lights that hang behind me, and let their warm glow nestle me into a magical grottoland where the minutes never matter and the harmony of the world only exists within my four-poster bed within the four walls of my bedroom.

It's so hot today, I wish I could flop facedown on top of it but I can't. I put on my aqua-blue denim dungaree dress with the high-neck vest top, which has a print of these cool little colourful fish all over it. It's a belly top, so my side fat rolls crinkle out in the gap of the dress. I scoop my hair into a topknot, take a fingerful of chocolate spread and leave for work. God, this so *is* a trashy diary about a moaning fat girl. Dove is SO right about me. Tragic.

# PLANET COFFEE

Is the place where I work. We sell coffee. I don't really like coffee. It's bitter and makes my brain go too fast if I drink it. We are located opposite the park, so we're usually full of babbling prams or work people in suits darting in and out. But people come to us for first dates too; old school friends catching up; interviews for new jobs; and too many of our napkins have seen the tears of a whispered breakup.

I don't hate it at Planet Coffee except for the fact that they don't sell my ultimate favourite, millionaire's shortbread: a dense little piece of architecture—a foundation of crumbling Aztec sandy base, slathered in salty caramel, with a shiny tiled roof of chocolate insulation to top it off. But it's all right because we don't have to wear a uniform or a hair net or anything bizarre, but on my first day the manager, Alicia, did say this to me (to be said in an Australian accent):

"You'll love it here, BB. We have a nursery across the road and some of the nannies that come in eat so much, they'd make *you* think you're anorexic."

As though it was a compliment, something to look forward to. But that was brilliant. Really. When somebody says something like that to me I am usually elated. I know that sounds odd but let me explain: meanness is a sign of weakness. You have to truly loathe yourself to be so horrid. Alicia is NOT my species. Camille thinks it's because I'm allergic to Australian accents but it's not. I'm just allergic to rude people who also wear toe rings. People say sometimes that boys are the ones we need to worry about when it comes to people aesthetically judging girls' sizes, but I go to a girls' school and TRUST ME, I find more of this sneering actually comes from girls and Alicia is one of the worst. I hate girls who don't love girls. Girls who aren't Team Girl. Boys will just say "you're fat" to me, which is a fact. I can accept that. Girls at school tell me I'm "hot" or "beautiful" and compliment my figure—"oh, I wish I had your big bum"—but in real life if they had an actual chance to swap bums with me they'd sooner swap bums with a rabid baboon that's just fallen into a cluster of snarling cacti.

Alicia is somebody who would describe me as "bubbly." Bubbly is a secret code word for fat. It doesn't even mean funny or sparky or eccentric or confident, like the word was invented for. If somebody says, "I met a lovely girl the other day; she was so bubbly." They mean to say that girl was fat with a smile on her face.

GROSS.

It's not fair. Some grumpy people are described as "bubbly" when they're obviously miserable as sin, but they're fat, so the word *bubbly* becomes them too and we all hang out as chubby bubbles in the Bubbly Bubble Gang. It's so lazy.

I actually think Alicia's quite "lonely" but I don't go around calling her that. . . . *Have you met Alicia? She's so lonely, isn't she?*

Then again, this is my diary not Alicia's. Bye, Alicia!

Even though I'm just sixteen I'll be running this place in no time. Because Alicia doesn't see me as a threat I can skulk around pretending to be *stereotypically* "bubbly" and *stereotypically* distracted by the cakes when secretly, really and truly, I'm crowbarring myself up the ranks through the sneaky guise of an innocent apprenticeship to really then be the only reliable person who knows what's actually going on. Meaning I'd be trusted to make all the decisions. Which would be a good thing because I hate the cold, stark, white-washed, art gallery walls, the try-hard "exposed" faux east London brickwork—so EXTRA—and cheap halogen lanterns. If I were going to run a coffee shop I would do it properly, and that means cake that isn't dry because it is pre-sliced, plus making sure that cream cheese frosting is on pretty much everything and that we sell good-quality chocolate chip cookies the size of dinner plates.

AND MILLIONAIRE'S BLOODY SHORTBREAD. Even . . . I dunno . . . thousandaire's shortbread would do.

But I'm not quite there yet.

# SICK

"Move, move, move, move, I'm gonna be sick, I'm gonna be sick."

It's Alicia, running towards me, holding her hand over her mouth. Wish she didn't have to be doing being sick right now because I need to ask her to apply for my apprenticeship. Jeez.

I try to suck my belly in as she wrangles past me to get to the backstage toilets. I call them backstage toilets because sometimes I think it's funny to pretend the coffee shop is the stage and the staff room etc. is backstage but now that I've said it out loud, and then also tried to explain it, I realise it's really not that funny at all.

She misses. Splashes of custard-sick fog the floor, bubble like melted butter, pop. Gross. It stinks too. Alicia is always very dehydrated; her lips are always crusty and look like shrinking fried cod. Maybe that's why she's always a moody cow, cos she's so thirsty? Flecks splatter my Converse. I'm kind of glad. I needed an excuse to test out my more comfortable and less flattering collection of old-lady orthopaedic sandals that I found for a fiver in the Salvation Army charity shop all strung together with elastic bands—this can be *that* excuse. They are in my locker; I'll go get them in a sec.

"Oh, Alicia, are you OK?" I bend down next to her, talking like a ventriloquist so I can hold my breath at the same time so the sick smell doesn't creep up my nostrils. I hold her hair up like how you're meant to do for a friend but Alicia's hair is really thin and childish and there isn't much to grab, and plus, she's not my friend. Would this be the right time to ask her if she can sort out all this paperwork to say I'm a legit apprentice or . . . ?

"Get the mop, get the mop," she cries. I get the feeling everything she is about to say is going to come in sets of two. "Don't let anybody come in, don't let anybody come in!" she adds. Thought so. OK, *so* not the time.

"I won't. I won't!" I reply, to see if I want to play this game too, except it makes me feel like I'm maybe just trapped in a horrible musical.

"Alicia, do you want me to call somebody?"

"I'm fine, I'm fine." She wipes her mouth.

"What about your mum?"

"No, no, I don't want my *mum,* BB." She winces. "Plus, it's very expensive to call Oz." I literally would be calling Australia every day on the work phone if I was the manager of a coffee shop with a landline. "I'm fine, I'm fine, just get the mop, hurry, hurry, don't let anybody come in."

"Do you want anything? Some water maybe?"

"Yes, please," she whines.

"OK, let me get you some water." I fill my chipped *101 Dalmatians* mug (when you have Dalmatians everybody seems to get you stuff to do with Dalmatians) with tap water from the industrial artist sink that we have backstage from the toilet that the customers aren't allowed to come into. It's a big copper tap that hisses out water.

"Eugh, no, no, not government juice!" she squeals, batting the cup away. No wonder she's sick. No immune system, I suspect, from snobbery.

"What's wrong with this?"

"I just . . . I just . . . ," she cries. "Maybe a Coca-Cola?" Ah, I see, *her* job perks are stealing the refrigerated drinks from the main stage of Planet Coffee, not calling Australia on the Planet's landline. She's still on the floor. She's wearing tight jeans, little black kitten heels, a stripy T-shirt. Kind of high-street trying to be French but mostly looking a bit like you work at Pizza Express. The thread's so cheap it's already worn on the bust, showing the print of her dotty bra.

"I'll get you some water," I reassure her.

I head out front. It's a busy day. It's always a busy day. A busy day stuffed with "earthlings," as Alicia calls them (that means customers, or sometimes she calls *us* earthlings if we aren't working hard enough, to try to threaten our jobs as aliens and somehow demote us to the level of real humans).

"Is she all right?" That's Max. Another *alien* from Planet Coffee. Except he is a quite beautiful alien but that's not for now, obvs. I'll just park that there nicely.

"Yeah, think so." I steal a bottle of water from the front fridge and can't help but smile. Because I've got a sneaking suspicion that Alicia is pregnant. ~~Preggers McSmeggers.~~ God, that's annoying. Is it too late to cross that out?

And you know what that might mean, don't you?

50

That Planet Coffee might have to find itself a new manager. I'm going to aim much higher than a silly apprenticeship—that will give Julian from Careers a shock.

I slip on my orthopaedic slippers and they feel like the squidge of success.

# POMEGRANATE

Camille meets me on the common during my lunch break. She has a giant red stain down her front like she's gouged someone's heart out.

"Don't ask."

"What is that?"

"I tried to have a picnic by myself so I could get on with my bikini designs and an accident happened."

"With what?"

"My picnic. I was trying to be healthy and have a salad, which I made at home—"

"What flavour?"

"Like, an exotic mix-up."

"'K."

"Then I walked past a fruit and veg shop and they had all these amazing slices of watermelon that really caught my eye but they also had pomegranates and just recently I've been noticing they've been putting pomegranate in all the salads at the supermarket, so I thought, *Oooh that might be nice,* so I bought it."

"For some reason I don't think that's the end to this story, is it?"

"OK, so . . . I couldn't get into it. Its skin's really hard; I guess to protect all them gems—have you seen pomegranate seeds?"

"Beautiful, aren't they? Like little alien pods."

"My gosh, they are . . . they are like treasure, gems like costume jewellery. Anyway, I tried stepping on it and using my teeth but . . . nah . . . so I went over to a tree and pressed the pomegranate in between my chest and the trunk and sort of squeezed the—"

"You hugged a tree?"

"Yeah, well, I can see how it would seem like I did."

"And it burst on your top?"

"Yeah. It's dry now, though. Salad is such effort, and they wonder why people don't eat enough of it."

"It's goddess food, apparently, pomegranate."

"Really. Knew there was a reason I was attracted to it." Cam scrunches her nose up at me and pokes out her tongue, posing for a second like a goddess before failing miserably and shaking her head in dismay. I wrap my arm round her neck.

"Come up with any good bikini designs?"

"Yeah, bikinis with tassels, and ones that go right up your bum so you can get a tan on your bum cheeks."

"Who wants a tan on their bum cheeks?"

"Oh trust me, there's a market for it. Then in, like, five years I'm gonna go to fashion week. Paris, New York, Milan . . . that's the plan, anyway . . . and Dubai too. Have you ever been there? It's mental. It's like futuristic and caveman at the same time . . . like all these crazy metal fancy shiny buildings just built on a desert."

"Sounds like *Flintstones* mixed with *The Matrix*."

"Yeah. That is kind of it. You feel like the birds are clockwork and you could unscrew the sun." Camille lies on her back. She's already caught the sun. Flecks of fish-food-like freckles dot her nose, speckles of neon pollen crown her Afro.

"So guess what?"

"What?" She bolts up.

"Mum's agreed."

"To what?"

"I don't have to go back after the summer."

"What?"

"Yep. I don't have to go back to school."

"SHUT THE FRONT DOOR!"

"No. Serious."

"Flip! B! That's huge. WOW!"

"I know. Hasn't quite sunk in yet."

"Have you told school?"

"Mum's dealing with it."

"What'd your dad say?"

"Not much. Not much he can say, is there?"

"Whoa, Bluebelle, this is mad. So what you gonna do?"

"I actually don't know. I have to technically do an apprenticeship cos I'm sixteen, like, make up the hours doing a skill. . . ."

"You could go into business with me!"

"I'd LOVE to be your apprentice! What would I do?"

"Make bikinis for girls that have massive boobs?"

"Yeah! With great patterns on them like . . . I dunno . . ."

"Toads or something."

"Yeah. Toads."

"I feel like a toad bikini could be my compass to decide if a girl could be my friend species or not."

"Oh totally, same for me with the shop, like if a customer walks in and doesn't like the idea of wearing a bikini with toad prints on it, then *GET OUT OF MY SHOP—you're not my kind!*"

I laugh.

"So I'm gonna work at Planet Coffee for a bit but . . . I need to persuade Alicia to offer me a barista apprenticeship scheme." I kick my shoes off; air licks my swollen toes. "Look at my trotters, bloody hell." I laugh. "These shoes are meant to be comfy." I squint at the sun. "But I couldn't ask her today cos I think she's pregnant."

"WHAT?"

"I know."

"Poor kid." Cam tuts. "Why can't we just do stuff like work as mechanics like they do in films?"

"You need a form for everything these days. You can't just *fall* into a line of work because you one day get on really well with a plumber and they're, like, *Hey, kid, why don't you just be a plumber like me? I'll teach you everything you need to know.* All has to be forms and stuff."

"Yeah, but it's a bit much. How are you meant to know when you're a kid what you want to do for the rest of your life? You choose your subjects for your exams when you're SO young without realising that those exam results could shape the rest of your whole future. It's bonkers."

"I know. And just think, I scribbled around my fruit bowl in art in black charcoal. Great." With my toes I claw at the grass. "How do you know where the right spot on the planet is for you? Like, how do I know I'm meant to be here, right now, doing this? How do I know I've landed in the right spot? My calling could be . . . I dunno . . . in New Zealand or St. Lucia or Mexico or New York or Berlin—"

"Or Dubai?"

"And I wouldn't even know it. And that makes me think life is too short. I don't have the time to test all these places out and find out where I fit."

"You can't spend your whole life hopping round to see if you fit in somewhere or you'll never be able to settle and see if it suits you or not because you won't stick around long enough to find out." Cam lies on her back and closes her eyes. "Anyway. You fit in here just fine; this is your home."

"How do you know that?"

"Just do." She picks up a daisy and twirls it in her fingers. "You belong with me."

A girl struts past in a pair of short jean shorts, cut off on the bum cheeks, wedges and a belly top. "Jeeeez, that girl is feeeeeeeeling herself!" Cam nods at her. "You go, girl!" she shouts.

"Good for her." I smile at Cam. "But back to me."

"Heaven forbid the subject would detour from you for a milli-second. Sorry, yeah?" We laugh.

"And, like, I'm only sixteen but already there are some things that I'll never be able to do."

"Huh? You're doing that thing where you start a sentence with 'and' and I'm meant to know what you're talking about."

"OK, like, I'll never be the best ballet dancer in the world. I'll never be the best violinist. . . ."

"Not true."

"Yes, Cam, because some people started learning to do these things when they were literally two years old. You've seen those shows with the child geniuses. It's too late. I have to get a wiggle on. I have zero life skills."

"Well, what do you want to do? What do you want to be the best at, BB?"

"I need time to decide."

"Take your time, then."

"I need to think at what I'm, you know . . . good at."

"OK . . . well, what are you good at?"

"Eating."

We giggle. Bellies jolting up and down. Up and down.

Cam pats the grass next to her. I lie, my head touching hers. Listening to the squealing sounds of summer. Kids in the paddling pool, dogs yelping, laughter, the nostalgic shrilling bell of an ice-cream van and the angry honks of hot agitated drivers from the road nearby.

After a little while we dust the blades of grass off our bums and pick the wheaty fluff from each other's hair. The press of grass thatches our elbows.

"I'll call you when I finish."

"I'll walk you back but not to the door. Don't want to see Alicia today, not with the aftermath of the open-heart surgery pomegranate."

"Fair enough." We hug and say a *love you.*

"Fudging hell," Cam grunts. "Everyone is so buff in the sun."

And I look behind me and that Max from work is wheeling the bin out onto the street.

# CHEESEBURGERS

You are a normal person before you get on the bus, then the moment you pass the driver you become a part of the Bus Community. Bus Club. Knighted for your annoyance at the sight of a coin of bubble gum puckered to the side of a fuzzy armrest, waiting for an issue to allow you to eyeball-roll and tut with a stranger. It's about survival, building relationships, I guess.

The bus always smells of cheeseburgers . . . cheeseburgers or wee or sweat or cold cheese and onion pasties but actually I think all of those things could also smell like a cheeseburger. When it comes to burgers I like to keep it simple. It has to have cheese. The bun has to be brioche and just as sweet as a cake. The meat has to be good quality, juicy and seasoned really well, the outside a bit blackened and charred. I love mine with a gherkin. If you can't get the best version of a cheeseburger that you possibly deserve, then you should just sack it off and have a cheese toastie instead.

I can't get a window seat and I'm looking over the heads of everyone to see where Dove is. Suddenly I see her blond ribbons of hair pegging it towards the next stop. Dodging and skirting and ducking through the streams of people like a skilled security guard dressed as a Christmas Fairy running after a shoplifter. My heart clutches as I watch her get on safely; I hate anybody that doesn't let her pass with ease—*just move out the way.* She's red in the face and panting but quickly gets over it. I'd be on the floor, wheezing, if it was me. Well, let's be honest, I wouldn't be running for a bus in the first place.

"You could have just waited for the next one?" My voice feels loud on the bus. Everybody is sweaty. Even with the windows open the heat sticks to us.

"I wanted to get the bus with you. You already waited for me."

We are literally going eight stops.

"Do you always get this bus?"

"Not really, mostly I run. Whatever the boys are doing. Sometimes they give me a backie."

"You *run* home?"

"Errr, yeah, walking's so long."

It is cute that we both go out of our way today to get the bus home together. Dove's nose is ruby-red with sunburn. The hairs on her arms and lashes have gone swan-feather white. I'm so jealous that she's getting to enjoy the six-week break to its full potential, UNLIKE me, who got conned into working a job like a full grown-up adult beast and yet still, for some reason, has to keep a food diary like a baby child.

"Think we can persuade Mum to get a takeaway tonight?"

"Not sure, all she's saying is how broke she is the whole time. Think she's worried in case her and Dad never sort it out and then she has to be a single mum."

"Dad will still give her money, won't he?" Dove looks worried.

"What money? Dad doesn't have any money either. Plus, if they break up, he'll probably use all of his money for some soul-searching trip to India." I grip her hand. "We'll be all right," I say. Luckily it's the same time the bus swings around a sharp corner, so it masks the grip as for support rather than affection.

"Do you reckon Dad is Mum's biggest regret?"

No. I think I am. She could have got *that* part if it wasn't for me.

"Probably, yeah." I change the subject. "Do you ever think about the supplies you have in your bag and think, if this was the end of the world and these were the only people left, who would you share your supplies with? I have nothing on me, so I would have to be really sucking up to all these strangers." Dove takes the question in; she looks quite serious, chewing the inside of her mouth aggressively. I carry on, "Imagine the contents of everybody on this bus's bags tipped out into a pile. . . ." We watch the people, stereotyping their bags by their mannerisms and clothes. "In her bag I bet there's hand moisturiser . . . chewing gum and . . ."

"Cigarettes . . . ," Dove adds.

"Why cigarettes?"

"My teacher always has gum and moisturiser in her handbag to mask the smell of the cigarettes."

"Ah, well spotted!" I nod, smiling. "OK, so we'd have hand cream, gum and fags. What else?"

"That man's got a pram, so he'll have loads of great stuff . . . wet wipes, rice cakes, apple juice, grapes . . . milk, maybe!"

"Good call. I'm sticking with him. But look, she's got bags of shopping full of stuff. Most of it's frozen, but in this heat . . . Come on, those Smiley Faces will be defrosted in no time."

"You'd kind of need to go round, wouldn't you, like a buffet, and take what you needed. Or exchange?" Dove offers.

"They all probably think I have loads of food in my bag. People always think I carry food with me."

"They'd be disappointed," Dove replies.

"Nobody would share with me. They'd think I'm greedy, I bet. They wouldn't dare share half their limp cheese sandwich with me just in case I snatched it and inhaled it. Like a giant, plopped it on my tongue to dissolve like an edible postage stamp!"

Dove laughs, then does an impression of some dinosaur-like hungry beast, groaning, "MORRRRRRRE!"

"Exactly. People think fat people can't get full up. EVER. Like our stomachs are massive everlasting gobstopper laundry bags."

Dove frowns. "Really?"

"Yeah, they think that's why fatness is connected to sadness, because we never feel full. Like, we eat to fill an empty void. This is what the stupid teachers at school say about me—that's why I hate that place; they never talk to *you* about Mum and Dad breaking up, because you're a thin person. The idea is so far-fetched, it's annoying."

"You're not sad at all. You never seem sad to me." Dove looks concerned. "Does that make you angry?"

"No, it makes me laugh." Because it does. That people think that to be fat you also have to be sad. Like sadness is the reason you're fat. It's what all the girls and teachers from school think. "Oh, BB's OBVIOUSLY fat because she's sad and she's OBVIOUSLY sad because her parents are breaking up, again."

My weight has NOTHING to do with my parents. What actually makes me feel sad, if anything, is others assuming that. Like I have no control over my emotions.

The skinniness-equals-happiness myth is just a terrible sum created by the media and brands to make women believe that if they are thin they are leading a perfect, carefree, successful life. That being slim means you are also automatically blissfully beautiful, intelligent, liberated, popular, cool, kind, disciplined, motivated, high-achieving, witty, spontaneous, adventurous, strong, courageous and ambitious whilst also being seriously deep in love with the person of your dreams and probably rich too, from being your own boss at your ideal job.

How, also, does this make thin people feel? Like they aren't allowed to be unhappy?

They are making money out of our insecurities, knocking us down by shoving an unachievable airbrushed model in our faces eating low-fat yoghurt and making us believe that THAT is who we need to be in order to be all of the above, to make us buy their stuff, read their magazines.

In other words, they are suggesting that being thin means you're winning at life.

And if you are otherwise, you are, well, losing.

And all of that is an utter load of absolute bad stinking rubbish.

"So this lot can go round thinking that I'm the greedy one, when in reality, if it turned to cannibalism, in desperate times, they would eat me. Everyone on the bus. Stand around me, sharpening their Oyster cards like makeshift cutlery, stomping some horrible bloodthirsty barbaric song, and then try to roast me over the engine of the bus . . ."

Dove is laughing so much little tears are building up in the corners of her eyes. "I've always wanted to eat the little fatty bits of flesh that hang over the top of your bra at the back, by your arms."

"Oooh, tender morsels there. Proper fillet. There would be a fight for those babies."

"Tossed in a bit of butter . . ."

"You'd probably ruin it by slathering it in ketchup."

Dove nods, giggling at the same time. "You'd taste so good, plumped up with all that superfood goodness you eat."

Our laughs fizzle out to a comfortable silence. Sisters. Both boiling hot and clammy. Sticky and grubby with sweat. Do people think we look alike? No. Probably not. My whole skinny family look nothing like me. But I feel strong with Dove by my side. Her arm reaching across my chest to hold the rail.

"Oi, quick, there's two seats. . . ."

# SQUASH

People avoid sitting next to me on the bus, so I usually avoid peak hours. Not because I'm embarrassed, I just CANNOT be bothered with the beef of people accusing me of treading on their toes or squashing their egg boxes with my calves. Quickly throwing their laptop bag on the chair next to them before I can sit down—"This seat's taken by my boring black bag." I once had a woman *snatch* the end of her coat from underneath me as I went to sit just in case once I sat, that would be it, she'd never see her coat again. That my bum cheeks would STEAL it. Vacuum it up with one gust of air.

I'm quiet, thinking about what the strangers have in their bags; are they wondering what I have in mine? But I bet they're just thinking, *She would be really beautiful if she lost a bit of weight.*

I've heard this before: "You're tall, BB. If you lost a bit of weight, you *could be* a model."

I don't want to be a model. Stop acting like it's a golden ticket to get through life for free. I'm not cussing models. I once watched this reality TV show for models and realised that being a model is actually kind of long. Standing around pouting and slitting your eyes, thinking about all the other things you could be doing rather than this, thinking too hard and long about how you look. It must be exhausting. After a day at Planet Coffee my cheeks are paralysed from smiling at everybody. I could do with more neutral face hours.

Imagine being a model, though. I don't want to wear clothes in magazines for companies to show girls how to *wear* something. To demonstrate how something *should* be worn. You should wear a piece of clothing how YOU want to wear it. It's like serving-suggestion pictures on food packaging . . . and nobody EVER listens to a serving suggestion. Ever.

"You never asked me what I had in my bag!" Dove yelps. "Because you're in luck, you're hanging out with the right passenger on this journey." Dove dips her hand inside her rucksack to reveal a shiny golden chocolate bar.

# CHEESE TOASTIES

The kettle boils, the toastie maker light pings on green.

"Do you think people won't take me seriously in life cos I'm fat?" I don't know why I'm asking the opinion of a thirteen-year-old.

"No, I do not think that. I think they won't take you seriously because you're sixteen. Sixteen. And dumb. Duh." Dove bites straight into the block of cheese. I pretend I don't see her doing it, disgusted. She continues. "Why would you say that, anyway? This fat talk is getting so long. It's all you talk about, fat, fat, fat. You talk about fatness quite a lot for somebody that doesn't care about being fat."

"No, I just like to point it out before somebody else points it out to me."

"'K. All I'm saying is, it's kind of annoying, just get on with it." Dove licks her thumb. "Like, it's not the only thing about you."

"Yeah, I know that, thanks, Dove." I snub her with sarcasm.

"So act like it. Jeeeeeeeezzzz."

Not 2B headbutts me in the back of the knees. "I have to go on about it because of this apprenticeship thing, I really want to work and earn money or whatever so Mum gets off my back and I can do what I want to do, which is I don't know what yet, which is fine too."

"It's good to know what you want to do a bit too, though . . . I know what I want to do." I watch Dove reach for the jam and smear it across a sliver of cheese. I then follow her hand as it lifts the concoction towards her mouth. Too much.

"Gross."

"Delicious."

"Go on, then, what are you going to do?"

"Be a stuntwoman for action movies."

"Fine, OK, so you'll be a stuntwoman for action movies, great, but you actually have a good shot at being that, Dove, because you basically already *are* a stuntwoman, but it's different for me with wanting to be a boss or run a company or start a business or something."

"Why?"

"Because, Dove, people don't like putting a fat person in a position of power—the addiction is too obvious. Like, a gambler can hide gambling or a cheater can hide cheating. You can hide smoking or even a drug habit—you don't have to wear it on your body—but as far as the world's concerned I *wear* my addiction, my vulnerability. I'm decorated in my weakness . . . like some tinfoil padded sleeping bag that I can't get out of."

"Hmm. I think it's better to know what somebody's weaknesses are from the start. Then there's nothing to hide." She sucks her thumb.

"Like battle scars."

"Kinda, yeah." She has worn blisters on the palms of her

hands. They look like craters on the moon from grabbing and gripping all that brick. "They should get a palm reader in for job interviews."

"Yeah! A CV palm reader." We laugh. Dove pushes her weight on the toastie maker; it sizzles. I wonder if anybody would know that Dove can climb buildings with her bare naked hands just by looking at her palms. Probably not. Those idiot members of the public probably think she rides one of those scooter things to school.

"Do you think I'm fat, Not 2B?"

"Eugh! Can you *stop* putting such emotional stress baggage on the dog?"

"Wait, I want to see his answer. Bark for *no* and sit for *yes*."

"Not 2B, SIT!" Dove yells.

"DOVE! Stop messing with the test."

"It's not a fair test anyway, you idiot. You're asking a dog if you're fat . . . It doesn't get much sadder than that. . . . Oh look, he's sitting."

"That's just mean for no reason."

"Oh my actual God, BB, look. . . ."

Warm, melted, gooey cheese gloops out of the toasted bread like a scene from *Ghostbusters*. Blond, stringy, salty creaminess. Rahhh-hhhh. I feel my heart beat like I'm in a romantic film and me and the cheese are the main stars.

"Ummmmmmmmmm."

"We should have added beans." Dove tuts as if we've made the effort to go to a party that's ended in disaster. *I knew we never should have come. . . .*

But I don't mind it without. The comforting thwack of savoury, salty, cheek-sucking butteriness dissolves onto my tongue. I follow Dove through to the living room, where our steaming cups of tea are waiting.

"Shall I go and put some beans on?" I ask Dove.

"Probably for the best," Dove replies.

# BAKED BEANS

I clearly remember a person from Manchester once say I was "sick for beans." As in, I was mad about beans. And they'd probably be correct because, in my mind, baked beans go with absolutely everything. I like them cold with salad, dumped into spaghetti or shepherd's pie, or mounds of them on toast. I remember once reading in the newspaper about a man finding a dead mouse in his beans. I remember the photograph of the sopping-wet blind mouse, dripping in bean juice and death. He got compensation—the man, not the mouse. The mouse just got to drown in bean juice. Pretty good way to die, to be fair.

Not gonna lie, though . . . it put me off for a bit but it wasn't long before I was back on the bean wagon. I loved them again, with potato waffles, with melted cheese. Although my first memory of beans, really, was seeing how many I could stuff into my belly button as a kid.

And let me tell you now, it was a lot.

# SUMMER ROLLS

"I'm basically broke," Camille says as we slurp fresh lemonade at the Vietnamese. We like to feel like we're so posh going out for a lunch that isn't a horrendous sausage roll from the baker's and this place is cheap but still has table service. The lemonade is so tangy and sweet at the exact same time and the sugar and citrus muddle together with the ice chips so gently, one slurp is freezing and the next is almost warm. It's like swimming in a pool on holiday and some areas are hot and others are cold from where the shade of a tree has leant over the water.

"I shouldn't even be here," she continues. "If my brother sees me he'll tell my dad and I'll be grounded. This money was from my uncle. Dad doesn't even know about it."

"I'm broke too."

"Yeah, but at least you're an alien."

"I dunno if it's what I want to do with my whole life, though."

"To be or not to be? As your dad would say," Camille jokes.

"THAT is the real question."

Cam leans on her wrist. She wears the friendship bracelet I made her. It's brown now and tatty. "I really wanted to get a job for the summer, but nobody employs a teenager for *six weeks*. It's too late now. It takes six bloody weeks to get to know the people and stop getting everything wrong."

"It's true." I nod. "I wouldn't have got Planet Coffee unless I went in there every day and pretended I knew how to use the coffee machine. Which, by the way, is really hard. Anyway, you have the Indian restaurant."

"Come on, Bluebelle, it's flyering once a week and it's a joke."

"Better than nothing, considering you talked them into giving you the job."

"You're so lucky you don't have to go back to school."

Am I?

I have a feeling I'm going to regret it. I can see it now: Cam graduating in one of those excellent black capes with the square hat, going on to become a brain surgeon, and me sweltering inside a kebab shop for just enough money to buy a kebab.

Our summer rolls are brought over. Four bulging snake-like rolls in sticky translucent rice-paper skin, stuffed with a stained-glass window mosaic of orange grated carrot, lettuce, fresh prawns and coriander and then sprigs of mint. The combination is the lightest summery bite of wholesomeness, dipped into sweet chilli sauce or a more-ish peanut dip. Camille dunks hers but then talks some more. She resembles a meerkat about to munch the head off a scorpion.

"They glamorise jobs for teenagers anyway; they make it feel like you can just roll up to any restaurant and just, like, get a job immediately while you're, like, becoming an actress or whatever, but it's not true. Actually, you need a reference. You can't just rock up somewhere and expect to have a dishcloth thrown in your hand and begin work. That you can somehow do a day's work and still find the time to go on to be a rock star or an actress or a prime minister. It's all changed."

"I know, and the classic 'Have you got any experience on your CV?' NO! Of course I don't have any bloody experience, that's why I need a job!"

"Exactly!" Camille bites into the roll. "Oh, shut the f-*ront* door, these are so banging. You know, the second I bite into them I just feel the need to order another plateful."

"So good, they actually taste of summer. I think more food should be named so poetically. You know, named after the feeling it gives you." I shake my head. "See, this is the only reason why I even want money, so I can eat out."

"Cheers to that!" Camille clunks her summer roll against mine as if we are cheersing flutes of champagne. "I tried to make these before but you know this rice-paper stuff is *im-poss-i-ble* to work with; it sticks to your *everything*. I don't know how they do it."

"I once tried to make fish cakes and basically ended up with a pair of salmon and mashed potato mittens."

Cam laughs at me and I laugh back—but not too hard—I don't want to lose any of this beautiful food to a nostril snort. I take another bite. I even like to dip the garnish in the sauce. The bush of lettuce, the strays of cabbage. I like it when they turn the vegetables, like the carrots and cucumbers, into roses and stuff, but they don't do that here. This place is too slapdash.

"I would be an amazing prime minister; I'd give out free jacket potatoes at bus stops because at least the homeless people would have something to eat."

"Oh yeah!" Cam claps. "Think about how sick it would be, though, coming home from a night out when you're broke and knowing, worst comes to worst, you're guaranteed a hot potato at the bus stop."

"Worst comes to worst? BEST, you mean."

"You love up a JP, innit? Where would the potatoes get stored?"

"Just like a vending machine built into the stop," I say, as if it's the easiest thing to do in the world. I have a vision of every London street turfed in soggy wet mashed potato.

"Great. Sounds great." Cam nods, completely convinced. "Do it!"

# PHO

Our king prawn phos arrive. Big, steaming bowls of fragrant broth full to the top with prawns and rice noodles and then you get to dress it yourself, which is my favourite bit. Bean sprouts, chilli, leaves of coriander and Thai basil and a big squeeze of lime. I shove everything on mine and every mouthful is soothing and sharp and sweet and spicy. It makes your nose run and your eyes water and gives your throat a serious massage. We slurp and spiral noodles together, splashing tails of whipping chopsticks. I am full-blown addicted to pho. Cam rants on.

"You know as well, jobs are so tight anyway these days, that you're not even just going against people your own age anymore. Like, you could be going for a job at a clothes shop that, like, a forty-five-year-old mum is going for too. And you don't really actually have a choice, it's like you can't get work, so you go into education to then be whacked with a load of debt you can't pay and nobody will even give you a job while you're at college or uni because, errr . . . MAYBE you're AT COLLEGE and when you're not there, you're studying or, let's face it, you're getting drunk. It's a trap. Then ONCE you get your qualifications all the jobs are taken or have been cut and then you're just there, trying to get the same job you applied for all those years back when you were sixteen, just this time you're way too overqualified and broke. Unless your parents are loaded or you come up with some amazing idea and become a millionaire, or win the lottery . . . you're screwed."

"A millionaire isn't even a millionaire anymore, Camille," I add. "You know how long a million pounds lasts in London these days? Zilcho nilcho. The flat next door to us—*flat*—just went for over half a million . . . HALF a million. And you've seen the state of my road. So a million is probably only gonna get you a small house. You know, when I was young and I imagined what a million-pound house looked like, straight up, I saw a castle!" Camille laughs into her soup. I snort but I'm deadly serious. "Like, honestly, Camille, I saw myself in the Disney palace, you know, that one from the start of the films. Not the cruddy house split into five flats down the road. It's a joke. My parents did well to get ours so long ago." I worm a clover of coriander from behind my molar. "I don't know how people even afford to live, let alone buy houses."

"It's a harsh time to be sixteen, BB." Camille takes a purple flower from the glass vase in the centre of the table and puts it behind my ear. "But we'll be all right."

Camille is right. It is a harsh time to be sixteen. But I'm going to spin this on its head. I don't know how. But I am. I'm not going to waste this world. We WILL be all right.

"And the worst isn't even over yet." Cam tips the bowl up to slurp the remainders. "We've still got our exam results to come. What a way to ruin the summer holidays."

Oh. Fudge.

# HONEY

I'm on the bus on the way home. The sun is beating down, making the top deck feel like a greenhouse and me, a great big fat tomato, swelling on a vine. I am still a bit red-faced from the pho too. Weird how in hot countries they eat hot things to sweat it out, like India with curry and tea.

I always, ALWAYS sit on the top deck and that is because the top deck is the deck that frightens me the most. You should, especially when you know people sometimes poke fun at you, sit downstairs, where you can avoid eye contact and confrontation and be all cosy with the bag ladies and babies. But I like to face my fears. Once a girl threw a chip at me on the top deck of the bus and sniggered, "Eat it, fatty." I just ignored the hot offensive stick of oily potato as it miserably flopped off my school blazer, and looked out of the window, holding myself together until I got off and cried so hard I nearly died. Every day I hate myself for not picking that chip up and throwing it back at her . . . or better yet, taking it, going over to her ketchup and dipping the chip in it. *Lovely.*

So, to challenge my fears, it's ALWAYS the top deck.

It's pretty much empty on the top deck because it's early after-noon and the summer holidays. There is a man in full leather reading a book called *The Dark Art of Street Magic.* He must be boiling hot.

All of the windows are open.

A boy a bit older than me gets on. He's wearing a cap and crisp white trainers. He has a hard face with sharp features, like an open toolbox.

I sit and put my headphones in and look out of the window to the street below. I watch kids playing on the pavement, bikes and skates. Dogs pulling on their leads. Men arguing over a car. A dad pushing a pushchair with twins inside. I see grannies hobbling. A woman in a purple hijab telling a story to a woman in a mint-green supermarket uniform on her break, smoking a cigarette. A road sweeper. A sweaty postman. A boy laughing with his friends.

Then I think I hear a voice behind me.

I ignore it. It's that boy; he's probably saying something rude.

He goes again.

Oh, maybe he's trying it on with me.

I suppose I do look quite hot today, and, if I'm honest, I am flourishing in my young-adult age, curling out from my cocoon like some wonderful butterfly. I'm wearing my baby-blue *maybe I work in a garage in the U.S. in the 1950s* two-piece that shows off my stomach.

I don't turn around, though. I'm not interested in being wifed off when I have a world to overtake. Becoming somebody's baby mama with kids right now is NOT the plan.

Then, obviously sick of being ignored, he taps me on the shoulder.

I snatch my headphones out and turn to face him. "Look," I say, "I'm very flattered but I'm not interes—"

But he jumps in there before I can finish with his rude-boy south London drone—"Derz a bee dyin' on yr hed."

"I'm sorry, what did you say?"

He kisses his teeth. "I said"—he gets louder—"THERE'S A BEE DYING ON YOUR HEAD!"

WHAT? The flower! It must have attracted a bee! I bat my head: he's right, tangled in my hair, caught in the strands, is the biggest, fluffiest bumblebee, wings fluttering, dying, struggling.

"WAAHHHHHHHH!!!! AHHHHHHH!!!!! Is it out? Is it out?" I panic, elbows flapping.

"Stay still," he says, and begins to rake my hair.

"Sorry, my hair is quite knotty."

He doesn't reply.

I really don't feel like getting my scalp stung today. NO THANKS. My head becoming some tortuous war zone/makeshift ambulance bed for dying insects.

"There we go." The boy has the bee's wings in a pincer grasp. The bee *zzzzz*es and eventually falls dumbly drunk on heat and, full from city pollen, purrs and sinks out of the window, looping sideways Os into the summer day.

"Thanks." I smile. "My friend put a flower in my hair so . . . maybe it was . . ." I begin to explain but he plugs his headphones in and starts texting on his phone. He doesn't care.

I can already imagine the message he's writing. And cringe. So I make up my own version of the text I'd write:

You can't blame them bees for loving honey, I guess. . . .

That's even worse.

# I REALLY AM NOT SURE ABOUT MY OWN PERSON-ALITY.

Honey is amazing. If you eat local honey, it can protect you from illnesses and hay fever; it's really good for your immune system.

You know, bees work so hard. There are worker bees and the queen bee that bosses all the other bees about and then there's this big bloke bee whose only job is to impregnate the queen bee. I always wonder if the other worker bees ever dare knock him off his pedestal and steal the queen for themselves, like, make a riot in bee land? Do you think there are ever scandalous affairs in Bee Town? Or gay bees?

Bees don't mean to sting you; quite amazing if you think they only have one chance to use their sting and they use it on you. If you're stung, that's quite an honour, really.

It's pretty cool that honey tastes of the flowers and plants near it, like blossom or eucalyptus. So you know when they build all those tall blocks of flats for all the office people in London, *they say* (I don't know if *they actually do it*) that to give back to the environment they put beehives on top of all of them, to make local honey, because you know that honey-bees are an endangered species? But basically the hives are so high up that by the time the bee travels all the way down to the flowers on the ground it will be so exhausted that it won't be able to make it back up anyway to make the honey. So it's horrible. And cruel. And they can't put flowers on top of the high-rise buildings because no flowers even grow in conditions that high.

Stupid idiots.

# SCONES

Scon. Sc-o-ane. Scon. It's scōn. Isn't it?

We do scones at work. Thick, they are. With or without raisins. Once I had an actual real-life proper, proper scone. It was at a hotel for my mum's birthday. We had afternoon tea. A big clothes-horse apparatus of a thing decorated with little fancy cakes and pastel-coloured macarons, perfect chocolate éclairs and frilly cupcakes—and then there were the scones. I'd only ever known them to be chalky baseball-type things with machine-made frills around the edges, pale and hard and heavy with little icicles of raising agent worming through the crumb. Impossible to warm the whole way through without burning the top and singeing the raisins to bitter rat poos, toasting them. Illegal. After you eat them you're left with a syrupy glue, a sort of cream-cheese paste at the back of your throat that hangs on the roof of your mouth like a hammock for a spider. Totally vile.

But these scones were warm, for a start. In a toasty napkin enve-lope, all their eyes peeping up like baby chicks . . . The tops of them glazed with a golden brush of egg yolk so they looked shiny and smart, their shapes individual, unique because they were made by somebody's kind hardworking hands. Once you broke them, they crumbled apart, their insides soft, fluffy, almost melting under the press of a heavy posh silver knife to wax with clotted cream and pippy posh jam.

Ours here are beach pebbles painted to look like ostrich eggs. Well, they may as well be. You get your "scone" with a tincy pot of jam that is so stingy the makers should be put in prison for the offence. The opening of the jam pot is too small for either spoon or knife, making it even more hateable, and not even one pot is half enough jam to cover half of a half of a scone. Stupid. The cream isn't clotted. It's a foiled tablet of cheap salted butter. BUTTER.

Don't order the scone at Planet Coffee; you might think you're eating *moon rock*. I wouldn't even put it past Alicia to go that far with the space theme. That's what makes me sick.

# MUFFINS

I REALLY like using the squeaky pen to write the menu out. *Squeak. Squeak.* I stand on a chair to do it. A metal one. One that I trust. The screws and I have forged a solid relationship, and the chair, she carries me well. Her metal works like scaffolding and I'm a big statue she's helping to lift towards the sky.

Our cake selection is actually pretty good but it's our muffins that made me want to work here in the actual first place. *Muffin* is my favourite word to write with the squeaky pen because I enjoy writing the word with the *M* really over-the-top, extra *M*-y, all joined up and loopy like the first letter of an old-fashioned fairy tale, then down to swoop low for the *u* and then making the *f*s join up like music notes. They are tall and come in little paper cups; the muffin swells out all over the top. These muffins are the reason that juicy hips got the name *muffin tops,* I'd say. Because of these beauties. They do look like a brilliant gorgeous girl with a giant bum spilling out over a pair of too-tight jeans.

The top is cracked and hardened with little sugar grains or oats or cinnamon, depending on the flavour, and inside it's all moist and crumbly and soft with a jammy, gooey middle. The chocolate one is double chocolate, so not only is the cakey stuff deep and dense and cocoa-y brown but it has these huge squares of chocolate chips running through it too and the centre is like a fondant. Moist and smooth. The blueberry one has giant sweet blueberry freckles throughout that are gummy and bleed into the soft white cake like a leaky biro onto a love letter, and the inside is so smooth and light. There's a healthy oaty one, which is soooo good, and then there's my favourite—banoffin—which is . . . you've guessed it, a banoffee pie muffin! Sweet caramel and banana sponge with cream cheese frosting with little toffee nuggets and banana chips sprinkled on top. The centre, a butterscotchy caramel whip. I mean, SERIOUSLY. WHAT THE ACTUAL HELL?

Alicia struts out. She's so annoying. She's one of those people that just eats to live. Not because eating is amazing. I'm the other way round. I'm sure you've worked this out. She loves up those really large uniform Bourbon biscuits and Jammie Dodgers when, sure, OK, they look great but they're not a delicious slice of home-baked cake. I like to see the effort: the peak of whipped cream and golden crumbling sponge, the bronzed goo of a baked peach that's caramelised the top of a tart. The rubble of toasted nutty mounds. She also thinks cakes are "real cute" if they are, like, overly iced turquoise cupcakes with glitter and plastic butterflies on top. A semi-edible greetings card. The sort of stuff people hand out at terrible baby showers. Also: Glitter is for eye shadow. Festival eye shadow. I really don't fancy seeing glitter in my poo left over from some hideous fairy cake that was decorated by somebody that should work in greeting cards and shouldn't be let near a bakery.

"Morning, aliens!" she whines in that annoying voice. She doesn't even have to put the pretend Martian voice on. Look, I'm not being mean about Australian accents, I promise, just in case you're Australian. "So, guys, how'd ya reckon you have a good day up in space?"

"Errrrmmm . . ." Max and I look to the ground. Marcel doesn't care; he's greasing his hair into a topknot. He's French; he does what he likes.

"I'm talking to you, Marcel?" She tells him off like a question.

"I'm French," he says. "I do what I like."

"You have some coffee and then you PLAN-ET!"

"Huh?"

"It's a joke. Planet. Like *plan it.* A good day up in spa—as in *plan* the day . . . but planet, because we're Planet Cof— Forget it." She straightens her face like she couldn't look more serious. "A bit of humour from time to time goes a *long* way, gang." Her nostrils flare like a dragon's. "What's wrong with you guys? Let's get the schedule up."

We set up and I go "backstage" to check I haven't got something on my head, as Alicia is one of those people that sometimes talks to your forehead or above it. She follows me in as I open up my locker. (I don't know why we have lockers; nobody ever locks them—we just dump our stuff inside them. Still, it's a cool place to keep pictures. I hang recipes in mine: *courgette and lemon spaghetti, butternut squash with kale and parsley, king prawns with chilli and red sauce.*)

"Bluebelle, can I have a quick word?"

"Sure."

"I just wanted to say thank you for the other day. I don't know what happened to me back there but you dealt with it totally professionally and you were a real good nurse."

"Don't be silly, it was my pleasure."

"Not many girls would clean up somebody else's sick like that"—meaning herself—"but you just rolled up those sleeves, got right down on your knees and scooped that vom up like a trouper."

GREAT. She slaps my arm. She does it with extra vigour; it's like she thinks because my arms are big that I won't feel the force of her bitchy birdy violence. That the nerves are numbed.

"Ouch." I rub my arm.

"Sorry, I've been doing kickboxing. Well, self-defence. You know, if a kidnapper ever approaches you on the street you just do this. . . ." Alicia closes her eyes, palms pressed together, and begins to do some sort of pointy hand actions that are meant to be t'ai chi, I guess. She sort of looks like she's massaging somebody's back.

"And what if that doesn't work?"

"It will."

"It might not."

"No, it will. Trust me."

"'K."

"Don't worry, though, babes, no one's gonna kidnap you anyway. Imagine trying to shove your ass in the boot of a car. I mean . . . let's be honest, that's one advantage to being, you know . . ."

Have you ever wanted to bite somebody's face?

I want to scratch her. Eat her. Then howl at the moon.

The worst thing is, she definitely meant that as a compliment. She does an awkward hum of some terrible song. "I'm sure it was probably food poisoning anyway. That made me sick. I had a bad chicken burger from Mandy's Diner and a few too many wines the night before." She unfolds a little hand mirror out of her pleather handbag and smudges kohl eye crayon on her lower lids, her wet mouth gaping open like she's a gasping fish. A line of spit connects her dry lips.

Everybody knows Mandy puts sleep-eye crust in her chicken burgers. Although I always think she must have to do a LOT of sleeping to gather up THAT much sleep crust. Also I don't think Mandy even exists.

"Probably that, then," I reassure her, but secretly I am body-waving inside wanting to throw her a baby shower ride all the way OUT OF HERE. I feel bad; Mum told me that women always want other women to have babies as immediately as possible to get them out of their career way, because in some places of employment there's a shortage of jobs for women, so they are all nipping at one another's feet all ugly, praying they'll take those high heels off and out from underneath that desk and become a mum, making space for the next one to come along. How horrible is that?

Anyway, now could be my chance. . . .

"Alicia, I wanted to ask you if you've, if Planet Coffee have ever considered taking on an apprentice? It's really quick; there's just, like, this application you can do . . . to, like . . . see if we can maybe apply for a barista apprenticeship? For me. And, like, this other let-ter . . . it's already typed up . . . just to say . . . well . . . it's from Julian in Careers, it's basically to say I can be an apprentice? You just have to sign it." I pull the little folded square out of my back pocket. I am sweating. Why? Alicia doesn't take the letter.

"Who's Julian?"

"Julian in Careers. He works at my school; he's, like, the career guy. I know that's not something you do here, but Julian says that some of the major coffee shops can apply for a scheme to have an apprentice and I thought—"

"Stop there, sweetie. You know that we pride ourselves on not being a major coffee chain, that's why our customers love us."

"No, no, I know—this is different. I was just saying that it's possible, that there is such a thing. You can apply for the scheme for me to be an apprentice, and that way—"

"Now, hon, I know you're in the summer holidays now and you're wanting to take a gap year to go find yourself or whatever"—IT'S NOT A GAP YEAR—"and if you're struggling for money and you want me to poke around in the rota and see if I wangle you out a few extra shifts here and there, then you got them. We all need a bit of extra pocket money, don't we?"

"Ah, thanks, Alicia."

"Not a problem, chuck, no worries, least I can do. We love having you around." She grins. "Now let me have a gander at this letter from your little Jools in Careers."

She whips it from me and clicks her tongue like she's calling a horse. "You scratch my back, I'll scratch yours, baby. But I'm not promising anything."

No, not "baby."

Shudder.

She balms her lips in pawpaw cream and smacks her locker shut. "By the way . . ." She puts a sympathetic claw on my shoulder. "Have you lost weight?"

OH. The most obvious. Most boring. Most overused fat girl compliment in the history of time. As if I'm going to suddenly spin around to Alicia with my palms under my chin and my eyeballs all big and gooey like a musical star and screech, *"OH MY GOD, DO YOU REALLY TRULY THINK SO? SAY IT'S SO, HAVE I LOST WEIGHT? HAVE I?"*

No, I haven't lost weight between now and the two seconds ago when you were just saying how fat I was. No. Weird, that, isn't it?

But instead I reply, "I hope not." And Alicia shakes her head as if she's a really bad actress in a soap and she's just found out that the man she loves is "not who I thought you were."

And then I see her pop the letter into her back pocket.

Her clip-cloppy kitten heels clap out front.

For comfort, I kiss myself on the shoulder, where her hand was.

Max catches my eye when I step out but then pretends to be pouring milk into a jug. It spills a little onto the floor by his feet. Teardrop white speckles splatter.

All day I see the top of the letter from Julian in the back of Alicia's pocket. And I watch it like it's a kitchen door at a restaurant and I'm waiting for my meal to come out. But it doesn't come out. And I fear it will be there all day. *And* the day after. Until the folds become fluffy. Until the dye from the denim bleeds into the white paper. Until it whizzes around the washing machine with all of Alicia's other bits of worn-out clothes and clogs up the arteries of her machine like a dirty tissue from a cold.

# APPLE

Apples are saintly, crunchy goodness donkey food. The hero fruit. If an apple were a person, he'd be that bloke that everybody likes that gets an invitation to more than one party on a Saturday night. Reliable. Loyal. A team player.

The only way to eat an apple is aggressively and splashily.

My body is like an apple. One that's maybe been rolling around the bottom of a handbag for a while, covered itself in glitter and hair and taken a bit of a bruisy bashing.

I want to bring this apple out with me but I don't want to eat it now because I'm not hungry and I don't want to hold the apple in my hand all day but I'd really like to not have to wear a bag today. I rub the apple against my leg, almost wishing it would magnetise itself to my clothes somehow, sort of latch itself on.

WHY don't girls' clothes come with pockets like boys' clothes do? Do we not have stuff too? I'm starting a campaign for dresses with pockets. Even guys get to go down red carpets and weddings with pockets and WE just have to shove stuff down our bras. It's so annoying. There's only so long you can hold a pound coin in your cleavage.

I'm wearing my off-the-shoulder leotard and dotty shorts. I feel like everybody is staring at my thighs. But I think it's because humans in England aren't that great at seeing naked flesh. We just aren't used to seeing that much skin. I have a massive bruise on my thigh too from work, which I forget about until I see somebody react to seeing it. Then I'm reminded of the swirling greeny purple tie-dye flower of it. I don't shave my thighs because the hairs grow back all dark if I do, so they are nice and blond now from the sun.

I meet Dad at the Lobster, a pub. He is sitting outside, in the shade, crumpled up over some Penguin Classic that's really famous that everybody lies about reading to sound intelligent but nobody has actually read unless it comes up in some school syllabus. And they still, even then, once it's been explained fifty thousand times, don't get it.

Dad always gets irritated by the heat. He scratches his ears like a flustered dog. He likes to sit all wound-up and suffering in the shade like a depressed teenage vampire. He likes to scribble down ideas and thoughts with a pencil in the pages while he's reading; he also, sometimes, licks the lead of the pencil before he writes. I have no idea why he does this. It's well extra.

"Hi, Dad."

"Bluebelle, what a beautiful day, isn't it? That's a nice lipstick . . . very . . . *bright*. You look very . . . pink."

"It's called Candy Yum Yum."

"Candy what?"

"Candy Yum Yum."

"OK." He accepts the information, logs it, and then I watch as it sails out of his head again, through his earhole into the universe to live with all the other unimportant information that parents have been told.

"Do you want this apple?" I hand it to him; it's inconvenient to carry but I don't have the heart to throw it in the bin. Sometimes I feel that fruit has feelings and I get guilty.

"I might have it in a bit, sure, leave it there. I'll pick at it." You don't *pick* at an apple. "I've got a beer here." He sips it, leaving him with a frothy stache. "Dove coming?"

"Should be."

"How's Mum?"

"Fine."

"Has she mentioned me at all?"

"Of course she mentions you." Dad looks relieved. I leave out, "Not in a good way."

"That bloody artist hasn't been over again, has he?"

"What artist?"

"That one with the ponytail."

"Keith?"

"Keith. That's the one. He fancies her, you know."

"Dad, Keith's about ninety-four years old and smells of damp."

"Well, she likes an older man."

"Don't flatter yourself. She's after younger men now!"

"No she's not. Who?"

"I'm winding you up." I feel my knees lock. "Ah, look, there's Dove."

Dove is wearing neon orange shorts and a white vest top, her long blond hair sailing behind her. She's tanned. She's never ever had to touch exfoliator or moisturiser in her life. She wears headphone buds in each ear.

"Doveling!" Dad says.

"Hi, Daddy." Dove for a second evolves from tomboy to ballerina as she leans into Dad's arms and kisses him, unhooking a head-phone.

"*Daddy.* She still calls me Daddy; you're such a little baby." He chuckles. He treats her like she's still three and I'm the big crashing horrid gargoyle of a sister, too big to call Dad *Daddy* without it being awful and weird and people thinking I'm like his girlfriend or whatevs.

"You look pretty," he says to her. Meanwhile I look "pink." Dove finds a chair and sits on it cross-legged.

"It's hot, isn't it?" Dove says, fanning herself. "It's going to thunderstorm tonight. I love a thunderstorm."

"That explains my headache." Dad rubs his head, trying to make out that he's so spiritually synchronised with the weather. "Do you not tie your hair up or anything when you do all that running around?" *He's still on this one.*

"No."

"Doesn't it get in your way?"

"Sometimes, but if it does I just wrap it into a bunch and bite it. Like this." Dove gathers all her hair up, twists it and clenches her teeth around the hair, biting down like a mum cat would carry her kitten.

"You odd girl," Dad says, picking up the apple. "So . . . which younger men is Mum after, then?" Jesus, DROP IT.

"Dad, look at my video!" Dove cleverly changes the subject. "Look, that's me, look, watch . . . doing a *front.*"

"What's a front?"

"A front flip . . . See?"

"I missed it. Show me again; hold it still. . . ." Dad fumbles with his glasses. "Start it from the beginning. Go on, wheel it back."

I watch Dove lose her patience. "OK, watch here. . . ."

"Which one's you?"

"That one."

"Here?"

"No! That's Tommy."

"He looks like a girl. His hair is longer than yours."

"Dad! You missed my front again."

"It's so shaky."

"That's because it's on a GoPro, Dad, strapped to somebody's head."

"A *go* what? I don't like the sound of this. It looks too dark."

"It *is* dark, Dad. It's a night mission."

"A *what* mission?"

"*Night,*" Dove stresses, "MISSION."

Dad looks frazzled. "Mission? What sort of mission? Is this legal? Do the police not . . . do you not wear gloves or anything?"

"No, Dad, it's frowned upon. You can't wear gloves because you have to get calluses, toughen up your hands for grip. You don't wear gloves."

"No helmet?"

"No, Dad."

"What if you fall?"

"Yeah, sometimes you bail but . . . you just try again."

"They only do low jumps, Dad," I reassure him. "Don't worry."

"*Low* jumps! Ha! It's not so babyish, Bluebelle." Dove's eyes light up. "I know someone who got *concussion* doing it."

"Good grief, Dove, what does your mother say about this?"

"She knows. I'm getting a crash mat for the garden to practise on."

"Yes, but there aren't any crash mats out on the streets of London!" Dad tries to be cool. "Why can't you just get one of those scooter things that commuters use to get to the office? Aren't they cool?"

"No, Dad."

"Huh?"

"Just. No."

# NOODLES

We wander into a vintage clothes shop on the way back from seeing Dad.

"It STINKS in here," Dove moans. "It smells of armpit and musty mothballs and . . . Chinese food. Why do you come here?"

"Because the clothes are unique and special and have history. You don't have to worry about sizes or being compared; nobody is going to point you out in the street and say that grandma from the 1950s pulled that nightie off SO much better than you. New clothes judge you whereas vintage clothes hang out with you like a friend who stands by you, whispers in your ear and keeps you company." I flip a velvet shawl over my arms. "Plus, I don't like being the same as everybody else."

Dove picks up a Fez hat and tries it on, does a face at me and then puts it back. "It's too hot in here. I'm waiting for you outside."

"'K."

I'm kind of glad anyway. I don't need Dove pinging back out of every mirror looking so effortlessly Miami eighties beach babe and trying things on for a laugh and managing to look like she's rolled out of some blog about *how to look so absolutely great a hundred percent of the time.* She would try on these vintage clothes for a joke and still look the best in the whole shop.

The music is nice and chimey. Little funny sixties melodies. My eyes are dotting about, struggling to settle. I love the clashing of prints and colours, the tumble of patterns, the out-of-place mismatching scramble of straw hats and flowery head scarves, ski suits and plimsolls, feather boas, kimonos and sparkly capes, the blend of fancy dress and genius.

"Hi." The girl looks up at me from her box of noodles. Where'd she get noodles from in a red box like they have in American films? Do you know how desperate I am to eat noodles from a box with chopsticks? Thus why the place smells of Chinese food. She's so cool. She has blue hair and a hoop through her nose and is wearing a butter-yellow polo-neck jumper not as a joke. Even in the summer. But she's pale. It's clearly her look.

We could be friends. We could have noodles in boxes and go for a drive to the countryside if she has a car. But then she ruins it. As most of my girl crushes do.

"Just to let you know . . . ," she begins, like she's being helpful, "most vintage clothes come up *pretty* small and the sizes aren't *always* what they say; they might *appear bigger* than *they are.*" I stare back, like HUH, sorry WHAT? So she adds, "Some pieces come from abroad and the sizes might be confusing. So don't be afraid to ask for help and if you want to try anything on, just ask before you try and squeeze into something."

*Just ask. Just ask* PERMISSION before you tear the seams. Before you enter, raging, like a grotesque exploding dinosaur made of hot boiling lava and ruin or eat all these bespoke "pieces," you absolute gargantuan FREAK.

"Oh, I'm leaving," I say. "My sister's waiting for me. She says the shop *stinks* of Chinese takeaway anyway. . . . Maybe it's those noodles?"

I bet she wouldn't say anything about sizes to Dove.

# SHEPHERD'S PIE

"Isn't it a bit hot for shepherd's pie, B?" Mum peers over the pan.

"Stop being so hawky judgey, Mum. Here I am just trying to pay my way and contribute to the *homestead* and this is how you repay me? With extra-rude remarks?"

"Homestead," Mum mutters. "Idiot. It smells very nice."

"AND guess what?"

"What?"

"Alicia has my apprenticeship letter and she's gonna sign it." Mum doesn't look impressed enough, so THEN I add/lie, "*And* also she's gonna apply for Planet Coffee to take me on as an apprentice."

"Well done, that's . . . good news. . . ." She is folding washing and decides to deliberately fold up a towel at this point to hide her eyes from me. "And any news on joining the gym yet?"

"God, Mum, I do one good thing and you have to throw it back in my face."

"No I wasn't, but it was part of the bargain, Bluebelle."

"Yes, I know that, thank you very much. I'm just trying to

99

prioritise and be a successful 'Power of Right Now' businesswoman. Some support wouldn't go amiss."

I really don't need the food to be tainted by my bad mood. I have to shake off Mum's rudeness so it doesn't infect the meal with all its bad feelings of bitterness and neglect. Because I am really good at making shepherd's pie. Like, really good at it. I use proper meat from the butcher. I'm one of those people who would rather spend my money on a good bit of meat than a pair of shoes. Are there many people like us? Anyway, mincemeat, not lean, the real one. If I can't find the best-quality meat available, then I make vegetarian shepherd's pie. I fry up the mince with good oil, of course, in a heavy pan. When the meat turns brown I drain off all the extra fat in a sieve and rinse the pan and dry it so it's clean. Then I pour in new oil, heat it up. When it's hot and goes all shiny I add one diced Spanish onion, chopped celery and chopped carrot. Once the onions are as clear as glass I add the meat back in. Now I raid Dad's cupboard and all of its treasures. I usually add Marmite, Worcester sauce, a bay leaf, a tin of Heinz baked beans, obvs, red wine if we have it, beef stock and seasoning.

I use baked potatoes to make *my* mash. It's hideously smooth. I add heaps of butter, a bit of milk and an egg and salt and pepper. I whip it up so it looks like a golden cloud. When the sauce has reduced and the meat is tender I pour this into our ancient olive-green casserole dish and then top with the mash. I love to spread the mash out like I am icing a dreamy cake. I sometimes like to rake a fork over the top to make little grooves in my starchy terrain. Then I grate creamy mature Cheddar cheese all over the top of it. And it goes into the hot oven.

I love the way the warm smell of it floats through the house, bloating the kitchen with comfort. I love watching the bubbling cheese and molten brown lava spots of meaty filling popping through the white mash.

The thunder outside begins to crackle and pop. And the rain tumbles down. Mum will be grateful for the pie now the storm's coming. Dove bounds down to let the dogs in, who immediately start catwalking the kitchen searching for odd ends of carrot tops and escape-peas.

"Oh FOR THE LOVE OF—" Mum shouts.

"What?"

"Which one of you little moos invited Dad over?"

"I didn't," I say.

"Well, why's he running towards the front door, then?"

"I felt bad for him, Mum," Dove admits. "He's all by himself."

"He's not all by himself. He's got his big fat ego to keep him company. Bloody hell, Dove."

"Sorry, Mum."

"It's fine. He's your dad, I suppose."

"And anyway, then you two can get back together."

"Ooooh, over a romantic sexy shepherd's pie and a summer thunderstorm," Mum jokes. "Go on, let the old rat in."

Dad enters; sodden, with a soggy *Guardian* newspaper over his head. I bet he LOVES looking this rain-drenched, bet he thinks it gives him real hunky charm and artistic neediness.

"Hello, my darlings," he almost sings to us in an overly good mood, and then he goes to the dogs, scruffing their ears. "Smells good, Bluebelle." I dump the hot pan on the table.

Mum has hers with peas. Dad, the bedraggled lost property jumper of mankind, has his with buttered bread to mop because he constantly has to feel like a downtrodden, mule-riding travelling-man-with-no-money-peasant that's turned up at an inn in the middle of the night for bread, cheese, ale, stew and a straw bed to sleep in. Which basically is an accurate representation of what he is. Dove has hers with a big splodge of ketchup.

But I like mine just exactly like this. On its own. No distractions. Just warm melty strings of chewy cheese, clinging to buttery salty mash, protecting the more-ish stew beneath.

And I pop the pan back in the oven for whoever wants seconds.

"Dunno where you keep it, Dove. It's like you've got worms or something," Dad jokes at Dove's massive fruit-bowl-sized portion, which she hugs close to her chest as though she's about to be mugged for it.

"It's good," she grunts, like an ungrateful nana over Christmas dinner.

"'Tis," Dad agrees. *'Tis.* We're not in a period drama now, Dad. It's too hot for him; I can see him tossing the hot potato around his mouth, hooting out steamy air.

"You're a very good cook, B," Mum chips in. She's obviously just trying to make up for her mediumly rude and unnecessary gym comment.

Admittedly, even with the press of a storm, it's a way-too-hot, clammy day for shepherd's pie but you can't rely on English weather, so you just basically have to eat whatever food you fancy whenever you fancy it. Plus, for London, summer just means overstuffed bins in local parks with half-eaten tubs of houmous frothing out of the top of them. So eat what you like. The whole time.

I am looking at Dad. We all fully know that he came not only for a hot meal but also to patch things up with Mum. Dad likes to look at Mum like she's melting his heart right before his very eyes. I wonder if that's how he looked at her when she was a student and he was her tutor. I can't *imagine* fancying one of my teachers. Maybe it's different when you're nineteen and your armature dramatics teacher on your funny little course is a kind of hot teacher. Not that Dad's hot or anything. You know what I mean.

I do quite like it when we're eating in the quiet like this. Knowing we are all experiencing the warmth of the same hot meal. The summer rain pattering outside. That we have something in common.

A four. This is us. Complete. But he just can't help himself, can he?

"That farty-arty Keith guy been over recently?" Dad asks Mum with an ugly jealous tone in his voice, and that's all it takes.

Mum and Dad are at it again. Rowing. And the sink is full of a snowstorm of starchy watery clumpy potato pellets that never seem to wash away and fill me with gloom. Luckily, Planet Coffee has taught me the importance of owning a pair of "dinner lady hands" and not to be afraid of touching old food of any kind.

# EGG-FRIED RICE

It doesn't hurt to shield the ducks' eyes from cooking eggs.

"They don't know what they are, you idiot," Dove moans as she thumps the wok down.

"You don't know that," I say, trying to wrap my fingers over their quacking heads. We have three boy ducks. However, we actually thought they were girl ducks at first and named them Mary, Kate and Ashley . . . (yes as in those Olsen twins, which I know is old-school but *It Takes Two* is probably one of my favourite *I feel sick I want to watch* . . . films), so we tried to give them boy names but we kept forgetting, so we just call them their maiden names. I would say Ashley came off the best. Mary, not so much. Anyway, they are all annoying and actually *all* rapists. I don't trust a single one of them. I've seen them do it. Hence why we have no girl ducks but, oh no, trust me, that *does not* stop them. Still, doesn't mean it makes it any easier to watch an egg being eaten.

"Anyway, they're ducks; these are hens' eggs," Dove points out.

Mary isn't even letting me cover his eyes, so I get bored of being nice anyway and sling the ducks outside.

"Eggs aren't anyone's babies, you know, BB. It's different. They aren't chicks." Dove curls her body down into some odd yoga move and peels back up.

"Dove, an egg is a chicken's period."

"Seriously? That's gross."

I make pretty much the best egg-fried rice, bar the boss at Happy Garden takeaway, than any other human. I rinse and then boil the basmati rice up—small tip: do NOT use cheap rice—then leave it to chill; once cooled, refrigerate. Then, when it's all cold I heat up sesame oil and when it starts to smoke I dump the chilled rice in until it toasts and crackles. Then I add two (OK, four) eggs . . . scribble the yellow around with a fork or chopstick, add lots of salt. I like the rice to catch a bit on the corners so it goes golden and crunchy. While it fries, I quickly slice two spring onions in horse-ear shapes and turn the heat off, sprinkle on top and serve with soy sauce. It's nice to let people add their own soy. That's how you're meant to serve it.

"You never put peas in!" Dove moans.

"You're not meant to," I argue. She rolls her eyes and digs her hand into the Crunchy Nut cereal, pouring it into her mouth.

"Don't eat that, it's gonna be ready in literally two minutes."

"Well, I *literally* can't wait, so . . ."

"You won't be hungry."

"Trust me, I will."

I know she will be annoying if I don't get the peas out of the freezer and add them to the rice. I have to put the kettle on too to defrost them.

We eat the rice. It's obviously amazing.

"Was nice having Dad over, no?"

"Yeah, I just wish he wouldn't always make dumb comments like that to rile Mum up. I can see why she finds him so annoying."

"Hey, do you remem—" Dove starts laughing so hard she can't get her words out.

"What? What are you laughing at?"

"Do you remember when we used to play that game Bum Tills?"

"Oh my G—" And we are both crying with laughter. Paralysed in a shuffling squeeze, heads tipped back so that the laughter is a mouth-open silent fit.

# BUM TILLS

Bum Tills.

I am going to take you back to my childhood. When bath time was playing pubs and mermaids, and our bedroom became the supermarket. The shelves were adorned with fabulous supermarket treats, where one-legged Barbie posed as a carrot or Marshmallow the Teddy Bear acted rather impressively as a convincing loaf of sliced bread.

I would always be the cashier, because I was oldest, obviously, AND it was my idea. Dove, being the recessive, would play the till.

Let me explain. . . .

I'd set myself up, on the bottom bunk, a fistful of empty carrier bags from a real actual supermarket behind me, flattened by a heavy book to look legit and fresh from the box and not crumpled as they are normally in the cupboard.

And Dove would have to lie over my lap with her trousers down and her pale little bum sticking in the air.

On the cheeks of her bum I would draw a till: various buttons dotted in felt-tip to push and prod, a keypad of numbers and a little screen for the total amount to roll through. I would draw this in ink and use an ink eraser for reality so I could change the amount for each customer every time. It was pretty much exactly identical to a real-life supermarket checkout.

Our school friends would come over and pretend to buy stuff from the supermarket, filling up carrier bags with the odd shoe or sticker book, instrument or tennis racket. They'd browse. Sometimes I'd hum some valid pop tunes I knew to make the supermarket seem even more authentic but nothing too cool or distracting—it was a supermarket, after all, and had to seem genuine.

BUT the best bit was to come. When the school friend shoppers came to the cashier—yes, me—it was my time to truly shine. I'd drag out the paying process, scanning each item, tallying it over Dove's flobbering little bum cheeks. She'd squeal and giggle while I prodded the numbers and talked to the shoppers about their "plans" for the week and asked them if they noticed the recent promotion on the toilet roll, did they have a club card (fingers crossed) and did they find everything they needed. When it came to paying, they'd all, of course, want to pay with a "credit card" (a playing card, dad's driving licence or . . . anything card-shaped lying around). And I would take the card and swipe it through Dove's bum cheeks, like at a real till point.

The transaction was complete.

# BACK TO RICE

The dogs sniff around for scraps. We eat until we hear the fork scraping the china of the bowl.

"Right." Dove stands, stretches and begins packing a bag.

"Where you going?"

"Parkour."

"Oh, Dove!"

"What?"

"Can't we be cosy in our sloppies?"

"No. Dylan has borrowed his dad's drone, so we're gonna film ourselves jumping off the bus shelter."

"LONG!" I moan. "I HATE parkour. It always steals you away."

"You could come do it with me? Why don't you try it?"

"Dove, in case you haven't noticed, I happen to be fat."

"What, and that means you can't move?"

"I have asthma really bad and I'm fat, so no, I can't go running around jumping off roofs and bus stops and stuff."

"There's always an excuse with you."

"Plus, I don't own a sports bra. My boobs would be, you know, all everywhere."

"Sports bra? I never need a sports bra."

"Dove. There's a big difference between you and me. You are thirteen. A lot can happen in three years."

She glances at my chest. "No thanks." She wraps her hair in her hands. "Better be getting your sports bra soon, though, for the old gym or else Mum will be livid."

"Don't remind me." I press a worm of rice with my forefinger, smushing it. "Off you go, then, to your best friend *parkour*." I begin tidying away. "What've the London streets got that I HAVEN'T?"

Dove blows me a kiss and skips upstairs. She moves like she's constantly on a pogo stick. "Thanks for dinner." Her voice pings off the pans—that I have to wash up.

"Be careful!" I yell after her.

"You be careful," she shouts after me. "You're the clumsy one!"

I fill a spoon of rice and lean it back like a slingshot towards the dogs. The rice spills up into the air like confetti and the dogs leap up to grab it. Wet mouths and clunky teeth, slobber and chatter.

Dogs don't even chew. Their mouths open like singing Muppets; they breathe in a gust of air and close like pedal bins.

# CAMOMILE TEA

It's hot in the cafe. Even with both fans on and the windows open the air seems to be bloated and stuffy. I'm wearing my pink-and-orange giraffe print shirt with my long pink Mexican-style skirt. My hair is up in an electric-blue rag. I loved the look of tying it up in the mirror next to my bright orange nails. I think about all the dirty air I'm breathing in, rinsing through my lungs and puffing back out again. We are quiet, so I'm giving the cutlery a polish. It's nice to eat cake with a fork. That's how you know it's good cake. When it forks away in crumbles.

Alicia's got Max and Marcel cleaning out the shelves behind the counter. They go all the way up to the ceiling, glass jars stuffed with loose tea leaves and coffee beans. Old dust-filled water jugs and glass vases. They do say pregnant people like to nest. I hope she isn't planning on nesting here too long.

Where is she, anyway? Has she even sorted out my application form yet? I really don't want to have to start considering other options.

Marcel is perving on the girls tanning in the park. AGAIN.

"Oh man, oh man. These girls are KILLING me today!" he sleazes. I roll my eyes. "Girls love cake; come in here and get some cake. I'm going to write on the board 'FREE CAKE' and watch the girls run in." I wish I had earplugs.

"Oi! Marcel! If you're gonna hold the ladder, then HOLD the ladder!" Max orders.

There's only one ladder and Marcel has already made it clear that he's not "risking his life for a cafe." Fair enough. I wouldn't have minded getting up there on the shelves but Alicia didn't ask me to go up the ladder, probably for obvious reasons. It's too hot anyway. I sit on my favourite metal chair to write the menu and watch Marcel hold the ladder as Max creeps up with confidence. He's tall enough anyway and could probably reach without it, his long octopus arms stretching to the layers of dust and junk. Swirls of powder wisp out in circles, the rows of fairy lights dancing as his hands gently brush them. He's delicate. His hands poke and shift as though the objects are soft fruit on a bush he doesn't want to damage. He's careful not to drop anything.

"Come on, man, why are you so slow?" Marcel sweats below. "I want to smoke a cigarette and talk to some ladies."

"Just don't hold it, Marcel. It's more annoying with you half holding it," he replies breezily without even turning round.

Watching Marcel, this hot little ball of frustration, sweating beneath the tall calm willow tree of Max is making me laugh. He then starts to tell us what he looks for in a girl.

"Big breasts. Big buttocks. Small waist. And long hair." I switch off after he adds, "Nothing makes me more sad than when a beautiful woman cuts all her hair off short like a boy."

"What about her personality?" Max asks.

"Huh?" Marcel replies, genuinely shocked at this.

I'm going to start bringing my headphones in to work.

Max, above, from behind, his low jeans, his Calvin Klein boxer shorts peeping out . . . I find my eyes looking longer than eyes normally need to look at anything . . . unless you're reading a really good book or watching a great slice of TV. Does this make me as bad as Marcel? Perving on Max? Is this perving? Or appreciating? Would it offend me if Max was doing this to me? NO. I'd love it.

Marcel, yes. Gross.

Max's mum is from the Philippines and his dad is Irish, so he has almond-shaped green eyes and buttery skin. Splattered in a supernova spray of camouflage freckles. That match his shorts. The sun makes him appear golden, like light breaking between clouds.

I wonder if Max has a girlfriend. He never talks about girls. Maybe he's gay?

Then I start to realise that actually maybe Max doesn't even talk as much as he's COMPLETELY—SOLIDLY—ALWAYS present in my mind and that makes me think that perhaps, just maybe, I might just talk *at* him quite a lot of the time. And maybe with all my talking at him, I think that we've had a conversation, when chances are, we probably haven't. It's just me, obsessing.

He starts to pass the mottled glass jars down to Marcel. The lids are thick with grey fuzz. Marcel moans, exaggerating the weight of every jar, lining them up along the counter. A customer walks in and Marcel serves him and begins to make coffee. Max stays up on the ladder, rooting through the shelves. With Marcel busy, Max looks back at me, cheekily grinning, and mimes a bullet to his brain to demonstrate what it's like doing a chore with Marcel, and I giggle. When he laughs these new dimples appear. Oh. His teeth are fish-bone white and sharp at the sides like little daggers. He touches everything with respect. Gracefully.

"Oh, fresh camomile, so much better than those tea bags we do here."

"Probably so old now, been up there so long; must be like drinking dead moths."

"Shall we find out, Blue?" I love it that he just called me Blue. "Fancy a camomile tea?"

"Sure, why not?" I smile.

Max hops down off the ladder. Marcel doesn't look impressed but Max ignores his fuzzy-eyebrowed glaring and starts fiddling around with a tea strainer and the urn. I like to watch the way Max does everything; it matters that he thinks it all matters. The way he carefully spoons out the golden dried-up flowers, choosing which cups we should drink from. His long fingers lingering on the clattered saucers. Smiling the whole time. I feel myself blush. With a butter knife as a mirror under the table, I secretly check the redness of my cheeks.

Max reappears before me with a steaming teapot and a broad smile, his eyes eclipsing the world behind him.

"Well, good news . . . it smells like camomile," he says, happy with himself.

"It's gonna send me to sleep; camomile tea relaxes you." I bite my lip, setting out the cups and saucers he's carried over to the table.

"Does it? I find all tea relaxing." Our eyes wrap around each other. I find him relaxing. Like hanging out with a cat or something.

"Some loose teas are really strong."

"If you brew them too long."

"It's too hot for tea!" Marcel snaps the moment shut and we are disappointed to see the customer exit the shop with her takeaway cup, leaving Marcel as our spare wheel, making things wonky.

"No it's not; tea makes you sweat, it actually cools you down," Max argues.

I LITERALLY MADE THIS POINT IN MY OWN BRAIN JUST THE OTHER DAY. WE ARE SO SYNCHRONISED.

"You should try some, Marcel." Max winks at me; he loves winding Marcel up.

"I don't need to cool down, man. I don't need to." Marcel shakes his head and then does an exaggerated stress yawn.

Max whispers to me. . . . Three, two, one . . .

And on cue Marcel grunts, "I need a coffee."

Max nudges me in the ribs. "Always know when he *needs* one."

I open up the teapot. The gravelly sound of ceramic grinding; the smell of blossom.

"What's the tea saying?" Max peers in. His face is so honest and open; he's bashful but confident in his own way. I like the way he dedicates himself to a task, no matter how small, and concentrates on it. You get the feeling that when he's talking to you, all he is thinking about is talking to you. He's genuine. And kind. His kindness evaporates off him, competing with the steam from the pot of tea.

"Let's give it a go," I say. Looking up. We are both pretending to really care about this one pot of tea he's made. We are invested in it, like it belongs to us. It is a device that we can pour ourselves into. Something simple and sacred that we have in common.

Yellow liquid gold fills the cups; two loose petals float to the surface of my teacup, riding the waves and rocking on the ripples. The potpourri dried bundles are revived.

"Do you want honey in yours?" Max asks.

"No thanks, I like it as it is."

"Bluebelle's sweet enough!" Marcel jokes, all corny.

I realise I've been polishing the same teaspoon for seven minutes and my thumb has got cramp.

"I could just sit here all day," I say. "Couldn't you?"

"All life," Max giggles. "I think I could probably sit here all life."

# ROSE WATER

"Chop-chop." Alicia slices through us. "Come on, come on, none of this chilling-out-time little tea party. You're not in the school common room now, guys."

Max and I jump up and snap back to standing. Max looks at me for a lingering second. I almost feel him deep-sigh as he breathes me in. I could swear he wants to be annoyed at Alicia for splitting up our romantic tea date but he'd never show it. He sees the good bones in everybody.

BUT.

I don't. Not right now. ALICIA! SO ANNOYING. (Sorry I know this is not about food and here I go again but I really just need to get this off my chest like SERIOUSLY GRRRRRRR. You know when a chick just really wrestles with your patience and messes with your life, it's, like, help a sister out here. DAMN!)

Maybe Alicia just has no social empathy. Perhaps she has no radar that shouts MAYBE THIS GIRL IS TRYING TO DO A FLIRT HERE AND I DON'T NEED TO SABOTAGE IT.

It would make sense, the way she doesn't understand food; she has no sense of style or taste when it comes to eating.

I know Alicia doesn't care about cakes properly because she likes weird horrendous flavours like rose water and that's just not a cake flavour ANYBODY would choose to eat. I hate rose water. It stinks. I hate it. It tastes of old ladies. It ruins all cakes.

Rose. A beautiful flower. A lovely perfume. But not a food.

We separate across the Planet floor as customers come in. A couple hunting for coffee after jogging. Rosy-cheeked and breathless. Their forefingers in a loose knot around each other as they scan the menu. My handwriting in scribbles.

Max goes over to them. He shares that same smile he gave me. I am so envious of their eyes getting to see his smile up close. It's wasted on them.

The blur of the radio remixes with the beat of my heart. The people darting about outside in their summer colours. Lost in the heat. The peak of summer.

And here we are. Thrust against the greenhouse of the coffee shop where it's hot and sweaty and sticky. With the face-clogging cloy of coffee. The way the black speckles from the grind get under your skin, the hit of it at the back of the throat, the bitterness of its smoky ash-like density. Then there's the scrapes and turns of metal on metal. The crumbling clouds of carrot cake almost seem to collapse under their own sweet softness, icing melting to the point that sugar granules seem to give themselves up willingly. And Alicia, snarling. Red lipstick over the lines of her lips, arms folded, eye twitching.

And so I am handed a wet sponge.

I feel my flesh rolling over my clothes. It's a pressing tightness that I like. I think chub rolling out of fabric is quite a pretty look. The idea of Max maybe watching my body makes me feel prettier even though my eyeliner is realistically probably smudged but I've learnt to love that look a bit too. I am buzzing after talking to Max. My body still shooting white stars through my bloodstream. I am scrubbing the front window, watching Max make coffee in the reflection. I can almost see the camomile tea running through his blood and veins like hot liquid gold to the point that he begins to shine, like a lava lamp through his skin. And to be on the other side of the room from him after coming so close feels sad and wonderful at the same time, like the nostalgia of coming home from Disneyland after the best day ever.

# TURKISH DELIGHT

Do NOT even GET me started.

# RICE PUDDING

It's gross. I wouldn't touch rice pudding with a ten-foot pole. It's foul warmed-up sick. It's always gloopy, it's always lukewarm and it does nothing for jam. It actually makes jam taste worse. Dove eats so much rice pudding. Then again, Dove eats so much of everything. Her food diary would be a thousand-page novel in comparison to mine, so be grateful. She has about nineteen sugars in every cup of tea—the spoon can stand up straight on its own—and *every* meal comes with a starter warm-up pack of cheese and onion crisps and gets chased with a jam tart or an iced bun, yet she is the size of a small fairy imp. I don't get it. I quickly imagine her one day being a grown-up mum with three kids and she *still* isn't fat. Not *even* then. She could turn into one of them old nans and get really into puzzles or doll's houses and never get up and she still wouldn't even be fat. Not EVEN then. Even if my brain tries its very best to accessorise her with the extra folds and bulge, it won't stick. She won't ever know heaviness like me. Ever.

"How'd you stay so skinny, Dove?" I ask her but I'm careful how I ask because I don't want her thinking that I want to be different from how I am. PLUS, I don't want her to think that I think she's *too* skinny, like *bad* skinny because also *skinny* gets as much of a bad rep as fat does. Like when people say "You're so lucky you're so skinny." If they don't want to be skinny, that's just as offensive as calling somebody fat. Funny how people think it's rude to go round calling people fat but not skinny. Skinny people get self-conscious too.

I watch her leapfrog off the back shed, swing into the tree, hobble up to the top, launch herself onto the fence, dangle her way along the sandpapery edge of the duck shed and, catlike, hop up onto the window ledge of her own bedroom and crawl inside. "Who knows?" she pants, and smiles, shutting the window behind her.

I reach for my inhaler and take a long, deep drawn-in puff. No matter how much I'd like to say it doesn't bother me, I do sometimes flirt with the idea of being tiny and how much easier that might make my life. Because maybe it would make it easier for others. To not have people second-guess if I can do stuff. To not have to make comments about moving around me.

To not make me then second-guess myself.

To not feel like I'm in the way.

# STALE POPPADOMS

We have three ways of making money between us, Camille and me. I have Planet Coffee and babysitting. And Camille flyers. Literally standing outside, handing out leaflets to strangers. When she first told me about the job I thought it would be flyering for cool things like club nights and gigs but because she's under eighteen she flyers for an Indian restaurant, the Lancer of Bengal. Three nights a week she stands in the doorway of the restaurant, handing out flyers. And I go, when I can (be bothered), for company and a morale boost. Mostly it's just us. Shivering. Sharing a pair of headphones, one in each ear, bouncing away to a song.

The money is terrible, and what is more terrible, they don't even give us free curry. Once, when it was cold, we got a cup of chai and a basket of unhappy-looking stale poppadoms that were basically thrown at our heads like we were desperate pigeons. We still ate them because we *were* desperate. Because we will literally eat *anything* put in front of us, let alone *thrown* at us, and because it counted as a freebie from the restaurant and we've been desperate for a perk of Camille's job ever since she started there. Something we could tell our school friends to legitimise us—"Yeah, I ALWAYS get free poppadoms." Plus, stale poppadoms are delicious. I love it when they get soft like edible salty paper. It's like the flavour of the sticky bit on an envelope. Amazing. The chai was all right too.

"Help me. It smells amazing," Camille moans. "They are so tight. I'm so starving. Why can't they just feed us, man? They make vats of the stuff. I don't get paid enough for this crap." She groans, staring into the window of the Lancer.

"Why don't you just ask them for a little cup of dhal or something?"

"You ask, they *like* you."

"They like you. It's your job, Cam."

"I've only got the job because nobody else is enough of a mug to do it. They literally pay me enough for my bus ride to get here." Camille clicks her tongue. "They probably think cos I'm mixed race I can't handle the spice. My dad literally fed me hot sauce as a kid. It's so insulting. I'd eat their hottest curry as a dare!" Cam grunts. "Go on, go tell them to dare me, BB."

"You want me to walk in and ask them to dare you to eat their hottest curry?"

"Yeah." She begins to crack up at the ridiculousness of what she's asking me to do.

"You know they give chillis to people in rehab? Apparently the rush of the heat is like a buzz."

"FEED US!" Cam suddenly screams at the door.

We both laugh so hard. Camille kicks the bricks of the Lancer.

"A bit of wee just pushed out."

# TUNA

"Not even one onion bhaji, not one; how bad is that?"

"Pretty crap."

"I'd even take the burnt stuff."

"Ooooh, I'd love a peshawari naan right now, wouldn't you, though?"

"I might buy one."

"Cam, you can't *buy* one, that's letting them win. You really would be a mug then."

"You're right. Least it's not cold." She sighs deeply, scratches her head. "People always overorder. I'd take the scraps."

"It's just the smell that's making you want it," I remind her. "See, this is when my jacket-potato-at-the-bus-stop idea would really come into its own."

"Oi, go look desperate at the window. Hungry eyes, go on, like a peasant from the Victorian days at Christmas. Make the customers feel guilty." We rehearse our hungry faces. "We look *insane*." She laughs. "I want your face, like that, as my wallpaper." She pats her pocket. "I actually did bring a tin of tuna." She wriggles her eyebrows. "But I haven't got an opener."

"A tin of tuna? What? Why?"

"Yeah. I love a tin of tuna, little bit of protein on the go. I thought I picked up a ring-pull one but it's the other one. I hate that. Why would they make any tin without a ring pull?"

I always like to think of "they" as the people we assume do all these things for us in the world, like bottle our ketchup and pack our crisps, when really those people called "they" could just be us. The consumers, *they* might like ones without ring pulls. No, *they* would not.

"I hate it when they put tuna in brine."

"JEESH! Me too. The order goes: sunflower oil, then spring water and THEN brine."

"Bit dog-foody isn't it, though, with the ring pull?" I grimace and Cam crinkles her nose up. "Yuck, that's the worst, when the dog-food cans don't have ring pulls and then you see the slime of that gross gold jelly glooping out of the top of the can. Like a pork pie."

"That's disgusting. Shut up. You're putting me off my tuna." Completely not caring that people in the street are now staring.

"Well, you're putting me off living. You haven't even got an opener."

"I know but I'll find something. Can maybe use a key or . . . I dunno."

"How you gonna eat it? What you gonna use?"

"With the lid. My fingers. Dunno."

"That's gross."

"I'm starving. See what lows this restaurant has led me to?" She moans and then knocks on the glass with her knuckles and says, "See what you've led me to? This is desperate measures!"

I shake my head at the audacity of her.

Cam delves into her pocket and reveals the proud round disc of tuna. "Dolphin friendly." She grins. "Thought you'd appreciate that." She then takes her door key out and kneels down on the ground, the stack of flyers for the Lancer in a powder-pink pile next to her. She kneels, the blunt key at an angle; she tries to cut, stab, prod, scratch.

"It's not working." She bangs the tuna can on the ground. It dents. "These things are indestructible." She bangs it again. A gust of wind drapes past from a too-fast car and picks up a few of her flyers, skipping them across the street as she crawls forward like she's playing a game of Twister, spreading her body weight out, pressing her fingers and knees on top of the pile. "Whoa, nearly!" She laughs in relief and I help her ruffle the flyers back into their stack and she leans back and sends the can of tuna rolling across the pavement.

"That's my tuna! Here, hold these." She shoves the leaflets in my hand and runs after the can, which drops into the road as a car approaches. Cam screams, "STOP! That's my TUNA!" before the driver runs it over, popping the metal with a thump, and speeds away. Cam screams from the heart in a blood-curdling bellow, and then an *ah* in surprise.

"No WAY! BB! Best can opener ever!" Cam giggles in delight and runs into the road.

"Watch out!" I shout.

"I am, BB! Look, nothing's coming." She crouches and peels the smashed can of tuna off the ground. It's a mess of elephant grey and elephant-ear pink. Splattered. Cam holds it like a dirty tissue; thick fishy oil is dripping onto the ground in greasy dots.

"Can you actually BELIEVE it?"

"You're not really going to eat that, are you?"

"Course! Life just gave me a blessing; are you serious? This can of tuna could change my life. It's a sign."

I watch her picking off the lid with her nail: shreds of grey metal.

"Watch your fingers!" I warn.

"I am." She picks at it again; the tin vibrates. "The lid's not coming off properly still. Pass me the key again, if I just dig it underneath maybe I can . . ." I watch the staff of the Lancer peering through the window at the commotion. They must think Cam's opening a safe what with the concentration and excitement on her face. "Let me just press that down like that, then this bit might tip up."

I watch the yellow price sticker darken as the sheen of oil bleeds over the top. Fish smell everywhere, simmering in the summer-evening air.

"Cam, just throw it in the bin."

"This is a good can of tuna here, BB. You don't just *throw* it in the bin."

"It's been HIT by a car. I'll buy you a new one, with a ring pull."

"That's not the point." She grits her teeth. "I want *this* can of tuna. Look, see? I nearly got it. Can you just hold that bit? Maybe just put the flyers down a sec and hold that bit for me."

"All this for a can of tuna, come on. You're getting oil on those great culottes." Cam winks at me and has to stop prising the lid off just for a second to spread her legs and show me how excellent it is that her bottom half could pass as skirt *and* shorts.

"It's not about the tuna anymore; it's the principle." She tuts. "Help me. I'd do it for you."

I put the flyers down and I have to hold the bent lid down as Cam uses the edge of the key to flip up the other side. The lid slowly begins to creep up, opening.

"Yes! Yes! Yes! BB! That's it! Press a bit more. . . ."

*SMOSH.*

The can of tuna lands facedown on the stack of flyers. Fish oil soaks into the paper, and coats our hands, fish-stained and glossy and tacky.

Cam just breathes in. Picks up the leaflets with the can of tuna on top, scoops up the whole lot and dashes it in the bin.

"Oi!" she shouts at a waiter, who peeps his head up sheepishly over the window. "Yes, you, I quit!" She storms over to the door and roars through the Lancer's letterbox: "This is long and you never give me any free curry; it's a disgrace."

And we stomp home back to mine absolutely starving and stinking of canned fish.

My hands are stinging with the wetness and awfulness of the tuna stains. They feel heavy. I have to keep my hands open like claws and away from my person, stretched out. The smell follows us home like the smell of vomit.

And without even enough money for a bus, and out of principle, we have to walk the LONG way home.

# OLD SHEPHERD'S PIE

"There's no way I'm gonna be able to find my keys in my handbag with all this tuna on my hands." I peer into the opening of my bag to see if I can make them out among the litter in there. All I can see is a lipstick, a tampon, a dog-poo bag and a tangerine with white dots on it. "I'm gonna have to wake Dove."

"Do it."

"DOVE!" I shout. "DOVE!" I pick up a stone and lob it at her window. "DOVE!"

Wait.

Her bedroom light pings on and she comes to the window and stares down at me. Unimpressed.

"What the actual hell?"

"I'm locked out."

"Why don't you have your keys?"

"I've got tuna on my hands."

"I don't even *want* to know."

"Can't you do that climby thing you do and get down the drainpipe and let us in?"

"Or how about I just climb down the stairs?"

"Or that." I smile. "She's so clever," I growl proudly at Camille.

Dove, livid, opens the door. She's wearing pyjama shorts.

"Wash your hands," Dove orders.

"All right, bossy. We're starving," I announce.

"Have you been to that Indian restaurant thing *again*?" She looks disgusted. "And did they not feed you *again*?"

"No, they are so tight. Don't rub it in."

"You're so pretty," Camille tells Dove. "Your legs are like bread-sticks." People are always telling Dove how pretty she is.

Dove rolls her eyes. "Mum's gonna be raging at you." She *loves* saying this as she stands over us making sure we scrub the tuna oil off our hands with washing-up liquid, like some evil guard at a prison.

"What is there to eat, then?" Camille suckers the fridge door open before snooping around inside. "I wish we had money for a pizza."

"Who on earth has a job at an Indian restaurant and doesn't get free curry? I don't get it. You two are idiots." Dove leaves us and heads back up to bed.

"The cupboards are bare." I puff my cheeks out.

"I hate it that your mum isn't *that* mum."

"Me too."

"Wait. . . ."

And that's when I remember the most best greatest thing in the entire world. There is half a shepherd's pie in the oven.

"Oh my actual days, we are saved!" Camille grins, already beginning to peel the cheese from the roof of the pie.

"Reckon it's all right? It's, like, really *days* old."

"Sure it will be, it's shepherd's pie. It's basically industrial. Don't these things get better with age anyway?"

"Hmm." She might be right. "But I didn't have it in the fridge."

"Oh come on, B, this is basically medicine compared to the dirty dog-food kebabs I usually eat after working."

Camille's right. And an oven is basically a fridge's understudy, so . . .

And the forks dig in. The mash is cloddy, almost frozen into a starchy iceberg and very baking-tray tasting but the flavour's still there. Ish.

"Oi, shall we whack it in the microwave?"

We fill our bowls and try to ram both of them into the micro-wave at the same time. They clunk and boff off each other, clanking round clumsily as the glass plate beneath jerks off its pivot.

"It's not heating. We have to take turns so it gets ALL the heat."

Camille puts her hand into the Alpen and scoffs a handful of ashy snowy flakes. It dusts her chin in powder. Impatiently we take turns to heat our bowls until we can barely take it any longer, forking our mash down lukewarm. Camille douses hers in brown sauce, chilli flakes and then a spoonful of mango chutney. I just have mine on its own.

"I am unemployed." Camille balls a fist under her chin.

"Don't worry, something will come up again soon."

"Why can't I keep a job?"

"Because you're too wild, that's why."

"What *are* you doing?" Camille asks me in a tired voice.

"Writing something down."

"What? Why are *you* writing?"

"I have to write down what I'm eating in this stupid book."

"It's a shame that what happened, happened. Otherwise you could have written down tuna," Cam says wistfully.

We share a toothbrush and head to my room. We go to sleep curled up like a balled-up pair of odd socks.

It feels like we have been asleep for four minutes. . . .

"BB!" It's Mum. "BB, wake up."

"Huh?" My eyes are clamped together with mascara spiders. The sun is beating through my curtains. SUMMER. YESSS.

"I need some help with the ducks."

"I hate it that you have ducks," I whinge. "They can't even have cute babies because they're all boys. They just quack and be annoying. I just want to sleep."

"Please help me."

"Mum, I just want to sleep."

"Bluebelle, if you think this not-going-to-college malarkey means you going out and sleeping in until eleven every day and not helping me around the house, then you have *another* think coming."

GRRRRRRRR! I think about arguing how amazingly consistent and good I've been at keeping my food diary but (a) it doesn't exactly mean I've been on a diet and (b) I don't want her to bring up the fact that I still haven't been to the gym. It was the deal, but OF COURSE you know that and are probably thinking YOU'VE DONE NOTHING EXCEPT EAT.

"Mum, technically, it's the summer holidays, so I haven't really *left* school until the holidays are over. I'm entitled to a break after my exams as the new school year hasn't technically begun, so you're kind of being unfair by taking away my rights." She ignores me and walks away. "Where's Dove, anyway?" I demand. "Why can't *she* help?"

"Jumping off buildings somewhere, no doubt."

I sink my head into the pillow. I hate this family.

Camille rolls over. Her Afro is in my face like sleeping next to a giant microphone. "Let's help your mum, come on. She's good to us."

Zombie-like, we plod to the kitchen. The sun streaming in through the window is making me feel all boiling hot like I'm stuck in a tent, trapping our skin all claustrophobic, like we have hair gel smeared all over our faces. Camille is wearing a bikini top and boy boxers but I don't think they belonged to a boy, ever. Her golden belly pops out like a little troll's. I could just pop a magenta gemstone right in the button of it. She's so lucky, she tans so beautifully in zero point one seconds. I am in a full matching set of pyjamas. So I doubt I could get a tan anyway. I love pyjamas.

"Thank you, girls. Basically, I need one of you to come with me to the pet shop to pick up straw because you can't park there and last time I got a ticket, and the other one to clear out the duck shed."

"Oh, Mum!" I moan because I know it's going to be muggins here that has to clear out the pooey shed.

Camille laughs as she hides her hair under an orange hoody and shoves some sliders on her feet and heads out with Mum.

"The shovel is out there."

"Oh *thanks*," I shrill sarcastically.

"And remember, the dogs can't be left alone with the ducks."

"Yeah, yeah."

"Enjoy the sun!" she teases, knowing I'm fuming.

# DOG FOOD

Mary, Kate and Ashley quack around me. Oh, NOT NOW. I'm so tired. My eyes burn to a crisp in the harsh light. Sizzle like burnt onion skins. It's so sunny. I'm so thirsty I could drink an actual lake.

Mum thinks she's so creative because she found an old bath on the street and turned it into a makeshift pond for the ducks to swim in. They have to take turns but they quite like it.

The dumb Dalmatians are here too. Sniffing the garden. Taking unnecessary wees to show off their freedom and trying to suck up to get treats and snuffling up the odd bit of duck food.

The shed is full of poo. Thick, feathery, leathery clammy streaks of wet, cloddy straw that is all sodden together and heavy and neon from duck wee. The rake claws mightily. I feel sick. My brain is swollen from the heady stench of *bleugh*. Maybe this sort of manual labour counts as going to the gym anyway? It's this sort of toil that earns you a torn muscle or a hernia or whatever. I imagine my back being torn apart like strips of streaky bacon, all the fat separating as I shovel. I'm like a farmer. Maybe THAT'S my calling?

"Hello, Bluebelle!" It's my neighbour Farhana, from next door. She's all right. "Lovely day!"

"Yeah!" I smile, a big one.

"Everybody is out on their balconies today!" She grins. "I've got to water my plants—look at my thyme; seen better days, right? It's so hot!"

I look around. Farhana is right. Everybody is out on their balconies. Watering their plants. Reading their newspapers. Saying hello. I always loved it that we have balconies on our houses. It makes our homes feel Mediterranean because it is so rare to have them on London town houses. Even if the view is mostly pigeons and flying crisp packets. Ah, it's quite nice really, on a day like today. Except ours is the worst balcony. Everybody else's is all smart metal, painted and lovely with plants and tables and chairs and mini barbecues. Ours is more like a ramp. A leaning ramp, hanging on by woodworm-snacked puffs of wood that almost seem to dissolve when you touch them. Decorated in bird poo and fag butts from the neighbour.

I lower my head. Continue to shovel. It's times like this when I could do with more limbs. Holding the bin bag open to tilt the wet straw in is proving to be hard. The dogs keep grunting around, gluey noses poking into the bag. "No, it's not for you," I tell them, wrestling with their big spotty sides.

"Eugh! That looks tough!" It's Gerald, the other neighbour. He's an author who looks *nothing* like his author photograph because it was taken twenty-five years ago. I know: I've researched him. He stands, proud, pregnant-looking and smug, on his balcony like it's a stage. "Rather you than me!" he jokes, balancing his mug on his gut.

"Ha!" I shout back, mainly because my brain isn't working enough to comment.

"Still, I suppose you have to pay your way somehow, even if it *is* just to Mum. When I was your age I had to do a paper round AND get the coal *AND* give my mother money for rent." He stretches his arms like he's some kind of hero. Why is he showing off that he had to give his mum money? Weirdo.

Camille is so lucky. All she's got to do is sit in the car and wait for Mum. Dove's the real lucky one; she never has to do stuff like this because she's always busy. I need a hobby or a club. Like how Dove has gymnastics and parkour. Yes, yes, I know the gym exists but that's NOT a hobby, that's a punishment. What club can I do? Wish I wasn't too old for Brownies. Brownies was wicked. Could really do with a squad of goody-goody Brownies cheering me on right now. Even more so now that my days are long and never-ending. I can't just work in a cafe all day. Twix club? Baked bean club? Garlic bread club? Key ring club? Something to get me out of thi—

*Oh dear, no.* Suddenly it's like the bottom of me has fallen out. I need to poo. Badly. I feel my organs sliding away from each other like the polar caps in the Arctic, melting, making way for a lava spill of furious hot poo to gallop out of me. *Oh what, why?* I smile politely to Gerald and try to act normal. I might have even mumbled something like "I forgot to . . . erm," but I can't be sure. I drop my shovel to the ground, where it lands with a dollop. The ducks look startled. Wet-mouthed, I shake. The dogs follow me, as we all know dogs double up as police officers and dustbins, to make sure I'm not rushing inside to either murder a burglar or drop a vat of gravy onto the floor. But it's just to get to the toilet.

I can feel the shepherd's pie banging on my insides like trainers in a tumble dryer. I knew we shouldn't have eaten that rank old rancid thing.

The heat of the sun is making my temperature rise, basically cooking the whole thing in my stomach. Melting it down. The disease of diarrhoea is punishing me. I've been POISONED. By my own self. Suicide. Death by shepherd! I run to the back door. . . .

It's locked. It's locked. I try again. Wrangling the door. It won't open. What? WHAT?

WHY DID SHE LOCK THE DOOR? WHY DID MY STUPID MOTHER LOCK THE DOOR? I DON'T UNDERSTAND!

Meanwhile, my bumhole is anything but locked. It is a wide-open discount store that is screaming "SALE! EVERYTHING MUST GO!" Sweat beads begin to squirt out of my forehead. My hairs all spike up and my toes curl as my body is shuddering. 2B grunts, Not 2B is bored and walks off. Disappointed there's no intruders or gravy. Their Dalmatian spots begin to blend and merge. I'm losing my mind. I need to poo so badly I'm losing my actual real-life vision. This can't be.

The ducks quack.

POO. POO. Actual, literal POO. Threatening to force its way out of me like a Mr. Whippy ice-cream machine. I trap it in.

I run around like a sweating headless chicken among ducks and dogs and overgrown weeds and the annoying pond bath and all this gross hay. Sweat is pouring off my face. Can I find somewhere to do a poo in the garden? But how, without being noticed by my nosy neighbours who are all enjoying the sun?

I've also left my phone indoors, so I can't even call Mum or Camille and get them to rush home and let me in.

They'll be back soon. The pet shop isn't far. Even though my mum takes a batrillion years to shop, I'm thinking Camille might've had the same reaction to the old shepherd's pie and they might have turned back.

I just need to hold it. Hold it. And breathe. Focus. Think back to that woman who came and spoke at school about mindfulness and meditation. Blank it out. What was it she said? *You are on a beach. . . . You can see the sea. . . .* NOW RUN, RUN INTO IT AND . . . POO!

Wah. Breathe. It won't be long until they come back. I tremble. I feel *sick*. Wet mouth. I spit. The bulking bashing of squishy, hot poo in my insides is terrorising me. I try to look calm. But I feel like I have a wet handbag filled with warm brown goat's cheese slamming about inside my guts. My bowels are a punching bag being beaten. A bagpipe of mud.

And then it only gets worse.

"BB!" It's Farhana. "Your mum's out the front. She says can you let her in. She's locked out."

What the actual hell?

"Sorry, what?" This can't be. I feel dazed. Feverish.

"She's left the front-door keys on the kitchen table; she's just asked me to ask you if you can let her in."

"Farhana!" I scream. My voice garbles; I feel like I'm talking gibberish, my mouth as lose as my bum. I can't be bothered to be nice to anyone anymore, no more pleasantries from me. "SHE'S locked the door to the garden from the inside! I'm locked out; I can't get into the house!"

AND P.S. MY BUM IS ABOUT TO EXPLODE!

"Oh dear! What are the chances?" Farhana bites her lip. *Well, don't just stand there.* "I'll let her know." She runs back inside and I squirm. 2B and Not 2B glance at me. L-o-v-i-n-g the drama. Smugly toilet-breaking liberally to spite me. YOU DO NOT NEED TO SQUEEZE THAT FAKE ANXIETY-WEE OUT, 2B. I have to find somewhere to go. I have to try the door again even though I know it's locked. *Maybe the heat made the door swell? Perhaps my hands were too clammy?*

"Bluebelle!" Oh no, not Gerald the author. He dangles his head over his balcony, mug balanced cockily in his hand. "Your mum's outside, she's—"

"I know, I know!" I snap. I KNOW! Shut down.

I can't do this anymore. I can't.

I need to get this disgusting Trojan horse of a shepherd's pie out of me. It's toxic; it's poisoning me. Why couldn't it come as sick? Then it wouldn't be so embarrassing. I could just lean over into a bush and be sick. Pop stars do it on stage all the time. Come on, if I could find somewhere to turn upside down it might come out of another hole. I can barely move; I'm walking cross-legged. Hopping. Bum cheeks clenched. I don't dare fart. It would rumple out of me. HELL. OK, THINK. . . . Right up next to the back door, there is an alley, only small, with a cupboard door where the lawn mower is kept. I creep around there, crouch and prepare to poo—but it's all decking. I can't just go freely like that. I don't know what's going to come out of me. What if somebody walks out at the wrong time? Yes, maybe my bare bum will be out of view, but the eruption of poo might not go so unnoticed. It might spill out of me like a glass of spilt chocolate milkshake. Crap, I need a *thing* to crap into.

The dogs look like they're looking around for me too. But I know they're not. They don't care. *Just DO IT. Be natural and free and animally like us!* they think. It's so tempting. But I'll never live it down. I'm meant to be becoming a woman. Not needing a *baby nappy*. I'll never be a manager of anywhere. I think about the annoying smug nurse from the doctor's laughing in my face. Alicia from Planet

Coffee tutting at me in disgust. The girls from school. Blegh . . . *She's so fat and gross AND she poos herself.* These stories don't just go away, you know?

I can't. The poo is bellowing, desperate to begin its grand exit and thunder out of me. Why do I feel like it's taking over my body, drip-feeding poo into my veins?

I'm so hot. I have to smash the window, break into the house. I take my pyjama top off, so I'm just in my once-white-now-looks-like-it's-been-retrieved-from-a-Victorian-ghost tea-stainy bra, and wrap it up around my elbow. I am so impressed I know to do that and not punch the glass through with my fist like an actual idiot, which I CLEARLY am. I size up the window, ready to punch the glass. But I can't. I'm tingling. I feel so weak from the necessity to poo that I have no strength. If I do a punch, I'll surely do a poo too. No woman-power at all. I have to grow up.

This is my moment. *You are a responsible adult now, BB. You got yourself into a jam and you're gonna get yourself out of it. Let this be the start of the new you.*

I go back to my spot, breathe in deep and pull my pyjama bottoms down and then I spot it. The dog bowl. Sod it. I drag the bowl towards me; at least then it will be contained. It scratches, metal on the tiles. Not 2B hates my guts—*Not in there, no, not in there, BB, THINK!*—but whatever, he needs to be brought down a peg or two. Sorry, Not 2B.

Shoving the metal pan under my bum like a potty, I, without much choice, release hot sloppy poo into it. The dogs whimper.

Gerald pops his head out onto his balcony to say something

but I point a finger at him from my crouched position like a possessed demon giving birth to another possessed demon, Possessed Demon the Second, for example, and roar, "GO BACK INSIDE, GERALD!"

And he skulks back in as I continue the big smushy relief. Eyes closed, it gallops out of me. I am rattling with the sensation. Trembling. So elated I feel I could float. Actual heaven. Pull my bottoms up.

Now. I am back to life. A superhero. Capable of anything. I breathe. Wrap the pyjama top again over my elbow. Focus on the glass like a bull's-eye target, smash the window; it shatters in one go. I am SUCH a badass ninja. I use my other hand to unlatch the bolt. Clank. Yet again, absolute boss. Inside, I run through the house. It all looks so basic and inferior to me now that I am a legend capable of breaking into houses and just as I reach the door the key inside the lock twists. Mum and Camille enter with Dove.

"Dove let us in. I told Gerald to come out and tell you. Did he not say?" BLEUGH. WRETCHED FLASHBACK OF GERALD SEEING ME POO! The eye contact. Shudder. Mum continues: "Sorry for locking the door, it's just habit. How did you get inside?"

"I just . . ." I feel frantic. "I just smashed the door with my elbow."

"You smashed the glass? BB, we were only outside for two minutes. I just rang Dove, she ran back with the key. Couldn't you have waited?" Stupid Dove with not even one bit of sweat on her stupid perfect forehead after running in the heat.

"Not really. I . . . had a bad tummy. Did you, Camille?"

"No." Camille laughs, carrying through the stack of straw. She looks perky and fresh. She's got bagels under her arm. We couldn't be in more different places at this moment.

"Is the shed clear?"

"Sort of, but, like I said, I had a bad tummy." I follow her through to the kitchen, where she unpacks her shopping.

"It's hot, isn't it?" She reaches for a glass to fill with water, rolling her eyes at the shattered glass on the floor. She looks out into the garden . . .

Where there are bloodstained white feathers everywhere.

Mary, Kate and Ashley . . . OH NO!

Those dogs do NOT hang about.

"Well, we won't be needing this anymore, then." Mum throws the bag of straw down and I run upstairs to shower.

# TOAST

Toast eases most things. Even toast from crap white sliced bread—
that and a cup of tea and you can fix quite a lot.

But not three dead ducks.

Or having to hose out a dog bowl full of your own poo.

It's later that day when Dad comes over.

"It's Not 2B!" Mum yells. "He thinks he owns the bloody place."

"Don't blame Not 2B!" Dad yells. He's wearing a flat cap these
days and he flops it off like a prop and slams it on the coffee table to
show he's annoyed. I can't help but judge all of his actions like he's
been directed to do them. "What do you expect? If you get three
ducks with two Dalmatians there's going to be carnage. They *are*
dogs, you know, Lucy. They hunt."

"They are badly trained."

"Oh, see it as the equivalent of you being left on your own with
four hundred glasses of chilled white wine and being asked not to
drink one."

"Excuse me?"

Meanwhile, the toast is amazing. I can drown out the thought of the ducks' murder and the poo incident and them arguing with the delightful lullaby of pale, salty butter. The smushing soft, warm press of a doughy mattress, the crumbling of salty Marmite rubble, collapsing under each chew, the crisp toastiness, washed down with tea. It's my fault. I never should have left the ducks unattended.

Then the pair of them *really* begin to row.

"Where are you going?" Dove says as Dad gets up.

"I'm leaving. Your mum's being a septic *cow*." And then he walks out.

Mum turns to us and laughs. "His hairline is so receding," she says. "I don't know what I ever saw in that bloke. Honestly, girls, never fall for an older man, because it seems fun and mysterious at the time and then you turn around and before you know it you've gone and made babies with your granddad. They say they have money but it's a lie; you end up paying for *them*." She rubs her eyes. "I'm sorry, girls, I shouldn't be mean; I know he's your father but I just need to get this off my chest." She rubs her neck like she's about to say something she's been holding back for a too-long amount of time. "Your dad is a deluded, arrogant, egotistical, self-pitying old pig with a drinking problem." She catches her breath, clears her throat and begins again. "He looks like a tub of butter, an old one, that should be in a museum. It's laughable." She strokes the dogs' heads. "What on *earth* was I . . . ? Dove, go pour me a glass of wine, would you?"


Turns out toast can't fix Mum and Dad either, but I love each and every mouthful.

# CORNISH PASTY

"No, I know what he looks like." Mum sips the wine; it's clearly giving her clarity. ". . . a Cornish pasty. Your father looks like a soggy Cornish pasty . . . sweating . . . in a paper bag."

You know, in the olden days, you used to be able to get Cornish pasties that were half savoury and half sweet so the farmers could take them to work and have a main and a pudding in one filling lunch. I think they should bring that back.

# LATTE HEARTS

It's not that I fancy Max but maybe I think I fancy him.

Quite an actual lot.

Max and Marcel like to talk for hours about the coffee beans. I know I *a bit* fancy him because I'm jealous of the coffee beans. I am jealous of how Max talks about them like it's his genuine passion. I am jealous of the way he holds the beans so gently in his hands, how he smells them, breathes them in. *Flirts* with them. I want him to talk to Marcel about me like I'm the coffee beans. Saying how great and unusual I am.

I flump next to the two of them. Next to my rival, the beans. Knuckles pressing into my chin. I have on my alphabet shirt. It's covered in coloured letters. And high-waisted pink leggings. The boys have a little thermometer thingy that they dunk inside the milk frother, and challenge each other to do designs on the top: leaves, fans, flowers, birds, presidents' faces.

"Teach me how to do one of those," I ask Max. And by "ask" I mean "BEG." Oh, I feel like my mum, perving all over him. OK. Time to admit it: I FANCY MAX. IT IS OFFICIAL. OH I HATE

HOW I'M WRITING. HOW I'M BEING. THAT YOU'RE READING THIS IN MY FOOD DIARY AND IT CLEARLY HAS NOTHING TO DO WITH FOOD BUT BLOODY HELL THIIIIISSSSSSSSSSS GUYYYYYYYYYYYYYYYYYYY. TOO FIT. TOOOOOOOO FIT.

"What, Bluebelle, you've been here ALL this time and you STILL can't make a coffee?"

"Shut up, Max. I want to do one of those designs on the top."

"Latte art!" Marcel smiles proudly. GO AWAY, MARCEL. "I can do boobs."

Max tuts at Marcel. "I'll show you." He smiles at me. Sometimes he looks at my mouth when he speaks. His head is newly shaved. I want to say *Have you had a haircut, Max?* but I'm a bit worried that it's slightly forward.

"Do the boobs if you want to get a better tip!" Marcel interrupts.

"It doesn't make the coffee taste any better," Max argues.

"But it shows you care!"

"Oh look, here's your chance!" I point as an old lady with a sausage dog wanders in. "Go earn your tips, Marcel!"

Max laughs and walks me over to the machine. "OK, your milk has to be all shiny and silky like this. You know if you have an espresso in the bottom of the cup, it's about trying to get the milk to go over the top of the espresso, so that it cuts through; it's what's going to get you that ripple effect, see?" I watch him gently curving the cup in his palm, swivelling the side of it round, angling it so it slides into his hand. "It's about pouring it from a height; then you begin to get closer. . . . When you've got that, you tip it up, here—you have to move quickly—and then . . ."

"A heart!" Could I be any more delighted?

"Yeah. You try."

"Let me taste it first," I say. "Bleugh! No, still vile."

Max laughs and hands me a fresh cup. The coffee machine churns. I do the same, following his precision. "Yeah, that's it, but relax your hand a bit more. . . ." He hovers over me like he wants to reach out and take the cup out of my hand. DAMN MY HANDS FOR BEING SO UPTIGHT. "Can I?" he asks gently.

"Sure," I say shyly, thinking he's about to snatch it off me, finding it unbearable to watch me mess up his passion.

But suddenly, instead, his warm hand is cupped *around* my hand. My tremor. The coffee flutters. I feel my heart racing a bit. Feeling a bit nervous.

I thought all you had to do was do your life and go to sleep and wake up and eat and drink and be happy and work and your body would work it out for you if you fancied somebody or not. I thought it just did all the sums for you while you slept and gave you the results in the morning, in your private time, when you were alone. Not when you're in front of the suspect, when you're at work trying to make a heart on the top of a latte.

Oh, how did I get here? I HATE MYSELF.

"You're shaking."

"I'm nervous."

"Why are you nervous?" BECAUSE YOU ARE LITERALLY MADE OUT OF CARAMEL AND ARE BRINGING ME OUT IN HIVES. DUH. "I had to do this hundreds of times to get it right." He takes my hand. I feel like the coffee is doing that thing the water does in *Jurassic Park* in the scene with the car when the *T. rex* is coming. BETRAYING ME. Absolutely throwing me right under a bus.

BANG. BANG. BANG.

Before I know it I am saying what I just thought out loud. Oh, hideous brain, you deceive me. "Ah, it's just like that scene in *Jurassic Park* where the *T. rex* is coming, you know, with the plastic cup of water . . . you know . . . the ripples . . ." *Oh shut up, BB.*

"I haven't seen *Jurassic Park*."

"You haven't seen *Jurassic Park*? Sorry, do you live under an actual rock? I just . . . Am I meant to still be your friend or . . ." PERHAPS YOU COULD GET UPGRADED TO BOYFRIEND.

Gross. I'm so easy to hate.

"Come on, it's so old."

"But it's so relevant. The effects are still so good. Like how you use the thermometer for the milk? Well, *Jurassic Park* has basically become my thermometer to tell if films are good at effects. Like, if it's a new film with a massive budget and the effects *still* aren't as good as the effects in *Jurassic Park,* then it is a hundred percent a bad film."

"OK, I'll check it out." He pretends to write on his hand with his finger as an imaginary pen *"Jurassic Park"* and then pretends to throw the imaginary pen over his shoulder. I giggle and it's the most annoying laugh you've ever heard.

"It's also become my thermometer to decide if I like somebody or not. If they haven't seen-slash-enjoyed *Jurassic Park,* then we can't be friends and they aren't my species."

"Hold on . . . you can't go round saying 'slash' in real life."

"I can say exactly what the hell I like."

"You're quite cocky, aren't you?"

HUH?

"Me?"

"Yeah."

"No, I'm not."

"Yeah you are. I'm not saying it's a bad thing or anything, you don't have to be offended, but if it's a weapon, a defence mechanism or whatever . . . all I'm saying is, you don't have to use that weapon on me."

I stay silent. I watch the coffee out of the corner of my eye. I can't shout at him because that will count as another weapon.

"I like how you are. You can be—SLASH—SHOULD BE—yourself, because being yourself is good and please don't rule me out as a member of your species because I haven't seen *Jurassic Park*." He whips the coffee cup up in the U-bend of his thumb. "And there you are; you did it!" He raises the cup like a potter spinning a jug on a wheel. "A sort-of-ish heart!" he announces. But I don't think I can listen because my heart is raiding around my chest looking for an exit to physically thump onto the ground, grow legs and run to the chapel to be wed.

"It looks like a broken heart to me." I laugh and go to tip it down the sink, embarrassed.

"No, no, wait!" Max says. "I'll drink that."

I watch him sip it, pleased as punch, if punch was ever pleased. That's my coffee going down his throat and into him. Sorry about me.

"You OK?" he asks.

And then I just say it, don't I?

"Er . . . have you had a haircut recently?"

He rubs his head. "Yeah, went to the barber's this morning."

"It looks very . . . barbery."

"Barbery. OK." He grins and Marcel snorts. Shut up you, Marcel.

And I have to put my whole head in the fridge to stop the blushing. My hand curled into a C-shape, frozen, from touch, recovering from THAT.

# VINEGAR

I care a bit too much about vinegar. I completely love it. I love so much vinegar on chips that the hairs in your nostrils shrivel up, your ears block and your cheeks pop. Any kind too.

I have an actual physical and emotional relationship with vinegar. I love vinegar MORE than I love boys.

And I need to remember that, should I need to put things into perspective, like I clearly do now.

When we were younger, we used to go to this after-school club. It was basically a church hall with chairs and tables and table-tennis. They did supply some games and stuff but you weren't cool if you touched the baby games, sticky with the touch of five-year-old bogey fingers. Gross. Kids NEVER wash their hands.

There was also a little hatch shutter thing that was pulled down as in the daytime the hall doubled up as a cafe for old age pensioners. There were little woven baskets stuffed with sachets of sugar, ketchup, brown sauce, tartar sauce and vinegar. I never tasted the food there but I always wondered what it was like.

Most of the boys and girls would sit in corners, thinking they were being really discreet, and do first-time kissing and over-the-clothes feel-ups.

But I just used to sit on my own, with the odd ends of fuzzy felts, making a farm or a beach scene, sucking on a sachet of tartar sauce or vinegar like it was an ice pole.

That's the sort of girl I am. A not-cool one.

I like vinegar more than boys. Can somebody please make me a T-shirt with those words on it? Because I think I need reminding.

Because maybe . . . MAYBE . . . I like a boy a little bit more than vinegar.

# COLD PASTA

The feeling has not worn off. I know I fancy him. Max. Because I am wearing a very big baggy T-shirt. That is how I know I am in trouble—and I do NOT want vinegar. And it's not just ANY big baggy T-shirt, it's one that has an astronaut body on it and when you wear it, your head becomes the head of the astronaut. Yes, it is THAT bad. I am wearing skanky old leopard-print leggings and manky old espadrilles and not one single stitch of makeup. This is the ONLY way I can know if Max fancies me back.

If he fancies me back when I look like this, then it will be genuine and our romantic love affair can begin with a road trip to somewhere great like, errr, maybe actual heaven. (I hate myself and every word that comes out of my mouth.) Or maybe I'll just TRY for one second to play it cool and reevaluate what to do next based on his actions.

If not, then I can get over this messy hindrance of my personal excellence.

But then why am I looking for Max's name on the schedule? Why is he not in today? Why am I walking past the odd jumble of left-behind coats and jumpers on the hangers to pick up his fig smell in case one of them belongs to him, even though it's full-blown summer? Why did I make myself fancy him? *Get over it.* You don't need to stoop this low like some hideous fangirl. OK. Do something productive with yourself, write a novel in your head, make an album, learn how to be a scuba diver or make a wristwatch with your bare hands or become a calypso dancer . . . anything but wasting your days obsessing over a BOY. Boring. OK? OK.

Fine.

Over.

No more.

Done.

I might just steal his number out of the staff contacts.

No. Psycho. Absolutely not.

I hate him. I actually hate him. I do not even like him. He's not even funny. Goodbye. Goodnight. *Adios, amigo.*

OOOOOH, what's Spanish for *Will you be my boyfriend?*

NO! STOP IT!

Calm the fudge down. Wish so bad I could take a nap so this nonsense could blow over.


The day is so dry at work. Alicia insists on listening to the cruddy playlist entitled "Chill-Out" or "Sunday Morning" on shuffle. It's not even relaxing: it's just the album tracks of pop stars that you would skip, which are only decent when an actual cool band or artist performs them for an ironic unexpected cover. It's quiet today because the weather is sunny and nobody wants to sit in Planet Coffee roasting their bums off when there's sunshine in the park. I think it's funny that we're like particles that have to be charged by the sun. We are just simply plants.

With the place empty, Marcel is on the takeaway coffees, so I'm, in Alicia's words, "giving the place a spruce." She *so* is pregnant. What the hell? I have to wash and dry tea towels, mop the floor and then clean the fridge out, which I don't actually mind because I can just imagine that me and Max are meanwhile running away to Japan to eat those cute cakes and go to those excellent cafes where there are cats just freely around and available for you to stroke whenever your heart desires.

The fridge inside the staff room is way more interesting than the big fridges out the front. I like poking through the old lunch boxes and seeing what gross things people have left behind, and working out people's personalities from that. There are two more members of staff that I don't ever really see because they work on the days I don't, but I guess soon I'll get to know them more. So for now, I judge them by the stuff they've labelled: carrier bags shoved in the back of the fridge containing just a wilted pear, now soft. Odd crusts of half-eaten sandwiches and orange-stained Tupperware. Healthy packaged salads dressed with good intention before they've been sacked off for a McDonald's instead. My favourite labels are the ones that say "MINE. DON'T EAT!" ultra-aggressively in black marker, as if there is some sort of feeding beast that works here that just HAS to eat ALL the homemade Tupperware-packed lunches. . . .

There are some boxes that stink, so I have no choice but to throw them away, the contents and the box. Old curdled milk, wedges of hardened cheese mottled in furry blue dots that crack like worn heels. Browning fruit and straggles of tinfoil, half-sunk juice cartons. Labels wallpaper themselves onto the fridge walls but my worst is cold pasta. Pasta that cements to the fork in clumps, that snaps and rejects sauce.

There're no leftovers from Max. There's no label saying "MAX." How dare he leave this mysterious untraceable trail for me? What is he, extinct? Is he really that chill that he doesn't have anxiety about spending lunch money like the rest of us?

Doesn't he want me to obsess over him? Doesn't he want to go to Japan and stroke all them cats? Doesn't he know how brilliant it would be to have a cool girl like me fancying him?

I see what he means about "cocky."

I hold my breath and reach further into the fridge for the odd crinkled-up stalks of tomatoes and soft grapes. I run a damp cloth around as far as my arm can reach without straining too hard. I mean, I like to do a good job but I'm not gonna clean it like it's my *own* fridge.

There's an itch on my nose but I don't want to scratch it because I don't want all these fresh fridge germs to touch my pure innocent face and my nails aren't long enough to have a good scratch without any cell-on-cell action. I mean, it's not like I'm working with a freezer here where these viruses get killed off; I reckon they thrive here in the lukewarm, puke-swarm fridge.

"Hello, BUM!" Alicia shrieks. HA-HA-HA. Slow blink. I imagine the view she must be witnessing, me face-first in the open fridge, like the back of a horse in a stable munching on a hay bale. She steps forward, bumping hips with me. "I'm on my lunch break, got to make a few phone calls and take some stuff to the bank . . . might pick up some sushi. Doesn't this weather just make you want to get wasted?"

"I . . . errr."

"I just want to sit in the park with a few wines and relax, you know?" She rubs her belly. "I'm exhausted." Cracking her neck she grabs her purse. "And I meant what I said the other day . . . about the shifts *and* the weight-loss . . . you're glowing, looking totally rad." And she heads out.

Not again. REALLY? I don't look "rad." I look horrendous, deliberately. Just hurry up and fill out my stupid form and sign my letter so I can take it to Julian from Careers already. So my mum gets off my frigging back.

# TONGUE

I wait for her to leave and then I poke my tongue at the back of her head and then think about sticking my fingers up at her but then wonder if perhaps she watches the security videos, so I get anxious about that and poke my tongue out again as if I have food on my chin or something I am trying to get off. Then I become conscious of that and pretend I have a tic. I figure six or seven tongue pokes over the next hour should cement the fact I have a possible tic.

I feel like my hands need a hundred scrubs after touching all the butter-cold whiteness of the staff room fridge. My fingers are stale and pink and prawny, ripe with bacteria. My hair smells. I go out the front, watching Alicia trip-trap down the high street, placing her Ray-Bans over her eyes. Bopping down the road like she's some insane female detective with baggage.

"Let's get this music off!" I say to Marcel. "Quick, change it."

"Hallelujah!" He rushes to the laptop.

"That doesn't mean *you* can put something on," I warn him.

He listens to house.

"What about a movie soundtrack?" he suggests.

"Sure."

I stretch. I crick my neck; it cracks like a walking stick being dragged along a set of railings. Not ideal.

"Can you please make me an icy hot chocolate?" Which is exactly as it sounds.

"Anything for you, my darling." Marcel is in a good mood.

"Thanks."

I think Marcel could make a good feeder, like if someone was into that. He always puts extras on everybody's everything. My icy hot chocolate is going to have cream and sprinkles, I can already tell. I don't ask him to not put the cream on, though, because I don't want him to make a comment like "Watching your figure, are you?" I just don't like cream on my hot chocolate. I scrape it off with a tissue and flush it down the toilet.

I watch the boys and girls flutter about in the summer sun. Vests and skirts, shorts and sunglasses, box-fresh trainers and new fold-lined T-shirts. Girls suffer in new sandals that rub and blister the backs of their heels and squeeze their toes in to reveal varnish-chipped stubby, hangnail trotters. Pale legs or sunburn, red-raw dots of fresh-shaven skin. The soft touch of inner thighs. Dry skin on knees. Dark patches. And kids, melting-lolly chins and hats and premature freckles, ice cream spilling into fatty folds on joints. There's always one in a car too fast, music too loud, the roof down, top off like we're on Venice Beach.

And then it's a bit like staring at a painting, I suppose, say of a river . . . and suddenly the river begins to glisten and move. Tall, white T-shirt, tanned skin, green eyes, big smile. He is eating one of those Calippo lollies, the classic orange, a cool ice pole.

"Hey, Maxy!" Marcel jumps up and fist-bumps with him. He smiles, all dimples and scrunched nose. "What you doing here on your day off, man?"

"I was just passing through." And then our eyes lock.

And I am fat.

And hot.

And flustered.

And I smell of cheese.

And I'm wearing that stupid astronaut T-shirt. I mean, I knew I wanted to look normal today, but not Normal Minus.

"Hi, Bluebelle." Max licks his lolly. Oh to be that lolly for a day. Jealousy rattles my big bones.

"I've been cleaning the fridge out," I say. Grinning, breathlessly proud, weirdly. He smiles back. *With those teeth.* "What you up to?" He rubs his shaved head and I say, "You off somewhere nice? You look nice."

OH HOLD ON WHILE I JUST CUT OUT MY TONGUE AND SWALLOW IT SO IT CAN'T SPEAK AGAIN.

"So do you," he says-SLASH-lies, ". . . two both."

TWO. BOTH. TWO BOTH? I look at Marcel, who probably looks better than me, actually, but the pair of sad rejects that we are stuns me. Marcel's eyes are caffeine crazed like a wild hyena's and I look like I've just given birth to a titan without losing the tummy fat after. And I dwarf Marcel with my grand height. I honestly am like a cathedral standing next to him. Hardly looking *nice* like Max the hot . . . god. God of . . . hotness.

Hold on. No. Why is my voice in my own head that I'm not even saying out loud now sounding like my mum: *god of hotness*? Oh, sorry, did I forget to give myself the memo that I am so cringe? This is cringe. Clichéd. Ugly. Put the book down. It's terrible. Still, I can't help myself, eyelashes up, pupils pop and . . .

"Then I'm going to a gallery. My favourite artist, Elouise VuMart, has an exhibition. . . . Do you know her work?"

I shake my head in a *no* because I've had far too much experience of people asking me if I've heard of someone cool and me saying *yes* to only find out it's a made-up person to trick me into looking like a try-hard IDIOT.

"I think you'd really like her paintings, Bluebelle. They are special." *You are.* Gulp. Gag. "Plus, the gallery will be air-conditioned. It's so close out there today."

He nudges his head backstage.

"Alicia around?"

"Nope, break," Marcel answers. "At last."

"I need to change my schedule." To work more shifts with me, he means to add. "S'OK, I'll give her a bell."

I WANT A BELL, MAX. GIVE *ME* A BELL.

Our eyes meet again.

"See you guys soon. . . . Sorry you're inside on a day like today."

And he vanishes, looking left and right onto the oncoming traffic of shiny happy people, before folding himself into the stream of humans as simple as egg whites into cake mix.

And before I know it, I am back here, scribbling everything down in my book, frantically raiding the schedule. . . .

I have to take Alicia up on those shifts. I need to work every day to make our shifts chime so that we work together every day, EVERY day. Every single day, boy.

# TACOS

Camille picks me up from Planet at the end of the day. I'm not gonna tell her about being morbidly obsessed with Max. He's a boy. We don't really DO boys. I find myself snapping back to us. We survive on the triumphs in the pleasures around us like music and eating and TV and talking and films and clothes and each other. We don't need any boy sucking us into the endless timeless vortex of insecurity and doubt and wasting endless hours on falling in love and . . . feeling special and happy and . . . euphoric weightlessness. OH, WHAT THE . . . WHO AM I?

"Greetings, earthling!" Alicia jokes. "You know, this could've been you, Cam!" She presents me to my friend with a back-slapping like I'm an exhausted unwanted prize on a game show, mocking the fact that Camille had a one-day trial at Planet Coffee and wasn't asked to come back because she drank A LOT of coffee and when somebody asked for an extra-hot, decaf soya latte with no foam she laughed in their face and pointed to the jug of tap water instead.

"Greetings." Camille LOVES to take the micky out of Alicia's alien chat.

"Where you girls off to, then?"

*Don't tell her,* I mouth to Camille, slicing my neck with my finger-tips and widening my eyes.

"To a really . . . boring . . . place."

"Well, let Bluebelle treat you, babes! She's gonna be working around the place a little more, ain't you, doll face?" She squeezes my cheeks in her spiky hand. HOW ABOUT FILL IN MY FORM, THEN? I swear she's holding this apprentice application over me like some kind of power. "And doesn't she look *so* great?"

Camille tries not to laugh. "She looks like she needs a taco."

"You GIRLS!" Alicia snorts. "You kill me. You've got to be a good supportive friend, Cam!" Cam IS a good supportive friend. "You've got to help BB get that bikini body."

"She has a bikini body!" Cam fires back. "She owns a body AND a number of bikinis." Alicia crinkles her nose in disgust at this. It's probably the idea of me flobbering around in a bikini making her feel sick.

"Alicia, I see a beach once a year for two weeks, *if* I'm lucky. What's the point? Forget my bikini body, I'm working on my *jumper* body!"

Cam laughs. "Same! Although, you know, I read this article on how to look good on a beach? It said to get to the beach before everybody else, dig a hole and place your towel into it so you only look half the size."

"That would never work because what about when you got up to have a swim; it would just be a nasty shock for everybody," Alicia argues, as if she's ACTUALLY considering it. "It's a good idea but it just ain't practical. Soz, beb."

"Alicia, it's the dumbest thing I've ever heard," Cam snaps. "I wasn't taking the article seriously."

"Yeah, just no carbs, I'd say! But plenty of wine! Laters, girls. Don't do anything I wouldn't do."

FAT CHANCE OF THAT.

Alicia then wrestles with her bicycle, pedalling away with her heels rattling over the sides, wobbling maniacally down the road, cars beeping and honking her.

"She's mental."

"Annoying is what she is. She drives me mad."

"Is she telling you you've lost weight again?"

"She thinks it makes me feel good. It's so insulting, it's her *banter* apparently."

"Oh, she's vile." Camille laughs.


The Mexican is nice. We like it. Turquoise walls covered in Mexican art, plastic flowers and painted clay skulls. Red waxy floral tablecloths loaded with hot sauces and a candle in a mottled red jar. And fun music. You could almost pretend you were on holiday.

"I've got NO money," Camille says. "Why am I here again, remind me?" she asks one of the skull head ornaments. She makes the skull talk back to her: "Because you live in a dream world where you think you are a millionaire and a basketball player is your boyfriend."

I laugh. "Your face is nice," I tell her. "You have a nice face."

"Thanks, babes. You have a nice face too."

Cam winks at me. And then before I know it, it's happening.

"Have you ever heard of Elouise VuMart?" I ask, looking down over the menu.

"No, who's that?"

"An artist."

"Oh no, is this one of those trick questions when you ask someone if they've heard of someone cool and they say yes and then you go . . . *Hahaha, they don't exist, loser!* Because it better not be. Once a girl in school asked me if I had heard of a band called Carrot Cake and I said yes they were my favourite and it turned out to be a setup to make me look like a total fool."

"I love you. That is all," I reply, but THEN I am becoming a boring basic cliché girl and I say it, I can't help myself, it's happening, it's happening, it's . . .

"OK, so you know the one I made the broken-heart coffee with?" (It's happened.)

"Zac?"

"Max."

"Sorry, Max."

"The boy from work."

"Boy? BB, sorry, are we talking about a BOY? You never talk about boys."

"Yes, well, I might ask him out to see if I do want to talk about boys."

"Just like that?"

"What do you mean?"

"You're going to ask him out? On a date? Just like that?"

"Yes. He called me Blue." I grin; Cam rolls her eyes. "Why? How else are you meant to do it?"

"No, no, B, that's great, I'm just a bit . . . Girls don't normally . . . I dunno, it's just . . ."

"What? Am I doing something wrong? This clearly reminds me of the time I asked a boy out in primary school. I knocked for him at his block of flats and he opened up his little bathroom window, shoved his hand out and physically 'sprayed me away' with Coral Peach air freshener as if repelling a frigging mosquito."

"Oh that is *sad*."

"I knew it was Coral Peach because my granny used it too. It was hard to go over there for a while after that. Still, I'm gonna roll my sleeves up and ask him . . . Wait . . . why are you looking at me like that? . . . I'm doing something wrong, aren't I?"

"No. It's just . . . quite forward, that's all. I've never really . . . Wow . . . OK . . . you're actually gonna . . . OK."

"Go on. . . ."

"Guys usually do that asking stuff. And what if . . . You know what?" She snorts. "Ignore me. You're amazing. Go for it. I love you."

"Camille. I don't know how this works. Isn't it just . . . you fancy somebody . . . you ask them out?"

"Yes, that's what it is. What it SHOULD be. It should be as easy as that. But it . . . You know what? Ask him."

"Should I?"

"You should."

"OK. Yes. I will."

"You're a braver girl than me. Wish we had something better than a tap water to cheers with. I can't even afford a Sprite."

"What are you even talking about, I am obsessed with tap water. Cheers."

"Cheers. To Princess Charming."

I take my hair and shove it between my nose and top lip to make a moustache. "Thank you, my dear."

"And the worst that can happen is that you get sprayed in the face with air freshener . . . pshhhhhhh!" Camille mimes spraying a canister of air freshener in my face.

"I know how that feels anyway, didn't hurt too bad . . . psshhhh!" And I pretend to hiss a can back at her.

Our tacos arrive. Soft blankets stuffed with golden fried fish, bright green creamy guacamole, herbs, blackened juicy chicken and spicy ground beef. We have tortilla chips and a big bowl of more blobby guacamole with shreds of red onion and jalapeno.

"Man, that's so buff."

"Oh it's hot, pass the hot sauce."

"Jeeeezz! SO banging! Wish I could cook like this."

We chew, warm spiciness zipping around our mouths like fire-crackers. I swallow and say, "Camille, if you had to do an exercise, what would it be?"

"I do do exercise."

"Huh?"

"Yeah. Course."

"When?"

"When I'm not dicking about with you."

"But you're always with me."

"OK, but when I'm not with you, I find time."

"You never told me."

"It's not a thing to tell, is it?"

"What do you do?"

"This exercise thing on YouTube."

I feel so betrayed. I gulp.

"Where?"

"Just in my bedroom."

I cannot imagine Camille working out in her bedroom. I am so shocked.

"I thought you just did nothing, like me." Although Camille doesn't look like me. She's toned.

"It's easy. I'll send you the link."

"No, don't."

"Why not?"

"I won't use it."

"Come on, B, it's fun."

"I don't think so."

"You just use cans of soup for weights and I turn the sound down and play my own music."

"I don't have any gym stuff to, like, wear or whatever."

"You just wear your bra and knickers, you can shower right after, you don't even need to leave the house." She stuffs more food in, licks her finger, winds it round the bottle of yellow sunshine sauce. "Want me to send the link to you?"

"I'm fine." I sip my water. My cheeks blister in an angry rash. "I'm fine how I am."

"You don't have to feel weird about wanting to keep fit, BB. It's good to be strong, nothing to be embarrassed about."

"I KNOW that, thanks," I snap back.


I'm angry at Cam. Why do I feel so annoyed? I guess I didn't really think we could survive our whole lives eating what we wanted and ignoring exercise but I guess I just kind of hoped we, I dunno . . . could.

Why does exercise feel so alien to me, anyway? Why doesn't it come naturally to girls like it seems to come to boys?

I look about the restaurant. People seem to be eating what they want, laughing, talking, drinking alcohol, having fun, but they are all normal-sized. . . . Eating food like this is maybe a treat to them, but I don't even question it.

Is it just me or does it feel like every girl is secretly on a diet?

I thought we were all in this "eating what we want when we want" revolution together, but I've got a sneaky fear that I'm the only one actually taking it seriously.

Or maybe even doing it at all.

# TEA

Mum and Dove are sitting on the couch when I get in.

"Hello, peach. Tea?"

"Yes please, Mum."

"You hungry?"

"I ate with Cam."

"Ah, nice."

"Spending my whole day's salary in one sitting."

"Always the way. You had fun, then?"

"Yep." I fan myself with the post. "Did you guys eat?"

"Yep." Mum gives me that look. "Dove made Carbonara."

Dove looks up at me proudly, big smile on her face, eyebrows wriggling, all cocky. Meanwhile, Mum, behind Dove, mimics throwing up, her face in contortion, shoving her fingers down her throat. I try not to laugh.

"Oi, you better not be being mean about my cooking." Dove rears up and points at Mum. "I'm serious."

"I wasn't. As IF I would. BB, I wasn't, was I?"

"No!" I defend Mum, my mouth curling into a smile. "She wasn't."

I throw myself down next to Dove.

"You stink of garlic," she snuffles.

"You stink of burnt pasta," I snigger, looking at her face.

"It *was* quite burnt," she admits.

"How do you even go about *burning* pasta?"

"It's when the spaghetti is too long for the pan of boiling water and sticks to the side and the ends go black and it stinks like that time you burnt your thumbnail on a candle."

"Oh well." I sigh. "I quite like the taste of burnt stuff." I close my eyes. "Burnt fish fingers, yum; burnt toast with Marmite, yum; burnt toast with peanut butter, yum; burnt noodles, yum . . ."

"All right, we get it, you like the taste of burnt."

"Exactly."

I lean into Dove and she would lie and say she didn't but she *definitely* put her arm out for me to scoot inside and let me lean my head on her tiny bony shoulder. The lights are low and the TV is blabbering away. Squares of silver, blue, gold and white illuminate the room. Mum comes in with three steaming cups, holding two handles with one hand.

She sits next to me and we all bunch up together, holding our tea close to our chests.

I like the idea of a house full of girls. Maybe you don't even need a man to come in stomping around and being all *there*. Maybe I could love a woman? Maybe I'll end up with a woman. We are humans. Men and women. You don't know who you're going to fall in love with; we fall in love with a person. Not a sex. And looking around, it seems women are just pretty cool anyway. But Cam and Dove might get jealous—I can really imagine them both giving my soul mate future wife a hard time.

We've all fallen asleep on the sofa. The soft silver light paints Picasso edges on Mum and Dove.

I creep up to get a glass of water before waking them both.

I crumple up my receipt from the taco place and dash it into the bin so I don't have to look at it tomorrow and feel guilty about eating out all the time and spending all my money on food. It lands softly on top of about fourteen thousand eggshells, flour, burnt spaghetti, raw fatty grey bacon, massive chunks of onion and a clump of scrambled egg.

And underneath that I see some of Dad's clothes.

A tired Dove stands in the doorway having already seen what I've seen. "She's slowly getting rid of him, you know. Bit by bit. It will be his head in the bin next." She stretches, showing her stomach, her ribs stacked neatly on top of one another, poking through her top. "Well, night, then."

"Night," I mumble back.

# PANINI

Some things in life are really hard.

I'm not being all first-world problematic about it except I am. But they are. Like fifteen full buses going past you in the pouring rain and then one empty one comes and you get all excited only to find it's not in service. But nothing competes with the daily struggle of having to toast, slice and serve a panini that doesn't belong to you.

That is something that truly tests your willpower and strength to the absolute maximum.

*Ohhhhhh.* When the bread toasts and the mozzarella squidges out and the pesto hits the grill. When you slice it, the cheese smacks the knife and tears away . . . and you aren't allowed to pick the cheese off the side because people watch you. Customers. Making sure you don't cough or breathe or fold your hair behind your ear and touch the bread and certainly don't plop any delicious scrumptious melted cheese into your mouth.

"You make it harder for yourself," Max says as he leans over me while I stuff the ciabattas. "If you don't want to eat them, stop making them look so tempting."

*Was that a hint about how hot I look?* I do look hot. Am I *tempting?* My mum tells me that electric blue brings out my green eyes and makes my skin look glowing. STOP BEING COCKY. How have I turned a comment about a sandwich into a compliment about myself?

"I don't like to give stingy portions. It's not fair. You have to leave a bathroom the way you would want to find it, and make a sandwich the way you would want to eat one."

Max nods and smiles.

"That's true." He peers over my shoulder. "It says quite a lot about a person, the way they make a sandwich."

PLOT TWIST. "Does it?"

"Oh, for sure."

"So what does this sandwich say about me?"

# MELTING PANINI

Let's talk about Max. If I'm weighing him up as somebody who could potentially have their tongue in my mouth we need to discuss him. Properly . . . *Firstly, is he too pretty?* I realise you can't see him and this is just a conversation between my head and me, but the risk that he could be *too pretty* is actually really important for me. We are all beautiful, but pretty is a completely different word with an entirely different meaning. I don't want to make him my boyfriend and every three steps we'd have some annoying model-scout girl ask him if he's "ever considered modelling." Perhaps he *has* considered it and is waiting for his moment to shine? His jaw *does* have the same angles as a packaged sandwich. I don't know. I guess you can't judge a person by their "alien" clothes either because this is stuff they don't mind getting covered in the soot of coffee and the splat of bleach. But he always wears cool trainers.

And he smells of figs.

"I think it shows that you clearly understand the good things in life."

He's right.

"I never understand why anybody who works in catering of any kind would ever want to shortchange a customer with their portions. It's not like the money is coming out of our personal accounts! There's no excuse to be tight. That actually stands for everything. You're going to get further in life if you're generous. In EVERY sense of the word."

"Wait, I haven't finished psychologically analysing you by your sandwich making. . . ." Then he snatches the panini from the board and bites into it.

"MAX!"

"Ummmm . . ."

"Max! That's for a customer! You can't do that!" But he doesn't care.

"Oh yeah, the vision is coming across much stronger now. Oh yes, I can really taste the personalities and character of the—"

By now a few hangry faces are staring at us. The panini-making machine is so slow too.

"Max, you're gonna get us in trouble."

"Oh sorry, my bad. It's just when I'm . . . summoning up this kind of . . . energy from the sandwich-making spirits I can't have anything . . . you know . . . disrupting my flow. . . ." He closes his eyes, opens one to see if I'm still looking and tries not to laugh. His lips are pink. Full. Bee-stung. "It means your . . ." He starts again. The queue of people are tutting angrily. I should be getting on with it, making new paninis, cutting bread and dicing tomatoes . . . but I want to know what Max is going to say about me. I don't want him to use one of those ugly fat-people words like "caring" or "motherly." I realise I hate the idea of him deciding if he fancies me. . . . *Is she too fat for me? Too bubbly?* I don't want him to usually only fancy skinny girls and then make me his wild-card exception to the rule and that I should feel *grateful* for that. I don't want him deliberating over me to his friends, asking their advice on whether they'd date a fat girl or not. I once had a situation with a boy I really liked. We'd spent all day kissing at a skate park in the sun only for him to turn to me on the walk home and say, "My friends think you're fat." As if I was meant to advise him on the tricky situation he now had on his hands, like I could help him out somehow. Half expecting me to respond with, *Well, should I lose weight, would that make your dilemma easier?* I was so embarrassed, I didn't even tell anyone.

Just tell me what you're thinking, Max. SPIT IT OUT. GO HARD OR GO HOME.

Is he really going to tell me if he fancies me or not by using the metaphor of a sandwich?

I do hope so.

Maybe he's having the same image right now: us walking side by side on a sunny Saturday only to be stopped by a plus-size model scout who asks me if I've ever considered being a "curvy model."

I'm just gonna ask him what he's thinking to save myself. I can do that. I think I look pretty today. And I'm nice. And kind. And interesting. And I've already proved that I can make a pretty decent sandwich. Equalling a completely stunning life partner/love of your life/mother of your future children.

But how to say the words?

"Oi, Max, so is this a thing or . . . ?" WEIRD. WHY AM I TALKING LIKE THIS?

"Huh?"

ROLL WITH IT. A few customers lose patience and walk out. Others stare.

KEEP GOING. OH CRINGE. WHAT AM I DOING?

I've turned into my dad and he's a complete tit. Blush. Blush. Prickly red map-shaped rash darting up all over me and why have I even opened my mouth? My teeth feel all loose and wobbly and weird and my eyes are jolting left to right like a lizard. Where do I stare? Where do I look? Where am I meant to look when looking somebody in the eyes? Wait, where do I normally look? How do I normally look at somebody in the face? Your eyes can't look everywhere at once—hold on, in the middle? At the edges? Why am I being so . . . Just look in the middle, the top of the nose. I'm cross-eyed . . . I'm cross-eyed and—*just shut up* and carry on . . .

"What I mean is, if this is like a *thing* . . . "

I can hear Cam telling me to shut up, Dove pointing and laughing, Alicia snorting.

". . . there's a lovely place near me, well, sort of near me, that does vegan crepes. . . . It sounds horrible, but it's not. I'm not a vegan. I mean, I couldn't be vegan, not that there's anything wrong with vegans; in fact, if you're a vegan I think that's totally cool . . . because obviously I know all about the fact they fake-impregnate cows and stuff to make milk and all the boy chicks that are born they just, like, whizz into a blender to make a meaty milkshake . . ." Max looks disgusted. "Horrible, HORRIBLE . . . but if you wanted to, if you fancied it, like, if you're free and . . ."

"GREETINGS, EARTHLINGS!" Oh, here comes Alicia. That woman has the worst timing. "Want to know why I've called you earthlings and NOT aliens?"

OH NO, ALICIA! NO. YOU ARE NOT DOING THIS. You're blatantly pregnant, you've had your time to shine, let me at least have a chance of TALKING to a boy without you getting in the way.

HERE SHE GOES. . . .

"Nobody wants to have a guess? OK, sure, let me fill ya in. You've spent sooooooo bloody long standing here cruising like tourists that I've been left like Neil Armstrong bloody walking the moon on me lonesome. And it's only school holidays! And there's a queue. A big one. Marcel is about to lose his rag. Come on, aliens, get to it. Snap, snap, let's get to work, BLAST OFF!"

"Sorry," I mumble, and watch Max walk away from me. Behind Alicia he turns, widens his eyes and pushes the whole panini into his mouth in one move. Then he grins. Mouth full of squished bread. He coughs. Chokes. Splutters. Alicia turns around and growls. And I am laughing my head off but secretly melting, like a soggy panini gone soft.

# CHEESE

The day goes on FOR-EVER. It's like it's stopped in time. I have a totally new understanding of the phrase "school holidays" now that I see it from the other side of the desk. School holidays mean HOT, BUSY and STRESSED. It's long, hard work. A chaos of mums and dads and nannies and babies and prams and soggy bread crusts and tiny hands clutching raisins and smushed-up grapes and flattened Wotsits. And kids just coming in like they own the place. And me, making green tea after chai latte after peppermint tea after stupid babyccino. And gossip and leggings and iPads and nobody eating. Just sip. Sip. Gossip. Gossip. This is so dry. Nearly as dry as the brownies that I've suggested a new recipe for to make them more gooey. And every baby is crying because it's so hot. I find myself counting nine months backwards from August so I know for my whole entire life how never to have a baby born in the summertime so I don't have to stare at their screaming red scrunched-up face. I realise how jokes it is that I'm writing this all down in a doctor's journal. I never thought I'd get so into writing this thing. How cringe it is that I'm now writing about a boy too. Well . . . I don't want to keep you in suspense. . . . Plus . . . it's kind of nice talking to you, really; it's like having a little friend.

All I'm thinking is Max and trying to figure out if he's my species or not. He's never seen *Jurassic Park*. But he's still not mentioned anything about the crepe place or me or being vegan, even though he did eat a panini, but I can't quite remember if it was a cheese one or not—no, it was, I know it was, but anyway, why does it even matter and I'm just going mad and my eyes are slowly blinding. Blurred by sweat and exhaustion and more sweat that's giving me rings under each armpit and my thighs are scraping against each other in scabby agony and I feel like a hideous monster walrus cattle girl and why would anybody like Max fancy me when a trillion and one astoundingly beautiful girls of every kind come into our coffee shop every day? And I am just here, taking up ALL the room. Conscious of the bobbly cheese-grater red dots on my arms that make my skin feel like the crust of a seeded loaf. Conscious of the fact that my boobs might be sweating but I don't have the guts to even look down and check because if I see hideous half-moons of sweat under there I will begin to believe I am as horrible as the rest of the world might think I am.

I am a tree trunk.

A grand piano.

I puff my Ventolin.


It's the end of the day when Max comes up to me and says in the cutest voice ever, "So if it's vegan I'm guessing no cheese, which is gonna be hard as cheese is one of my all-time favourite foods, but it's a sacrifice I'm willing to make, Blue." He grins. "For you."

OH BOY.

It. Is. On.

# MOULD

I have to take the bus home. My thighs are rubbing like mad. It's like rubbing your cheeks on tree bark. Plus, the sweat is making it so sore; every step sticks and chafes. The bus is so hot and everybody is covered in a gammy sheet of glueyness. But I don't care. I am going on a date and I can't help but feel really good about that.

Obviously I want to get home and just put a soaking wet bedsheet over my whole body and watch TV and eat ice cream but Mum doesn't seem to have the same agenda. Plus, the only ice cream we ever have in our house will be a quarter tub of something old that has thawed so badly it will have snowflakes, or a gammy singular solitary ice lolly dating back to the early 2000s. The front door is wide open and both dogs are yawning and scratching around the front garden. The house is ripe with the throat-thwacking stench of bleach and Mum is padding around in Dove's Nike sliders and a pair of yellow gloves.

"Right, BB, get your gloves on. Come on, we're having a clear-out."

Dove looks at me with one of *those* faces and I can see she's already been put to work by the grot and grime all up her arms and on her cheeks. I don't even *own* the gloves she means.

"You two can clean the larder out; it's full of all your dad's crap. He hasn't touched half the stuff in there for years."

I don't want to remind her that I used Dad's larder to cook the shepherd's pie the other day but that obviously made me poo out the whole of south London into the dog bowl, so I keep quiet and say, "Yeah, but what if we throw away stuff he, you know, *wants*?"

"I don't care if his bloody dead mother's ashes are in there: out. OUT. OUT!"

Harsh. I raise an eyebrow at Dove.

So I guess Dad isn't coming home yet, then.

Dove holds open the bin bag and I open the larder door. It's the same height as me, like an airing cupboard, and stinks of spices and savoury musk. It's the cupboard of every ingredient that can change a tin of tomatoes into a chilli, a curry or a bolognese. The cupboard where everything and anything goes. The cupboard you don't dare touch in case it avalanches on top of your feet and breaks your toes. In fact, both dogs have had injuries from the cupboard: 2B once ate a whole sack of sugar and was sick for days and Not 2B had a tin of golden syrup dropped on his head.

It's floor-to-ceiling chaos. Jars of spices balanced on top of vinegars and oils, tins shoved in in all directions, some upside down and slanted, and open packets of lentils, rice, flour, almonds and pasta ready to roar open at you and skittle across the floor.

We travel all around the world inside the globe of Dad's larder. Yellow turmeric and baking powder, shreds of saffron, smoked paprika, vanilla essence and Tabasco, sticky Marmite and banana ketchup, oregano and fish sauce, coconut milk and cayenne pepper, balsamic vinegar and palm sugar . . . We find doubles of almost everything, triples in most cases: three open bags of couscous, three jars of curry paste, three bottles of soy sauce. And the whole thing, nearly everything in there, is all out. Of. Date. Crawling with fluffy reels of dust and strings of spider webs carrying spools of flies. I sneeze as the mixed itchy-scratchy powders irritate my nostrils. My eyes water and bleed my makeup as I reveal what should be jars of dried coriander leaf that are now a muted gunmetal grey and turned to dust. Flour is damp, vinegars are dehydrated and sauces are pungent and ripe, gone off.

The jars of jam are thick with mould sporting hay bales of silver fur.

I feel crap about chucking it out, to be honest. Plus, some of this stuff is really good quality. Even if it is out of date. Dad would still use it but it seems every time I try to hold something back, Mum glares at me like I'm thrusting a knife into her shoulder.

Everything is . . .

*Best before* . . . when Dad still lived here.

*Best before* . . . when Mum and Dad were happy.

And it all goes in the bin.

# SPRING ONIONS

People always say how much Mum and Dove look alike. Having a mum smaller than you makes people look at us like I've given birth to a mum rather than the other way round. Imagining me squeezing out of her is like imagining a sausage dog giving birth to a desk. I watch Mum and Dove move around the kitchen, hopping like little robins looking for somewhere to settle.

I'm a pregnant cow.

A gaggle of spring onions hold tight like hugging girls in the grasp of an unnatural blue plastic band; their spindly legs are strangled around one another, bruised and brown and wilted. Have you noticed that, if you look closely, spring onions wear pin-striped power suits? Mega babes.

"Why are these bloody things in the cupboard?" Mum *very over-the-toply* roars. "Bin. NOW!"

"All right, calm down."

"Don't tell me to calm down, Dove. I'm sick of this man's rubbish *everywhere*. He's not even here and he manages to infest the whole place with his everlasting debris of sh—"

"You don't need to throw all of this stuff away, Mum. Just cos you don't want to live with Dad doesn't mean you have to throw perfectly good food away."

"Perfectly good? Perfectly good? I can't see what's perfectly good here. What's the point in buying all this stuff if it just goes in the bin? Do you think I like seeing food go to waste?"

"OK. OK. Calm down!"

"I am CALM."

She's not. What is WRONG with her tonight? I am wondering if there's any natural yoghurt or ANYTHING in the fridge that I can slather on my thighs to take the venomous sting away. Does it have to be in date if you're just rubbing it on your thigh chafe?

"What's wrong with you tonight?" Dove ventures. How brave. I mean, I was thinking the exact same thing but, like, I'm not dumb enough to say it.

"What's *wrong* with me?" Mum says. "What's *wrong* with me? I'll tell you what's wrong with me. Your stupid father is an absolute incapable moron who lives his life like a student and can't sort himself out and thinks just because he is an old man that he can patronise me and squish me into compromising conditions so I'll buckle. You know, he hasn't got a clue. Do you know that? Not one clue." Her voice gets louder. "He's an egotistical parasite," she barks. "And then, to top it off, I've got you two taking a FULL three hours to clean out a larder that I already said needs completely throwing out!"

"We didn't want to throw away anything edible, anything Dad might want."

"Oh, Dad wants it," Mum snarls. "Dad wants it ALL!" She throws a tea towel onto the table. "But Dad doesn't live here, and I, me,

MUM, am asking you to throw it all away, all of it. You both suck up to him nonstop. Why don't you ever listen to *me*? It's MY house and I want that cupboard and everything in it gone, do you hear? And I want to start fresh without that ugly rancid rotting jungle looking at me. I can't even make a risotto without the whole thing crushing my foot. LOOK AT MY FOOT."

OH. So this was the trigger. A bright-purple swelling of a bruise shines on Mum's toe. The pan is burnt, lined with burnt onion, the elderly cousin of the spring onions. (Why do Americans call spring onions "scallions"? It's such a diversion . . . like, how an aubergine is an eggplant, and coriander is cilantro. Aubergine—all day. *Egg*-plant, though? A plant of eggs. No thanks.)

"It wasn't Dad's fault that happened, though, Mum. Stop shouting at me just cos Dad isn't here to bear the brunt of it."

"Bluebelle, don't even start with me. He stacked the cupboard like an absolute boob. Dad is NEVER here to bear the brunt of ANYTHING!"

"Yeah, cos you kicked him out."

"Is that what he told you? Seriously, I'm not in the mood. Helping me clear up is the least you can do. You still haven't kept your side of the bargain." *Why is the knife turning on me now?*

"Mum, I use the stuff in the larder too, you know, not just Dad." I feel my chest tighten. I feel it clench. My breathing becomes all short and sharp.

"You said you'd go to the gym; you still haven't gone. You said you would. You promised."

"Mum, it's not that—" My ribs are aching. My words are constricted.

"I don't want to hear it. Do you have any idea what a big deal it means for me to just *let* you not go to school, to just *believe* in you, trust that this is the right decision for you, to maybe not get your grades like everybody else your age? Have you not thought about that? Your exam results are going to come knocking on our door any second and it's like you don't even care. That's not normal. For some kids these results change their whole career path, determine their entire future, and you haven't even batted an eyelid! That's over ten years of education for what? Nothing!"

"Not *nothing*," I say. "My brain's not a sieve, I've not forgotten all of this, Mum. I *am* smart, in my own way."

"I didn't say you weren't smart. I never once said that, but THINK, for a second, please, how it will look in the future if you're not happy and you turn around and say to me, *'Mum, why did you let me quit school? I was just sixteen.'* Do you know the guilt I will feel if you can't become the things you want to be because you don't have the grades? I'll have to live with that. Not you. You probably won't even remember."

"I will. I will remember. This was my decision, Mum."

"Course you won't. Trust me, Bluebelle, I've *been* there; *I've been you.* Thinking the world will give me a massive paycheque, that everything will be all right. But you won't remember. I don't remember my decisions when I was sixteen, because I was SIX-TEEN! All I knew is that *my* mum told me I would NEVER make it as an actress, ever, that I would never be onstage and, you know, she was actually right, I didn't."

Because she got pregnant with me.

"I didn't make it. And I didn't do my exams because I concentrated on performance. And then I was left with nothing. And I had to pay for that, in my own way. So I'm letting you take one. I'm letting you do what you want to do, but there were conditions."

"I know, Mum, and I've told you I'm grateful. I said to you, didn't I? I said I'm so grateful for that." I feel myself getting short of breath.

"And your *one* part of the bargain, aside from keeping the diary thing—"

"Which I'm doing, I'm doing—ask Dove—aren't I, Dove?" I panic; Dove panics; we're all panicking. This has come out of nowhere. Mum's gone mental. WHERE'S MY BLOODY INHALER?

"*Aside*, I said, *aside* from keeping the diary, which is the easy bit—anybody can keep a diary—was going to the gym."

"Mum, I—"

"I'm not asking for rent money, no contribution towards bloody toilet roll, nothing. All I'm asking is for your word, your promise. And you can't even give me that."

"It's not like that, I just . . . I haven't had the time. I'll go, I will, I'll go."

Dove pretends to read the back of a crumpled packet of flour. The ingredients being . . . flour.

"And we're just gonna go back to the doctor's, like *all* those times we've gone before and nothing would have changed with your health and it will be my fault, again. Because I was too lenient. Then I'm going to look, YET AGAIN, like I'm the world's worst mum and your dad is just going to love that, isn't he? That you've given up your education and I've *allowed* you to; I've failed and you can't even get your lazy bum down the gym three times a week for me!"

"I will. I'll go, I'll go for you!"

"Don't go for me, Bluebelle. That's not the point, don't you see? Go for you, go for *yourself*!" She shakes her hands wildly and then points right in my face. "I look bad in this but you're the only one you're cheating!" She looks at me in disgust. I find my inhaler and breathe in. And again. I hate the look she's given me; it makes my bones go cold. "Listen to you. You can't even breathe."

Ouch. Tears form; one slides down my face. I wipe it off. Breathe in and face her.

"You think I'm too fat, don't you?"

Dove lifts her gaze to Mum, wide-eyed.

"Oh, what is this now?"

"No, Mum." I jut out my jaw; my voice rasps. "If you think I'm fat, just say. If you want me to get to the gym because you think I'm fat, then just tell me. Don't pretend it's because it will make you look like a bad mum if I don't go. Sorry I'm not a skinny-minnie like you and Dove, sorry I can't eat a whole burger and chips like you two and not feel the fat physically attach itself to me, sorry that people laugh at me and point at me and make comments about me, that I'm embarrassed whenever I point you out as my mum and have people stare back at me in disbelief and make cruel jokes about me because I'm so BIG. That it's a miracle that YOU pushed ME out. That I didn't *break* you. I hate it that I can't share clothes with you and Dove. That we can't even go shopping together because I don't want people to comment on us. That some shops don't have my size, even. That I tower above you. That I can't even get on some roller-coaster rides, that people describe me as 'big,' that they assume I'll want a 'large' of everything, assume I'm a liability, that I'm a whale, that I'm not a girl, that I can't be gentle, or feminine, or myself. Because that's all I'm being, Mum, myself. Or I'm trying."

I can't help it: the tears roll down my cheeks fast now and my voice cracks and trembles. "That's all I'm trying to do."

And she drops the bin liner to the ground and we hug and we are both crying. Mum strokes my hair and I don't even care that our fingers are covered in old food and bits of grossness.

"You know you never know the answer, don't you?" Mum holds my face, wiping my tears with her thumbs and says, "You never really grow up. It's a trick; everybody is wandering around just as lost as the person ahead and the person behind. We are all winging it. You are always waiting for somebody to tell you if you're doing it right but you never know. Ever. Me and Dad don't know. None of us know what we're doing in this life. But we are proud of you for asking for more. We are. And I don't think you're anything except beautiful. You're so beautiful, I can't even begin to take in your beauty. You've always been beautiful. I don't know what I'd do without you."

Mum yanks Dove into our hug too and we are holding tight, bedraggled, tired and worn, but still so close, still holding on, together, like the girl gang of spring onions we've just thrown in the bin.

# MARS BAR

"Don't burn it!" I yell, smacking Dove's hand out of the way.

"Sor-ry! Calm down."

"It's only meant to be thirty seconds."

"It's not *my* fault the stupid thing only sets in minutes."

"Take it out."

"Stop bossing me about."

"If you did it right, I wouldn't have to."

"OH! YEAH BOY! IT LOOKS AMAZING!"

"Let's see, then, share the wealth."

A warm bowl of melted Mars Bar. Hot caramel, chocolate and nougat. Sticky, fudgy, warm.

"Ice cream?"

"Here."

"Swirl it in, B."

"Yum!"

"More!"

I stir in the vanilla ice cream and it begins to melt straight away, bleeding into the caramel, softening and collapsing. A whirlpool of edible paint.

"Want to stay in tonight and watch a film?" Dove asks, slinging me a spoon. We both stay silent for a moment, mouthing the ice cream into little quenelles with our tongues, eyes fixed on each other in perfect contented smiles.

"You never want to stay in with me."

"Well, I'm asking you now. . . ."

"I can't."

"Oh. Why?"

"I've got a date!"

"A date! What the hell, with who?"

"This alien from Planet Coffee," I say. Dove snorts. "What's so funny?"

"I love it that you're eating a melted Mars Bar and ice cream the day you are going on a first date."

"Why, what's wrong with that?"

"Ha! Nothing's wrong, it's just not what other girls would do."

"Why, what would other girls do?"

"Probably starve themselves. All the girls in my year are just selfie-obsessed, none of them eat. Tania Gray chews paper."

"Weird." I lick the back of my spoon, the balance of hot and cold dissolving on my tongue. "It's so sad. We're all so vain."

"I wouldn't say you were."

"Dove, all I bang on about is how much I love myself."

"That's not vain, that's just healthy, isn't it? That's what you always say. And I think it's true."

Our silver spoons battle like tusks as we scramble for the last milky dribble of dessert.

"So what film are you gonna watch tonight, then?"

"Maybe *Snow White and the Seven Dwarfs*."

"Really? Why that?"

"Just feel like watching it." Cute.

"If you had seven dwarfs to your personality, what would they be?" I ask her.

"Errrrmmm . . . Playful. Sarcastic. SO COOL . . ."

"So cool? It can't be two names."

"So-Cool. It's double-barrelled."

"Fine."

"Playful, Sarcastic, So-Cool . . . ," she relists. "How many more?"

"Four."

"OK." She smiles. "Cheeky."

"Annoying."

"You're annoying!"

"Maybe we both have that personality trait."

"Hungry."

"Ha! We share that one too."

"And outdoorsy!"

"OK, now do me."

"OK." She bites her lip nervously, as if she's an apprentice that's finally being trusted for the first time. "But don't shout at me if I get them wrong."

She looks me up and down. . . .

"Annoying."

"Yes."

"Hungry."

"Uh-huh."

"Confident.

"Bossy."

"Bossy?!"

"You said you wouldn't shout."

"Fine. Carry on. . . ."

"How many more do I have?"

"Three . . ."

"A liar."

"A LIAR!"

"You told Mum you'd start going to the gym as part of your deal and you still haven't gone yet."

"That doesn't make it one of my dwarfs, Dove. That's like a phase one of my dwarfs was going through; it's like a choice one of my dwarfs had to make when it was . . . I dunno . . . out of choices. It wasn't a lie because I'm not actually ever going to be going to the gym . . . so . . ."

"You lied again, then. Anyway, it's good to have a double-barrelled dwarf name like me . . . *A-Liar.* Quite a pretty name if you say it out loud like that, rolls off the tongue, Aliar . . . See?"

"Then it's not double-barrelled, though, is it?"

"OK, B, it's up to you how you want to say it; it's your dwarf."

"'K. Two more."

"Stubborn. Kind . . . no, actually . . . *Kind*ofcool."

"Awww. I think."

"No, awww is right." Dove nods. "I was being nice."

"You forgot fat."

"OK. Which one do you want to swap for fat?"

"Aliar."

"Fine. Swap Aliar for Fat, then."

We stare out of the window. The sun beats into the kitchen.

"It's a nice day for a date."

"Not for me, I'll be sticking to everything like a melted candle.

This hot weather does not work for my fat and my cheap clothes." I flap my arms to make air. "And my thighs are gonna probs be rubbing like mad."

"You can borrow my headscarf if you want," Dove says. She knows I like her fruity headscarf.

"What, to tie around my thigh as a chafe barrier?" I joke.

"No. For your hair! Do NOT put my headscarf anywhere near your—"

"I know, I was joking. Thanks, Dove."

"You're welcome." She is pleased to offer it to me, I can tell.

"It seems too nice a day for a movie night."

"Yeah, maybe you're right."

"The sun won't go down till nine!"

"Yeah. Maybe I should go play out instead, might see what the boys are doing."

"Do you always jump off the same things?"

"What do you mean *jump off*?"

"Like, is it just, *let's jump off the bus stop again* or is it more . . . advanced . . . like, are there stages and stuff?"

"Some of the boys like to perfect a jump before they move on to the next, others just care they made the jump and move on. Depends how stupid you are, I suppose."

"Or brave."

"Or brave, yeah."

"Which one of the two are you? Stupid or brave?"

"I dunno."

"I'll come watch you . . . you know . . . throw yourself off buildings or whatever soon."

"K."

"Have fun."

"I will."

"Wear sun cream."

"I will."

"Oh, and Dove?"

"Yup?"

"Be brave."

She folds up the sleeve of her T-shirt to reveal her biceps. It's like the curve of a prawn. She kisses it and holds her fingers out to me. I touch them with the tips of mine.

"Tell you what . . . ," I offer. "If I don't get back too late, we can watch *Snow White* in my trifle when I'm home?"

"Midnight feast?"

"Midnight feast."

And then she pokes her pointy tongue out and gallops upstairs in pony-like boniness, her blond hair swimming behind her like a torch of light I'll never be able to capture.

# CREPES

I am wearing a too-tight two-piece, which sucks my fat in in places and plunges it out in others. It looks wonderful standing up but I hadn't really considered what sitting down was going to look like. I can already visualise the red lines crimping around my waist later like I've been singed with the edges of a piping-hot pie. My hair is all ruffled from faffing around with Dove's headscarf—which I ditched and decided not to wear and instead have it oddly tied around my wrist as a makeshift bunchy bracelet.

"I'm early" is all I say to Camille after I punch her name into my phone.

"Early where? Were we meant to meet?"

"No. To meet Max."

"What the? You nutter! I thought you'd tell me when you were seeing him."

"I'm telling you."

"What are you like? What are you wearing?"

"My candy-stripe two-piece thing."

"The pink or the red?"

"The red."

"Oh."

"Why 'oh'?"

"Ohh in a good way. Ohhh as in NIIIIIICCCCCE."

"OK."

"How early?"

"Three minutes."

"That's not early."

I pace the high street: Chinese takeaway, Caribbean food take-away. A hair shop. A deli. A pub. London is buzzing with the romance of summer; you can feel it in the air, the delight of some-thing good just around the corner.

"OK, I'm going in."

"No! Make him wait a bit."

"Why? I'm here, why would I wait?"

"Power, B!"

"Ewww!"

"Come on! You have to be late!"

"Why do I?"

"Dunno, it's just a thing, you have to, honestly, B, give it two minutes."

"How many dates have *you* been on, Cam?"

"My aunty told me all about this stuff."

"'K. 'K. Pass the time. . . . Let's play a game. . . . Guess the name of the restaurant?"

"The Happy Vegan?"

"Good guess. The Smiling Whale."

"No way."

"No, not really."

"Am I guessing or are you?"

"Sorry."

"The Melon?"

"Nope."

"The Disgruntled Lemon."

"Idiot. Ha!"

"The Lonesome Mug?"

"I love that one."

"Can I have a pint in the Lonesome Mug?"

"Haha!"

"Ooooh, prawn cocktail crisps and a—"

"I think he's calling me. . . . Oh no, it's just Mum. Can I go in now?"

"NO! I mean, you don't need my permission but . . ."

"Cam. I'm bloody excited to meet this boy. I don't see why I have to pretend I'm not."

"You're right, you're right, go . . . go . . . GO! Have fun. I love you."

The place is a concrete shell. Like a shop. You can see the kitchen. A woman is flipping crepes on metal stoves. The music is loud. Happy. There is bright graffiti scribbled all over the walls and wilting film posters. The furniture is mismatched. Scrubby. But comfortable. Like a living room. The menu is simple. But not. Simple because it's short but not simple because I've never been out for savoury crepes before as my dinner. It's just crepes. Sweet or savoury. But not just "vegan" cheese. There's sweet potato, chilli, potatoes, spinach, avocado and tons of spices.

And there's Max too. You could almost forget the place was vegan he's so beautiful.

We hug hello. He smells of fig even more today. I suddenly freak out that I have orange lipstick on my teeth and the fear of it is ruining my personality.

"I just need to use the bathroom." I smile with my lips closed.

He smiles back but his teeth are lovely and big and white and open and broad and honest and natural. And he is familiar and new at the same time. Like spending Christmas abroad.

The toilets are shabby but it's OK. I have amazing hovering skills. I undo my button for a second just to let my stomach hang out. Feels so good. MUSTN'T. GET. TOO. USED. TO. THE. RELIEF. Just as anticipated, a belt of prints from the elastic is embossed on my waist. I find imprints in skin really pretty. I always love it when I get prints in my face from sleeping on creased sheets. I prepare to suck myself back in again to my outfit—

Wait.

*Why do I have so many missed calls from Mum? Dad too? And Camille?*

And I know. Before I even call them back I know that something's not right.

That something has happened.

Something bad.

# IRON

I gulp.

I taste iron.

Breathe.

My hands shake a little.

I frown.

Click my tongue.

What could it be?

Did I leave the taps running again?

I'm scared to call back.

Another girl steps into the toilets. She has a beanie hat on and a piercing between her eyebrows. She says a small *hi* to me. She smells of tobacco.

I try Mum again. No answer.

I try Dad's phone. And Dove's and even the house phone—which nobody ever answers. . . . It rings out.

OK. I check my makeup. I think I look nice. Like a snapshot of how I'd like to look in somebody's mind if they thought of me.

*Sometimes, with certain people that you love, I think it's to do with*

*magnets, something happens and even if it doesn't happen to you physi-*
*cally, somehow, you feel it in your bones. A numbness, a rush of some-*
*thing missing, a blind slip in the darkness, a weightlessness, an alarm,*
*a flashing sudden strike. Like a fuse popping. And you know. A syn-*
*chronised crossing in the stars and you are in the right place at the right*
*time . . . or completely the wrong one.*

I just knew. My bones felt too light to move, too weak to use. So
soft they bowed slack like loose strings on a violin.

The phone rings in my hands and makes me jump. It's Mum.

She's crying. Muffled tears.

"Mum?" I ask. My voice doesn't sound like my own. "Mum?
What's going on? Where are you? Mum?"

"Dove." She cries, and then her voice breaks again before she
regains control of it. "Dove's had an accident."

I don't even say goodbye to Max. I run out of the door and he is
left behind and everything I know slips into darkness as my chest
is filled with the concrete of the ground and I find it impossible to
catch my breath and my fingers are too shaky to even reach for my
inhaler, only thumb her headscarf tied to my wrist and tremble.

# POWDERY HOT CHOCOLATE

Sleeping Dove is a wounded sock rolled in a drawer. A bird with a broken wing. A delicate spool of cotton. She isn't wearing her own clothes. It's a shock to see her. She flits between looking ancient and tiny. Her eyelids are puffy, yellow and shiny. Her lips look tender and sore, swollen, split, bloody. Her eyebrow is cut, her left ear is trickling with a sticky leak of wine-red blood from underneath the bandage. Her arms are whipped in a tie-dye bloom of bruises. Hands are bruised too, nails bloody. I can't see her legs because she has a blanket over them. But I bet they'll be bruised too. Under all that mummified wrapping. Her heart beats *bu-boom. Bu-boom.* It's well boring in this place with her asleep. She would've loved to watch all the people.

Dad kicks the door ajar with his scuffed brown shoe and hands me a beige cup of something more beige. He dramatically tiptoes in to try and lighten the mood. Mum rolls her eyes at him and shakes her head.

"The coffee here is diabolical, almost as bad as yours!" he jokes in a whisper to me. I smile back. Dad secretly LOVES my coffee. It's organic and farmhousey, that's why.

He acts like a little boy, pretending to poke the wires and prod stuff in the room. Mum growls at him. He looks told off. Trying not to laugh. Winking at me, he picks up a stethoscope and wraps it around his neck and pretends to examine me in silence, to not annoy Mum. Scribbling down pretend information and scratching his head and frowning. He's always so good at impromptu acting like this. When Mum looks at him he freezes up and holds his breath like one of those mime artists in Covent Garden. He's so bad in awkward situations. But I'm so glad he's here.

He sits down and sips his coffee. Cups it in his hands and begins to tap out a rhythm, probably something from Radio 2, and then realises that's probably annoying too. Mum side-eyes him and he places a finger over his mouth.

"This really is my favourite coffee shop," he says with sarcasm, again, unable to sit still and face Dove. "I take all my meetings in the local hospital, you can't beat it. Nothing like a stiff plastic chair and a machine-made coffee to really get you pumped!" The gap in his teeth looks bigger than ever. He looks like a child. An awkward one. Suddenly not knowing where he fits in the world. Mum sighs. Deeply.

"Well then, Dove," he whispers close in her ear in this funny naggy jobsworth voice he puts on when he's pretending to be pedantic or taking the mick out of our neighbour Gerald. "That was your final warning. You really are making quite a racket with all that big heavy loud lying there and doing nothing! Can't you keep it down? I'm trying to drink my coffee in peace!" He jabs her gently in the shoulder with his index finger. "I'm not used to seeing you so . . . still."

And then in an instant his smile breaks upside down and looks really, really human. Not like an actor at all. He leans into her head and sniffs a grown-up sob into her hair. This makes both Mum and me cry a bit.

We clamber around the bed and hold hands. We can't believe we nearly lost her.

Dove would *hate* to see us all over her like this.

Hospital hot chocolate is just brown water. Until you get to the end. Then there's a heap of overly sugary powder at the bottom. Dove doesn't wake up. But when she does, I'm sure she'll have something to say about these terrible drinks.

Won't you, Dove?

Won't you?

Dove?

# CAULIFLOWER CHEESE

"Hello, Alicia?"

"Trouper! You're more than two hours late. You better have a good excuse or I'm blasting you back down to Planet Earth faster than you can shout cake!"

"Sorry . . . it's my sister. I just wanted to let you know in case you were wondering where I was today. I'm at the hospital."

"Crikey, chuck, what happened?"

"She fell. From a building."

"WHOA! Bloody heck!"

"I know. I'm sorry, I should have called earlier but we didn't know what was going to happen."

"Oh bubba, this is terrible. Is she . . . gonna . . . Will she? . . . Is she . . . How is she?"

"She's resting now. But we're all just a bit shaken. It was quite a high window, where she fell from, so . . . her friends are quite shaken too."

"I bet."

"So if you don't mind, is it all right with you if I just let you know when I'm able to come back in again?"

"Sure. Sure. Just keep us aliens posted. We can get cover; who knows, maybe even your little mate Camille will have to pull her stripy socks up and get to work! Ha! I'm just kidding; I'd NEVER let that girl work here again." She snorts. "OK, just let us know if there's anything we can do."

"Will do. Thanks."

"Oh, and give that Maxy a ding; he's worried sick about you!"

"Yeah, just say hi."

I hang up really quickly after that, a bit like how I imagine gangsters do when they never stay on the phone long enough to say a proper goodbye.

Least work's off my back; one less thing to worry about. I think about calling Cam. And then Max. And then I decide not to. I know I can't avoid them forever and I don't want to worry them, but right now I don't want to speak to anyone.


Mum and Dad go to talk to the doctor and I wait. Staring at Dove's plastic tray of "in case she wakes up" creamy cauliflower cheese go from steaming and silky to developing a strange cellophane-like skin. The cheese, curdled, and the cauliflower itself looks square, like it's manufactured, connecting pieces to a toy that you might try slotting together. If you were to eat it, it would be congealed and salty and heavy.

My phone rings straight after that. It's Cam. I can see the texts from her and Max building in my phone. It's not that I'm deliberately ignoring them, I just don't have anything to say. And I just tried speaking on the phone and it turns out I didn't really like it.

I use this time to talk to Dove a bit, but I'm not even sure she can hear me, and then I write in here. Dove has sun freckles speckled over her nose. I knew she wouldn't use sunscreen. Her forehead's got a red line where she was obviously wearing her stupid GoPro camera strap thing. *Idiot.*

Open your eyes. Idiot. *Cough, cough.* WAKE UP!

Dove always laughs at how I can always stomach all food, and that goes for service food too. I actually really enjoy service food. Like aeroplane food and school dinners. And if I was in prison, I'd probably go ahead and enjoy that grub too. I love those little foil trays you get on an aeroplane, stuffed with something that's always really squidgey and hot with teardrops of condensation and always-terrible salty cheese and soggy vegetables. I like the silver triangle of Dairylea soft cheese that when you unwrap reveals a block that resembles ice-cold moisturiser, perfect slathered onto a wheaty, salty cracker with the ridge of a plastic knife. It fills the mouth like paint. The claggy press is cloying against the teeth. And school dinners . . . yum. Especially chocolate cake and gloopy skin-on chocolate custard. Jerk chicken and rice'n'peas. I even like the savoury squareness of a dense spongy cheese flan. Where you can't even taste the cheese and it's just a bland plain egg square.

Here, they stuff as many calories as they can into everything. I guess it's because when people are sick they might only be able to manage a mouthful here and there, so every bite has to be jammed with calories.


I press my hands up to the glass like binoculars and see Mum chewing her lip outside, talking to a couple of Dove's friends. They are using their hands to demonstrate Dove's fall. One of them reaches up scarily high. I shudder. The boys look washed-out, like Quentin

Blake illustrations: wiry, spotty boys with greasy fringes. I keep meaning to stand up and go say hi but my body is heavy and numb. My big bones feel extra big today, playing up. I always feel extra huge in front of Dove's mates, like I'm the actual BIG sister they use as the butt of their jokes, accusing each other of fancying me. Not in front of Dove, though; she'd never stand for that. I consider them some more. Maybe it's because they are all so weedy. I could crush them. To them, I am a terror of a woman. A King Kong.

Mum holds her face in her hands and then brings the boys in for a hug. I watch them in silence. And then steal my eyes away to look at Dove some more and this little quiet room. My phone rings in my bag. Cam. Again. I let it ring out.

The room is light blue. The sheets are white. There are some children's books in the corner and one of those games where you slide the wooden coloured beads over the twirly metal rods. There are also a few badly painted pictures of Disney characters on the walls. They all look like evil-twin versions of the real thing. Scary. It occurs to me that Dove is still a "child." Dove's body, still not finished. So fragile. And how I am growing so fast. Would I be on the other ward on the other side of this giant hospital? Next to grown-ups who have to do all of scary life on their own . . .

I realise I've been sitting on my hand for ages. It's gone numb and there are creases all over it. I don't like seeing the creases today. I should have just watched *Snow White* like a normal, unselfish big sister.

"Can I tell you a secret?" I ask her. But she says nothing. Just lies there with those closed shiny veiny eyes. "When I was younger . . . ," I begin, "I used to steal the good bits out of people's lunch boxes at school. I'm not even a thief. But I used to do it. They always had such good treats in their lunch boxes, stuff Mum would never buy, like Fruit Winders and Crunch Corner yoghurts and mini chocolate chip cookies and animal crackers. We never had all that, did we? I mean, I didn't even really like cheese strings but they tasted like the best thing ever when they were stolen from some poor kid's Winnie-the-Pooh lunch box. Why is that? Do stolen things always taste better?"

Dove says nothing.

"Course, I'm not a thief." Her silence makes me cry. "But you can call me one if you want to. I won't mind. I really won't." A tear plops onto Dove's cheek.

"Please call me a thief." I press against her. "Please say something horrible to me."

I clamber up next to her and try to shuffle onto the bed beside her. I feel too tall and too big. The bed squeaks and the wheels judder beneath me. I feel the bed tilt from the weight of me. We never could play on the seesaw together in the playground; it used to have to take Dove plus two of her friends to balance a seesaw with me. "It's because I'm older," I would say. It wasn't. It was because I was fat. And my bones are big. I clasp my arms around her so tight.

"What did you do, little bird?" I ask her. "Why did you have to go flying around the city like that?"

She has little calluses on her palms. Rough. Like verrucas. Her head is bruised. Ouch. Blood still in her hair, cuts on her brow, her cheek grazed. It makes my knees turn to jelly.

There is still some glitter and mascara on my hands from where I wiped my makeup tears away. I think about when she was a little girl and was still able to fit into the baby chairs in shopping trolleys. I would stumble alongside with undone shoelaces, desperate to clamber on up beside her while she was babied, and how Mum and Dad let her play that game. I think about all the grown-ups that never minded carrying her home from stuff, letting her creep up onto their shoulders to get better views at concerts and the fair, sitting on their laps on the train or bus. I'd cling to the pole, knowing nobody would ever want me on their lap. Knowing I'd squash them. Give them cramp. Nobody called me "cute." Or let me balance on their toes while they danced me around the living room, or swung me up or tossed me in the air at the park or piggybacked me or launched me across the swimming pool in a fit of giggles. I was big-boned. She was the little bird made for flying. It should have been me that was broken. I wrap my arms around Dove and sink my face into her neck and I don't recognise her smell today. And I just love her so much. I just love her so much. And my heart is cracking. And I was wrong about what I said before. . . . I can't eat when I'm sad.

I can't even write.

# READY BREK

Ready Brek is the first food Dove manages to swallow. She has a big dollop of jam in the middle AND chocolate chips. She eats every mouthful. I love watching her eat. I'm so grateful to see her chewing, moving.

"I'm sorry," she tells Mum. "I didn't mean to—you know?"

"We're just happy to see you awake," Mum reassures her. Mum's doing well not to be mad at her because I would be ONE MAD MUM!

"I'm an idiot. I lost my balance; I got scared." She sighs.

"We know, darling."

"I ruined your date, didn't I?" she asks me.

"Just a bit!" I joke. "I don't care. I had a peppercorn in my tooth the whole time anyway, so it's a good thing probably."

Dove manages to laugh at my lie but then winces in pain. The sound is contagious. It's like she's been hit with a tuning fork and we all feel the vibration of her pain tingle through us.

Ready Brek smells so nostalgic and familiar. Oaty and sweet and comfortable, like a blanket. Like being a baby again.

I don't hear the words the first time. When Mum says them.

"Dove. You're going to have to get used to living in a chair for a little while."

"A chair?" Dove's face nearly slides off. She wasn't expecting it and her shock smacks Mum round the face. Mum wants to cry but holds the tears back. It's like having a horrible coughing fit in the theatre when you're squeezed in between rows of people and you're sweating and panicking and wishing you just had the guts to let rip and cough and cough and cough until you threw up. She sucks the tears back again. "A wheelchair, sweetheart, just for a little bit . . ." And then she says it again, this time without dressing it up; this time she says it hard and loud so she can hear it said too, clears her throat: "A wheelchair."

Dove is motionless. Her face screws up in anger. She looks down, afraid of looking at us. She shakes her head. I reach for her hand but it's limp in my palm like a dead mouse.

"It'll only be for a short time, Dove, but you've broken your legs. The bones are—"

I butt in; I can't help but interrupt. "Mum, hold on, you haven't even let her have a chance to walk yet. Let her walk, why can't you just see how she gets on first? Get her out of that bed and you'll see."

"Bluebelle," Mum snaps. But I keep pushing.

"No! Mum, you haven't even let her have a try. Once she gets home she'll be absolutely fine. If you just let her get up, she'll be running around and—"

"Bluebelle. ENOUGH!" Mum yells, and it shuts me down. I turn around and cry. I'm angry. I can't believe what I am hearing. Of course Dove is all right. It's DOVE! She doesn't need a chair. Why would she need a chair?

"It's OK, BB," Dove says, and a small tear runs softly down her cheek. Dad holds Dove's hand so tightly. "I wouldn't even know how to walk today anyway."

My brain launches out of my skull like a camera on a wire, X-raying her body: a jigsaw of snapped bones, a train set with a missing track. A squashed bird, crushed in the hand of a giant.

She's broken both of her legs.

Dove closes her eyes and blocks out the world.

The doctor, a nice enough man with a broomstick stache and kind blue eyes, gently raps on the door and enters. He is already saying sorry with his little silent smile.

"How are we doing in here?" he asks in a chirpy whisper.

*We?* No, not *we*. I ignore him.

I turn to Mum and plead. "Can we please just try her legs again, before all this cast stuff goes on? Can we just see if she can walk a sec?"

"I'm afraid—" The doctor begins to answer for Mum but she interrupts and gets there first.

"Bluebelle! STOP now, no. These people do this every day and they know what they're doing."

My voice rises. "I don't understand why they're not putting her up on her feet and letting her just have a try at walking?"

"Stop it, Bluebelle, you're being ridiculous. She can't even get up out of bed," Mum orders.

"Of course she can!" She can do everything, can't she?

"Stop shouting."

"I'm not shouting. THIS is shouting!"

"Bluebelle!"

"She'll be fine and she'll recover but for now she has to rest," the doctor answers calmly, too calmly for my liking. "Your sister has had a lucky escape. A fall like that could've been fatal."

"I wouldn't call it lucky," I mumble.

"Bluebelle!" Mum cries. And then, "Sorry, Doctor."

"It's all right, don't apologise. Everybody's tired, you've had quite a scare and it's normal to be upset," the doctor says. "I understand this is a big change and a lot to take in but as I say it won't be forever. Dove will recover." I stare at him blankly. "It's OK. I'll give you some space; it's rather cramped in this room. The nurse will be round soon with something for the pain." Yeah, you just go home to eat lasagne with your girlfriend or boyfriend or whatever and walk your dog and forget all about us.

Mum smiles sweetly at him and mouths a *thank you*.

"I'll leave you to it, then," the doctor says, already halfway out of the door.

"Yeah, bye," I bark. I throw the diary at the wall behind him. It pounds off the smudged face of some hideous re-creation of a warped Smurf and flops open.

"BLUEBELLE!" Mum explodes, bearlike and gnarly. I've never seen her so mad. But it's Dad who turns on me this time. He rips his glasses off his face and glares at me. His cheeks show colour. I know he's only being like this to show off to Mum, prove that he has a backbone. A vein pulses in his forehead. He's fuming. He points at me.

"We've always let you be exactly how you need to be, Bluebelle, let you do exactly what you need to do, your mum and I and even Dove . . . and we let you get away with it. You manage to make every situation about yourself. But it's not about you today. This is about your sister and this time you've crossed the line."

"How is it about me? It's NEVER about me; it's always only ever about you and Mum, fighting like kids and—"

"ENOUGH!" Dad bellows, and I slam into silence.

Mum tries to perch on the edge of the bed and then apologises and mentions something about needing to call Granny back. "She's worried," she mutters, making no eye contact, backing against the door and turning away from us.

"Lucy, Lucy, don't," Dad says.

"I'm sorry, I just . . . sorry." Mum squeezes herself out of the door and I watch her flutter out of the room as quick as she can, almost in a jog now. To get away from me. Times like this remind me once more that Dove and Mum are small. And thin. And light. They have that in common. And I feel horrible. Like a stain.

My phone vibrates. *Max.* I cancel it.

He rings again and I cancel that too. I don't read the texts either.

"Dove? Dove?" I nudge her. I stroke her hair. She is drowsy, with her eyes half closed. She cranks one eye open like I've woken her from a dream. "'K, you sleep some more, then." I kiss her head.

We sit in the stillness.

Dad looks at me as if to say, "Well, that was dramatic." There's no space for being angry or stubborn. I can feel my face falling before it happens. Dad takes my hand and leads me out into the corridor.

And the moment we are away from Dove I fold into his arms and cry like a *T. rex* having a breakdown. I wet all down his front. Dribble and snot and hot red-raw emotion seem to have teamed up and kidnapped my whole body.

"OK, darling, my darling, let it all out. It's OK."

"I don't want to cry in front of Dove," I say. "I don't want to—"

"It's OK." He strokes my hair. He's been smoking. I like the smell.

It reminds me of being young. I breathe it in. I'm aware of people walking past us. We rock stiffly in a tense, sharp shake. I haven't felt hugged like this in ages.

"It's just everything. I know it's only broken bones. . . . I know it's her legs and they'll fix. . . . I know it's the bittersweet ending in comedy films and TV shows where it's funny after a big fall to end up with all your limbs in casts. I get that. I do. I just . . . I just don't like imagining her falling . . . hitting her head . . . being scared . . . lying there on the ground, on top of all that rubbish, the bin bags and spiky stuff and crap . . . by the railings . . . screaming for us." I can't stop crying. "And us not being there."

"Well, it's lucky the rubbish *was* there, Bluebelle. Probably saved our girl's life!" Dad smiles, holding my face, wiping my wet eyes with his thumbs.

"And it's just hit me, the shock, to imagine losing her. . . ." Dad strokes my hair. I cry into his chest. I miss him living at home. I miss being small and him carrying me. I don't even remember when that stopped. "I should stop crying. I have to be strong for her."

"You *are* strong." Dad has wet eyes too now. "My God, you girls are the strongest girls I've ever met in my life. I'm lucky enough to even know you, honestly, that's why I'm so desperate to come home. Because I'm so rubbish without the three of you." I laugh at him. "Look at me," he adds, drawing me out to face him. "I'm a right state." I laugh again, through wet drops of tears.

"Come on, don't be hard on yourself. We're all in this terrible soap opera of life together. Honestly, I wouldn't even act in it if I was paid all the money in the world. . . . Well, maybe I would . . . I *am* quite desperate and haven't done TV for years. Talk to my agent." He winks. "Now, where's your pump?" He pats my pockets.

I don't look up. I squeeze my eyes. I am trembling. He hands my inhaler to me. I take long, deep, wet-faced puffs.

"I thought she wasn't going to wake up too," Dad says. "So I'll take the broken legs, trust me." I laugh. "And besides, I'm looking forward to getting myself a fresh permanent black marker and practising the spelling of every single swear word I can think of on those casts. Two legs—now, that's a LOT of space to fill!" He kisses my head and shoves open the door with his side.

# CHERRY DROPS

Sorry. I wasn't expecting this thing to become an actual diary. It was only meant to be about food. And here it is, getting all . . . you know . . . heavy.

Really, I shouldn't be writing in you because it's a food diary and, well, I haven't really been eating.

Not that that's a good thing either. Undereating is just as bad for you as overeating. I know that.

Mum calls Dad to say she's having a cup of tea in the cafe and then she'll be back up. She'll be sorry because the nurse enters with a temporary wheelchair for Dove. It's kind of clunky and squeaky and not very comfortable and has some chewing gum stuck to the bottom of the seat. Still, I try to pretend it's the coolest thing I've ever seen.

"Whoa, cool," I lie. "Check it, Dove."

Dove says she'll "have a go" when she feels more awake. Dad offers me a cherry drop and I go to open Dove's one for her but Dad doesn't let me. He places his unintimidating dog-paw-like hand on top of mine and softly shakes his head. We mustn't mollycoddle her. And I leave the wrapped sweet for her, untouched, on the side.

Dad and I suck cherry drops as we take a look at the chair.

Dad, with his crackly actor voice that read children's audio books to earn a bit of extra cash. He'd take it really seriously, barging round the house, stretching out the words "Ru-mmmp-el-*stiltz*-skin" and "Rap-UNNNN-zel." When we were small we'd play them and let his "actory" voice read us fairy stories before bed. Feeling so superior to all the other kids because he was OUR dad and no one else's. Sometimes he'd sit next to the speakers, miming to make us laugh, stories of princesses and magic, of wicked witches and evil stepmothers. It sounded like Dad's normal voice except he'd just pronounce all the bits correctly and leave out all the swear words. Sometimes I'd get jealous that other kids went to sleep listening to his voice and he'd say, "Just think of all the little children without a daddy to read them a bedtime story before bed. It's very generous of you to share your dad." But that only made it worse. He was OUR dad. Not the generic comforting voice of *a dad* for everyone.

We are on our second round of cherry drops by the time Dove stirs. My tongue is red, soft and numb.

"What you guys eating?"

Dad nods his head towards the wrapped sweetie on her bedside. She grins.

"Well, well, well then . . . ," he mutters in his Big Bad Wolf voice, "want to know what I think about all this?"

Dove nods.

He continues. "I think it's a good thing to try jumps that are too high for us." Dad's voice starts to crack; his eyes go all watery. "It is, it's a good thing. You're bloody crazy but my word, babe, are you cool."

# SOME MORE TOAST

"**B**B." Mum knocks on my door. "I've left some toast out here for you, noodle."

"Thanks." I'm not going to be one of those bratty kids who says "I'm NOT hungry" because even though I've lost my actual appetite for life doesn't mean that I want to make Mum worry about me too. She has enough on her plate. Figuratively.

I take the toast, slide the plate in as the china growls on my wooden floorboards. A patch of the wood is covered in black fluff from when I spilt a whole bottle of Diet Coke over it years ago and didn't clear it up. It went sticky. Now it's covered in sock fluff and bobble.

I roll over on the trifle and stick my phone on charge. The screen flickers with messages.

Max: *Blue, really hope you're OK, thinking of you.* xx

And then: *AHHHH! Alicia is doing my head! Wish you were here.* x

I don't dare open the messages from Cam. The ones from girls at school. I think about sending a group message to everybody with some lame joke about all the things Dove can't do now that both her legs are broken, with some great emojis, but then delete the whole thing in embarrassment like I'm pretty much the grossest most unfunny person in the universe. It's probably better to say nothing.

The toast is hard to swallow and goes down like eating a shoe. I manage one of the four buttery triangles. Guilt runs through my whole body from doing absolutely anything. Because all I think about is all the things that Dove can't do. I have an image of finding stainless-steel silver sheets and wrapping them, conelike, around my skin, carving off the layers like those ham cutters at the deli. My flesh, thinly sliced, piling up in that waxy paper.

I can't stop thinking about Dove and how she feels and what she's going through, even though I know I should. If I think too hard about it, it would be like a tidal wave rushing through my mind and body and once I let the emotion in it would burst my bones and flood me until I was full to the brim and I would combust out of my body completely until my body was no longer a body and all of me would turn to absolute water without any bones at all.

I am useless. I am school-less. Max doesn't even know I don't go to school . . . so I'm uneducated too. A waste. A waste at sixteen. Who was I fooling that I was cute and cheeky and strong? I'm annoying and weak. People will see Dove in her chair and they will see me, the big sister, looming over her in my towering monstrosity and think, shame it was the little one. They will naturally resent me. Because Dove did everything with her body. And I do nothing with mine.

If I was in a chair, nobody would even notice the difference.

# QUAIL

Mum's upstairs with Dove, and Dad and I sit downstairs by the little coffee shop. I hate seeing sick kids. Worried parents.

I get a picture message from Mum. *D's getting her wounds re-dressed! X*

Dove's smiling in the photo but I am not and neither is Dad. "Zeesh!" he winces. "She looks like a bloody Francis Bacon painting."

Dad's right, her head is covered in weird shapes and muddy marks. We zoom in: there's this one bit of sticky dried blood that looks like black beans from the Chinese, all dehydrated and gross. Like chewed-up, spat-out licorice. Her hair is all greasy from where it can't be washed because of all of her dressings.

"We should text back," Dad says, rubbing his specs on his moth-eaten jumper. "A joke or something."


I wish Dad would stop using Dove's accident as a chance to flirt with Mum. Or use me as Cupid.

"Hungry?" Dad asks.

"Not after seeing that," I joke.

"Could stretch our legs, though, have a *mooch*?" as Dad loves to call it.

We head out of the car park, past the neon ambulances and wheelchairs, the stretchers and flustered visitors hailing taxis, towards the street, back to where the shops and normal people are. The people who don't even think about the hospital until they need it.

"Sure you don't fancy any lunch?" Dad suggests, snooping at a menu as we pass the high street.

"No. I'm not hungry." My eyes skim the bland, predictable menu. Overpriced. Ugly. Pretentious and uses weird words to mislead you.

"You have to eat. You've had nothing all day."

I say nothing.

"The eyes are off you now with all this—you don't have to worry about writing that diary anymore, Bluebelle. Mum isn't going to mind about that. Come on, eat something?" he offers. "When am I ever offering to buy you lunch? Me—what is it you call me? Mr. Tight?" I smile. "Come on. Spread some gossip about me and my generosity. It's a rare opportunity, one not to be missed!"

"I really don't want to eat, Dad."

"Well, can't hurt to take a peek at the menu." He tilts his spectacles. The place he wants to eat at is one of those weird actors' club member things, which I can't be bothered to go to because he'll just bitch about everyone in there stealing his roles and owing him rounds of beer and then be upset when he finds out that his signed headshot has been removed from the wall for not being famous enough.

"Hmm . . . quail." Dad considers it. "No."

"I've never tried eating a quail."

"Oh, don't bother." He almost physically brushes the menu away. "You're not missing anything; it's the most pointless food of all the foods. It represents the ultimate food for snobby toffs." He blows his nose on a scraggy tissue scrumpled up from his sleeve and briskly walks on.

"One time I went to a posh charity dinner where—honestly—thousands of pounds must have been spent on this luscious wine and complicated canapés and decorations . . . and the staff were impeccable—you know, first-class, and—"

"That's so weird, if it's a charity, why don't they just *not* spend all the money on the event and give it to the charity instead?"

"Oh, to butter up the millionaires so they part with their cash. It's giving a little to gain a lot, I suppose." He begins to walk away from the restaurant. "Or giving a lot to gain . . . more."

"But surely if they're that rich they should just suggest *not* having the meal and instead giving it to the people that actually need it and give the donation regardless?" I argue. "I think it's horrible that people need to be massaged to hand money over. If you can afford it, share it."

"Too right! Of course. But I wasn't one of the millionaires, don't worry." I wasn't. "I was reading a poem for the entertainment. They didn't even listen; they talked over me."

"Oh, Dad. Poor you." I felt sorry for him.

"I'm used to it, darling. These millionaires are used to fantastic wine and food and probably used to *good* theatre, so they don't care. Anyway . . . not my crowd. There were about eight hundred guests there, maybe even a thousand, and we all, apart from the vegetarians, I suppose, were given a quail EACH. A whole bird, a whole life right there on the plate."

"EACH?"

"Each."

"For one dinner?" I snarl, disgusted. "That many lives, wasted?"

"And let's be honest, how tasty can *anything* be when a chef has had to prepare eight hundred portions of it?"

"True! I bet EVEN eight hundred slices of toast wouldn't taste great, so why that many birds? At least with whole chickens you can share the meat, say spread between four, so that's, what, two hundred chickens, two hundred lives eaten—but EIGHT HUNDRED?! Were they even nice?"

"Oh, of course they weren't. Bony old things. They don't even have any flesh on them; they're not meant to be eaten. You feel like some wretched giant Viking when you eat them. . . ." He coughs. "Course, we all had so much wine we couldn't even really taste it," Dad adds. "Some of the people there couldn't even be bothered to mess around with all the bones."

"And I bet the people there weren't even grateful. Or impressed. This was just another fancy meal on another day that would end up squished up in their tummies and swirl down the bowl of a toilet."

The eggs of a quail, apparently, are as small as thumbprints, like those delicious chocolate eggs you get at Easter. You can't dip a soldier into an egg *that* size—you'd need to boil twelve of them before you'd even get a yolk flow going and imagine peeling the stupid things: Who's got the time for that?

"Why are we so barbaric?" I ask Dad. "Why do we think we can just take from this planet, pluck at creatures like they belong to us—bake four and twenty blackbirds, kill a squid just to make black pasta, force-feed a duck so we can get a bit of pâté? Why can't we be resourceful and if we take a creature, respect it, use it, all of it?"

"We are so greedy. And picky," Dad says. His voice is sad, defeated. "We are so picky."

I feel sick.

Food makes me feel so sick.

"On second thoughts . . . ," Dad says softly. "I think I'll just get a sarnie."

# BAD FATS

Max, again: *Please just let me know you're OK. That's all. X*

I go to reply but I don't know what to say. My thumbs hover over the letters . . . Maybe just an *X*? No. Always annoys me when I just get an *X* back. Oddly aloof. Maybe I'll reply later.

I always used to think in films and stuff when a fat actor playing a "fat" character gets called "fat" in the film or whatever—does it not hurt their feelings? But it's a fact. They know they went up for an audition to play a big person. It's not a shock to them the same way it's not a shock if somebody is old. Or tall.

It's not just because I have eyes that I know I'm fat. It's not even the fact that people think that because you're fat you're also gross. As if being fat means you'd eat something off the floor or have BO or stinky feet or are really lazy. As if you might keep a line of crushed, damp Doritos under the flab of your breast rolls. Sleep with a baguette in the crease of your elbow, *just in case*. All of that annoys me but it's not how I know I'm fat. It's not even the fact that the sensors of my cat-whisker hips don't work and my bum always ends up knocking ornaments off shelves in those weird little card shops or sends china salt and pepper pots flying in restaurants as I squeeze past a table. And we all know we've squeezed in that little bit too far at a table to overly *let the fat girl past*.

It's mostly because when I say I'm fat, people go, "No you're not."

And that means I definitely am. It's OK. I've learnt that people secretly like it a bit if other people don't like themselves because it gives other people power. It shows weakness. And I'm not going to be one of those people. EVER. Because the only person I'm not liking by doing that is me.

But right now I'm finding it hard to like myself. And it's unusual for me. And it hurts.

# COCONUT

I wake up to more missed calls from Cam and Max. Bleugh. *No thank you, anyone.* I let my phone run out of battery.

Bye, world.

Mum is at the hospital with Dove. Again. Mum's stopped asking me to go. Dad has been sleeping at the house on the sofa. He LOVES it; he can't believe that he's been *allowed.* He wears matching striped pyjamas and a dressing gown to show he's here to stay, that he's extra relaxed so there's no need to move him, and everything Mum asks him to do, he replies with "Not a problem."

He dumps the newspapers on the side.

"Here's that coconut water thing you asked for. It's crazy expensive. Coconut milk is so much cheaper—why don't you just drink that instead?"

"It's not the same; it doesn't hydrate you the same."

"For that price it should hydrate you all the way to a tropical island!"

I roll my eyes and open the carton. The cool, creamy water is smooth and tangy on my fluffy tongue. "The coconut is a perfect example of you how hard nature wants us to work for our food.

You have to crack through that hairy, heavy shell to be *rewarded* with the sweet flesh and water. Not just take, take, take off a supermarket shelf."

"I saw bananas wrapped in clingfilm once," Dad says as he unpacks the breakfast shopping, trying to act like everything's normal. I say "breakfast" but it's closer to lunchtime. Dad thinks that us talking like this will distract us from everything—from Dove, but also maybe the fact he's trying to move back in right under our noses. "Errr . . . *HELLOO* . . . that's why nature gave them a *skin*," he adds, pretending to be a girl my age.

"Did you walk to the shops in your pyjamas?" I ask him.

"No, course not," he says as if I'm crazy. "I rode my bicycle."

I wonder if Dad too has become really conscious of his legs and what they do. How they work and how they feel. Does he feel like he's walking in space, like me? Then other times like he's underwater, wearing one of those oversized old-school metal diving suits, like me? Drowning? Short of breath in either scenario.

I reach for my inhaler.

He makes a cafetiere of coffee. I still have no appetite.

"Come on, then, Super Girl, what you eating?"

"I don't feel like anything."

"Come on, look, I got avocado—you love avocado. Bloody things cost me a fortune," he jokes. "Expensive rascals, aren't you?" he mutters to the fruit. "So trendy, aren't they? Bet these things are cheap as chips wherever they're grown. They say ripen in the bowl but half of them look like meteorites and the other half look like they've been involved in a pub brawl."

"I know Mum made you go to the shops so I'd eat."

233

"Come on, at least a bit of toast?"

My brain finds an image of Dove's dirty hands, her bruised knuckles, her fingernails jammed with gammy dried-up blood.

"Why do we eat meat? We aren't meant to eat meat."

"Cavemen ate meat."

"Yeah, but they had to work for it; there was nothing else. And I bet when they killed something, like a wild boar or whatever, they made it last. It probably fed a whole family for a week."

"True. We are a greedy country of consumers. Why are you so interested in the economics and politics of food at the moment?"

I ignore him. But it's because I feel like I've had too much of it. I've robbed the planet.

"But why do we eat it?" I continue. "If we're descended from monkeys, then surely we should eat what monkeys eat? They eat soft fruit and vegetables. Nuts."

"Some monkeys eat meat." Dad plays devil's advocate.

"*Some* humans murder other humans."

"This is a bit of a deep conversation for this time of the morning but I have to say I'm rather enjoying it."

He'd love me to be vegetarian—that would be another thing he could sling across the plates at a dinner-table debate. *"Well, MY daughter's vegetarian, so . . ."* And then I think about Dove. He's got THAT to use now. I shake the ugly thought out of my head. Go away.

"Monkeys have short nails like us and flat teeth, molars, like us. They climb; their hands and feet are for climbing. We can't outrun an antelope like a lion or kill it with claws or sharp teeth. We aren't that kind of animal."

"True." Dad nods. He feeds Not 2B some raw bacon fat.

"And we can't even *digest* raw meat; in fact, it makes us sick."

"Steak tartare?"

"Oh yeah, cos I eat THAT every day." I'm being difficult.

"We can't actually really digest cooked meat that well."

"See?"

"Although that is why man made fire. We made fire . . . We made traps to catch food, spears to catch fish. That's what makes our kind top of the food chain. Put a man in a cage with any beast and the beast wins . . . but throw a rifle in the cage, the beast wouldn't know what to do. It's evolution, Bluebelle. We need meat to live."

I hear the key in the door, which means Mum's back.

"SURPRISE!" she squeals. "Guess who's home?"

And I hear metal clanking against the step. Dove.

Dad leaps up excitedly. "Well, that *is* a surprise! We weren't expecting you back yet, my darling!"

And I don't know why, but I feel scared. I run upstairs to my room—like I said, I don't know why. I find all the Nutella jars and sling them out, even if they have knives and spoons in them. The sound of glass and metal. Clank. Clunk. Everything goes in the bin.

# MILLIONAIRE'S
# SHORTBREAD

It wasn't my choice, or deliberate, but I slept. Deeply. I think it was exhaustion that did it.

*I'm gonna do my shift today. Is that OK?* I text Alicia and await the annoying flurry of emojis that's gonna whack me in the face with her reply. She loves the little cartoon face with one eye closed, one open, with the tongue out.

I am actually looking forward to going back. I never thought I'd say that but it's true. Planet Coffee, where it only matters that the milk is frothed and the forks are clean. That customers get the right change and you go along with the rules that people expect in a coffee shop, the warm embrace of comfort and simplicity.

Max does a double take when he sees me. Green eyes blooming like a blossoming flower on a nature programme sped up. He's surprised.

Alicia follows me backstage. "Hey, honeybunch, it's good to see you. How you doing?"

"I'm OK, thanks."

"Did the flowers arrive OK?" Yeah, lilies: they represent death, you IDIOT. BB, be nice.

"Oh yeah, they're lovely thanks. They're still alive."

"Aw, that's good. And the choccies?" Yes. The "choccies" too.

"Uh-huh." She nods. Hands on hips, she breathes out. It's like she feels safe to just "let it all hang out" in front of me. Cos who am I to judge? Her belly is bursting, swelling over her jeans, the button straining at the seam. She's doing that whole *I'm denying I'm pregnant but I'm definitely pregnant.* I knew she didn't have food poisoning. It takes a lot to take down a cockroach like Alicia.

"You been eating?" she asks. *It's nice to give a fat person permission to eat.* I glare at her and say nothing. Alicia scratches her wrist. She then attempts a hug. "You look so thin." Erm. OK. My body tenses, rock hard.

"So how's she doing?"

"Dove's doing great. She's dealing with it much better than I am!" I chirp awkwardly.

"You look tired." She smiles.

"Yeah . . . well . . . I am." I AM. "I just can't bear the idea of her not . . . being able to do stuff."

"You can go home any time if you decide it's too soon. We've got it covered here, chuck."

"No, no, I want to be here. I was going a bit crazy at home. There's not that much use me being there."

"Oh, bubba, you must be going through hell."

The conversation's shifted from my weight to my baby sister's accident. She wants to hear the story replayed like one of those *Emergency 999* reconstruction documentaries. But I'm VERY protective. Defensive, almost. It doesn't feel the same as when she comments on my weight, because my fat is mine. Because I understand it. I put food in; it comes along for the ride. This is something completely different. Something that can't be fixed by writing down some thoughts in a diary. SO GO ON, THEN, ALICIA. SAY WHAT YOU WANT TO SAY. ASK WHAT YOU WANT TO ASK.

"So . . . like . . . do you think . . . she'll be, like . . . able to walk again?"

"Yes. She will be able to do everything. It's just two broken legs." I wrap my apron around my waist and tie it into a bow.

Did you sign the letter yet, though? Obviously not. Whatever. Don't even care anymore anyway.

I gaze at the tubs of brown squares in their Tupperware boxes, like jewellery under glass. I smile. "I see we've got millionaire's shortbread now. That's cool."

"Yeah, it was Max's idea. He said they were a must. I took his advice; thought we'd trial-run them for a bit, seeing as he was so SET on having the damn things." She shrugs. "I'm not such a caramel girl myself. But I think I know someone who is."

Me.

*Max.*

If I was thirteen and you weren't reading this, I'd draw a hundred love hearts around his name right now.

The idea of salt and sweet. Of the sandy base and squidgy caramel. I feel my mouth water in the wrong way. I feel sick. I don't want it. I've lost my love for food.

I've lost my love.

# SEASONING

At Planet Coffee, I watch girls and girls watch me. I find girls much more interesting than boys because there are so many diversions and versions of us. Boys get excited if their jacket has a hood or their coat has a patterned lining. Boys think they are *wacky* if they wear a pink shirt or sport a flash of red sock peeping out of their shoes, if their trainers have a blue air bubble.

We think we need things that make us recognisable and that we should be known for our things—our perfume, our hair colour, our style, our taste. So that other people know who we are. So other people can describe us to somebody new who hasn't met us yet.

Do I have the right trainers? *No.* The right hair? *Definitely not.* The right ringtone—*no way.* The right underwear or clothes or bag or nails or ideas . . . Do you have to decide who you think you are right now and then stick to that choice forever? Do you have to be pigeonholed? Which umbrella do you have to stand under? I just want to be a girl. Flavoured with my own seasoning that makes me *me.*

In the toilet at work I lift my top up and look at my belly. I prod it. Suck it in. Push it out. My ribs are there. And a line wants to be, down the centre. Women are like wardrobes, aren't they? We split down the middle; the doorknobs are our boobs . . . and then think about all the brilliant, beautiful stuff that you can shove inside your wardrobe of a personality. Colours, fabrics, textures ready to butter-fly out and show you off in your many versions . . . each telling a different story, a little history, a little shade of you.

The mirror in the toilets at work is two mirrors shoved together and if you stand at the right angle you can only see half of your body. Then I can almost, sort of, see myself as a thin person.

# CINNAMON

"Yeah, but how is she?"

"She's fine, go back to work."

"I am. I am at work. I'm still working; I just want to know if she's all right."

"She's fine, B. She's had tuna pasta, haven't you, Dove? Tuna pasta and cheese-and-onion crisps and now we're . . . Yes, BB. Do you want to say hello?" Mum coos at Dove softly; I feel like she's about to pass the phone over to a grandma or a toddler. "Hold on, BB, Dove wants to say hello. Hold on, let me just pass her over."

"It's OK, I just wanted to know she was OK. I've got to go now. Sorry, Mum. I've got to go—"

And I end the call just as I hear Dove's high-pitched, happy *HELLO*. My heart is banging out of my chest. I throw my phone on the top of my bag like a hot potato. I didn't have to go at all . . . Why am I avoiding her?

I scrub my dirty hands down my apron. I close my eyes and breathe deep. I shake my arms out. I think about calling back. I could say sorry. I could say sorry to Dove and listen to her properly, about her day of watching cartoons and not getting a moment to herself. Just sitting. Eating all the annoying gross fibrous foods that she doesn't like that the hospital has her on just so she can go to the toilet. Fibrous foods that make her so thirsty but she can't even drink as much as she'd like in case her bladder swells and hurts her insides, which then hurts her ribs. Ask her properly and listen properly too, instead of going through the motions, not really being there.

But I don't. I can't. I should ask her how the hospital visit went. How she is. How she feels. I should just talk to her like I'd normally do. Tell her about the millionaire's shortbread. Tell her about normal stuff. But I can't because everything feels so minimal and birdseed-tiny in importance. I should call, right now, and say: "Dove, you're my sister. I care about everything you're going through; everything you're going through I want to go through too. I want to take your suffering away. You're my baby sister, I love you so much." But I don't. "I can't watch Mum lift you out of the chair to shower you. To not get your casts wet. I can't watch Mum getting you changed and Dad lifting you back onto the sofa and in and out of the car." I chew my tongue and then I step out front again. I want to taste blood.

Back on the Planet my mind can be distracted. I stop thinking about how every bone in my body feels, bothered by my big bones getting in the way. Did you know roughly fifteen percent of the body's mass is made up of bones? Split that in two, top half and bottom half, that's like seven and a half percent for each. A bit more for the top because I think the head is well heavy. Mine is, anyway; it's like a bowling ball. So . . . let's say eight percent is the top half of the body and seven percent is the bottom half. . . . That's a LOT of body weight that Dove can't use. A lot of dormant bone to carry around, dragging her down like a ball and chain.

My legs feel light and full of water. Like jelly.

I hope for a busy day and lots of customers.

I go and stand next to Max. Hoping his conversation, just his company, will ground me somehow, give me a sense of purpose.

He is making chai latte. "Cinnamon?" he asks the customer, and she shakes her head and replies, "No, thank you."

WHAT IS WRONG WITH PEOPLE?

"You know, you can really start to think people are generally decent and then they go and do crap like that. Like when people don't have chocolate sprinkles on their cappuccinos . . . Surely that's the only real reason to get a cappuccino," he grumbles to me as he watches her leave.

I say nothing. I can't even think of what to reply with. I can't make eye contact with him. I'm nervous he'll bring up the date that we didn't have.

Max continues to serve and nods towards the counter in time to Alicia's terrible music. I look down and he's made me a hot chocolate with a "latte art" heart on the top. And next to it, a slice of millionaire's shortbread. And he doesn't ask any questions at all.

# SALT

I hear Mum crying in the bathroom. I want to knock on the door and comfort her but I don't know how. I feel like I've stolen something from her. I feel guilty. I feel like I've let her down. I think about us like we're characters in a doll's house, moving around, and Dove is just frozen on the sofa bed downstairs. It's not just the legs. It's the way she looks, swollen and bruised, her pretty face: swollen lips and puffy eyes, her skin tattooed in a greenish camouflage of hits. It's worrying how quiet she is, how eerily silent the house is without her pounding around and flipping off the walls. Her bedroom is empty.

We used to have bread in our doll's house. It was the size of my little finger, a little loaf, salt-baked. And painted. We used to take turns to lick it. I don't even know where the doll's house is anymore.

I wonder if Mum would feel as sad if it was me.

Sorry, I know that's an ugly thing to say. And an even uglier thing to read. I'm just being honest.

# HAWAIIAN PIZZA

Normally, I'll eat any pizza. I'm really not fussy. Of course my favourite is from a proper wood-fired oven. Pizza made from fresh dough and a real tomato-red sauce. I like it when the whole thing is covered in white rounds of mozzarella that go all brown and bubbled and the crust chars and black charcoal-mottled black spots pop. But Dove likes that terrible pizza from the takeaway that comes in huge boxes and the cheese is orangey and the crust is so heavy it's like a wrecking ball has knocked you in the gut. She likes Hawaiian best. So the whole pizza is covered in little plastic curls of dehydrated porky ham and triangles of tinned, luminous pineapple. The pineapple bit I get but I don't see what ham has to do with Hawaii.

This is why I'm happy to see those boxes now. All stacked up on the kitchen table, and twelve beaten-up trainers and all these scratched, stickered skateboards lined up by the front door. Because it means that Dove has asked for the terrible pizza. Her free-running parkour mates are here. Eating slices, drinking cans of fizzy drink and laughing. Trying to make light of the situation. A pack of grubby, spotty, greasy boys with dirty, bitten nails and smashed phone screens. Snorting and being insecure, with bent, bony postures and not knowing where to put their arms if they're not eating or drinking.

They take Dove out into the garden and take turns whizzing around on her lap on the patio. 2B and Not 2B are jumping around barking and trying to lick the grease off the boys' hands. They write all over Dove's casts with their funny tags. One of the boys, Florian, has called himself "Ghetto Gangster" and he is literally the poshest kid I know—I've seen his house, and his jumper costs more than my whole wardrobe put together. Maybe it's ironic.

"Don't you want any pizza, BB?" Mum asks.

I shake my head. No. I don't feel like anything. It's actually the first time I feel like eating anything—I think it might be that the shortbread has ignited something, but I know what those boys are like and they'll happily keep eating all the pizza in the world until the supply dries up. And I don't want them to look at me like I'm eating something that's theirs. That's something I don't need. It's as though people look at bigger people and assume we shouldn't feel the need to ever get hungry because we have enough fat stored up to last us until our dying day. As if we can nibble off our sides like we're made out of peach.

We watch Dove laughing outside, listen to her voice screeching. The boys crowd round her like she's a queen.

"They feel so responsible," Mum says. "They feel like it's their fault."

"It's not their fault," I grumble, knowing how stubborn and determined Dove is. She would only have jumped if she wanted to.

"No, I know it's not; they all do it. Hopefully it will make them think twice when they're out there doing that parkour business. . . . It's been quite a wake-up call for them all. It's just a shame it's my little girl who's had to be the scare." Mum rubs her eyes. "I was certain they were just hopping off bloody brick walls and climbing trees . . . you know? I thought it was so much better for her to be in the outdoors, running free with the boys than, you know . . . on the bloody internet getting involved in all that gossipy vain rubbish or being groomed by some murderer online. I thought the worst thing that would happen would be a few scabby knees. . . . I never . . ." She shakes her head again, holds her chest. "I wouldn't have let her do it if I thought it was dangerous, if she was doing anything that kids haven't been doing for years."

She strokes my hair. "She's lucky to have a big sister like you. She looks up to you so much, you know that, don't you?"

I know. I want to say, "IT WAS MY FAULT. I TOLD HER TO BE BRAVE."

But I'm not even brave enough to say that.

How dare I tell Dove to be brave? I'm not even brave enough to go to the gym.

"Anyway . . ." Mum breaks my thoughts. "Don't you get your GCSE results this week?"

And that's it. I text Cam: *Hey . . . you busy?*

# POPCORN

I meet Cam at the Odeon.

"Salt or sweet? Salt or sweet? Now, THAT'S the question."

"You sound like my dad," I reply spikily.

"I know, isn't that the point? What's up with you? We always say that."

"Oh, sorry."

"Salt or sweet?"

"What?"

"Popcorn, you fruitcake."

"I don't like fruitcake."

"Seriously?"

"Sorry. Whatever. I'll have whatever you're having."

"Well, I haven't had dinner because SOMEBODY gave me five seconds to get ready, so I'm starving; I'm literally blowing all my money here. I'm getting a large one and Maltesers *and* Minstrels and whatever that blue drink is saying for itself. Have you ever had these nacho things? The sauce looks a bit orange." Cam looks up at the menu. The whole cinema smells of popcorn. Of warm lights and apprehension. We come to cinemas to go somewhere else. To sit in the chair and rocket off to somewhere new.

You know, the reason you have popcorn in the cinema is because it's a quiet snack to eat. Crisps and stuff are too loud and crunchy, so that's why we have popcorn.

"Exam results Thursday," Cam says.

"I'm not gonna get mine."

"What?"

"I'm not going to get them."

"Don't be weird."

"It's not weird; loads of people don't collect their results. Think of all the kids that go skiing in France or whatever and aren't there."

"Yeah, but those kids probably know they've done all right; they probably have extra tuition and all that crap."

"A girl in my class, Ruby, it's her birthday on exam results day— think she's going to go into school to collect her GCSE results? Errr. No. She's not."

"Well, she might want to if she's done well," Cam says bluntly.

Rude. I know that comment was a bullet aimed for me.

"Yeah, maybe. Just don't see why anybody would want to go into school on their birthday."

"They'll post the results to your house. You can't just avoid them."

"Let them post them, then." I know I'm being nasty and difficult. I don't know why I can't shake this mood off.

Cam studies the menu again. "I'm starving," she moans. "I had a chewing gum on the way here and it's tricked my belly into thinking a steak and chips is about to land in there." I say nothing. "I didn't have time to put on mascara either; I look like a blind mole."

"No you don't," I offer, trying to be normal and nice.

"I do. Bloody hay fever, can't even wear my contact lenses. I have to wear my glasses in the cinema like a total geek."

It was a bad idea coming out. I am obviously finding it hard to be social. Wish I'd never called her. All of this pretending-nothing-has-happened-to-Dove business in fake old cinema land. But what am I expected to do? Bring it up with everyone ALL the time? I hate sci-fi films anyway. Idiot actors running around in metal chutes and pipes talking to one another in too-fast sentences of invented spaceish jargon that means absolutely nothing. I find it really hard to forget they're on a set. When we see a shot of space I just know they're filming this whole scene on some tinfoiled corridor in a studio in Swindon. Why am I so miserable today?

"Salty and sweet, please."

"I thought you hated sci-fi?"

"I wanted to get out of the house."

"Ah, nice. I want to come visit Dove. When can I visit her?"

"I'll let you know."

"So you keep saying. Does she not want visitors?"

"She does," I snap. Cam looks offended. Confused, she says, "I'll stop asking. Just let her know I'd like to see her whenever she's ready."

"She would love to see you."

"I was thinking she could come tonight? She loves films, she could've come to the cinema with us?"

"Cam, Dove can't just *come* to the cinema!"

"Why not?"

"Isn't it obvious . . . ? She can't come to the cinema. . . . She's . . ."
I can't really think of a reason why she couldn't come to the cinema,

actually. I'm talking like somebody I hate. I feel like the staff behind the counter is staring at me, shovelling popcorn into pop-up cardboard boxes and staring. Camille won't hand over her card to them until I've explained why Dove can't come to the cinema. A queue forms; I blush. "Well, maybe she *could*. . . . The accident's really changed her. She's different now. . . . She's . . . I don't know . . . she's changed."

"I'm not being rude to you, B, honestly I'm not, you know I love you, but do you think it might be *you* that doesn't want visitors? Do you think it might be that the accident changed *you*?"

"What?" I feel a lump in my throat, my insides falling out. "What do you mean?"

"Just because Dove is in a wheelchair for a bit doesn't mean she doesn't want to laugh or cry or enjoy a movie, that she doesn't want to do stuff like go out. She's not in a prison."

"I didn't say she was." I feel myself boiling up. "She looks like a monster. Like a different person—it's scary. And heartbreaking. Look, you have no idea how it feels to have this happen to you."

"B, that's the whole point. It HASN'T happened to you; it's happened to your sister. Your sister and, yes, that means you're going through stuff too, I know. But how many times have you moaned when people say rude stuff behind your back and you say . . . *Just because I'm fat doesn't mean I don't have ears*? Right? It's like you think just cos Dove's had an accident *she* doesn't have ears, a heart, a brain, feelings . . . like she doesn't want to live. It's a real bummer, I get that, six months is a long time to be in a chair, especially for someone like Dove, but she's gonna be all right because . . . bones mend." Her words cut into me and she doesn't stop there either. "Yeah, so you're right, it hasn't happened to me, I get that, but if it *was* me . . . No, actually, if you were being YOU in this situation, how you'd *normally* be, you'd be marching her round everywhere you went, bloody scratching her itchy legs with a whatever that thing is that you flip bacon with and helping her and demanding she saw the world as she did before, not hiding her away, acting like the world is over because of a wheelchair!" She shakes her head at me. "You're being selfish."

I want to throw the popcorn at her. And her stupid blue drink. And the ugly nachos. I hate Cam. She doesn't get it. She doesn't get it at all. I am so embarrassed and humiliated. Everybody is staring at me. I flush red; my ears tingle; my eyes fill, fast, with tears.

"I'm going home," I mutter, and turn away, expecting Cam to run after me and grab me and say "don't go" like she normally would, but instead:

"Oh, course you're going home. Course you are," she barks across the foyer. "Fine. Be a coward. Be a defensive coward like always! Don't bring your sister to the cinema, don't collect your exam results. . . ." She is screaming; she never minds screaming in public. She's shaking now. "LEAVING SCHOOL IS THE BIGGEST MISTAKE YOU'VE EVER MADE! YOU'VE GOT SOME SERIOUS GROWING UP TO DO, BLUEBELLE!!"

And as I run down the stairs of the Odeon I notice the accessibility badges *everywhere:* the chairlifts, the wide automatic doors, the ramp at the entrance. Things I never noticed until they apply to my family. I am so ignorant. I didn't like hearing Cam because Cam is right. She loves Dove too.

I'm making this all about myself and of course Dove can go to the stupid cinema.

She can do anything she likes.

My breath gets tight. Short. I have to over-breathe. In. Out. In. I scramble out of the cinema, down the steps, sliding. I think I see a couple of girls from my old school. NOT now. Can't handle the small talk. I hide in the alley.

"Was that Bluebelle?" I hear one of them say.

"No, really?" the other one replies.

"Her sister nearly died, you know?"

"No way, how?"

"Jumped off a building apparently."

"What? Why? Tryna kill herself?"

"Dunno, but . . . Bluebelle's not coming back to school."

"No way. Lucky. How'd you know?"

"My mum's friends with Miss Scott, in't she?"

"Ah, she probably works at the cinema now!"

"Ha! Probably. Free popcorn."

"I reckon she's pregnant."

"No!"

"Yeah, that's why she can't come back."

"She's not pregnant, Maliha. She's just fat."

I feel my insides clatter to the ground like a broken vase; I'm ashamed. My breathing is tight. I am fumbling wildly for my Ventolin. All blurry. I panic. Cheeks out and in. Puff. Chest tight. My fingers rummaging for my inhaler. I can't just barge into them like I normally would. With my head against the bricks I try to concentrate on breathing but my chest is so heavy and my head is everywhere. DOVE. The accident. Over and over. Her fall. Her fear. Her face. Her legs. Her body. Smashed. *Be brave. Be brave*, I said. I told her to be brave. . . . Mum. Dad. Coffee. Alicia. Glaring. Max. Puff. Puff. Puff. Breathe. Breathe. Over-breathe. And again. And again. I cry into the darkness. Trying to calm down.

I am alone and there's not enough air for me.

# TIGER'S MILK

Dove's sleeping on the sofa. I try not to disturb her while I make tea, gently pouring hot water on top of the tea bag, watching the triangle balloon beneath and the brown leaves whip up like a tree in a storm. The water, tinted immediately, a lagoon; the tea bag, a sleeping sea monster, waiting to surface.

Milk brings on a silent storm of rain and thunder and swirling skies. I spin the spoon quietly, not allowing even a tinkle. Mustn't wake my sleeping sister.

You know the tea we drink from tea bags is the leftover rubbish bits from excellent tea?

We basically drink ashtray tea.

I think about making a cup of tea for Dove but what if she wakes up and wants to talk; what if she needs the toilet and I get it wrong and don't know how to do it? Mum says the base of her back is all scabby like she's been burnt. I don't want to see it.

And then I notice 2B and Not 2B's baskets are empty. Their black fleecy blankets are speckled in silvery white dog hair, topped with their chewed grubby rubber rings and soft toys. The daily massacre of dog-toy fluffy organs, dissected and floating across the floor-boards like passing clouds. Dogs know how to just be themselves, be confident and secure in being simply animals. Know how to care when no words are needed. Just by being there . . . The two dumbest, clumsiest dogs in the world have better social intelligence than me.

Mostly, as I said, a cup of tea *can* fix everything. Even a lemon and ginger or a fresh mint. A hot chocolate can often do the trick. But it's the fridge that reminds me: in Mum's handwriting, magnets holding it to the front on a small scrap of paper, is the recipe.

Sometimes . . . when we need to heal and feel ourselves again, when we need a mug of warm comfort, when nothing else will do . . . it has to be Tiger's Milk. It's something my mum has always made us when we're feeling down or not ourselves. You measure out the cups of milk and warm it nicely, then you add the spices: ground nutmeg, ground ginger and a stick of cinnamon. Once the milk is simmering away you turn the heat off and add a big dollop of honey for sweetness. On the top, I place a fork and shake some extra cinnamon; that's what gives the milk the stripes.

And before I know it, I am gently stepping towards a sleeping Dove. I hear the faint muffled warbles of a cartoon. The dogs snoring next to her, just happy to be on the wood floor (Dad had to rip up the carpet in the living room for Dove's chair to move easier). Dove sits up when I enter.

"Sorry, did I wake you up?" I whisper.

"No. I was just dozing." She looks happy to see me.

"Resting your eyes, as Dad would say."

"Oh yeah, that would always annoy me. He used to let us draw on his feet with biro. . . . Is that Tiger's Milk?" she asks.

"Yeah, how'd you know?"

"I could smell it. I haven't had one in ages."

"Well, it's time to fix that."

I balance the mug to hand it to her, trying to twist the handle round so she can grab it.

"I've got it," she assures me. "It's OK."

She takes a sip and sighs with joy.

"Have you heard from the boys since they came over?"

"Hmm. I don't know if we have that much in common now that I'm like this for the rest of the summer. . . . I'm not gonna lie . . . I actually thought it was a bit hard talking to them. I spent so much time with them before but, like, we didn't really talk. You know, because we were always doing dumb stuff and, well, now . . . we kind of have nothing to say. It was a bit awkward. They're a bit . . . boring." She scrunches up her nose like the idea of the boys puts a bad taste in her mouth.

I nod. "Yes, I know what you mean." I want to stroke her hair but I can't look her in the eyes. I joke, "You might have to start fancying girls to fit in." And Dove does that smile—that hasn't changed a bit; it's always been there.

"The last thing I need is another girl to hang out with. You and Mum are total head cases." She laughs, one eye on the cartoon. "Have you seen Mum at the moment? She's lost the plot. So over-the-top! I mean, don't get me wrong, I know my bottom half looks like two giant rolls of toilet paper, but I'm not dying." She fingers her head.

"Don't pick, it won't heal."

"Can't help it."

"It's Dad that's making me laugh." I lie down next to Dove on the floor by the dogs. They immediately start stretching, thinking it's time to play. "Why's he acting like he and Mum are going to reignite their passionate love for each other by bonding over re-dressing your war wounds?"

"Proper begging it, isn't he?" Dove sniggers. "What a goat! S'pose it's quite amusing watching them cos it IS well dry being indoors all the time."

"Yeah, I should . . . We should hang out . . . sometime," I say.

"Well . . . I'm pretty free," she jokes. And her chin wobbles. She looks like she did when she was little. Harmless. Curious. Small. When it was my job to make sure she got home from the park safely and could reach the slide properly and I would leap up to catch her balloon if it floated away. . . .

"I love you, Dove," I say, and hold her so tight. I can't get close enough. I wish we could swap bones for a bit. She could have my big old lazy things and turn me into something wonderful for the summer. Somebody that would DO stuff with herself. She lets me hold her, which isn't very Dove-like.

"'K, drink your milk down. It will make you strong like a tiger."

Dove shuffles her hand under the quilt and brings out her phone. She doesn't say anything.

"What's this?"

"Just watch."

*It's the summer-night silver sky. The lights of the city glimmering like a mirror ball. The sound of laughing. Trainers scuffing. Panting and the whipping air. Then I see her, her blond hair a slash of gold, sparking under the flash of a camera. The boys say the words "cat leap." One of*

*them tells her not to. Another says "don't," tells her she won't be able to*
*make it. I hear Dove on the footage say, "I can!"*

*She leaps. Like a superhero. She makes it. The jump. Her grip, tight.*
*She hangs. It's an old, derelict house. The frame of the window, old*
*wood, crumbles away in her hands, into puffs, like Shredded Wheat.*
*Loose shards of paint splinter away. The boys shout her name. Try to*
*guide her with panicked voices. Dove's fingers try to find the grip in the*
*surrounding brickwork. I can almost feel her nails breaking. Her body*
*is small. A spider. She staggers. Wriggles. Struggles. I can't watch. But I*
*can't not. And then . . . nothing. I assume the camera is dropped.*

"Do you think I'm an idiot?" she whispers.

"Yes, of course I do." I snort.

"No, *really.* I lied to Mum. And Dad. And the doctors. And you.
I didn't lose my balance. I knew the jump was too high, BB. I knew I
couldn't make it. Even as I jumped I knew I wouldn't land properly.
I just wanted to do something big and brave like you said. . . ."

I feel the worst.

"It wasn't your fault. You still made the jump. It was the windowsill that caved in. It was old, the wood crumbled, you lost your
grip—you still *did* it."

Dove cries. I put my arms tight around her as she cranes her neck
into my stomach.

"I fell all the way down. It gives me nightmares. Why did I do it,
Bluebelle?" she asks me.

"Sometimes we do things even though they are self-sabotage," I
say gently, but I know, deep down, this isn't about Dove. . . . "Or
maybe it's the opposite. Maybe the realistic, sensible side of your

head told you that you couldn't make the jump but maybe . . . maybe a tincy, teeny-weeny bit of you believed in the magic of it. . . . Maybe that little voice told you to do it. Because you're brave. Because you're a little bird, you thought you might fly."

I try and sit as best I can beneath her head and stroke her hair. Her eyes close. She balls her fists and rubs her eyes.

"Grrrr. I'm nervous to go back to school, BB. I don't know what they'll say."

"What are you nervous about?"

"All of it." She gulps. "Mainly arriving for the first time, people staring at me with these two stupid things on my legs," she adds bitterly.

"Most of your classmates probably know what's happened by now. And are over it. Plus, they'll scribble all over your cast! You can just enjoy being the centre of attention for a bit."

"I don't want the sucking-up fakeness. It's so trapping being in this chair. And I don't like the idea of them all talking about how I did it. I don't want rumours to spread about me. I don't like being talked about."

"Well, there's a rumour going around at school that I'm pregnant, so . . ."

"Is there?"

"Yeah."

"God. You've never even *done* that, have you?" she asks, tipping the end of the Tiger's Milk into her mouth.

"Dove! That's NOT the point!" I shout. She passes the empty mug to me with a mischievous smirk painted across her face. "And anyway, I'm not talking about *that* with you." I laugh, yanking the mug out of her hand. "You have nothing to worry about. I promise.

The people that laugh and stare at others are the ones that aren't happy with themselves, and the ones who are sucking up are the ones who don't get enough attention."

"And I'll be thrown out of gymnastics and football."

"Not necessarily."

"And netball."

"No, I reckon you'll be all good."

"I'm not much use now."

"How do you know that? You might be the best."

"No, I think I'll just be thrown out."

"You won't be. And if, if, *if* you are, which you won't be, at least you were accepted in the first place to get thrown out. I was *never* accepted into any squad or club."

"I thought you were in cooking club."

I raise an eyebrow at Dove.

"I might just pretend to be pregnant anyway to get out of life." I sigh.

"I don't think being pregnant gets you out of life, BB. I think it gets you into a right mess. I mean, look at Mum!"

"True." I stroke the dogs' heads with my feet. "Ooh, I know what game we still can play, though. . . ."

"What?"

"A sport that you'll definitely be better at these days!"

"Go on. . . ."

"Bum Tills!" And Dove bursts out laughing so hard. She tips her neck back and cracks up, tears sprinkling out of her crinkled-up eyes and relief just rushes through me and it tastes better than anything I've ever tasted.

# A PATRONISING PASTRY

Alicia has me in the "sofa area" for a "heart-to-heart."

"I got you this, doll face." She slides over a soggy pecan plait. (She didn't *get* it for me; she literally just pulled the silver tongs out and shoved it onto a white plate.) It looks like an infected toe. Gammy and sore. Complicated to eat without little hardened nibs of burnt pecan toenails plopping off. "It's on me." She winks.

"Thanks," I say, but inside I am laughing. It's like I'm some voodoo witch doctor who's only going to open up to her once I've been gifted with an "offering." In this instance, a patronising pastry.

"You enjoy that, sweetie. You deserve it."

No, I don't. I'm not a dog. *Good girl.* Where's my apprenticeship form?

"Babes," she begins. "It's been so busy we've not really had a chance to catch up. How are you coping? With your sister's illness?"

She's not ill.

"Dove's doing really well; it's just the getting used to it."

"The pain?"

"No, it's the boredom. Dove's really active, so it's difficult for her, being indoors and not being able to do the stuff she likes doing." I watch as an impatient woman storms in and *demands* Marcel make the most overcomplicated coffee order the world's ever heard. "A decaffeinated extra-hot Americano with skinny milk . . . in a separate cup." She then tells Marcel that she's "in a rush," so can he "make it quick." As if he'd be slow deliberately. And then she adds, "I'm late for a meeting." I think there must be nothing more irritating than a person strolling into a meeting late, holding a piping-hot coffee from the coffee shop next door.

"Well, just know that we love having you here." Alicia suddenly burps. She thumps her chest. "Excuse me." It smells like paprika. "I mean, we all do. Poor Maxy is bloody crazy about ya! Hovers over you like a fly on poop!" She's trying to be nice, but really. . . .

I imagine myself being a dried-up slug of dog poo. And "Maxy." I shudder.

"I don't know about that."

"All I wanted to say is, if you want me to back off, or if you need some more time at home or . . ."

"No, we've just been adjusting at home and everything. Dove won't need help forever. It was a shock to begin with but I really do want to get this apprenticeship sorted."

"Sure. Sure. I get it. I get it." So . . . if you get it, have you done it, Alicia, OR . . . ? I do a bit of creeping. . . .

"I'm sorry if I've not been a hundred percent focused or whatever or let you and the . . . other aliens down."

"Bluebelle, I swear to God do NOT say that. Stop that right now. You do NOT have to apologise. You couldn't let us down. I was worried it was *us* that had let *you* down. I didn't want your alien commitments to Planet Coffee distracting you from your . . .

errr . . . mothership on Planet Earth." NO, PLEASE MAKE IT STOP.

"No . . . not at all."

"Phew. Great. I've been keeping myself up at night with worry about you, girlie." She sips her mocha. "So . . . there is some news."

Come on, please, make my day, you've signed the form and they've accepted and it's all great. Please . . .

Alicia's face lights up. "I know this will come as a complete surprise. . . ." Trust me, it won't. "But I'm pregnant!" She squeals. "Don't worry, it's decaf. Life is so dry these days."

"Ah, Alicia, congratulations!" I shrill. Quite good acting, I think.

"Steady on! Keep your bloody voice down, I haven't quite told everybody yet." Alicia looks about for paparazzi. "They'll be in complete shock." They won't. "I actually wasn't gonna keep it but my bloody sister told my mum. Course, once that cat was out the bloody bag it was all tears and *blah blah*. Before you knew it I was out choosing breast pumps and buying maternity leggings." She thumbs her left eye, which seems to be leaking. "It was a one-night thing—it meant nothing—but my mum, she's a bit of a wolf. As far as she's concerned, if you've got one of her little 'uns roasting in the oven . . . well . . . you're having it. It's wolf pack. That kind of thing. So, long and short of it, I'm going back to Oz. It's a better place to bring up kids; it's sunny and green and there's the beaches, and the people are less . . . you know . . ."

"I'm really happy for you, Alicia. Australia will be an amazing place to bring a baby up."

"You think? I think London's pretty cool too. I mean, look at you, doll face. You're a proper girl-about-town."

"I'm sure your baby will be pretty cool too."

"Thanks, kiddo."

"When will you be leaving?"

"Well, this is the dilemma. You can't fly when you're pregs over a certain amount of time and obviously it's such a long flight, I'd rather get it out the way than do it on my own with a screaming newborn!"

"I think you'll be amazing at being a mum."

"I dunno. Kinda scary bringing a kid up on my own."

"You can do it." And I mean it.

"I guess if I can manage this place I can do anything!"

"Hah. Yeah." I smile. It's polite, isn't it? But I don't have the energy to do another fake laugh.

"Which brings me to what I wanted to say . . . They want me to find replacement management before I leave . . . so I'm going to speak to the *powers that be* and do my very best to push this apprenticeship application forward for you and make sure that the next manager takes great care of your future as an alien, because, who knows, one day you might be running the ship!" She snorts. "I want to leave here knowing you're in good hands and being looked after."

"Wait, so does that mean you'll do it?"

"Sure does."

I feel a weight lift off my shoulders. What a relief.

"Thank you so much, Alicia." I smile. "You have no idea how much that means to me."

# FISH FINGERS, CHIPS AND BEANS

I LOVE chips.

Any chips.

Fat, soggy chips from the chip shop that smush into each other like hot clay. Drenched in salt and vinegar. Onion vinegar. Ummmmm. I like skinny fries that come with burgers—crisp slants that crack under the teeth—and the softer ones too, floppier fast food fries that you can pinch up in claws, grabbing several at a time like peanuts, and squash them into your mouth. I like posh chips, proper chips, with sea salt and rosemary, chips where you can see the potato skin on the edges. I like the proud golden ones that stand militant like a Boy Scout wearing a sash dotted with badges.

But secretly, one of my favourite ways to have chips is when it's just me and Dove and a whole bag of frozen chips. We whack the oven up really high, fill a baking tray with a WHOLE BAG OF HOME FRIES and leave them for over half an hour to sun-tan and crisp up in the oven. It says on the bag to leave them for twenty minutes but that isn't long enough—they're still too pasty; I like my oven chips to catch a little on the corners and the centres to get soggy when they absorb the vinegar. We like to put a box of fish fingers in too. We like our fish fingers really overcooked so that the middle is almost dehydrated and the cod is basically a puff of white dust that crumbles out like old toothpaste. The outside is golden brown. We like peeling off the lid of the fish finger, like opening a treasure chest. There's not much worse than a soggy fish finger. We like to pretend that we're on a cooking show while we make it, pretending we're making the most luxurious gourmet meal. We dump the chips in a huge tin bowl filled to the top and we take turns to rake our hands in like those arcade machines with the claws that reach for the teddy bears. We like it with beans, obviously, and a huge splodge of ketchup.

It seems a good time to make this. I'm hoping it stirs some crazy hunger up in me that makes me able to eat. Dove directs me with the oven, bossing me about from her throne like some queen.

I don't tell Dove about Alicia agreeing to take me on as an apprentice because I don't want it to seem like anything is going on in my life. I don't want to feel like I am flourishing in anything. Even though I know Dove would be happy for me, I don't want to rub salt in her wounds. Instead, I want salt on chips and to melt away like a pack of butter and do nothing except make Dove feel good.

But the chips sit in my throat like leather bootlaces.

Dove tumbles out a mountain of chips onto her plate.

"B," she says all of a sudden. "Can you do me a favour?"

"Yeah, course."

"Whatever happens, can you just be normal with me from now on?"

"I am, aren't I?"

"You are now, yeah, but I think you maybe weren't before and I hated it and I just don't know what I'll do if things don't go back to how they were before all of this. I want you to still make fun of me and push me around and stuff."

"I think I'll be *pushing* you around for a while," I joke. "I don't think I have a choice in the matter."

Dove looks upset. "That actually really hurt me, BB."

"Dove, I'm so sorry. I was only joking. Honestly, I didn't mean to . . . I thought you'd find it—"

"Don't worry, I suppose I deserve it. I always called you fat." She puffs her cheeks out.

"You don't deserve this. I'm sorry."

I look at Dove. Even trapped in a chair she's more free than I am. I keep seeing her over and over again, launching off into the air, letting go of everything like she had nothing to lose. She shovels a few chips in her mouth through a brave smile. But I know she's pretending to be strong about all of this. She doesn't need to be a hero.

"I do love you, Dove. I think you're so amazing."

"I love you too," she says. "But seriously, don't treat me any differently, will you?"

She lets a tear run down her soft face, her eyes watery and thick, blurred in the confusion of this challenge that she has to conquer in her own gentle way. "I'm sorry for crying," she says. "I just love how we were."

Dropping my fork with a clang, I hold her hand tightly, wiping my own tears away. "We weren't anything, Dove," I say. "I love how we *are*."

Where THE HELL have I been?

"Wanna go get some air?" I ask.

# CREAM CRACKERS

"Where is everybody?"

"I think we're the last ones here."

"So you didn't need to wear those sunglasses that make you look like a rich woman who just found out her movie star husband has died."

"Guess not." I take the sunglasses off.

"I thought you didn't care about your exam results anyway?" Dove opens up the packet of crackers we've just got from the newsagents, along with the ice poles, but we already ate them.

"I don't."

"Well, why are we here, then?"

"I just wanted to find out. Curiosity. That's all."

"Do you want a cracker?"

"Yeah, 'K."

Dove places one in my hand. The sun is beating down on our bare shoulders.

"God, they're so dry, they're making me thirsty." My tongue feels like sand.

"Do what I do," Dove suggests.

"What do you do? Do I even want to know?"

"Eat a cracker, chew it up and everything like normal, leave it in the back of your throat, then you can make a pâté-type thing by regurgitating the sick bit onto the next cracker, like how a bird would feed its baby, like a little hors d'oeuvre . . . ?"

"You are a frigging gross genius. But I'm not gonna do it."

I crumble up my cracker and leave it for the pigeons. Dove's made me feel sick. She happily munches away and says, "Imagine if you've done really well in, like, maths or something and then you decide to become a . . . Wait . . . why do people need to learn maths? Like, what job does being good at maths get you?"

"Accountant? Errr . . . newsreader?"

"You don't need maths for reading the news."

"Maybe if you want to be a maths teacher?"

"Why would you ever?"

We take our time. London in the summertime offers us a man hosing his front garden, two toddlers plonked in a paddling pool by his feet, giggling and splashing. A guy a bit older than me clearly scrubbing his first-ever brand-new car. There are two twelve-year-olds linking arms, sharing headphones; they look at Dove and then look away. There's a couple with a white fluffy dog taking photographs of the trees in the sun and two men with loads of dangerous-looking chopped-up wood strapped rather unsafely to the roof of their dad-car, blaring guitar music out of the window and singing along.

And there it is. School.

"Go on, then. . . . Let's see if you'd secretly make a great news-reader. . . ."

# GUM SHIELD

That night, my thirteen-year-old self haunts me. I'm angry at her for being immature. She wasn't like Dove. She was so insecure it went full circle and made her vain. Always looking in. Always comparing. Self-conscious. Unconfident. She remembers an older, pretty girl with skin the colour of a leather handbag, called Charlene, scaring her and a group of her friends in the toilets with the thrilling advantages of sticking her fingers down her throat. How good it felt to see screwed-up little *Z*s of pasta bows floating in the toilet bowl. She said the trick wasn't just to ram your fingers down; you had to moonwalk them on your tonsils—that would trigger the vomit in a second. All the girls thought Charlene was so cool. We loved her nose piercing and the way she ate chocolate bars and cheese melts all day. We all promised that after school we'd go home and try it.

I remember eating everything I could find at dinner. I had chicken and mushroom pie: a crusty, flaky top with buttery, golden sides that cascaded over the pie dish like Sleeping Beauty's hair. Crimped by Dad with a fork. The inside was silky, creamy, shiny, perfectly seasoned. It erupted out of the hole in the top of the pie, volcanic, whispering secrets of a warm winter's comfort. The chicken was so tender it would fall apart into shreds when you tagged it with your tongue. The mushrooms were woody and smoky. Little bombs of forest forage. Dad whips egg into our mash, butter, pepper, milk and snowflakes of salty crystals. The sauce floods the mashed potato Mountain of Dreams. And, of course, peas.

After that I ate anything I could find in the hatter-mad house that I live in. Half a tub of old (not even enjoyable) strawberry shortcake ice cream, a bowl of stale Shreddies, some ham that was meant for the dogs, crackers and cheese, a bag of Wotsits for Dove's packed lunch, toast with peanut butter *and* butter, cashew nuts, some tuna and mayonnaise in a bowl, a *luxurious* cherry yoghurt and some old Halloween pumpkin chocolates that I remembered being in a drawer in Dove's room. They tasted like hard dust. Still, I sat, and de-shelled all twelve of those smiling pumpkin moons. Just cos. Just cos it was *eating everything day* and soon I'd be sicking it all up. I was like the Very Hungry Caterpillar leaving a stream of food-shaped watercolour holes in my wake. I had a new skill that meant I could eat everything and nothing mattered. I was *Binge-Girl,* the all-time favourite eating disorder superhero. I was so full I couldn't even remember the swelling loveliness of Dad's wonderful pie anymore. It was just temporarily filling another hole on my scaled tongue. That would all go to waste.

When my family were snuggled down watching a TV programme I ran upstairs to the bathroom. I sprayed the room with a cheap girly deodorant Mum had recently left by my door with some sanitary towels and tampons, *just in case.* I think I'd only ever been sick four times in my whole life. Once on a ferry from seasickness, once from bad chicken kievs, once from bad lasagne and then the first time I smelt smoked haddock. I wasn't a sickly girl. Sick smelt disgusting and had to be masked. Or maybe it was my shame that reeked so bad this time.

I laid a towel down. I used my school swimming towel because I didn't want to involve anybody else in this horror. Dove would have been ten. I didn't want her getting out of the bath and wrapping herself in something that had seen what I'd done to myself.

Then I tied my long thick dark hair into a hairband.

The bathroom felt echoey. All my actions were clanging and loud. Muffled by the churn of my own guts, twisting.

I stooped over the toilet bowl and tried the moonwalking thing. No good. I tried again. Gagging. I panicked. Flushed the toilet really quick to drown the sound. Coughing, spitting. I tried again. *Walk, walk, walk, tickle, tickle, come on, come on, just like Charlene said . . .* More retching, some rice from lunch maybe but . . . nothing.

I could hear the wretched stupid girls from school. I knew they were talking rubbish but it didn't stop me from wanting to push a little harder.

And then I hear it, the ugly mean loud voice in my head that interrupts me when I'm at my most weak. The one that prods me in the belly, barking in its evil voice like some wretched twisted mantra:

**YOU HAVE ASTHMA BECAUSE YOU ARE FAT.**

**YOU HAVE ASTHMA BECAUSE YOU ARE FAT.**

**THAT IS WHY YOU CAN'T BORROW OUR CLOTHES OR COME ON HOLIDAY WITH US IN THE FUTURE. BECAUSE**

**YOU ARE FAT. AND WE CAN'T HAVE ANYBODY THAT LOOKS LIKE YOU IN OUR PHOTOGRAPHS. YOU WILL RUIN THEM. YOU WILL BRING OUR FRIENDSHIP GROUP BEAUTY STATUS DOWN. WE CAN'T BE HAVING THAT. YOU ARE FAT. AND THAT MEANS YOU HAVE NO SELF-CONTROL. AND THAT MEANS YOU HAVE NO SELF-WORTH. AND THAT MEANS YOU HAVE NO SELF-RESPECT. AND THAT MEANS NOBODY WILL EVER LOOK UP TO YOU AND RESPECT YOU BACK. AND THAT MEANS NOBODY WILL EVER CARE WHAT YOU HAVE TO SAY IN PUBLIC. OR THINK OF YOU. OR TRULY LOVE YOU.**

**AND THAT MAKES YOU DISGUSTING.**

I turn the volume down on it. It's not real. It's trying to trip me up. And then I remember the last time I kept a diary. And why it ended so badly.

*My eyes begin to water. I'm panicking now. Charlene said this would be easy, but it's not; it's terrible. More tears. Sweat. I'm so clammy. My knees hurt from being on the towel, little wormy imprints on my chubby kneecaps. I can't do it. I'm a failure. I can't even be sick. I'm not a proper, real girl. Real girls have control of their bodies. Discipline. And now I've gone and eaten all this crap that I didn't even want for no good reason whatsoever. It will stick to me, the new fat, calories*

*clinging to my face like hamster cheeks. I have to get it out. I flush the*
*toilet again, to seem convincing, on the off-chance any member of my*
*family is sad enough to think, "Oh, let's listen out for Bluebelle making*
*herself sick."*

*And I leap into my room with an idea. I have to get this vomit*
*out, NOW. I can't sit there in front of my friends and Charlene at*
*break time tomorrow and listen to them all purr on, grey-toothed and*
*greasy-eyed, exhausted from their icky evening of triumph, while I sit*
*there, a plump embarrassment. Chewing my hair.*

*Even if I lie. It isn't the real thing. I know. I can feel the weight in my*
*rolls of fat that I pinch sometimes until it bruises.*

*I reach for a coat hanger. In my wardrobe. It has to be the metal*
*one, from the dry cleaners, not the posh wooden ones. We only get those*
*ones by accident anyway, when clothes swap around; they are really*
*for Mum's and Dad's clothes. Then I bend the hanger, turning it into*
*a boomerang shape, twisting the hook bit down. It is the shape of a*
*gun. Then I lock myself in the bathroom again, run towards the toilet,*
*urgently shoving the hanger down my throat so fast I don't even notice*
*how it feels.*

*Except for cold. Mean. Not right. An intruder. Painful.*


The sick was disappointing. A few Wotsits. Some little squares of
Shreddies. Brown smudges from un-chewed chocolate. I'd violated
myself. I just cried so hard. I couldn't even tell Mum because she'd
just cry too. Or Dad because he'd cry even more. My teeth touched
the basin with a clink. Never had I wished I could undo an action
so quickly. It was like blurting out a secret at a sleepover.

I began to tidy my room so that I could throw the hanger away without it seeming obvious. This was the kind of sly, dodgy behaviour girls my age save for their first cigarette.

I couldn't wait to see the back of the hanger. It felt like a murder weapon. I already felt like it wouldn't be the last time I'd ever see it; it would show up again in a plastic sandwich bag, grinning at me, in the courtroom of *shame* as evidence.

I want to hug the young me.

But I left her behind.


*The next morning I wake feeling like a warmed-up corpse. I ground my teeth so badly my jaw is locked. The hinges around my face are tight. My teeth push against themselves. I could snap them off. Packed too tight. I just feel so grateful that my body didn't sink to the same level as my mind had. Good old Big Bones, refusing to throw up. To give me what I wanted. Sometimes it isn't mind over matter. Sometimes your body knows what's best.*


That's why I listen to it, that's why I eat what I fancy. And respect it.

I didn't hang around with those girls anymore after that day. I didn't really hang around with anybody at school after that day. I just put my head down and got on with it. I wasn't disliked. I waited for the rumours and abuse to start, but I thought that if any one of those girls tried what I did, regardless of whether they got results, they'd feel just as ugly about themselves as I did about myself. And they wouldn't want to speak about it again anyway.

I just got on.

The grinding of my teeth didn't stop. Mum got me a gum shield.

I had it fitted in a dentist's room with weird pictures of armadillos made out of beads on the wall. The dentist said teeth-grinding can be caused by anxiety. My parents splitting up for the first time may have been the cause of it. Little did I know I'd get used to that.

My mouth was filled with an overwhelmingly minty plaster, which I actually quite liked—the suffocation of freshness was a new sensation. It was like chewing on a bouncy ball. I felt like the dogs. A week later we went to pick up the clear shield. A jelly waxwork mould of my mouth. My bottom teeth splayed out like a fan.

At first the ridges cut and gnawed fresh gills into the insides of my red cheeks and I think actually made me grind more. Like I was chewing on those fish-bone clothes tags. I think I was scared of swallowing it by accident in the night and choking to death on it. I guess it couldn't have been worse than the coat hanger. But then I got used to it. Bit it down. The clear plastic became frosted and scratched, chewed so hard I made holes in the molars and my teeth would just clamp and grit against each other like rocks. Turning my teeth to sand.

Luckily I met Cam at Planet Coffee. She calls her trial shift there not a trial for a job but a trial for a friendship. Planet Coffee was just the right setting for two weirdo aliens to become friends. She says.

Once I met Cam, I didn't need to use the gum shield anymore. . . .

But I feel like I have to wear it tonight.

I got an A+ in art.

The rest was mostly Cs, Ds, 4s and 5s and actually one B.

An A+ for my charcoal mess.

# SCRAMBLED EGGS

I wake up and head downstairs, to see Dove at the stove.

"What you doing? You're not cooking, are you?" I accuse her sleepily. The counter is way too high for her.

"Course I'm cooking. I'm allowed to cook, you know."

"Sorry. Sorry. Course you are."

"So annoying. Don't baby me like that."

I want to defend myself but there's nothing to say. My jaw is tender. My gums are sore.

"Mum made me a drawer down here. Look, it has pots and pans and utensils, and I can reach the two front burners."

"OK, that's good."

"So pop the toast up, then."

"Ah, you made some for me?"

"Yeah, I made some for you. I've been waiting for you to wake up and I knew the smell of food would do it."

"You know me too well," I lie, rubbing my eyes instead of my belly, putting the kettle on. Even though I couldn't stomach a thing.

"It's done. It's in the other room, waiting."

"Oh amazing, thanks, Dove." I smile at her, watching her navigate her way around the kitchen: reaching, swivelling, her own revised version of culinary parkour. "What we having?"

"Scrambled eggs."

Dove isn't really a cook. So I'm completely doubtful. But how bad could scrambled eggs be, really?

"They're horrible," she says after she takes a mouthful.

"No they're not," I lie, forcing another forkful down. They are grey. Full of peppercorns that crack under your teeth like bombs.

"Don't lie." She presses the egg and milky water sinks into the toast. It's the colour and texture of nicotine-stained net curtains. Dove pushes the pan of eggs away from her. She growls a horrible noise from the pit of her stomach and angrily flings the wooden spoon across the kitchen, leaving little eggy sprogs across the tiles. "I HATE THIS! I CAN'T STAND IT! I HATE IT! I HATE IT! I just wanted to be able to . . . DO something!"

I want to, but I don't hug her.

I pick the spoon up off the floor and hand it back to her.

"Well, you chose the wrong thing to do. You were a terrible cook before your accident," I say. "Pass the eggs here. Let's try again."

"Just give it to the dogs," she grumbles, munching on the corner of a slice of toast, "and pass me the jam."

# HOT EGGS,
# MAYBE MEXICAN STYLE

To a pan of hot oil, so hot it shimmers, we add spring onion, chilli and the half-soft green pepper we have hanging around in the fridge. I throw in tomatoes and some Tabasco, cayenne pepper and smoked paprika. We let it cook. . . .

Dove's eyebrows unfurl.

We don't have tortillas but we do have pittas in the freezer. Dove toasts them quickly in the toaster; then we place them on the hob, charring them up all lovely to get the black bumpy, gnarly lumps on them. Then I dump the horrid eggs back in the pan. The whole thing sizzles. I find some Cheddar cheese and grate that into it, melting it down. Cheese and eggs are BFFs. They are both edible glue that bring everything together. Then I crumble a knob of feta on top. I say a knob. I mean a lot.

I snip whatever not-completely-brown leaves are left of some old parsley on top and hand the pan back to my sister.

"WOW!" Dove's eyes light up. "BB! This looks delicious!" She grins.

"I dunno how it'll taste."

"Delicious, I bet." She tears some bread and scoops the egg up with it. "Yum! How did you come up with that? It's so good!"

"I think your eggs are what made it."

While she chews she watches a neighbour's tigerlike cat snake along a fence, slink up onto the shed and then elegantly hop up onto our windowsill. Dove's face is red from the warmth of the spice. She smiles at the cat.

She looks over at me; her eyes are deep and serious. "Don't stop moving your body, BB, even though it's hard, even though you say it's not for you and you don't really like it. Keep moving. Run. Swim. Cycle. Climb. Jump. Dance. Whatever. Just don't stop. Ever," she orders. "Promise?"

I nod. I'm taken aback by her intensity at first but she's serious, and I only say, "I won't." I want to cry because she's hit a nerve. Because I know she's right. "I promise."

I wonder, in life, if I've ever made my own heart beat fast. Sure, I get nervous and flustered and angry and scared and excited but that's mostly out of my control and doesn't always feel good. I've never caused myself to sweat and rush for the sake of it, because I can. For release or pleasure or energy. I've never urged my feet into a run . . . never heard my heart thump in my head.

And I know . . .

I have to bite the bullet. . . .

I head upstairs to hunt for my swimsuit.

# FRUIT SALADS

I believe I have the best swimsuit in the world. It's vintage. Second-hand. Some people get weird about the fanny bit touching your own fanny. As if those little plastic covers you get on the gussets of swimsuits in shops when you try them on are any better. My suit is like industrial armour and it is architecturally beautiful. Pearly white dotted in navy spots. The cups make your boobs spludge out like a balcony but they never flop over the top. The waist stuffs you in all nice, holding you in tight so that your hips can swarm out. I sometimes can't help but imagine the woman who wore this suit before me. Probably in the fifties or sixties. I bet she was really cool and wore black cat-eye reading glasses with diamonds at the corners. I bet she had a body like mine and jammed it into pencil skirts and let her body dollop out and swell from the plunging V of an open shirt or slit at the back of a dress, mesmerising people all over the world with her wonder. I bet she was amazing and had a fantastic name like Dixie. Or Lucky. Or Scrunchie.

The only problem is . . . I've never worn the swimsuit actually swimming. So that's the first thing I'll try for my recommended exercise. To shut Mum up. To make Dove proud of me. I'll give this swimming business a go. Because I want to keep fit. I want to keep strong. I don't want to lose weight but I want to be healthy.

I find the suit at the bottom of an old beach bag that I planned to take to the lido last year but I think the grumpy English weather stole that chance from me. The bag just has the suit ragged up at the bottom and the confetti of about fifteen Fruit Salad sweets. A chewy candy that is meant to taste like, well, a fruit salad. I pop one in my mouth. It tastes like eating a brick of Lego. I chew it; I can actually feel my molar being sucked out of my gum. I swallow it anyway, and for ages I feel the little blob of plastic sitting there, rotting in my gut but not. He'll be in there for a while, that sweetie, the last one in the waiting room.

Really? Is it really happening now? Am I actually about to do this gym thing?

# SAUSAGE

They put everything in a sausage. The eyeballs, the trotters. The bum, even. Gross. You know once I heard of someone who found a bumhole on their pizza with hairs on it. Actual pig hairs on a pig bum on the pizza.

My bedroom looks out onto the garden. I see the dogs sniffing about outside. I close the curtains of my bedroom to change. I always think it looks strange when the neighbours close their curtains in the middle of the day. It looks so suspicious. I strip naked to try the swimsuit on. I catch a glimpse of myself in the full-length mirror. My body is wide more than anything. Plump, ripe, jacket potato-ish. Uncooked sausage-like. I have a spray of moles that decorate me like chocolate chips. A small mountain-peak triangle of a scar on my hip from the tip of the iron. My thighs touch like more lined-up uncooked sausages. I have stretch marks all over, silver silkworms like a map of roads drawn out on tracing paper. I imagine myself like the Incredible Hulk, bursting out of my skin, prising apart my tissue and muscle.

I take the mirror off the wall and lie down on the floor. I

hold the mirror above me. My face sinks back. My arms out, shoulder-width apart with the view of myself top to tip. I want to see how I look naked, lying down. My boobs slide off either side of my chest like gravy dribbling off the edge of a plate, my ribs rise and my belly dips. My thighs spread and swell in the flatness of lying on my back. I have red knicker-line prints etched onto my softness like a zip. I am a sausage. A red sausage sizzling in a pan. I crane the mirror about; it's heavy now, but I can't put it down. I angle it over me in beams of the sun cracking through the gap in the curtain, the yellowing patches of my body. The diamond cuts from the mirror reflection sharpen the roundness of me, like slicing into a birthday cake with a knife.

Maybe I'm not a sausage. Maybe I'm a birthday cake?

I place the full-length mirror to the side, leaning against the fridge-cold radiator. I roll over to my side like a half-moon. My belly gives in to gravity, sliding down, puddling to the floor. My chin looks big. YOU DON'T WANT TO GO TO THE GYM BECAUSE IT MEANS YOU ARE GIVING IN. YOU WORRY YOU MIGHT BE LETTING YOURSELF DOWN, THAT YOU'RE GIVING IN. YOU PUT ON A BRAVE, PROUD FACE EVERY DAY. YOU LOVE YOUR BODY SO OTHERS DON'T HAVE TO AND YOU THINK THAT THE GYM IS YOU THROWING THE TOWEL IN ON THAT SELF-LOVE. THAT YOU'RE AGREEING WITH THE REST OF THE WORLD THAT IT WAS A LIE ALL ALONG, A DEFENSIVE FRONT. THAT THEY WERE RIGHT ALL ALONG. THAT YOU *DO* HATE YOUR BODY.

BUT IT'S NOT RIGHT.

YOU LOVE YOUR BODY.

YOU ARE REWARDING YOURSELF BY GETTING STRONGER. IT MEANS YOU LOVE YOUR BODY MORE, BLUEBELLE. NO MATTER HOW BIG YOUR BONES ARE.

That's more like it.

# CHLORINE

Already the girls at the desk are looking at me.

I know *that* look.

"I'd like to join the gym, please."

I am counting the seconds until they offer to sign me up to a weight-loss programme or, better still, ask if I want to be introduced to a personal trainer. They like the idea of sitting there and perving over my transformation, waiting for me to reappear at the front desk one day wearing a pair of jeans that I can pull out to show a gap big enough for a whole other person to fit into and go "Can you BELIEVE I lost THIS much weight?" Carrying my spare, baggy skin around with me like a rucksack. The gym might make me their poster girl.

They've seen millions of *me*s before with our good intentions and high hopes.

"Sure." One gazes at the computer. "Have you done an induction?" She's typically *sporty*. Dressed like somebody who enjoys blowing a whistle angrily, while parading along the edge of a swimming pool. Probably showing off because *she* gets to wear her *outdoor* trainers *indoors*. The other one is a tiny dart of a female with cheek-bones that could spiralise vegetables. She has slicked-back black hair pulled into a face-lifting ponytail, and shimmery lip gloss. All she needs is a plastic bottle of something E-number-orange and she's partying in Ibiza. She looks me over, like looking for a snag of thread in a dress she is searching for a reason not to buy. Up and down. She can't stop looking. It's like she's addicted. Her narrow eyes try to take me in. Her pupils try to box me into their rings. I want to cower, so instead, to combat that, I hear Dove's little voice telling me to push my chest out. Puffing myself out all confidently like when you see pigeons out on the pull trying to meet a girl-friend.

"Yes," I lie. I look at the wall of personal trainers. Their faces are lined up like a hall of fame, posing awkwardly with white teeth and hormone-charged eyes. I don't want to know ANY of these people. That's the last thing I want, some built-up tanned man called *Todd* embarrassing me by showing me how to work these machines.

How hard can they be, anyway? *Press start.* Easy.

"What's your name?"

"Bluebelle Green."

Ibiza starts to look over the PE-teacher lookalike's shoulder now too, trying to find my name, squinting behind fake eyelashes. But also bouncing her head to the terrible noise of the dance music blar-ing out. One whispers to the other—they are never going to turn down the commission of a new member.

"Can't find you . . . How unusual . . . Anyway . . . let's get you signed up."

"'K." I flush bright red. Splotchy. I wonder why I'm embarrassed now, when I've blagged myself into the gym without doing the induction and not at the moment when I was actually doing the blagging. Is it because now I have to face it? Physically enter the vortex of physical activity? While I fill in the fussy membership form I think about the little me laughing at me now. Like I am betraying myself by joining a gym, how out of character that is. I think about all the times when I was younger, excused from sport at school, sat, fat and sweaty, panting on the wall or bench while the others played rounders or cricket. Half-moons of sweat under my *first-person-in-class-to-get-tits* breasts from doing absolutely nothing. I was last on the wall to get chosen for any sport—except for a bit in primary school, when I was good at being "in goal." The boys worked out that I could just stand there in the position of the boy's toilet sign and block balls like a giant gingerbread man. Until I got hit in the face and my icing smile turned to a frown.

"Because you're under eighteen there's no joining fee."

I should think so too! My money should be going on really great life experiences, not running it away in an air-conditioned torture dungeon.

"You don't look sixteen." The Ibiza one smiles; she means it as a compliment but I find it bitchy. Like she's trying to suss me out. Perhaps she is envious of all the clubs I could get myself into underage. If I ever wanted to do that, which I just do not.

They make me have my picture taken. At this point I feel my confidence steal away like Peter Pan's shadow. It suddenly whips off my back like a scarf in the wind and bolts for the door. I manage to grab it back. *Oh. No.* You are not going ANYWHERE. You're coming with me.

"Smile!" And I do. In a short, muffin-mouthed attempt, like a Cabbage Patch doll.

And off we go . . . me and my confidence locked into a gym membership.

"Do you need me to show you where the changing rooms are?"

"It's fine, thank you," I say. "I know my way. I'm using the pool."

*Course you are,* I bet they think. *She's just gonna flop about like a starfish hippo and sink to the bottom like a submarine.*

Swimming, they think, is NOT real exercise. They probably think swimming is what you do when you're taking a *break* from exercise. To recover. On the off-days when you've spent all week bench-pressing and lifting a . . . whatever one might lift.

Already I am regretting even coming here. *Why am I regretting coming swimming?* SHUT UP, BRAIN.

I find the women's changing rooms. It's different from when we used to go swimming with Mum. With Mum, it was fun. We would all pile into one family changing room and laugh as Dove wedgied me up the stairs. And we obviously didn't do *swimming.* We just dunked each other and played mermaids or pretended to work in a pub in a sea of beer and sink and float and gargle chlorine while Mum did breaststroke.

But now it's just me. Just me, trying.

Trying really badly to look like a grown, confident woman knowing what I'm doing when all I want to do is be in the family changing room with Mum and Dove. I'm not sure I'm ready to be grown up. Independent and alone.

The changing room is a gloomy, damp place. Full of black, coiled hairs, strong like hedgehog spikes, snailed around the bumpy-nippled floor. I am wearing my swimsuit under my clothes already and it's making me feel really hot and panicky and trapped. What do we talk about? Me and these women? Will everybody in here know that I'm a fraud? Will they judge me? This is the secret life of people who aren't at desks, this is the rabbit hole of the world. The swimming pool.

I feel enormously hot again and worried somebody might ask me if I need help and that will mean I've failed at my challenge of independence and keeping fit. I could faint any second and I cannot wait to get out of my clothes and into the water. I shove my stuff in a locker, dropping my jumper onto the disgusting tepid floor. Gross. The ground is so clingy. I forgot my coin too for the locker but no one's going to steal anything of mine, so I dump it all in, even though I'm tempted to just put all my clothes back on and go home. My thighs are rubbing a bit. They are also covered in purple-green trademark witch-coloured bruises from my constant clumsiness and misjudgement of small spaces. Anyway . . . you can't be expected to live in England and have evenly toned skin. It's cold: the heating dries us out and then it rains all the time, which is great for potatoes but it doesn't mean it has to make ME look like a potato. Rough and gnarly and knobbly.

*Splat. Splat. Pad. Pad.* Towards the pool. I LOVE that my toenails are painted green. They look so exciting next to the hideous beige of the floors.

I edge into the water. Underwater makes every part of everybody look like a mirage, a blurry painting, a circus mirror . . .

The fat under my arms is here.

The fat on my back oozing over my straps—here.

The print of my cave of a belly button squeezing behind my costume—also here.

The squiggles of silver stretch marks that sprint down the backs of my legs and arms. All here.

All present and correct.

Tromp. Tromp. Tromp. And weightlessness . . .

Swimming becomes calm. I find a rhythm. It's OK. So at least I haven't forgotten how to swim. Am I sweating? Wait, can you sweat in water? I imagine it to look like sun cream on the surface of the pool, oily and rainbow-coloured.

My baby curls tickle my ears as I breathe deep, arms swanning in and out, rippling the water, butterflying. I am not sure if I am enjoying this or not. Is that normal? To not know if you're having a good time or not? I think about the view of me from behind. The gusset of my suit sucking in between my bum cheeks and my two round legs. My big legs. Knees frogging in and out. I do feel short of breath. This swimming is not as easy as it looks. I keep staring at the clock. Why do the seconds seem to freeze? I stop.

I catch a glimpse of myself in the grooves of the pool's reflection. I lean forward and tie my hair up into a big topknot. A bony old woman with grey hair does a breaststroke past me. She looks at me and then tears her eyes away like she's seen something she doesn't want to see but is trying to be polite.

It seems that exercise has given me nothing but a belly full of chlorine.

# BANANA

My wee is boiling hot. I feel tired and energised at the same time and at last, actually, for the first time in ages, truly hungry. I feel taller. Great.

My banana is bruised brown and smushed. I don't really mind, it makes them sweeter. I eat it while I rummage for my inhaler. Swimming makes me starving. *Why is that?* I think of somewhere to sling the skin.

The showers are in this big communal steamy box of different women of every kind looming and cleaning like pecking flamingos . . . like talking trees . . . like willowy flamingo talking trees. Hanging goggles, splodges of creamy silver conditioner and chlorine-flavoured yellowing bikini bottoms, the snap of latex swimming caps. The ground, all urine- and shampoo-splattered tiles, peppered with more crop circles of hairs and toenail half-moons. The women look up as I go in. Swamped like squids smothered in clouds of fake vanilla-smelling foam. They herd together, like cattle. They mostly look like mums. I'm the youngest, bar the small toddler clinging to his mum's big cliff-face legs with sucky barnacle hands and the baby clutched in one of her strong arms. She has drooping ripe purple nipples that almost touch her pelvis, belly clumpy like soil. Quivering rivers of streaky stretch marks. Once a baby's house. A kangaroo pouch. A sacred nest for creation. Arms muscular and defined from carrying shopping bags and pushing prams and swimming lengths of breaststroke. Wheeling shampoo into her knots of fuzzy hair. She has bumps and lumps earned from living. Hips like the Big Dipper. Great for that little boy, I bet, for driving toy cars up and down. The little boy stares at me. At my body. I'm in my swimsuit still. I feel like a child. I wonder if the mum is thinking I'm a child too. They dry off and leave, the mum talking nonsense about rice cakes.

Funny how women are the ones that suffer the most attack and punishment for their bodies when they are the ones that have to change the most. . . . What a weird world we're in.

There's *nothing* to be embarrassed about. Notice how when we watch a nature programme and see fifty elephants washing themselves by a lake and they all look the same to us, but really they are all unique, all have their own quirks and ways—but we can't see that; we just see fifty elephants. Well, that's us showering. In the grand play of the world, we all look the same; we are all a flock, a species, of quite beautiful women, just taking a shower, just taking care of ourselves. That's all.

I am proud to be a girl. Because that's a fact. But prouder that I love myself. Because that's a choice.

# CORN ON THE COB

Cam and I both have lipstick on our chins from the corn nibbling. Hers is purple and mine pink.

The salty butter dribbles down our forearms as we go in again for another bite each. Black charcoal flakes stuff our gums and replace our teeth with small golden squares. I know I have to say it. My heart thumps.

"I'm sorry I was horrible last week," I admit.

"You weren't."

"I was."

"You weren't. *I'm* sorry for speaking to you like that, BB. I just know you've got it in you to know how to deal with this properly. I know it's hard and every day is new, but Dove needs you. More than ever."

"I know I have to be strong for her."

"Not even strong; just be yourself, just be you, you know, normal. Annoying. Normal."

"You're right."

"And I'll be there for you."

"You are there."

"Smile."

"And you, let's see . . ." A grin of nibs and corn kernels and black stuff slathered in wet, buttery dribble.

"Kiss me, darling!"

"Oh, mwah . . ."

"Actually . . . speaking of kissing . . . what's going on with you and that Max?"

"I don't know. I kind of think that might be . . . you know . . . done."

"Why would it be done?"

"I think I messed it up, maybe?"

"Why? How? By leaving him in a pancake cafe?"

"*Crepe,* Cam. Not pancake."

"Whatever. You did NOT mess that up. Text him now."

"No. I dunno. I've got bigger things to think about."

"'K. Well, you haven't messed it up. He'd be mad to not be mad about YOU!" Cam licks her teeth. Little yellow studs of corn flick off her tongue.

"Alicia is gonna do my apprenticeship form. It's happening."

"BABE!" Cam grins. "That's amazing!"

"Yeah." I feel sick. "Is it?"

"Yes, completely amazing. What you wanted, isn't it?"

"It is, just scary. You know . . . to go off the beaten track . . ."

"You've always gone off the beaten track, that's your . . . you know . . . *thing* . . . and who wants to be on the stupid track anyway? It's all tracks. If you can put your foot down . . . it's a track and . . . if there isn't a track . . . you make one."

"I think I might want to go back to school."

"No you don't." Cam shakes her head. "I knew this was coming. You're just looking for the easy way out. Like you do with everything—with the gym, with Max . . . You know what you have to do." She licks butter off her thumb. "Anyway, you got an A+ in art. An A-PLUS! And if you want to go ahead and be an artist you can do that whenever you want; it's never too late. Mate, you've got your apprenticeship; you got what you wanted. It's absolutely brilliant, B. You smashed it."

Cam's right. Maybe I did.

# JAFFA CAKES

I try swimming again. Once, I saw a footballer run onto the pitch eating Jaffa Cakes, so I make sure I topple a few into my mouth before I climb into the swimming pool to look pro, like a true athlete. Dark chocolate that cracks when your teeth bite a half-moon into it, the little orange jelly disc, chewy and tangy and then the light soft cakey sponge bit underneath.

Today there are a couple of skinny women talking by the edge of the shallow end. They have their babies bouncing in floats in front of them and they are "yaaaaying" at them in between gossiping. They are both so tanned, their skin colour is like beech, their shoulders like highly polished doorknobs. I wonder if they know they have a stereotypically "better" figure than a sixteen-year-old and they've just squeezed humans out of their bodies. Then again, I've seen sixty-year-old women that have stereotypically "better" bodies than mine. I look like I'm about to give birth to kittens.

I begin to swim. I think about my skeleton. It feels like my bones are the parts of a ship. But they're not. They are just as delicate and small as the women with the babies.

Once I watched this documentary where this little boy had this horrendous skin disorder. His skin would just eat away at itself. It looked bloody and angry. Even the touch of fabric against his skin would be agony for him. A bath was so painful. He had to constantly be covered in thick healing ointment and lubricant to stop anything rubbing his fragile raw skin. He had to be bound, the whole time, like a mummy, in a complicated dressing of cushioning and bandages. . . . With clothes on he looked like a scarecrow—all the padding between the clothing and his skin made him look like he was stuffed. Like a child wearing a fat suit to a fancy-dress party.

I wonder if that's how people see me if they think of my skeleton. Like it's buried for protection. Hidden under fat.

I don't like to climb out of the pool using just my arms like they do in adverts because I always get nervous that my arms are too weak and I won't be able to drag myself out of the water and will end up looking like 2B does when he tries to climb up onto the high wall outside and topples backwards. Dogs get embarrassed too, you know? I use the ladder, even though the sides of it brush past my bum and the steps clank and clatter when I get out, as if I'm going to pull them off the wall. I ship water up with me. *That* makes people stare.

I wash stares away in spirals down the drain.

With my hair still a bit wet I peep my head around the gym. I figure with wet hair it will make it really clear that I am on my way out so Todd the personal trainer, or anybody else for that matter, can't try to coax me onto one of the cardio contraptions.

The room is spacious and white. And quite empty. There are rows and rows of the same thing. Hideous shiny machines, sniffing and panting and showing their high-tech muscles. I imagine what it must look like full: everybody moving their bodies at the same time, like ants. It must look like some Daft Punk music video. Full of robots. Silvers, greys and blacks. Dizzy pop music tries to lure me in, enticing me to step onto one of the machines and try my luck as my reflection pings all over the zillion corridors of mirrors. I look about, wondering what to do with these giant coloured blow-up bubblegum balls. I realise then that the gym is an electronic futuristic playground made for the same people that take double shots in their coffees.

I rinse my mouth out with water at the fountain and leave.

On my way out I walk past a room full of people cycling really fast on stationary bikes to really loud music, disco lights spitting off the walls.

A gym person walks past with a clipboard. It's a young guy, not Todd; he has acne scars on his face.

"What on earth's that in there?" I ask.

"*That* is spin class."

"Why don't they just go for a bike ride outside?"

He laughs but he doesn't find it funny. It's not a real-life laugh. "They *could*, but I don't know if you sweat as much. Plus, the music is all part of it; see how they go up and down and left to right? Can't do that on the road."

I watch some more. It looks fun. I think I'll say that out loud.

"It looks fun."

"You should try it," he suggests, but his tone feels rife with sarcasm.

"Fine. I will," I reply boldly. "When's the next class?"

"Tonight. But you have to get here early. It tends to fill up quick."

"Well, I'll see you tonight, then."

And I walk feeling like I'm in a music video and the gym boy with the acne scars is thinking, *Wow, oh my days, that girl is so cool.* But I think he probably isn't.

I start to run through all the reasons I can't go to the spin class tonight:

I've already been to the gym once today. I don't want to look like an addict—good reason.

It's too hot and sunny today—another good reason.

My room needs a tidy—completely acceptable reason.

My trainers are a bit old, they might not be so *spinnable*—valid reason.

I should spend some time hanging with Dove— Hmm . . . I think she'd prefer I was here, to be honest.

# GREEK SALAD

"Hi, munchkin." It's Mum. My phone screen is already sweaty. "I'm going to be held up a bit at work today; are you able to pick up some food for us?"

I pull the phone away from my ear and growl silently into the darkness. Why does she think because I'm at home that I'm automatically her PA/slave? It's so annoying. I don't have an endless stream of money, Mum, actually, and I also don't have buckets of time on my hands.

"Are you there?" she continues. "I was thinking a nice Greek salad: feta, olives, tomato . . ."

"I KNOW what goes in a Greek salad, Mum."

"Great. Is that OK? I would ask your dad but he'll never get the right things. I'll give you the money back when I get home." She never does.

"I can't," I say. "Sorry."

"Why not? What you doing, then?"

I breathe in deep. Because once I've said it, I can't take it back.

"I need to buy a sports bra."

"A sports bra . . . a . . . OK? That sounds . . . adventurous."

"Don't annoy me or else I won't go."

"All right, calm down. Where are you *going*, then?"

"I'm . . . going to spin class. At the gym."

"Oh! Well, that's . . . that's brilliant!" Her voice sounds a bit too happy. It annoys me MORE.

"Yeah, so sorry, I won't be around to get your Greek *bits*."

"No, no, course not, don't you worry. I'll get that and you enjoy . . . spin." Her voice tingles. "Go, girl!"

Well . . . here we go, then.

# ENERGY DRINKS

They are probably my food hell. I know it's not technically a food but I think they are gross. I just can't understand why anybody would need an energy drink on a normal day when we've been all right up until now as human beings living on just actual real-life food. People were giving birth, climbing mountains, hunting, making fires, writing novels, painting the ceilings of buildings, making sculpture out of marble, smashing the living daylights out of a . . . I don't know . . . harp or whatever and inventing things, all without energy drinks. I'd understand it a bit more if they tasted good, like how chocolate tastes good, but they taste like 2p coins and blood and make your breath stink. I can't believe how many kids I see drinking them. Like, actual twelve-year-olds just banging an energy drink. When we were twelve, if anything, we needed a tranquilliser.

Lots of the people in spin class are swigging from energy drinks before class. I feel like I'm doing something wrong with just my bottle of water. I am wearing tiger-print leggings and a violet sports bra with a T-shirt on top. Didn't realise everybody planned on dressing quite so gloomy. I feel eyes looking at me, taking in my size.

I am, by far, the fattest person in the room. Still, we board these bikes. Some people take an age, fiddling around with the rusty seat and adjusting the height. I jump on mine. I feel the saddle squash into my bum cheeks, losing itself in the crush of me. My thighs are clamped around the bony ridge of it. We wait for the instructor to enter, lots of awkward coughs and sniffs. A few "stretches" from people "prepping." One woman is wearing a visor. A visor. What the hell? Tour de France, is it now? And then she enters. She is NOT the man I saw before. It's Ibiza leading the class. Oh HELL! Her tadpole brows are stuck in a constant frowning glare. She greets us like we are a room of snotty babies who have just vomited squashed carrot all over the floor. I am already dreading her "tunes." I turn the pedals of my bike. They are stiff. The pressure of my feet won't turn the wheels. It's like churning concrete. Sticky. It MUST be broken. STOP! STOP! CLASS DISMISSED, MY BIKE IS BROKEN. The bike screeches back in agony like a disgruntled mule screaming GET OFF ME!

And she begins. Shouting at us over some hideous, as suspected, scribble of dance music, a white noise of frantic chaos that's clearly been designed by somebody who hates ears. Some kind of demonic dance-floor hell of programmed sound that deafens me senseless. The lyrics, aimless throwaways of "let go" and "hold on" and "lift me up." Not to mention the spinning. It's HARD. Tireless, unbearable turns of a wheel that doesn't want to turn no matter how hard you turn it. And we are sinners repenting for our midnight snacks and bus rides and drive-thru stop-offs. I want to unscrew my ankles and get new ones.

And then we're meant to lift up and then sit back down and up again. HOW? HOW ARE PEOPLE DOING THIS? HOW ARE

THEY SMILING? Why do my arms ache and my abs howl when my legs are the ones doing all the turning? And I am dripping in my salty sweat that is running into my eyeballs and stinging them like murdering a slug with salt and I can feel the veins throbbing out of me and my bones feel twisted like they might pop out of the skin like in a gory horror film where a bone just busts out of a limb like a hot dog in a bun. I feel as though my feet might bulge out of my trainers. And MORE sweat is POURING from places I didn't even know owned sweat glands. Panting. Coughing. Round and round. Struggling. Lifting bulk. My bum. My ill-fitting knickers, wedged up my bum crack. The seat: DRENCHED. Is everybody dead or just me? My fleshy thighs are burning in purple swells. I've drunk nearly all my water and my feet are strapped into these stupid stirrup buckle things, locked into the torture. Cramping up.

And the terrible, terrible music just goes on and on. RE-LENT-LESS.

"Right," the instructor says, "that's the warm-up done."

# CUCUMBER

"I can't believe you *faked* an asthma attack." Dove bites her lips, loving that I was so naughty.

"Dove, it was hell. I had to get out of there."

"Weren't you embarrassed?"

"No, that was the last thing on my mind."

"You shouldn't do that, B. It's bad karma."

"I think I've had enough real asthma attacks in my lifetime to warrant pulling a trump card."

"You're still bad, though." Dove bites a snag nail. "I actually bum-shuffled up these stairs today."

"Well done."

"Cheers."

Dove and I lie on my trifle with our feet stacked up on cushions and cucumber circles over our eyes. Dad made Dove this makeshift bamboo stick thing with a fork stuffed in the end for her to scratch her legs with.

"Do you have to *scratch* so vigorously?" I ask.

"Yes."

We are clumsily feeding ourselves Greek salad, chewing salty black olives and blocks of feta cheese.

"Don't tell Mum."

"Tell Mum what?" Mum demands out of nowhere. Where'd she even *come* from? Damn these stupid cucumber sunglasses for blinding me. I had no choice . . . I had to . . . I lie again. . . .

"That I had an asthma attack in spin class." I peel the watery circles off my eyes. I say the sentence really emotionless so she can't hear a crack of falseness in my voice. Dove flashes me an eye-piercing snarl of disapproval. I look away.

"Oh no! BB! Why didn't you call me?" The guilt slathers on thick like cream cheese.

"I didn't want to worry you."

"BB! That's not good, you have to be careful not to exert yourself." She rubs my feet, sitting on the corner of the bed, her forehead frowning with concern.

"I know. I'm stupid."

"Was it bad?"

"It wasn't great," I lie again in a croaky voice, feeling the burn of my little sister's eyes scorching holes in me. I avoid eye contact in case I burst out laughing.

"Oh, sweetie, were you scared? Were the people at the gym good about it?"

"Yes, they were good. It's a shame because I had to leave spin class early."

"Oh, love, you were so looking forward to that too. How was your new sports bra?"

"Hmm . . . sporty. Digs in a bit."

"Yes, they are very supportive, aren't they?" Mum coos in empathy. "Poor you."

Dove rolls her eyes; she can't help herself. "Luckily I was at home to help her, Mum. I've taken care of her all evening." Dove pokes her tongue out at me. Mum falls for it.

"Good girl. It's scary when she has an attack, isn't it? You're a very good sister. I love my girls, always taking care of each other." I could punch that little bird of ours right off her perch.

"That's us!" Dove sings.

"I've heard spin's *awful* anyway!" Mum mutters. "Meant to be the hardest of all the classes."

"My legs feel like they are going to drop off," I moan. Dove digs her nail into my calf.

"Your dad's got some of that salve somewhere. It's what the Thai boxers use, apparently; meant to ease the muscle pain. Do you want me to get you some?"

"Yes. Well. Seeing as though I am an athlete, it probably wouldn't hurt." And she leaves the room to go get the magic balm.

Dove elbows me. "*Athlete*. Shut up. You did the warm-up of ONE exercise class. Hardly ready for the Olympics."

"Excuse me, Dove, I've done swimming AND spinning in one day. I'm basically a tri-athalist . . . or whatever they're called. And stop pretending you've been taking care of me!"

Mum comes back in. "OK, roll your leggings up."

"She's not been at war," Dove sniggers.

"I'd like to see you do it," I bark back.

"HA! SPIN CLASS! EASY!" Dove nods towards her chair.

"She does have a point." Mum raises her brows.

"Listen, mate, this is my room and I can bum-shuffle you out of here whenever I want."

"You couldn't, cos you can't even WALK after riding a motionless bike for five minutes!" Dove shoots back.

"Girls." Mum wrinkles my leggings up. It pinches the skin.

"Ouch."

"OK, now this will sting a bit to begin with."

"What do you mean 'sting'?"

"It burns a little, when you first apply it."

"It can't be worse than what I endured today."

"Lie back and I'll rub it in."

It smells like mint but not natural, more clinical and aniseedy. A bit like root beer. It hits the back of my throat with a thwack. The sensation of it going on my legs is like Vaseline. It's a thick balm and quite bittersweet with having the tension rubbed out of my legs but also wincing at every touch.

"How's that?" Mum asks.

"Fine," I say, my head in a frown.

"It's not burning?"

"Nope. It's . . ." And then it hits me. It's like hot coals poured onto my body. Like the worst sunburn. Like . . . OUUUUUCH . . . OUUUUUUCCCCCCCCCHHHHH. "GET IT OFF! GET IT OFF!" I throw the cucumbers off my eyes, snapping up to sitting. Honestly, what kind of hellish day of torture is this?

"Calm down, calm down!" Mum taps me on the knee.

"Mum, it IS BURNING!" Dove is rolling around laughing at me. "You can shut up!"

"You're such a baby."

"If you think you're so good, why don't you try it?"

"Dove's used it lots before, after her free-jumping."

I HATE Dove right now. She looks at me all smug.

"It will go away in a minute, just hold on."

The pain eventually fades and I can start to breathe again even though I feel like an absolutely disgusting hot sweaty failure pig in a blanket with rogue dog hairs sticking to the salve.

I lie back down and let Mum continue to rub and it's nice now that my nerves have gotten used to the tingling burn of pure actual fire. I replace the buttons of cucumber over my eyelids.

"I think you might be right." Mum cuts the warmth of the balm with her voice. "The gym might just be a stretch too far for you, BB, with your asthma and everything. Maybe just stick to swimming for now, eh?"

I nod, feeling so sorry for myself. I grab a circle of cucumber, snatch it off my eye and drop it into my mouth, crunching, like some rich lady of some posh house being massaged and eating grapes. Happy, in the safety of knowing that I'm never going back to the gym again.

# CAPERS

Gross minuscule hunchback pond toadettes. What even are they?

# PESTO

You can make a pesto out of anything. I don't know what *pesto* exactly means in Italian but I bet it's something like "anything and everything sauce." I do mine just the regular way, lots of basil, good olive oil, toasted pine nuts, salt, pepper, a squeeze of lemon juice and grated parmesan, and the great thing is, because the sauce goes in the blender you don't have to bother with that tiny mousey grater to grate the parmesan!

"It's FINE that the gym is not for me. It's just *not.* Like how I'm not *that* into dolphins. I don't JUDGE people that are into dolphins and go all round the world to swim with them, the same way I don't judge people that like the gym. The gym is just not my thing. And that's OK. It's probably not really for loads of people. Anyway, I bet I walk about five thousand steps when I'm working a shift at Planet Coffee, so that should improve my fitness in no time flat. I'd rather swim to the middle of an ocean or climb up a rock like some wonderful strong Amazonian woman than be tasking it to the drill of some ugly dance song like some robot worker bee in the air-conditioned gym room. NO THANKS."

"Yeah, but you're a member now, you have to go," Dove presses.

"Dove, my bum is dead, do you understand? DEAD." Dove giggles at me. "AND I went YESTERDAY, Dove. Nobody goes to the gym this much in a whole lifetime."

I go on, making sure I'm not being insensitive, but my misfortune only seems to make her howl harder, so I continue. "That class has absolutely ripped my muscles to pieces." I de-wedge my shorts out of my bum crack. "It's dead. R.I.P., bum. The seat proper rubs your thighs too. I want to see the damage but I'm too scared to look." OUCH. OUCH. OUCH. I wrangle my way to the fridge, hobbling like I have a hula hoop attached to my hips that I mustn't drop. "I feel the need to sue them." Dove cracks up.

"Sue them for your dead bum." Dove pinches her nose and whines, *"I'm Bluebelle and I can't do anything because my bum has died,"* mimicking me. "I cannot unload the dishwasher because of my dead bum, I *can't* feed the dogs because of my dead bum, and I *can't even* enjoy any of this delicious pesto because of my dead bum."

"The last bit isn't true, though, 'K?"

"Someone's got their appetite back, then. Maybe the gym wasn't so bad after all?"

Maybe.

Yeah, my body is heavy and sore, but I suddenly feel a lightness tremor through me that almost gives me butterflies.

I think about Max.

I wonder if he's thinking about me.

# SOUP

After MY ONE ALLOWED DAY OF REST I know the expectation of the gym is going to start rat-a-tat-tatting on my door again, so when Dad suggests some soup for lunch I am well up for the distraction. . . .

I always hate the idea of soup but never usually mind it when I'm eating it. I always find that I'm pleasantly surprised.

"What soup is it, though?" Dove asks before she fully commits to eating it.

"Leaf."

"Leaf? Leaf soup?" I ask. "What do you mean, 'leaf'?"

"Are you following a recipe, Dad?"

"Course I'm not following a bloody recipe!" He rubs his hands together like he's conjuring up a master plan. "You girls, this time we live in, nobody does anything from their imaginations. Why do you have to follow a recipe? It's just soup. Soup! Just boil up some vegetables, add stock and season with a few magic bits and bobs. Yes, it's leaf. Leaf-flavour soup. What's the big deal?"

"Maybe that leaf doesn't actually really have much flavour. I've never heard of leaf soup," Dove says.

"Well, I'm sure you've never heard of turtle soup either but it's a thing," Dad smugly assures us, clapping down the lid of a saucepan to make his point.

So, leaf soup, it turns out, is all the bags of salad leaves and spinach from the fridge, boiled up, blitzed and turned into sludge.

"It's not done yet, there's more, I have to add my magic now. . . ." And I realise the same moment Dove does. Dad's larder is completely rinsed. Everything thrown in the bin. He just hasn't seen it yet.

"We can have it like that, Dad, don't worry," I say, but it's too late. I can hear Dad's heart shattering to pieces.

"Your mum did this, didn't she? I knew it, I knew it, I knew it!"

There follow lots of swear words and Dove and I pour ourselves a bowl of leaf soup and blow bubbles on our spoons, laughing hard. With some salt, pepper, a scrape of nutmeg and a blob of cream it's actually all right.

# SWEET AND SOUR

After "lunch" Dove's friends knock for her. They are going to the skate park. Mum gets all jumpy and panics and makes Dove a peanut butter sandwich in a rush, which Dove, being Dove, leaves on the side and forgets about. I'm so baffled by people who can forget about food.

And I am left with Mum and Dad, witnessing their sweetness turning sour. . . .

NO! The arguing is *too* much. Mum at Dad. Dad at Mum. Mum calls Dad a "loser." She says he takes it out on her that his career is "down the pan." He laughs and says "that's rich" coming from her and calls her a "parasite." She throws a book at his head. The dogs do stress yawning and clap their teeth. Dad calls Mum a "soppy teenager with emotional issues." He tells her she has "too many regrets" and "needs to let go and stop harbouring." Mum cackles in Dad's face and says that he's the "teenager." She calls him a "freeloader," a "failure" and a "joke."

Then Mum cries.

The house is on the boil like the soup.

And I have to get out. I have to feel something. Go somewhere I can take out all this BLEUGHHHHHHHHHHHHHHHHHHH and maybe that place could possibly be the gym?

Who knows, maybe I'll try it again?

You'd like that, wouldn't you, Doc?

Whatever, nobody is still going to be reading this, surely?

And I charge upstairs and pack my bag ready for the gym. But I can just hear them, rowing, rowing, rowing, and my room is a state and everything is everywhere and it's too hot and my thighs rub and my bones ache and my mind is all rattling and numb.

And then it comes . . . tight. My chest. I've got no air. Wheezing and coughing. Tightness. Sharpness. And I can't catch my breath. I sit down. Try to keep calm. Where's my inhaler . . . ? I can't find it. I tipped my bag upside down looking for my stupid gym bag. Where's my night one? My stronger one? NO! I grip the bedsheets, scramble around the bedding . . . Where's my . . . My chest is sore. Stubborn. Refusing to lift. I can't speak or even open my mouth. The panicking is making it harder to inhale. I don't want to make a fuss. This is my fault. Just calmly breathe in and out. In and out. In and out. In and out. In and out. In and . . .

You're fine.

You're fine.

You're all right.

I'm all right.

# DRIED MANGO

There is NO way in hell this stuff is completely natural. It is the sugariest invention of all time. If it really is just mango, like it says it is, why does it have to be so expensive? Why is dried fruit more expensive than fruit, when fruit grows on trees? I HATE it when people try to charge for nature. Like, you know when you go to book a hotel and they charge more for a "sea view"? It really annoys me because how can you charge more to look at the sea? The sea is NOT yours.

This mango is addictive. Are you allowed to eat the whole pack? Of course you are. You HAVE to eat the whole pack. I like it when you can see the imprint of the gauze that they've baked the mango in printed on the dried flesh. I like the chewy bits that are a bit burnt and golden on the edges.

I am chewing, still, as I go up to the reception at the gym. Just so I don't change my mind. Just so I stick to my guns and see this through. They look surprised to see me. They thought I was just another one biting the dust, whatever *that* means. It's impossible to bite dust.

"Welcome back," says Ibiza, glaring at me like some vile evil fairy-tale stepmother who thought she'd got rid of me (by means of a spin class) until I resurrect myself from the dead.

"One for spin class, please," I say proudly. The girls do a delayed . . . *OOOO-KAY* . . . as they hand me my pass.

"It's not me teaching it today, I'm afraid," Ibiza says, as if that fact should change my mind.

"Too bad," I say. Which I don't know why I say as it's not one of my typical sayings but sometimes we say things, don't we?

I don't hang around long enough to discuss asthma. And why should I have to? They obviously weren't *that* concerned with my well-being.

Spin. Right. OK. Fine. Not. A. Problem.

I bounce up to the changing rooms. Skinny, muscly girls clanking in lockers, hair dryers purring and the smell of perfume and coconut and moisturiser. It's all more threatening and serious up here than the communal spirit of the changing rooms for the pool.

I dump my stuff into a locker and see my phone is ringing. Max.

I don't answer it. I don't need a man getting in my way right now. It's time to spin and sweat and, dare I say it, I'm almost looking forward to it. . . .

# BLOOD

I am first in the cycle studio and take my time to organise my bike. Even though I have absolutely ZERO idea what I'm doing, seeing as I never made it past the warm-up before. The room smells of old sweat. Dehydrated glands squeezing out old beer and curry from people who probably call nuts a "treat." Damp towels. The floor has an extra layer of sticky sweat laminated over it. I catch myself in the mirror. The bike is a skeleton next to me. Hard. Cruel. Wheels smile at me with a flash. Like the ones I see at home.

I wonder if my boobs joggle around all the time, or just at the gym.

The bike's screws are orange with brown rust and don't seem to turn properly. I can just hear this awful screech every time I dare turn a knob. I hear the door open. *Forget it,* I'll just ride the bike the way it is. An older woman with a pixie face enters. She looks like one of those wrinkled hairless cats. She starts fiddling around with these weird trainers she has on that look like tap shoes. Bet she actually enjoys eating raw seaweed as a snack.

"Do you need some help?" she asks me.

"Yes, please."

"Have you been to spin before?"

"Sort of."

"Come here, let me help you." She taps over with her silly show-offy shoes. *Trip. Trap. Trap.* "You have to have the seat hip height and the handlebars need to be a forearm away, like this. . . . Stand there." She measures me. "Gosh, you *are* tall, so let's bring the seat up a bit. These things are quite rusty! They need oiling." She screeches the seat up with a bang; it locks into place. "Try that?"

I hop clumsily onto the seat. "Yeah, that's better." But the poor donkey bike beneath me groans in pain. *Shut up, you.*

"Good. OK, now pedal for me. . . ."

I start turning my legs. I feel self-conscious pedalling on demand; what if it's just her and me? One-on-one spin tuition. Surely that's a good thing but the thought alone makes me feel physically sick. "Your legs shouldn't fully lock when they straighten; you need a bit of give." I nod. "And when cycling on a resistance you mustn't be pushing too hard so that your knees are struggling. No strain, OK, knees always forward. You push and pull from here. . . . Yes, that's good." She smiles and swivels the gear dial around for me. "And when you're on a lower resistance, when we sprint, like this, you mustn't be bobbing round in the seat like you are now; you should be locked in, firm, you see? Engaging all the muscles, the core, the arms. Keep your form. You don't want to injure yourself. And breathe. You'll soon get the hang of it."

More people start to enter and the room suddenly fills. Phew. It's not just us. Thank goodness.

This instructor seems so nice, no wonder it's a full class.

She pulls a headset out of her bag. *Why's she got that?* There are a lot of people, I suppose. It must be quite hard to hear. Plus, her voice is quite soft. *Fine. OK.* I gently begin to turn and the wheels spin in response. Others begin arranging their bikes just like I was taught moments ago except they don't need guidance. I watch how everybody fixes theirs. People exercise for different reasons: weight loss, fitness, habit, depression, alone time, boredom, last-minute bridezilla panic, last-minute holiday panic. . . .

The instructor swings one leg over her bike at the front, which is facing us, like a cowgirl mounting a horse. Still, I'm glad we have an older lady taking the class, it should be nice and relaxed. Miles away from the nightclub Ibiza trauma.

She then affixes her microphone and peels her top off . . . Errr, why does she have a six-pack and a flat pair of breasts? If I tried to take my top off, while wearing a headset, I would be suffocated. But oh no, not her two little kidney-bean perkies popping out of her tiny yellow belly top. Her arms are muscly and toned. Her stomach is ripped, muscles pinging out of every square. I was NOT expecting that bod.

"She's had four kids, you know," a woman with a stache whispers in my ear. "Un-believable."

I gawp.

"RIGHT!" she roars at us—*awwwright, motor mouth!* "YOU LOT ALREADY DECIDED HOW MUCH ENERGY YOU WERE GOING TO SPEND IN THIS ROOM TODAY. I WANT TO SEE THIS SPIN CLASS SPEND YOUR ENERGY LIKE THE MONEY YOU SPENT IN YOUR GAP YEAR WHEN YOU WERE EIGHTEEN. . . ."

Can everybody stop going on about bloody gap years? I gulp. I'm not even seventeen. I haven't even got any money to spend today, let alone in a year. Still, I pedal . . . Everybody else is. I'm gathering by the class's reaction that this must be her weekly motivational speech.

"I WANT YOU TO WORK HARDER THAN YOU'VE EVER WORKED, SWEAT LIKE YOU'VE NEVER SWEATED AND DON'T STOP . . . UNTIL YOU CHUCK!"

Chuck? What does she mean? *Vomit?* Surrounding spinners pant like thirsty dogs, sniggering at the idea of being eighteen. *Chortling* at the thought of chucking. Meanwhile I feel food rising in my throat.

"LET'S GO!" And the music begins as she roars, "WELCOME TO HELL!"

The music is some sort of heavy death metal. Loud screeching electric guitars and terror-tomb drums. A big screamy high-pitched voice sneering away.

Oh. God. Oh. God. Oh . . .

HELL?

*THUMP. THUMP. TURN. TURN. MORE. MORE. HARDER. HARDER. GO. GO. GO. GO. ROUND. ROUND.* Heart is pumping. Legs are burning. Sweat is POURING. Head is spinning. Ears are blurring. Blinding. Eyes are watering. Nose is dripping. ROOM is tight. Air is NOWHERE. Sweat from my forearms. My chest. And all around me are other people. Competitively spinning and groaning and churning with gritted teeth and crinkled eyes and wrinkled foreheads and spinning legs that look as though they might take off like that scene from *E.T.* where they cycle past the moon. In fact, the man in front of me is cycling so hard that sweat is just squirting onto the ground. I'm trying to catch somebody's eye to do an eye-roll or something, any sign to be like . . . "HELLO?

ISN'T THIS HELL? IS IT JUST ME OR ARE WE ALL DYING? ARE WE ALL INSANE?"

But they're all locked in, spinning tight. Normal people, hypnotised. And I am on the outside, staring in at the discipline and strength, just thinking HOW? I look up at the instructor as she bellows at us to turn on another gear. Her six-pack is splattered in pearls of sweat, her taut, ripped body is churning as she tells us to go up again. Why is she not drinking water?

"COME ON!" she yells again.

And the whole room spins so fast that the sound changes to a whisking noise, like spinning cupcake batter on a high speed. I taste blood in my mouth. Rancid iron mixed with phlegm. I think of my remarkable sister. *I am spinning for her. Keeping fit for her. My heart beating for her.* For me.

The music is buzzing, vibrating through the metal frame, and I am pounding, spinning, sweating in my oversized T-shirt and I want to take my top off so badly but nobody else is. EVEN though it's boiling hot and all I have on underneath is my one sports bra. My boobs are so big, I don't want them flopping around, but the instructor, she's only wearing a crop top too, surely it's fine. Everybody else just seems to be suffering, panting away with red raw cheeks. Oh, whatever.

I take my top off. People stare. WHATEVER. Fudge off!

*THAT'S BETTER. PHEW.* I feel my boobs and arms rattling away. My back fat quivers. My sweat trickles into all my folds, leaking into the flesh but WOW I feel better. Stronger. My tummy fat rolls over my leggings and the lip of the elastic is all folded down. Teeth gritting. I'm like a girl in one of those adverts to show that girls can do stuff. Locked in.

GO! GO! GO, ME! YES! And pant. Pant. CLIMB THAT MOUNTAIN. CAN. CAN. CAN! A dot of sweat from my head lands on my wrist. I watch it splash.

And . . . as if by magic, it happens . . .

The endorphin hits . . .

I am alive. POW! WOW! BOOM! KA-POW! RAAHAHA-HAAHHHHHHHHHHH! I FEEL SO AMAZING! Like a wicked spell has been cast over me and I reel in the thrill of the drill of my heart as the music switches I realise I am smashing it to "It's Raining Men"! YEAH IT IS! *Hallelujah!*

And before I know it we are winding down, bikes are slowing. The music changes tempo, soft and simple. We can stretch. We can settle. Bones crack and creak like grandfather clocks, like fractured antiques. We clap. We say well done to each other and thank you. A fully grown adult man tries to high-five me but we miss; it's awkward because we're tired and also I've never really been good at high fives anyway, especially with a stranger—no, with anybody. They make me anxious. We wipe our bikes down. The mirrors are foggy with a mist of sweat and condensation. I can't see myself even if I wanted to. Pant. Pant. Red. Lungs crushing. Arms rattling. Legs zinging.

I did it. I actually did it.

I am the last to leave. . . .

"Well done," she says to me. "You did really well."

And I go over to the mirror and write the letters *BB* in the steamy mist.

# SUSHI

I grab one of those little sushi trays from a sandwich shop on the way to the gym. Japanese people must laugh at our sushi. Even I know it's embarrassing and I know nothing. But I like the idea of it as a snack and using the little plastic fish of soy sauce to dribble over my rolls. Mum and Dad think it's hilarious that kids eat sushi these days. It was so exotic to them. You know the wasabi, in most places, isn't even wasabi. It's horseradish dyed green. It's really hard to grow wasabi here. It's OK, though. Too cold. A bit cloddy. I LOVE horseradish.

When I work at Planet Coffee more I'll save up all my tips and take Dove to Japan to eat real sushi. I think of Max. And the cafe with the cats. Shame that never came to anything.

# BAGELS

Everybody fights over who invented the bagel but I can completely understand this because did you know bagels are poached for a bit in water before baking? Who even *thought* to do that? They are amazing.

# SALAD CREAM

I know it's gross but sometimes I really enjoy taking a page from the book of ham in the fridge and dolloping a splodge of salad cream inside it and wrapping it up like an envelope wonton parcel and eating it down like a snake would an egg.

I like the vinegary sweetness of it.

Salad cream really can bring any sandwich to life.

I think about calling Max back. But is he the kind of person I can eat salad cream ham wontons in front of? I just don't know.

Besides, these days, I might intimidate him with my own mighty wonder-self and badass strength.

# GREEN TEA

After basically being a boss at spin I decide to try yoga. Some people have brought their own mats. I don't even have a mat. I should get a mat. Where do you even get a yoga mat from? Can't you just use a towel? Will people judge me if I use one of the gym's mats? Why am I worrying? SHUT UP.

The teacher is an older man. The sort of man my dad would hate because he seems like the kind of person that is an accidental millionaire and just does this job for the fun of it. We start on our feet. Talking about posture. The gaps between our feet. Our hips. Breath and shoulders. We all watch our reflections in the mirror. Some can't do it. They avert their eyes. We are all different. With bits that go in and go out, that curve and fold. We are different ages, with different interests. The only thing we all have in common is that we all have bodies that we want to, or need to, take care of.

Yoga is actually quite hard. There are bits where my body shakes, my muscles trembling weakly under the weight of me. Sometimes the mat slips, my hand so sweaty that I slide forward. Sometimes I can't wait for a pose to finish so I can untangle myself and rest. My breathing is short and stubby in places; other times I find my breath has held itself all together and my jaw is so clenched that my teeth feel like they might be cracking and I have to remember to let the breath go. My knees stiffen. I can only just touch my toes. Some people can't even touch their knees but nobody is bothered by that in here. Once I warm up and relax I start to enjoy it. I like warrior pose, where the instructor tells me to pretend I have a laser beam of light shooting from my middle finger, and then in triangle pose I look up to my open hand pointing towards the sky. I let my spine twist. I like the animal names of the poses: the hare, the cat, the cow, the cobra, the downward dog. It's so visual. We put our hands to our hearts. We rub our hands to "make warmth," then we place the warm hands on our chest. It's nice.

I could get used to this yoga business, I think. But then, suddenly, the whole class betray me and zip up into headstands. HUH? WHAT? When did we become acrobats, please? Even the old people are doing it. And I'm just on the floor, in child's pose, out of my depth. The youngest in the room and maybe the least agile and flexible.

Great. Yoga is annoying anyway. Green tea tastes like fish-gutty pond water.

BUT THEN we get to lie back on the mats and relax. I do a position called "corpse." But I don't feel dead. I feel far from it. My mind is racing. Thinking about Dove and her life and her body. About what's going on in her brain. How small we are. I'm thinking about all the things I'm going to do this year. And something changes. I feel a small tear sneak out of my eye. They might call this reflection. I don't know what it is. Because it isn't sad tears. Is it OK to be this young and confused? I feel overwhelmed, flooded with promise. I think about how exciting and scary it is to be alive. Why it matters so much: because we care. Because it's all so important and precious. You know . . . whoever is reading this . . . confidence isn't something you can buy on a shelf in a chemist and roll under your armpits to protect you. Confidence isn't something you can simply dream up or manifest. It comes from a place deep down. It's a muscle, just like a biceps or the imagination, that needs training and attention; it can't go to sleep. Self-love needs reminding. Needs activating and strengthening. You have to love yourself. It's the start of everything. The rest will follow naturally.

# OIL

"I didn't throw the oil away. All the oil is there."

"That one we got in Greece, in the can, that's gone!"

"It's all gone because you used it; it was empty!"

"You could have asked me."

"You weren't here. You weren't living here before Dove—" Mum stops herself. "Why would I keep your stuff here if you weren't here?"

"It's still perfectly good food regardless of whether or not I'm here."

*"Perfectly good food?"* Mum laughs. "Bill, ask the girls, ask the girls if a seven-year-old jar of anchovies counts as 'perfectly good food.' "

"I've been putting this stuff in food for years. It's preserves. You don't have to worry about sell-by dates and all that rubbish—it's the supermarket's way of convincing you to buy more."

"I'm sorry, but we didn't all grow up in the olden days of black-and-white televisions where everything came in a tin or vinegar!"

"You're just being spiteful now, Lucy."

"You're just being unreasonable."

"Me? That was hundreds of pounds of produce."

"Hundreds of pounds. You'd get more for your moth-eaten track-suit bottoms."

And Dad bolts over to us both, kisses us both on the head, puts a lead around Not 2B's neck and storms out of the house.

It was actually me who used all that Greek olive oil, so that's how I know Mum's telling the truth.

I am well into oil. It has pretty much become one of my main actual factual interests. When I was little I thought of oil more like a cleaning product. I knew it was useful but now I could HONESTLY drink a pint of olive oil. I'm assuming no nurse has the time to read this whole diary like an actual book so it won't be a problem if I say that my favourite way to have oil is slathered over ripe tomatoes with salt crystals like snowflakes that are as big as clip-on earrings, or just fill a dish and plonk a wodge of crusty bread in and let it sail and sink in the silky green gloopiness.

The oil is always the main event.

Groundnut oil is one of the newest members of my squad. You know groundnut oil makes the best roast potatoes in the world? You have to buy Maris Piper potatoes, peel them, chop them into lovely coffin shapes, boil them up until you can poke a knife easily right through, drain them, bash them about in a colander and then let them cool. Completely. Overnight if you can bear it. The idea is to let them chill with all that fluffy crust around them. In the midnight air, they sort of become frozen yetis. Then smother them in groundnut oil, sea salt, garlic cloves and rosemary. . . . Makes the best potatoes ever.

I am not surprised it took me ages to re-like oil again. It was what

I used to smear in between my thighs to make the tops of my legs not rub when I was younger. It only made them worse and fried up my inner thighs like pork chops.

Dad will be back any minute because he really will regret taking that stupid stinking Dalmatian with him.

"Thank God, I thought he'd managed to move back in for a second," says Mum. "I was about to make up an elaborate lie that we had to get the whole house fumigated for termites so he couldn't come back."

The termite being—well, you guessed it—Dad.

# ICE

It's boiling at Planet Coffee. My mascara is dribbling down my face, weeping, and Alicia is fanning herself with every available makeshift fan she can find. Because of the insane weather we have a massive queue for iced coffees.

"Guys, guys, we need more ice," she orders, hands on her still pretty much flat belly. Sometimes it blows my mind to think there's an actual PERSON in there. "More ice, now, can you both go? We need a lot. A LOT, A LOT!"

Max and I, aprons still on, leave Planet Coffee and, waiting for the cool breeze, instead get punched in the face with the smack of more hot air.

"Wow, was the air con on in there? It felt boiling."

"It's warmer out here than in there!"

"OK, supermarket?"

We jog as quickly as we can towards the supermarket. Max is so tall and his strides are effortless and long and elegant and I'm like a hybrid of a turtle and a pug snorting beside him. Even though I've been going to the gym, I'm not like him. I'm panting, red-faced and sweaty. Even my top lip is sweating. My hair has gone frizzy and is sticking to my face. If I wasn't with Max I'd be calling Cam confessing that this was a major setback to my personal fitness. WHEN does fitness kick in so that you are able to just, like, swim the River Thames and not even feel it?

The closest supermarket is *completely out of ice* and the queues are so long too.

"What?" Max moans. "How can they be out of ice?"

"It is a Saturday and the hottest day of the year, Max. Barbeque day."

"I s'pose. 'K, let's try somewhere else."

We jog/die along the high street towards the express supermarket, which doesn't even stock ice cubes. Then to the garage, which has ice coolers but not ice cubes.

"No frappés today, then," Max says as we head back.

"Oh, what about in here?"

I spot a Turkish fruit and veg shop and the heat is beating down on all the fruit displayed outside. Pomegranates, yellow mangoes, limes, lemons, oranges, peaches, apricots. There are half and whole watermelons, juicy and rich and the sweetness of strawberries, tomatoes, kiwis and bunches of black and green grapes.

"It smells amazing," Max says. He leans forward to inhale. Ripe, natural sweetness.

A man with a fluffy moustache steps out in front of a multi-coloured beaded curtain that rattles musically.

"Hello, mate. Excuse me, I don't suppose you have any ice for sale, do you?" HE'S SO SWEET TO EVERYBODY. I LOVE HIM. STOP LOVING HIM, YOU LOOK TERRIBLE.

"Ice?"

"Yeah, ice."

"How many you want? One bag?"

"How much have you got?"

"Come."

We follow the man inside and the air is immediately cool. Three fans purr excellently and the air offers us welcome relief from the chaos of a sweltering Saturday high street. The man tells us to wait as he leaves us to go out the back.

"I think my friend Camille bought a pomegranate from here a while ago and she spilt it all down her front," I tell Max.

"Pomegranates are special," he says. "You know they say there are twelve segments in each fruit, six in half . . . You know, like the months? AND 365 seeds in each one just like—"

"The days of the year?"

"Yeah, exactly. One for each day of the year. They are proper in sync with nature. Mad, isn't it?"

"How do you know that?" I ask curiously.

"My grandma told me," he says. "Although to be fair she does also have a browning branch of a Christmas tree in a vase by the window from five years ago that she waters nonstop in the hope it grows into a whole new Christmas tree, so . . . It's pretty dead. So . . . she might be making this stuff up."

"I like the sound of her."

"Yeah, you would. She has a pet crow, well, a crow that visits; his name is Colin. She feeds him crushed-up Rich Tea biscuits. He apparently has a girlfriend too called Wendy but Wendy doesn't visit much. Too shy, apparently."

We browse the shelves. The shop is bigger than it seemed, with four aisles stuffed with cans and pots of spices and jars of stuff. Fresh mint and herbs line the front, with more fruit and vegetables and a fridge stocking coloured drinks. It's hard not to lick the glass. There are spider plants and palms and rows and rows above covered in garlands of fake flowers—pinks and yellows, reds and oranges. Fake plastic fruit too, shiny red apples and grapes and bananas dangling overhead. More beads. Coloured clothes pegs. Glass teapots and decorative mugs. There are ornaments, funny water fountains and comical dustpans and brushes and candles and incense, sheets of twinkling fabric, little embroidered silk shoes and doormats. The smell is rich with star anise and vanilla and frankincense.

"Well, I know where I'm doing my Christmas shopping this year," Max laughs in a whisper. "This shop has everything."

"It feels like we're on holiday." I am stunned, looking around in this weird magical paradise. I feel myself cooling down.

"Yeah, it does." We wander round, pointing and smiling, waiting for the ice. "So . . . haven't seen you for ages, are you OK?"

"Yeah, I'm sorry about that. I'm not avoiding you."

"Sure? I mean, I get it if you are. I can see why that night has bad memories for you; I just don't want you to . . . you know, associate me with bad memories."

"How do you speak so clear?"

"How do you mean?"

"You just speak with clarity. It's nice."

"OK?"

"Sorry. I was weird. I was. But I'm better now. I don't know. I promise I think nothing bad about you. I've just had things, you know . . . on my mind."

"You thought more about what you want to do . . . with your life?"

I shrug. I wander ahead. Wanting to touch everything. Suddenly I become so overwhelmed and grateful and happy and excited. I can't even begin to put my finger on it, but it rises up through my chest and I could just cry. I say, "I want to do so much. I want to live, really live. I want to do all the things you're meant to do in all the places. I want to . . . eat cheeseburgers and chips and milkshakes at an open-air drive-in cinema in America and laugh and wear boots and short dresses—" Max laughs but I'm not laughing; I'm just smiling. I carry on. "I want to drink black coffee and red wine and eat steak and baguette in Paris and have a lovely little shiny bob and be really good at eyeliner. I want to eat tapas, *standing up,* in a backstreet cafe in Barcelona, with a tan and loose-fitting clothes. I want a roast dinner in an old pub in the middle of nowhere in the countryside, with a watermill attached to the side and my stupid dogs to be well behaved and lie there while I look over the newspapers and let the cuff of my jumper curl over my wrists and my hair, tussled from the wind, be heavy with rain and hope. I want to eat street food in Thailand and wear those yoga pants that make you look like you've pooed yourself, and wear no makeup, and do a handstand in yoga. I want to go everywhere; I want to do everything. I just want to be happy. Do you know what I mean?"

And then Max kisses me. He has to arch his neck down just a bit to do it. It's warm and neat and not messy. He holds the back of my head, which is sweaty but I don't care, and his other hand is on my lower back. I kiss him back. My eyes are closed and if I even open them for a second I just see the blurring rainbow of all the wonderful things behind and the beautiful things in front too. I like this. And my mind is silencing out the whole world and I think about kissing and how it's the nicest thing I've ever tasted. And I feel truly beautiful, even though I am wearing no makeup. And sweating like I've been at spin class ten times over. My heart is hopscotching.

"Ice, ICE! Lots of it." We jolt apart, startled by the moustached man's enthusiasm. He rests one foot on top of the ice bags like it's land he's just claimed as his and with a grin on his face announces, "I see you kiss." He chuckles. "You want borrow a wheelbarrow?"

And red-faced and buzzing we barrow the ice back towards Planet Coffee with smiles on our faces, each sucking a cube of ice.

We near Planet Coffee and Max turns to me and says, "OK, here we are, back at Planet Hell. In case I don't see you because the day is going to be crazy . . . you know I still owe you a date?"

"I think I owe *you* a date. I was the one who ran off!"

"No way, definitely not. I owe you."

"OK, so when do you want to take me on a date?"

He looks at me cheekily. "What about now?"

"Max! We can't go now! The Planet is chaos, Alicia's hormones are all over the place, it's too busy. Plus, they need the ice—"

"You're right."

We cart the barrow to the shopfront, where Max unpacks the ice bags and begins to sling them into Planet Coffee. Strong arms slinging the crush of ice, sleeting and frothing. Already melting. All the while Alicia is moaning like a whiny cat that's been left unfed for days: "What took you so long, guys?"

And I begin to explain that we had to get it from the Turkish shop as Marcel robotically uncarts and stacks up the bags of ice for Alicia.

Max dumps down the last bag and looks up, flustered, fingertips red raw with the glassy ice. The faces of caffeine-starved customers grind into him, trying to transport him to the coffee machine with some kind of crazed telekinesis. He calmly puts his hands on his hips.

"Come on, then, Maxy. Chop-chop." Alicia claps her palms together but Max, instead, cackles, bites his lip with mischief, giggles and whacks me in the back of the knees with the barrow, jolting me, collapsing my bum snugly into the seat of the barrow like an armchair. Max whips the barrow up onto its wheel and pushes me out of the shop.

I *scream.*

"MAX!" Alicia shouts. "Stop jerking around, aliens. You're very close to shooting back down to earth with a nasty bang and becoming earthlings. I mean it! Come on, snap, snap." Another magic phrase that doesn't work. Max pushes ahead, steering the wheelbarrow and me. *Running, running, running, running* towards the common, dodging people, dogs, buses, prams, the angry snarls of Alicia. *Away, away, away . . .*

He whizzes me around the grass, the flowers, the fountain, the picnic-makers, the bumblebees, the little birds and paddling pool. I open my arms up, I stretch my fingers out. I close my eyes. Both laughing, we slide and skid and breeze, free and wonderful. Until he tips the barrow over and I topple out and we fall onto the soft grass, laughing more, too breathless to even think about kissing. We link fingers. Giggling. The single wheel from the barrow still spinning. And then Max turns to look at me, vampire teeth and dimples and says, "I've been thinking about this for a long time; I really want you to be my girlfriend. Will you please think about being my girlfriend?"

The words come out before I even hear them in my head. "Thought about it. A hundred percent."

# PIE

Dove is throwing leek trimmings at the dogs. Mum's making her famous, delicious cheese and leek pie; we'll eat it later, slightly warm with salad.

The house smells like a cuddle.

"Gym *again*?" Mum asks as I scoop my hair up into a topknot.

"Yep."

"Sure you're not overdoing it?"

"No."

"You've been every day this week."

"Yeah, but I mix it up. I don't do the same thing every day. Sometimes I just go to stretch."

"I used to know somebody at the theatre who had a gym membership with three different gyms because she wanted to go so often and so the staff didn't talk, JUST so she could work out three times a day."

"Well, I'm not like that."

"OK, just be careful. I know what an addictive personality you have."

She is referring to the one time I got addicted to the blackcurrant powder dilute drink that I used to get from the vending machine at the library when I was eight. The sugar used to make my heart beat fast.

I like to feel my heart beat at the gym. I like to feel the sweat trickle down my head. Now I walk past reception and swipe my membership card and they don't take a second glance at me and I don't at them. It's just normal.

Changing, I feel happy. I'm just so glad I decided to get fit now and not later in life. It's only going to get harder to make a big life change like that. I mean, look at my dad. And if I want to eat everything I want, I guess it's good to have balance; in fact, my happiness and enjoyment of food is basically why I work out.

I think about food when I'm working out. When I'm standing in front of the mirror, lifting a dumbbell, pushing a medicine ball, squatting and pressing, I'm imagining I'm a mushroom bubbling in a sauce. I imagine I'm a hot skewer of kebab being carved off a knife. Today, I'll think about Mum's pie. I love pastry. Pastry that is thick, wet, water-based . . . flaky pastry, puff pastry. I like all pies too. I wish we had sweet pie shops here like they do in America. Cherry pie and an iced tea and red shiny lips and red nails.

I like to feel my legs. I like to pound. I like to pace. I like to race myself and see if I can go harder. I like to grunt sometimes and snarl as my muscles flex and flip and turn inside my skin. Even though I can't see them, I feel them, building, bulging, bursting, clenching. And with every bad, tired moment comes a newfound wave of power. And when I attempt to do sit-ups at the gym my fat sticks to the mat and makes flumpy fart noises. Air presses out as my skin suckers my back. People stare but I just put my headphones in and smile. And if I still feel self-conscious or weak—

All it takes is another woman from across the room to smile back and I keep at it.

And if there's no woman to smile at, well, then I just have to smile at my own sweaty cherry-faced tomato dummy grin smiling right back in the mirror.

When I get home Mum, Dove and I eat the pie at the kitchen counter. We forget about the salad and just eat it out of the pie tin, taking turns to scratch the hardened molten lava of cheesy, creamy sauce that's got stuck around the outside of the pan. Sword-fighting our forks like tusks.

Mum and I wash Dove and sing Christmas songs, even though it isn't Christmas and Dove says we are gonna get bad luck but we don't care.

And we sleep well.

# BBQ

Dad's turned up, uninvited, with BBQ food. Bags bursting with sausages, burgers, buns and posh crisps.

"Bill, what's all this?"

"Food! For a barbeque!" Dad opens up his hands, delighted.

"We don't even have barbeque coals. The thing hasn't been washed for months; it's probably all rusty and covered in black bits."

"I'll clean it up in no time. Come on, Lucy, it'll be nice."

Mum rolls her eyes and Dad nudges me in the side. He's obviously delegated me as his win-back-Mum wing(wo)man.

"You should have worn the sausages round your neck, like a Tony Soprano necklace, then she would have found you irresistible."

"You're right; it's too late now, isn't it? Too obvious? Bit try-hard?"

"A bit, yeah." I nod.

"What's all this, then?" Dove comes into the garden. "You all right, Dad?"

"Dad's making an impromptu barbeque."

"Trying," Dad says as he looks at the trays of the BBQ as if looking under a car.

"You better have got those yellow Post-it Note cheese squares."

346

"Course I didn't. I'm trying to make it up to your mum, not put her off me forever. I got proper cheese. Expensive cheese."

Dove rolls her eyes. I can see why. It doesn't melt the same as the cheap stuff.

Two hours later we have a roaring fire and equally roaring bellies. We weren't even hungry until the idea of the BBQ was planted in our brains; now we're starving and we have to wait until the coals go all silver and ashy until we can cook anything.

"Isn't this the life?" Dad says from his chair. He has sunglasses on even though the sun is going down and it's getting a bit chilly. His legs are way too spread, his hairy chicken-drumstick thighs bouncing open and shut, his stupid sandals showing off his bruised big toes. He is sipping a beer. The fire does smell good. Popping and cracking into the sky.

Mum comes out with a tray of chicken she's cooked in the oven, with the dogs slobbering after her. She's also made coleslaw with apple instead of cabbage and even knocked up a potato salad.

"Finally!" Dove zombie huffs. "I'm starving."

"Don't eat too much; you're gonna want some real barbeque action in a minute!" Dad grunts in a "Texan" accent.

"I wanted it two hours ago," Dove says, biting into a piece of chicken. "And this one doesn't give you all black bits on your teeth."

We finish eating. The plates pile up, smears of oil harden; the coal from the fire is now snowflake white and crumbling under the breeze.

"So have you told Dad your news?" Mum asks, picking at some cold chicken.

"No, not yet."

"Go on . . . what news?" Dad's interested, even though I know he's trying hard not to take it personally that he's always the last to find out about everything.

"That BB's got a BOY—" I launch up, chicken bone rolling to the ground to be snuffled up by one of the dogs, and slam Dove's ginormous mouth shut with my hand.

"That Planet Coffee is going to take me on as an apprentice."

"So what does that mean?"

"It's twelve months. I get paid. Not much, but still . . . and I can still do my other shifts too. It's a barista apprenticeship."

Dad looks for Mum's reaction. Mum looks at me proudly, smiles and says, "She sorted it herself . . . and she's been keeping the diary from the doctors. *And* going to the gym . . . so . . . I can't really argue with that."

"That's very good, Bluebelle, very good indeed." Dad nods. "And your A-plus in art." Dad shakes his head, like he's about to cry. "My baby girl, all grown up. I remember when you only just started nursery and now you're finishing school. I can't believe how proud I am of you girls."

"I wouldn't be too proud, Dad," Dove says. "One of us has broken both her legs jumping off a building and the other is leaving school to learn how to make cappuccinos."

And we all crack up laughing.

Dad finishes his beer and is feeling rather pleased with himself. To impress Mum, he shows us some of the stage fighting he's been teaching the students at his summer school. He teaches Dove and I how to slap and punch each other round the face without actually making contact. I have to stomp my foot at the same time to look like I've broken Dove's nose. It's funny. Especially as Dad is well drunk and keeps slurring his words and tripping up when his sandal slides off. Mum is laughing, beer in hand. Dad does some karate for us and some other really strange physical theatre.

"Do a roundhouse kick, Dad!" Dove orders, and Dad begins spinning round in a circle and flapping his feet out. Dad is wobbling drunkenly all over the place on the decking. Knocking over the plants and falling into a thorny bush.

"Watch my lavender!" Mum warns.

"You try now, BB!" Dove says.

"I can't!" I say. "But I can show you some of the yoga I've been learning?"

"Ahhh, yoga. *Namaste.* I have an inner yogi in me," Dad says wistfully. "The lovely relaxing bit after all that action—what a perfect way to end a *blissful* evening in paradise." He looks at Mum for a sign of romantic gesture. He gets a side smile and a raise of the brows. I wouldn't start counting his hens too soon if I were him. The dog farts to add to the mood.

"So this is Warrior." I show him.

"Yes, yes, I know *all* about Warrior."

"There's one really hard one my teacher taught me but I can't do it."

"Which one?"

"The Crow Pose?"

"Aghhhh, the good old Crow, no problem, remind me. . . ."

Mum laughs, all flirty. *Awwright, Mum.* Calm down.

I squat down to the decking, spreading my hands. Then with elbows wedged in between my inner thighs I try to lift my feet off the ground, tipping my head forward . . . I hold it for half a second before losing my nerve and dropping back down.

"That's serious!" Dove laughs, impressed. "You can almost do it." Even though I definitely can't.

"Nah!" Dad waves me off. "It's a piddle. Say no more!"

He squats down. I hear his bony knees crick and he finds his balance and, using his hands, tips up. His grey hair floats up like a toupee; I see his bald patch like a little shiny moon twinkling on his skull. He looks old. Different from the frozen photograph I've captured of him in my mind. Mum watches, hand over mouth, trying not to laugh at Dad in his camo shorts and tropical shirt as he pouts his mouth and closes his eyes as though he is meditating. I can't even begin to imagine the photograph Mum has of him in HER mind. It must be a completely different person altogether. Do we hold on to the person we love as the person we see before us today or is it the moment we decided we loved them?

Dad suddenly, drunkenly, FOOLISHLY, tips forward, makes the pose and holds the position and we all whoop, impressed, until he gets too cocky and . . .

BAM!

His face hits the ground. He's tipped too far forward too quickly. SO drunk he couldn't think fast enough to put his feet out to brace himself.

"AHHH!" he yells, and he looks up and his nose is bleeding and he has cut the bridge of it, all bloody, and his lip has already swollen and his forehead is grazed and covered in black grit and his chin is scabbed and his eyes are already swelling. "OH. OH. NO. My face, my face . . ." He wants to touch it. "Is it bad? Is it bad?"

"No. No!" We lie to him. Sitting him down as Mum scuttles over, reassuring him.

"Come on, old man, let's get you cleaned up," Mum says as she leads him indoors. Dad apologising to Mum, desperately trying to remind her how good he was at yoga back in the day. The dogs follow, of course; they love the drama.

Poor Dad.

Dove and I leave Mum and Dad to it. We can see them in the amber glow of the kitchen from the darkness outside. Dad on the kitchen table and Mum dabbing his head. Dad's making Mum laugh, although I honestly can't say if it's intentional.

"B, want to see what I've learnt?"

"Sure."

And suddenly, Dove whips her chair up onto one wheel and spins around on the decking in a pirouette.

"What the hell was that?"

"I dunno. Does it look cool?"

"It looks amazing!" I hug her. "So cool!"

"I'm gonna learn more. I've been watching these videos. I'm also going to try out for a basketball team."

"Dove, that's brilliant news."

"Tell you what is brilliant news . . ." Dove glances over at the back window where Mum and Dad are hugging. I scrinch my nose up at them—they can be a bit cute.

"Really, really wish we had marshmallows," Dove sighs. "Always forget about how much I love them."

Ooh, sorry . . . What did we eat? . . . OK . . . well, the fairy lights shine a teary dream canopy over the orange flames and cindered coals, so we weren't entirely sure when things were cooked. I guess cooking with fire makes you feel so animalistic and caveman you can almost trick yourself into thinking you are able to stomach pretty much anything.

But I'll go with chicken. Moist and chargrilled on the outside, sausages that were herby and delicious, bread and cheese and cole-slaw.

And you're probably gonna tell me that most of that is bad for me, but I just don't care.

# MARSHMALLOW

"Let me just *squeeze* past your bot-bot." Alicia double-taps my side. "If you just breathe in for me there, babycakes . . . ," Alicia says as she unnecessarily inches past me to sit down. Exaggerating my size. I don't take it personally. I'm over it.

"Bluebelle, there's something I have to confess to you, doll face. A little bit of . . . *not-so-good news* . . ."

"OK . . ."

I watch a couple *sharing* an electric skateboard whizz over the zebra crossing towards the park. So annoying.

"I've had a call from head office . . ." There is no head office; it's basically a forty-five-year-old stoner called Daerren (yes with an *a* and an *e*) who lies on his couch with his iPad all day. ". . . and they"—that'll be Daerren—"are, regrettably, as I suspected, worried about committing to the apprenticeship. It's not something that we—*they*—as a small independent coffee house can take on. It's a big responsibility and, well . . . even though I've tried to convince them"—Daerren—"it also didn't look great that you've not really been here much; there's lots of blanks in the rota, which doesn't

353

look too pro, and when they asked why you weren't here a lot I obviously had to explain about your sister's illness and—"

"Not an illness," I interrupt.

"Sorry, beb, not illness, you know what I mean."

"No I don't. Not really. She had an accident."

"Errr . . . O . . . K, moody pants." Alicia looks put out. "I wouldn't be going round acting like that, giving it the biggun after your little stunt with Maxy boy. You're lucky I didn't tell them about *that* or you both would've been fired on the spotty-spot-spot."

I stay silent.

"And I didn't dob on you. *'Thank you, Alicia.' 'You're welcome,'*" she says to herself through gritted teeth as though she's being nice, even though she's being snide. "And you should be thanking me anyway because I've made sure you can keep your job after I leave. I had a lovely chat with HR"—HR? Give it a rest, that'll be Daerren's cat—"and we all agreed that. Perhaps you could speak with the new manager and he'll give you some more shifts?"

"Who is the new manager?" Not that I care. (But obviously I do.)

"Marcel."

"Marcel?"

"He's great with the customers and he makes a hell of a cup of coffee. Have you seen his latte art? I mean, it's totally off the chain!"

"He draws BREASTS with hot milk, Alicia."

"Well . . ." Alicia sucks her cheeks in. "I've never seen the breasts."

The cakes stare back at me. Their silence speaks volumes. I feel betrayed by the whole building and everything inside it. It's almost the start of term and I don't have an apprenticeship. I don't have anything to go back to. I told Julian from Careers, I told Mum, I told Dad and Dove and Cam and Max. And now I'll have to face them all.

"Don't be upset. Have a hot chocolate and help yourself to a pastry."

"I don't want a *pastry*."

"Why don't you just pop yourself in the diary more, like we talked about, get those shifts up, and when you're eighteen maybe you'll get the chance to even be manager yourself? If that's not an incentive, I don't know what is. Maybe you could even apply before you turn eighteen? That way you've got something lined up."

Suddenly I see myself: washed-out. Working as the Planet Coffee manager until I'm forty. Earning more money for Daerren at a business I could run myself. My kids at the table, slurping their babyccinos as my boobs begin to look less and less like the ones on Marcel's coffee froth.

"You can't do that."

"Beg your pardon?"

"You said you'd make sure you had the apprenticeship lined up for me. I've told my school. . . ."

"Yes, I know, which is why I've *kindly* taken the time to write this letter to your school to say there was a miscommunication on our part."

She holds the letter out in front of me. I reach for it. Alicia snatches it back.

"Aha! Not so fast, earthling. Less of that attitude, missy. I've got you out of a hole here."

"Not necessarily. If you hadn't left this so late, I could have found another solution." I am so hurt. I don't know what I'll do now. I've been working so hard at everything, only for life to kick me right in the teeth.

"I didn't say it was a *definite*, Bluebelle." So then why does she look guilty? "Now, are you going to stop playing the blame game and calm down so I can hand you this letter?"

"I am calm."

"You don't sound it."

"I am."

"Give me one good reason why I should give it to you."

"How about: I've made hot drink after hot drink, sandwich after sandwich, scrubbed the toilets, scraped bogies off the walls, cleaned the fridges, I've emptied bins and mopped up YOUR SICK. I've smiled when I've not wanted to smile and gotten dribble on my hair and chewing gum on my dress. I've put up with rude comments from customers and never once been rude back. Once."

"Oh, newsflash, shock horror, it's called WORKING IN A CAFE, princess, get over it. Sorry it's not good enough for you."

"Whatever, I'm going home."

Alicia's jaw drops off. "Oh no you don't."

"I'm sick of proving myself. I don't want to be here right now. I want to go and so that's what I'm doing. I'm listening to myself."

"If you leave now you don't have a job. Not even a weekend one. You will be an alien no longer. You can wave goodbye to THIS planet once and for all, and let me tell you, Planet Earth will not be as lenient with you as I've been."

"Fine. I quit."

"Oh, soz that you just decided you don't want to work here right now because things aren't going your way, Little Miss Choosy Brat-Face, but that's not how real life works. If you're leaving, it's called TWO WEEKS' NOTICE. Read the small print."

"Life is too short for *small print*, Alicia."

Alicia frowns. She tries to reach her hand out to me. "OK, here's the letter." She boots her chin out to stop it wobbling from nerves. "Now, if you wouldn't mind just bleaching the back b—"

"I've just told you I'm leaving," I say. Alicia looks at me like she's been slapped round the face. She turns ugly immediately.

"I'll rip this letter up right now, right in front of you, missy moo. Then you'll be sorry." She is shaking; she has worked herself into such a stupid frenzy. Her wrists are rattling.

"Rip it up, Alicia. I don't care. It's just a stupid letter from you that will mean absolutely nothing. I could die in this place. I've got things I want to do, so . . . I'm going."

I unpeel my apron. Alicia cries out some annoying dramatic gasp that I adore to ignore.

Marcel comes in from a break, smelling of stale fags and chewing gum.

"Where you off to?"

"Home."

"Did you hear the news? You're talking to the manager of Planet Coffee! Imagine all the girls I'm gonna get!"

"Yes, congratulations. I'm leaving now."

"I thought your name was on the rota. Aren't you meant to be working?"

"Nah. I'm going to hang with my sister." I pick up the glass jar of dusty pink, purple and white mini marshmallows by the till. "And I'm taking these too."

Both Alicia and Marcel stare at me, mouths ajar, in absolute shock. Alicia runs after me, her clip-cloppy heels and annoying voice yelping behind me.

"Wait!" Marcel shouts. "You have to ask me! I'm the manager!"

"Yeah, well, you've not even started your job and I already quit. Great managerial skills."

"Unbelievable."

"Oh, and Marcel, just a few tips . . . Your breath stinks of de-hydration: drink more water. Which reminds me, if you ever want to get a girlfriend maybe stop being such a sexist pervert?" I bark. Marcel and Alicia stand stunned as I turn to leave. "AND will you widen this bloody door so wheelchairs can get in and out, and lose that stupid step, get a ramp? Seriously."

And I just manage to hear Alicia say to Marcel, "Well, she's not wrong, is she?" And I smile in the end-of-summer sun.

# THAI RED CURRY

I think one of the worst things that could ever happen to a person would be for a bottle of fish sauce to smash on their dress. Imagine that? IT ABSOLUTELY STINKS.

I help Dad with the curry. We make a paste out of ginger root, lemongrass, garlic, chilli, sugar, oil and fish sauce and add it to fried onion. The broth is silky-smooth coconut milk and stock. The king prawns need their gross horrid grey veins scooped out of their backs. It's the nerve. That gets the information to the prawn's head.

"What information does a prawn even need?" Dove asks innocently.

"Information that says . . . *AAAARRGGHH I AM IN A POT OF BOILING HOT WATER* before dying," Dad shrieks.

"Dad, did you just act out a prawn?"

"Yes, I've perfected it, I'm waiting for my call—*Prawns,* the movie."

Dove takes a carrot from the fridge and chomps off with it.

We plop the prawns in at the end, top with coriander and a squeeze of lime. We have it with steaming jasmine rice. Some people HATE coriander, it's like one of those things that you're programmed to either love or hate. I think it tastes different to different people. To me, it's aromatic, but to some people it's like skunk stench.

Mum and Dove join us at the table. Mum and Dad have beers; they offer us one each too but we say no.

The curry is warm and friendly, a comforting spicy bowl of heat.

I take another spoonful of the aromatic curry. The prawns feel fleshy and human, like eating fingers.

Dad proudly places the bottle of fish sauce in the larder. He can begin restocking it.

Dad's nose is already starting to crisp up, thanks to the sun. It looks like it's healing. Thank goodness. I've had enough of him walking round like he's earned the injury like a member of the Mafia, replying to the neighbours' questions, "Don't you worry 'bout where that came from."

He's just happy he feels a sense of community. Of belonging.

But really, though . . .

"BB?" Dove asks. "Was it you that left a jar of marshmallows on my bed?"

"Maybe."

# BREAD

"What would be your last meal on earth?" Max asks as we picnic on the trifle.

"Hmm. Bread. Any bread. Farmhouse tin loaf with crusty edges, stale bread, warm bread, tiger loaf—did you know the crackly bit comes from ground toasted rice?"

"Yeah, I heard that."

"Isn't it great? I heard that a little girl wrote to a supermarket and said that the bread looked more like a giraffe than a tiger and so they changed it to giraffe bread instead of tiger. How good is that?"

"So good."

"Or . . . warm baguette—the ends, the knob bit, with a wedge of thick cheese or butter, *ooooh,* or even cheap sliced bread, toasted, buttered. Garlic bread with warm, leaky butter—cheap garlic bread where the garlic butter is sponged into the centre and it's pre-sliced . . . don't care; it's a different taste, ready for a different day. Or those half-baked baguettes that come in the plastic packets?"

"Ah yeah, my brother likes those."

"Complete lifesaver, full of raising agent but can transform a lunch when you're too scared to face the rain. Olive bread, studded with little black and green nibs wearing treasures of salt crystals and the toasty top. Cheese bread. Ummm. Cheese and ONION bread . . . *mmmmmm*. I like ripping the inside out of bread, rolling it in between my hands into doughy cigars, housing my hand in the new mitten."

"Hahaha, Bluebelle, you're so funny."

"I want to try fool's gold loaf, have you ever heard of it? It's the sandwich that Elvis Presley would order and gobble with champagne. It's eight thousand calories per serving!"

"Huh? What the—how come?"

"Errr, because he can have whatever sandwich he wants. He's Elvis!"

"Fair enough. What's in it?"

"Basically it's a whole loaf of white bread with all the soft middle innards scooped out so you are just left with the outer crust, then all that middle stuff is replaced with the filling. First it's smeared with butter, then it's stuffed with fried bacon, peanut butter and jam. Then the whole thing gets wrapped in foil and put in the oven. I would so eat that. Just to taste it."

"Me too, sounds unreal." Max nods. "Any other bread?"

"Focaccia. With rosemary needles and olive oil. Wafer-thin ham and milky cheese. Ciabatta, stuffed with mozzarella, tomatoes and pesto. Any bread. At any time."

"Yeah, I think bread's a pretty good last meal. You know those people who do the no-carbs diets? That's crazy, I could never do that."

"I know, so unhealthy. So they can eat a whole entire plate of cheese and salty bacon and fatty sausages but they can't eat ONE slice of bread. I just think that's mental."

"I can actually make bread."

"Can you?"

"Yeah. When I was younger I used to be well into it. Now I only bake every so often. It just takes so long, with the yeast and everything."

"PLEASE bake me some bread."

"OK. I'll put your order in." Max goes quiet. "I'd like to be a baker, actually."

"What? Really?"

"Yeah, it's so therapeutic working with dough. Really calming. I'd like to do brioche and croissants and buns and all that."

"How did I not know this about you?"

"I just . . . I dunno . . . Planet Coffee kind of sucks all that stuff out of you, I guess."

"I think you'd make an amazing baker."

"How'd you know? You've never even tasted my bakes!"

*"My bakes!"* I imitate him.

"What?" He giggles. "That's what you say."

"Did you know you shouldn't feed bread to ducks in the pond because sliced bread from the supermarket has calcium in it and ducks don't like calcium? It's bad for them. Maybe it makes their beaks grow bigger and it weighs them down so much and drowns them."

"I did not know that."

"My last meal on this earth would be bread and butter made by you. Then I'd die happy. I'm so happy anyway. Without the bread."

# CHOCOLATE CORNFLAKE CAKES

Dove stirs the cornflakes into the chocolate and they soften under the weight of the warmness and wetness.

"Gimme one of them, then?"

"No, they need to cool down in the fridge first and then I put the chocolate eggs in the nests."

"Come on, Dove, I'm going to yoga; I'll be starving!"

"Go on, then. . . ."

Warm, melty chocolate on my tongue. The soft, golden flakes dissolving, cracking apart on my tongue, crowning my teeth. Sticky goodness buckling from the golden syrup. "You're not the worst chef in the world; these are AMAZING!"

"Ah, thanks!" Dove smiles, smearing chocolate from the wooden spoon onto her cheek.

In yoga I manage to do a headstand for the first time in my life ever. I wasn't even aware I was doing one and then I basically just was. I pretty much got tricked into doing a headstand and loved it. At school I wasn't one of those girls who could just flip upside down in front of a wall. But here I am. Belly out. Boobs by my eyes. Holding a headstand. It must've been the power from the chocolate cornflake cake.

I feel the blood flood to my head. I grin with pride.

The yoga teacher winks at me.

I watch myself in the mirror. I am pleased with what I see. A thousand pairs of eyes staring back that aren't really there . . . I don't need to worry or wonder why the world stares at someone like me; *they* need to worry and wonder why THEY stare at someone like me.

And if I could talk to little me now, I would tell her that she'd matter more to me than anybody will ever matter. Look at you now, Bluebelle. Just look.

# MIDNIGHT FEAST

I come home after seeing Max and Cam for enchiladas by the river. The house is a blue moon and still. Dad's flat cap sits on the banister. I lift it and smell it. *Wax. Age. Musk. Familiar.* His beaten shoes are by the door; he likes to be barefoot, feel the ground under his feet. I'm glad he's here.

Dove's casts are getting really dirty. Covered in tags and glitter and scribbles. The silver brightness of her laptop shines a pale moonbeam glow over the room. I poke my head in her downstairs room. . . . She's got her eyes closed like she's sleeping. The screen is playing a wheelchair basketball game.

"Dove?" I whisper. "Dove, you awake?"

"Ah. Hi, B." She turns. "Yeah."

"So . . . I don't have an apprenticeship at Planet Coffee."

"Oh."

"Alicia didn't give it to me."

"What a chief."

"I know."

"What happened?"

"She's basically a modern-day crook." I shake my head like I've been absolutely taken for a mug. "She said she'd sort me a job and basically didn't. She took me for a fool." I add, to enhance the drama, "But it's OK, I'm not going to let her incompetence stop me."

"So what now, then?"

"Hmm . . . remember before . . . I said we'd watch *Snow White*?"

"Errr . . . yeah?" She smiles.

"I think I just want to do that for now."

Dove smirks. "Well, that sounds ideal. Why don't you go and get them cornflake cakes; they'll have set by now."

I crawl into bed next to her. Elbow to elbow. The plate of wonderful chocolate nests in front of us.

"Actually," I say, "let's not watch *Snow White;* we've seen it hundreds of times."

Dove looks disappointed. "Fine. Are you gonna go up to bed?"

"No way! Let's watch your basketball. I want to know all about it. . . ." And her face goes into a wide smile.

"Really?"

"Course."

"Well . . . ," she begins.

# SANDWICHES

I hate it when they put raw red onion in these sandwiches. It makes me so livid. It repeats on you all day like some annoying oniony TV jingle.

Dove's made hers for lunch without onion. Because she's not insane.

I decide to wear the rainbow kaftan with the black leggings and the pom-pom shoes.

"You look like a girl I snogged at Glastonbury a LONG time ago." Dad sniggers over his morning coffee.

"Hideous." I ignore him, filling a mug with water; my mouth is so dry.

Dad's eyes glaze over like he's trying to see her face and relive the moment, a big grin splattered across his dummy face. I'd rather he didn't. "What was her name now . . . Barbara? No, not Bar— Deborah? No, Donna . . . Sure it was Barbara, Barbara *Glaston-bury*," he establishes like it's her legitimate surname. "Anyway, she was *wild*, whatever her name was. Yes, you look just like her."

"Although I bet she was about ten times thinner."

"Hmm." Dad considers it. "I was too drunk to remember." He leans against the sink, uncrosses his arms. "But I know for a fact she wouldn't have been half as gorgeous." He backs the rest of his coffee. "Not with these genes!" We laugh. Dove enters; she is in her school uniform. "Speaking of genes, here's more proof of my talented puddings! Doveling, you ready to fly?"

"Sort of."

"You look smart. . . . I like your hair like that; you look like a wrestler." Dad's never been one for compliments.

Dove knows this only too well and replies, "Thanks, Dad."

"Right, you two ready, then? Sure you don't want me to follow behind?"

"You're not our security guard, Dad." Dove shakes her head.

Dad puffs his shoulders out and puts on a New York gangster voice, his two swearing fingers in a V shape at his eyes and then on us. "You know I'll be watching you, don't you?"

We roll our eyes but we can't help but laugh.

"B, are you really wearing *that*?"

"Yeah, why?"

"It's my first day back *and* . . . well . . ."

"Dove, you're in a wheelchair with your legs in two casts. Do you think anybody is gonna care what I'M wearing?"

"Actually, I reckon she *should* wear that. Everyone is going to be SO concerned with Miss Barbara Glastonbury's terrible outfit they aren't going to *care* about Dove!"

Mum comes down. "Ahhhhh, you both look brilliant!" She applauds us.

"All right, Mum, we're only walking down the road!"

"I know, I know but I want to get a photograph of you both."

"A photo? *No*, Mum, why?" I howl. "You see us every day."

"I want a photo," Dove says, "to prove to my kids that I broke both my legs when I was thirteen."

"Come on, then, let me see if I can *ugly* myself up a bit so you girls don't feel intimidated." Dad ruffles his hair up, muscling in on the photo. "I don't want you girls to feel a laughingstock next to me, eh?" His coffee smell is a toasty wave of comfort; his bad jokes seem to warm me from the inside out.

"No, Bill, I want a photograph of the girls, not you, you big naan bread." Mum moves Dad out of the way.

"You know *naan* actually means *bread*? So when you order a naan bread at the Indian restaurant you're basically ordering bread twice?" Dad smirks cockily.

"Bread bread." I laugh.

"See? Joke's on you." Dad clicks his tongue.

"Whatever, Bread Bread, I've got MORE than enough photos of you. Out the way!" Mum shoves him now.

"Do you?" Dad manages to somehow find flattery in this and stands back, pretending to read the week-old newspaper.

"That's it, OK . . . right, closer, OK . . . Now, girls, on the count of three say 'Cheese!' "

"Ready?"

"Three. Two. One."

"CHEESE!"

Cheesy indeed.

Cheese is delicious. Cheese is mould. I don't like cheese with blue veins in it.

# BLUEBELLE'S

The world is the same, tumbling on as we whoosh by. The shop-keeper waves, the faces stare, smile. Dove is looking at her phone, not even looking up as I pant and sweat behind her, little teardrop beads squeezing out of my head. Hasn't this gym business paid off yet? My God.

"Ahhh, look at this message from Lottie, isn't that cute? Ah, look, Echo liked our picture and Reena, ahhh. They are so cute." Dove coos. "Ah, and Jordan . . . and Olivia. Oh . . . I can't wait to see everybody."

"That's good. That makes me happy."

"Are you nervous to see any of your old school friends? They'll all be there for sixth form, won't they?"

"Yeah, I hadn't really thought about it, actually." I had. I can imagine them now. Clucking and screeching. Excited. I am happy for them. They'll run to Dove; they'll want to push her around all day. They'll want to ask her about me. And I know she'll say nice things about me. Tell them I'm doing well.

"What is wrong with you? You're shaking like a leaf," Dove says as I fix her hair by the school gates.

"I'm just nervous. . . . I don't know."

"Why are you nervous? There's nothing to be worried about," Dove reassures me.

And I hold her so tight and she wraps her arms around me and we say goodbye.

"Good luck." I kiss her head.

"Thanks. Love you."

"I love *you*, and remember, be a firework."

"Be a shooting star!"

"Be a rocket ship!"

"Be a stick of dynamite!"

"In real life, though, be the candles on birthday cakes, the ones that never blow out!" I pretend to blow candles. "Until the icing on the cake is just covered in spit."

"Ha! Yeah! Oi, you, be a cannonball!"

"That I can be!" I crouch into a ball and Dove cracks up. "Drive safely!" I shout after her. She spins round and whips her wheel up at me, skidding a tyre mark on the ground.

I watch her leaving me, heading towards the crowd. Towards the long hair, the short skirts, the plaits and braids, hijabs, the glasses, balls and singing, the sweets and crisps and snapping of biscuits, the unscrewing of bottle caps, the screaming and hugging and shouting, the hearing aids and braces, the whispering and gossiping, the cussing and hugging and kissing and music and phones and lip gloss and hair gel and unbuttoned shirts and plaster casts, the howling and laughing . . . and Dove. A confetti-stuffed grenade I've had to let go of.

I walk along the high street in my rainbow kaftan and pom-pom shoes. I walk along, past the people, past the faces.

I sit in a coffee shop, one I've never been into before. They have a ramp at the entrance but the door is a bit narrow.

Their cakes look all right. I could do better.

Mine will be called "Bluebelle's." It will serve proper iced coffee and proper coffee, without boobs on top. We will serve real cake with proper icing and a proper crumb that is baked fresh every day. The whole place will smell of sugar and coconut and banana and toffee. We will do meringue angels, Victoria sponge, blueberry loaf and polenta cake. We will serve macaroons and apple pie and proper jam tarts. Moist cupcakes and cookies and brownies that are soft and squidgy. Millionaire's shortbread EVERYWHERE. We will smile when babies come in and open up the windows and invite the sunshine inside and the breeze and the thunder and the storm and blankets and heaters for when it's cold. There will be seats outside and a garden, and dogs are allowed. And breastfeeding. And I will write "muffins" in a swirly pen with the *f*s joined up. The sandwiches will be stuffed full and delicious, the soup homemade. The Bakewell tart slices will have *toasted* almonds on top. Not pale soggy fingernail ones. The flapjacks will be soft and full of seeds and nuts. The sugar won't come in packets. Tea won't be a ridiculous price, even though I'll give people a whole pot to themselves and it will always be made with those lovely cotton tea bags, unless they like the dregs—people like what they're used to. The camomile tea: *flowers;* the bread: *freshly baked on site.*

This became more than a food diary. But eating is a story of your life, so when people say food is a comfort, they are right in a way; it's always there with you. It's always a friend. Your favourite foods travel with you your whole life, taste everything you do. Even if you're crying over a plate, the plate is still there.

Full of hope.

# PISTACHIO ICE CREAM

It's not a flavour you would choose, I know, but it's the only flavour ice cream Mum actually likes and she gets it from the Italian near us. She says it's the ONLY flavour worth having. I get chocolate. It's dense, rich and sweet.

"Want to taste mine?" Mum asks, offering me a lick.

"No, it's only because you want some of my chocolate because you're regretting that green flavour."

"No, I'm not. Come on, try some. . . ." She barges the thing in my face.

"I don't like it."

"Come on, this is the year of new things."

I give her ice cream a lick. It's green, nutty, almondy and tart. It's actually delicious.

"WOW. That's so nice."

"Told you!" She licks it. "Uh-oh, you like pistachio ice cream; you know what that means, don't you?"

"What?"

"You're turning into your mother!"

She laughs.

"Shut up, you, do you really need to say that before I'm about to get weighed, as if my day isn't depressing enough as it is?"

"Do you really need an ice cream before being weighed?" Mum comments.

I laugh. "I do, yeah."

"And I love that about you." She strokes my hair.

# VITAMINS

"You again!" The nurse grins when she sees me, her gold tooth glinting.

We are back here, back in her office. Surrounded by the anti-smoking posters and the five-a-day reminders and the various ways to check your boobs for breast cancer. I probably need to start doing that too.

Vitamin adverts are everywhere. I'm sorry. I know you lot probably think they're all good, don't you? But I don't get why you'd not just eat the actual food instead of having a dehydrated powdery tablet version of something good for you, because they didn't have vitamins in the olden days and my grandma is still alive and she's, like, nearly a hundred and has properly never had a vitamin in her life. I hate them anyway. Who in their right mind wants to spend the whole day with a pod of fish organs lodged in the back of their throat slowly dissolving? NOT ME. And anyway, I've heard that actually the vitamins aren't even effective once you've got them home because all the goodness in them dies on the supermarket shelf, which kind of makes sense; nearly all the healthy good stuff should be served fresh. When you get those little white lines on your nails, is that *really actually* to tell you that you need more calcium? You should know. And why is it just calcium with the warning sign? Like, why doesn't your skin get covered in little orange dots if you need more vitamin C or whatever? Maybe you doctors look for those signs and know how to find them—perhaps to you deficiencies are really easy to spot? I find it mad to think about how little we know about the human body.

"So." The nurse sits and stretches her legs; she lets the back of her Crocs slide off her heels, the cracked dry backs of them like elephant skin. "What's been going on?"

"You can read it all here," I say, sliding the beaten-up book towards her. She lowers her glasses, peering over the frames, locking eyes with me.

"You did it?" She shakes her head.

"You didn't think I would?"

"I won't lie. No, I did not." She places a hand on the book, the book I've written in, a friend. "To be honest, Bluebelle Green . . ." She raises a brow to Mum. "You've surprised me." She smiles at me. "And how did you find it?"

"It was OK."

The nurse lifts the diary and begins to flip through the pages. "Oh my word."

"What?"

"I thought you were going to list your food, not"—she looks again, eyes wide—"write a whole . . . book!"

"I kind of had a lot to say."

"I suppose I have to read it now, don't I?" She slaps her leg. "I stitched myself up there, didn't I?"

She won't read it. As if.

"OK, let's get you on the scales."

"She had an ice cream on the way here, so don't be too hopeful," Mum volunteers. Oh shut up, Mum. THE ABSOLUTE BETRAYAL.

"And she's got a boyfriend!" DOUBLE BETRAYAL. What is going on here?

"MUM!" The scales yield underneath me.

"Ooooooooh! So you're a happy girl, then. See, I told you you have a pretty face."

"Surprised you two haven't been texting, such best friends."

She winks at me. "You've lost weight."

"I haven't tried to."

"Well done." She slaps me on the back.

"Don't 'well done' me. It wasn't deliberate."

"She's been exercising." Mum strokes my back. "Plus, I guess she's just growing up."

Mum looks me up and down. I see myself in her; for the first time ever she looks just like me, and me like her. I gulp. I know I have something to tell her. . . .

"Mum, I didn't get the apprenticeship at Planet Coffee," I tell her.

"Uh-oh, not again." The nurse walks away. "Leave me out of this."

"Sorry?" Mum's face slides off.

"It didn't happen." I shake my head. "Alicia didn't sort it."

"But I thought you said it was all happening. For a year. That you were being paid, that it was all fine with Julian from Careers."

"No, they lied. It was fine and then it wasn't. They said it was too big of an ask of them or whatever and that I had missed a few too many shifts, but that was a bit because of Dove and everything at home." Mum looks horrified. "And then stupid Alicia started practically making me BEG for this letter to take back to school to explain that it was their fault, not mine, but she was being so nasty about it. She's also pregnant and in a horrific mood because she's sick quite a lot and can't drink white wine like it's going out of fashion anymore. And I wasn't going to be the brunt of that. So . . . I quit. I walked out of there and told them to get an accessibility ramp." The nurse chuckles at me; Mum does not. "And then I maybe stole a jar of marshmallows."

"You stole *what*?" the nurse says in disapproval but Mum just says nothing.

So I carry on. . . .

"Look, I know you're mad and this wasn't what we agreed and I sort of exaggerated it and made out as though the apprenticeship was a done deal when it wasn't completely sorted but that's just what I was led to believe, Mum, and also I wanted you to be proud of me and think I could sort stuff out for myself and I know this isn't exactly what we talked about when we made our deal and you've been so cool about stuff and supportive with me and had a lot with Dove and so I've just decided—if they let me—that I'm going to go back to school and do sixth form. I've got my A-plus in art so I think if I can go back and just talk to Julian from Careers, then—"

"No. No. No. Hold on." Mum puts her hands out and closes her eyes to take it all in. "Just stop there. . . ."

"Sorry," I say. The nurse sits down to enjoy another episode of our family show, and has the audacity to go ahead and pop a mint into her mouth.

"There is no way you've come all this way and done all this to just not do what you want to do because of that absolute idiot." I feel her look at me like she's looking at an adult, not her daughter, not a child at all, and she says, "I had to grow up so quickly when I had you, Bluebelle, that I didn't get a chance to think about what I wanted to be when I grew up. Sometimes I wonder if I actually ever will grow up at all, if it's too late and I missed it all. But if I ever do get a chance to grow up again and do it properly . . . I hope I grow up to be like you. It's all I could ever ask for."

My eyes water.

"If Dove taught us anything, it's that life is too short. If going back to school is what you want to do, then please do it. But I don't believe that that is what you want. I want you to do exactly what you want. And maybe you don't know what that is yet, but let's find out together." She reaches out to hold me. "You won't have to do anything on your own."

And I fall into her and hug her.

"Oh dear!" The nurse reaches for a packet of tissues out of her handbag and wipes a tear from the corner of her eye.

We are all laughing and crying at the same time. We are a mess, basically.

"What am I going to do?"

"I don't know, but it's not like we've ever had a plan before and look at us; I reckon we're doing all right, us lot," Mum says. "You're a girl. And you can do whatever you want. The whole world belongs to you."

# A FAVOURITE RECIPE FROM THE AUTHOR (BB LOVES IT TOO!)

**Salmon Tacos with Mango Salsa and Toasted Sweet Corn**

This is one my favourite recipes. I made it up as a complete accident and it has become a home necessity! These tacos are like a theme park in your mouth. They feel like party food. My boyfriend loves them. My sister stole the recipe. They're fun and messy and great to bring to the table. Pretty healthy. Vibrant. Colourful and quite easy to make, and they look impressive. You can use chicken or vegetables if you don't eat fish, and they're a great low-carb option for people who are into that stuff or are gluten intolerant. You can serve them with green rice and quesadillas or just munch them on their own. This is playful yummy relaxed handfood that I like to eat!

# SALMON TACOS WITH MANGO SALSA AND TOASTED SWEET CORN

Serves 4, making 2 large tacos or 3 to 4 smaller tacos, depending how big your lettuce leaves are.

## FOR THE TACOS

4 salmon fillets (I use ones with the skin.)

Olive oil

Cajun spice mix

Sea salt

Romaine lettuce leaves (You want outer leaves that you can stuff, so pick large, healthy green leaves. You can use the smaller inner leaves in a salad another time.)

2 avocados (or one big one), thinly sliced or mashed

## FOR THE SALSA

1 large mango, diced

2 limes (one for serving)

1 bunch of cilantro

1/2 red onion, chopped (Sometimes I leave this out.)

## FOR THE SWEET CORN

1 large can of sweet corn

A chunk of butter

1/2 teaspoon of smoked paprika (more if you like hot)

Sea salt

# METHOD

Start with the salmon fillets. Place them skin-side-down on a baking tray lined with foil. Cover the fillets with olive oil and the Cajun mix and salt to taste. Bake for 15 to 20 minutes in a 350-degree oven, until the fish is firm and cooked through.

Meanwhile, get your corn on.

Melt a chunk of butter in a medium frying pan. Drain the sweet corn and add it to the butter and sizzle over medium heat. Try to flatten out the corn evenly so that all the kernels are touching the base of the pan for that gorgeous charred effect. Add your paprika and salt to taste, and then let the corn toast. It can burn quite easily, so watch out! You want it not quite black but with nice golden-brown edges.

You've got your fish in the oven, and your corn is sizzling. Now you can turn your attention to the salsa. In a medium bowl, mix the red onion and mango together and squeeze in the juice of one lime. Add a good handful of chopped cilantro. Set the salsa aside.

Take out the fish and leave it to rest for approximately 5 minutes.

Prepare your tacos by setting out your lettuce leaves on a platter or board. Fill each one with some of the avocado and the salsa.

Break the fish apart into flakes—they should slide away from the skin (you don't want to serve that). Fill the tacos evenly, and don't be at all worried about making them look clumsy or overloaded. They should look appetising, generous and scrumptious! Top with the toasted corn.

To finish, sprinkle your tacos with cilantro and splash a good amount of mild hot sauce across them confidently. If you want extra heat you can top them with fresh chilli. Serve each taco with a lime wedge.

For even more flavour (and mess!), you can add sour cream, beans and cheese!

# ABOUT THE AUTHOR

Laura Dockrill is a performance poet and novelist. She is the author of the CILIP Carnegie Medal–nominated YA novel *Lorali* and its sequel *Aurabel;* the Darcy Burdock series for younger readers, which was nominated for the CILIP Carnegie Medal and shortlisted for the Waterstones Children's Book Prize; and her debut children's poetry collection, *My Mum's Growing Down.* Laura Dockrill lives in London. Visit her online at lauradockrill.co.uk and follow @LauraDockrill on 🐦.